Acknowledgments

As always, many fine people sacrificed their sanity and busy schedules to help me complete this book. I would like to thank Norma Kay Justice and Scott Falkner for their inside knowledge of television news—any errors are completely mine, not theirs. Jeff Strand for taking time out of whatever hilarious and gruesome novel he's working on now to read this. Megan McKeever and Eric Ryan for their editorial expertise.

Books by Ryan C. Thomas

Novels
The Summer I Died

Novellas
Elements Of The Apocalypse
Undead: Headshot Quartet

RATINGS GAME

A NOVEL
by
RYAN C. THOMAS

Cohort Press

For Gram

Ratings Game. Copyright 2007 by Ryan C. Thomas. All rights reserved. Printed in the United States of America. No part of this book may be used or reproduced in any manner whatsoever without written permission except in the case of brief quotations embodied in critical articles and reviews. For information, address Cohort Press, 1143 Northern Blvd, Clarks Summit, PA 18411

First U.S. Edition

ISBN 978-0-9777196-3-1

RATINGS GAME

Dog eat dog
Read the news
Some will win
Some will lose
Up's above and down's below
And limbo's in between
Up you win, down you lose
It's anybody's game

— "Dog Eat Dog," ACDC

CHAPTER 1

It was a New York Monday, mid-January, eleven in the morning. A bad luck kind of day, Stone thought, wishing he'd leapt off his tenth floor balcony instead of heading into the office. The dog had left a yellow puddle on the kitchen floor which he'd sloshed through in his socks, there'd been no cream for the coffee—a pathetic can of Folgers at that, left in the dark recesses of the top cupboard by his hell-spawned ex-wife—and to top it off, a large pink bunny was currently firing him. Well, sort of.

Stone grabbed its ears and yanked its oversized head toward him.

"What do you mean I'm getting fired?" Through the mesh eyeholes he could make out the shadow of some wannabe actor lurking inside. "Where'd you hear that?"

"Let go, man," the bunny yelled.

Stone stood in disbelief, waving his coffee cup like a grandstand conductor. "Tell me!"

The pink bunny threw its hands in the air, backed away. "Hey, chill, bro, I'm just saying what I heard, ya know?"

"What did you hear?"

"Cheese said the new guy was out. Not drawing an audience. I don't know, could've meant anything, could've been talking motherfucking baseball. Who am I, Sherry McClaine? Shit."

"Shirley McClaine."

"Whatever. Where's my carrot, I got a promo to tape. My ears better not be bent, man."

Cheese was firing him? Not a big enough audience? This was bullshit. In the few months he'd been anchor he'd received nothing but supportive mail; people liked him.

He pushed past the bunny, stormed off down the central hallway of the WWTF News offices, and took the corner like a NASCAR driver, black coffee spitting out of the drinking hole of his travel mug.

"Hey, Stone!" he heard from behind him. But he didn't turn around. Not because he was in a rush—which he was—but because his name really wasn't Stone. It took the second time to get through.

"Yo, Stone!"

He spun around, found the giant pink bunny following him. It lumbered down the hallway like a child's nightmare.

"What?!"

"Hey, man, for what it's worth, I liked you. Your sign off—'It's your news, I just tell it'—good stuff."

"Yeah thanks, Bugs." He was feeling as appreciative as a child getting socks for Christmas. Some half-hearted words of encouragement from a guy in a foam suit weren't going to change that.

"Yeah, well, screw you then," the bunny replied. "Asshole."

Down the hall he sped, up to Cheese's door, and stopped dead. Inside he heard voices, male voices, a female voice—a female giggle. Ah shit, he thought, so it's true. It had to be, his life always went to shit around giggling women. A giggling man in the boss's office was just a kiss-ass, a giggling woman was a piece of ass looking for a handout.

He knocked.

From inside: "Who is it?"

"It's Stone."

The door opened. Cheese stood there, impeccably dressed as always in an Italian silk three piece—imported on a ship made of gold, no doubt—Bruno Maglis reflecting the shine of his cosmetically-bleached, perfectly straight teeth. His hair was streamlined, his gold-rimmed glasses so clean you couldn't tell if they had lenses or not, his aftershave so perfectly subtle Stone thought of angels wafting Mediterranean spices in the subliminal places of his mind.

Cheese, the king, the News Director, the man who made it all happen.

"What can I do for you, Stone?"

Behind Cheese sat a pair of legs, female legs, outstretched and shaven to silk. The kind of legs that made Stone want to strap on goggles and go skiing down them. He couldn't see the woman's face, but she was no doubt the giggling broad of his doom. He was curious.

Cheese cocked his head. "Stone? Problem?"

Against the wall, leaning like George Raft without the character, Duncan Willis pretended to wind his fake Rolex. It was rare he even had time to lean with all the menial tasks Cheese had him running. For some reason Stone felt embarrassed in front of him; normally he was just embarrassed for him. What a prick.

"The pink bunny told me I'm fired."

"What pink bunny?" Cheese asked.

"In the hallway."

"We have a pink bunny?"

15

"He heard you say the new guy is fired. I'm the new guy, right? At least as it pertains to an audience?"

"Why is there a pink bunny in the hallway?"

"Am I fired or not? Who's the broad?"

"This is Miss Pastore." Cheese moved aside and introduced her with a sweep of his manicured hands.

Rising like a heat wave, she walked towards Stone, posture tall and straight. Blonde hair, red lips, black suit with pin stripes down both jacket and skirt. She took his hand, which was covered in sticky coffee, and shook it twice.

"Pleased to meet ya," she said. Said in a southern accent no less, which in New York City is somehow a lot sexier than it should be.

"Likewise," Stone replied. She opened her mouth to elaborate but he cut her off. "The bunny, Cheese," he said, desperately trying to ignore Miss Pastore's moist lips and butterfly brown eyes, "what's the deal?"

"Good question, Stone. I'm not sure. Duncan?"

Duncan snapped to attention, suddenly useful. "Yes?"

"Why is there a…what color did you say it was?"

"Pink," Stone replied. "But that's not—"

"—A pink bunny roaming my hallways?"

"Kids segment," Duncan said, "after the food bit. You wanted to attack the younger demographic before school began."

"Jesus H. Christ, you're right. There you go, Stone, there's your bunny."

"Fired, Cheese. Am I being fired?"

"God no. What? The bunny told you I was firing you?"

Cheese was dancing around the subject. One thing about bosses is that they don't get to be boss by being dumb. They rely on those around them being dumb. Like Duncan, who suddenly pretended to rack his memory.

"We fired the janitor last week. Maybe you're confused."

"Fuck you, Duncan. The bunny said the new guy was getting it. That's me. Then I come up here and this…woman…is in your office giggling like you're high school sweethearts. Do you think I'm dense?"

"Relax, Stone—"

"Farques."

"Around here it's Stone, and if you don't settle down you're going to see why I am the Head Cheese. You're not fired, but we are doing some rearranging."

"Rearranging?"

Duncan went back to playing with his watch though Stone could see what he was really doing was trying to look down Miss Pastore's blouse from behind. Couldn't blame him, really. What a prick.

"Look, I was planning on talking to you later today," Cheese continued, his eyes focused with a kind of casual tyranny that made Stone wonder what kind of leather chaps he wore around his basement dungeon. "I had a meeting with corporate a few days ago and they're worried about ratings, but nothing that involves pink slips."

"How about pink bunnies, then?"

"I told you—"

"Charles," Stone said in his best don't-bullshit-a-bullshitter tone, and also because people only used Cheese's real name when they wanted to talk serious dollars with him, "she's here to replace me, isn't she?"

"Not replace. Not at all."

"Replace Swift?" Claymore Swift, the other anchor. African American man, sharp as a tack, had the looks to go with it too. Cheese would never lose him.

"Of course not."

"Then what?"

"Accompany."

"What, on air?"

"The shareholders think bringing in a new face will attract more of a following."

"You mean you're brining in tits to attract the drooling blue collars."

"What can I say, Stone? We're losing to WYNN and that shitstain Doug Hardwood."

"Screw him," Stone said, though his point was lost.

"Exactly," Cheese replied. "We can't have that. So we're doing this. Sexy women attract watchers. Watchers make our ratings go up, and if our ratings go up we get better advertisers. Better advertisers means more resources for the station. It's all money in the end, Stone, you know this. Christ, don't take it personally, you're a good anchor, just not what we need right now."

"You said accompany. Where's that leave me?"

Cheese straightened his cuffs, gave a quick glance at his gold watch. Before he could speak Miss Pastore leaned in.

"I'm hoping y'all can be my counterpart. You know, banter with me, whimsical BS like on the Hollywood newsmags. Or like Jay Leno and Branford Marsalis."

"Branford stands off camera."

Miss Pastore sat down facing him and crossed her legs. She left enough of a gap he could just about see her panties. He thought of the Beach Boys lyric, *the southern girls with the way they walk*...Jesus, she'd have them eating out of her hand.

"Charles and I were thinking you could do a new segment called Stone's Moans. Different moan for whether the story is a rant or a rave. Local op ed stuff. And when you're not doing your thing we cut to you for a joke or two."

The bitch was here one day and she was deciding his career path for him. He hated her, and wanted her.

He looked at Cheese, who was smiling with approval. "Miss Pastore had a big hand in putting WMMS on the map," Cheese said.

"Where's that?"

"Louisiana," she said, pronouncing it Lewseeana. "We did the same thing there. Folks ate it up."

Cheese winked at her. She winked back. "What do you think?"

"My ratings are that bad?"

"Stone," Cheese put his hand on Stone's shoulder, pulled him close, "we had to bring in a bunny. What do you think?"

Stone turned and walked out of the room.

CHAPTER 2

When Amanda Pastore was twelve years old, she squeezed a bunch of lemons into a pitcher, added some sugar, set the pitcher on a card table at the corner of her driveway, and waited for the farmhands under her daddy's employ to come throwing down quarters for some homemade lemonade.

As far as she could do the math, she'd added the right amount of sugar, the right amount of lemons, and the right amount of childhood cuteness, that by the end of the day she'd be buying that new Linda Ronstadt album she wanted so badly and still have enough left over for a down payment on a luxury tree house.

But by the end of that first business day she had made a mere fifty cents, a pathetic amount that certainly wouldn't afford her a new record let alone much of anything else, and decided that business was not her thing. Perhaps she would do better spying on her brother—who was four years older and more than likely up to no good with that so-called friend of his, Red. Barring that, she'd just ride her bike down to Main Street and look for change on the sidewalk, maybe listen in on the Coopers while she was at it. The Coopers owned the grocery and were never short on colorful names and descriptions to call each other during a fight. (Amanda's favorite of which remained to this day, as provided by Mr. Cooper one Sunday afternoon: "You lucky you got that never-healing ax wound 'tween yer legs or I'd smack yer mouth right off, you loud-mouthed she-devil!")

And that's pretty much what she did for the next four years. Until she turned sixteen, when puberty, as her daddy put it, set things a-changin'.

The most notable change was the addition of a full set of curves to her body. Every boy in school now wanted to be her friend, and it was all she could do to get them to not throw money in her direction. She couldn't walk down the halls without the entire football team shuffling behind her like mules after a carrot. At first it was creepy as hell, but soon all that devotion got her thinking on her failure in the lemonade business. And so, after a couple weeks of leading a bunch of lemmings around the school, she decided a little experiment was in order.

Wearing her baby blue bikini—the skimpy one that Mom didn't know she had—she pulled the card table out of the garage, made up a pitcher of lemonade, sat it next to a sign saying LEMONADE 25¢, and proceeded to make thirty-seven dollars...

...in two hours.

Business, for Amanda Pastore, had never made so much sense.

Taking a cue from that experience, she set her sights on a journalistic career that would be both lucrative and exciting. Once she entered the world of nightly news, her blue-bikini body toned and tanned, she knew she could pretty much count the days on her hand until she made anchor.

Now, sitting in Cheese's office, she marveled at how business then was no different from business now—it wasn't what you sold, it was how you sold it.

There was a twinge of regret at seeing the anger and disappointment in this Stone guy's face, but she wasn't about to let emotion get in the way of her paycheck. She'd worked hard for her body, and her career. After he left the office, she turned to Cheese and said, "He's pissed. But I guess I'd be too."

"If he looked half as good as I imagine you do when you wake up, I'd sit him at the desk and let him make origami. He understands. He's a smart guy."

"You treat all your employees with such allegiance?"

"Depends. What does it get me and my show?"

"Hmmm." She glanced sideways at Duncan, making no attempt to pull her blouse closed despite his rapt attention to her cleavage. "Duncan, would y'all be a dear and get me a coffee. Cream and sug—"

Duncan was out the door before she finished the sentence.

Cheese sat down at the desk and lifted up the morning's newspaper. The front page story had something to do with the police arresting a popular nightclub owner for drug solicitation.

"See this," he said to her. "This is going to lead off every news segment on every channel tonight. Know why? Because it's political, that's why. It's got shit to do with drugs. The mayor thinks he staged some kind of coup, thinks he'll get votes from all the white-haired ladies living above the park who're afraid to come into the area where this club even is. So WYNN, WBMS, CNN, MSNBC, all of them are gonna show it because when politics stomps on the little people, viewers tune in to bitch. And my job is to make sure the people watch *our* story. Which means coming up with an angle. And that, to bring me back to the point, is where Stone was failing. He was shit with angles. That's where you come in. You've got angles as well as curves, so help me out."

"What are y'all thinking?"

"Well, I could put the chief of police on TV—"

"And die a slow death, Cheese."

"Okay, talk to me."

"What you want to do is get the club owners shouting a mantra. About how the mayor is trying to shut down the one thing that draws people to this town: the nightlife."

"Keep going."

"Closing down nightclubs in this city, hon, is on par with prohibition. We get the owners to say the dance clubs are next, with bars soon to follow, and now you've created a zeitgeist."

Cheese cocked his head. "I love big, sexy words."

"Bring the public close to panic, get them irate, and they'll be tuned in every night."

Cheese sat back and put his hands behind his head. "I like it. So long as we give it attribution—"

"Sure, then nobody can complain. Hell, maybe someone gets so amped up they threaten to kill the mayor even. Not that I'd condone such overblown sensationalism, mind you. But that'd give us a lead story, that's an angle."

Duncan returned with a cup of coffee and handed it to Amanda. "Thanks, sug," she said, taking a sip and licking her lips.

Both Cheese and Duncan watched in fascination as her tongue

played across her bottom lip before darting back inside her mouth. She was used to the staring and let it go without a word.

"What are you discussing?" Duncan asked. Once again, he pretended to be caught up in his watch while trying his best to secretly look at Amanda's chest.

"Murder, Duncan," she said. "The best way to get ratings short of a war in this city."

"Was somebody murdered?" he asked.

Cheese stood up, put a hand on Duncan's shoulder, handed him a slip of paper, and pointed him out the door. "Stop asking stupid questions. Here, check on this for me."

"No sweat, Cheese. What is it, a lead?"

"No, it's the name of a book I ordered at the Barnes and Noble. Go pick it up for me. And be quick about it, I have other shit I need you to do for me."

Duncan read the title out loud, "How To Stop Giving Women The Best Sex Of Their Lives."

Cheese turned to Amanda and sniffed. "It's a little problem I have. I'm trying to solve it."

"Cheese," she said, "you're a pathetic man. Thank God you know how to run a news room."

"So how quickly can you get me some club owners bitching about the mayor?"

"It's eleven o'clock now…how about y'all give me till two. I should have something by then."

"I'm gonna call promotions and set up a taping…say, three o'clock. How's this: Disco Infernal, the War on New York City Nightlife."

"That's a blue bikini."

"Blue bikini?"

"Never mind. It's great," Amanda said. "I'll be back in time. And if you could, Duncan, get Stone some joke books at that store. Viewers like a witty op-ed piece, and he's as funny as a Republican rally."

"Now that's witty."

"I know."

"Stop staring at her chest, Duncan."

"Sorry." Duncan crumpled up the paper and put it in his pocket.

"No worries, sug," Amanda said, smiling at him. She opened the door to the hallway. "I'll be back by two." She raised her coffee cup as she left the office, toasted to her new boss and his Igor. "Here's to change, hons, all for the better."

CHAPTER 3.

The five o'clock newscast went just like Cheese said it would: a total nightmare. The thinking was that it would take a few days to iron out the kinks, and in the meantime Miss Pastore's cleavage would compensate. They had already written Stone a story about a dog that rescued kittens from an abandoned building downtown. Probably they got the damn things from the pound and shot B-roll in another state for all he knew if it was true or not. He read the damn teleprompter like a robot, utterly pissed off. "...and that's a moan of love from me, Roland Stone, here on Stone's Moans."

Pride is not something you ever plan to lose, so it takes a moment to sink in when it does. Walking off the set, Stone felt it sink in real quick. It wasn't temporary, like when a subordinate co-worker suddenly becomes your manager, and you end up working harder to prove to the higher-ups it should be you with the new gold name placard. This was a downright eradication of any and all self-esteem. It was humiliating. His pride may as well have left a note in his brain that said, sorry, these things happen, I wish you the best in life but you're just not what I'm looking for right now.

Pride. You don't even know you have it till you lose it.

After the newscast, Amanda approached him fearlessly, an assertive manner that instantly put her in charge. She gave him a patronizing kiss on the cheek. "I know y'all hate me right now for taking your spot. But Cheese has a plan, and I think it's a good one."

"It took me three years in the field reporting on this same kind of horseshit to get that anchor job. No offense, Miss Pastore—"

"Please, it's Tricia Mason now."

And so it begins, thought Stone, she has a screen name. "Miss Mason, you understand if I'm not too pleased here."

She patted his shoulder. "You'll see, hon."

And with that she smirked and sauntered away doing this thing with her hips that hypnotized everyone in the room.

Cheese sidled up next to Stone, Duncan Willis at his heels holding a cup of coffee for his master. "Numbers are coming in now from sales. We're already up from yesterday. Wait till word of her gets out. I'll be fucked if Nike doesn't buy air time from us. Or Rolls Royce."

"Rolls Royce doesn't advertise on TV," Stone said.

"They will now. She's got something special, something ripe and fresh. What do you think, Duncan?"

Duncan agreed, but Stone expected nothing less from a man who could say Yes Boss in twelve different languages.

"I can't do this, Cheese."

"Yes you can. You're a big boy now. That Stone's Moans bit was pretty good, I thought. Duncan?"

"Yes, sir, pretty good."

"Shut up, Duncan," Stone said. "How long?"

"For what?" Cheese replied.

"Until I get back up front. Because Stone's Moans is pathetic and you know it."

It looked like Cheese was going to say something prolific the way he sighed first, but Frank Dorey, the studio director, ran up with some papers and cut him off.

"Numbers, Cheese, just got 'em."

Cheese took the pages and flipped through them, found the part he was looking for. A smile as long as the Mississippi stretched across his face. "She's got something special."

Defeated, Stone walked away, went up to his office and took out the flask of Crown Royal he kept in his lower drawer for special occasions. It was cliche, but it suited his current self image—old and used. He downed two big gulps and coughed as the alcohol lit up his gut. That was that, he thought, he'd been ousted. Shit. First his wife, and now his job. Bad things come in threes, right? What was next?

To top it all off, he had to repeat it all for the ten o'clock segment. Which he did, slightly drunk.

It was almost two in the morning when he hit O'Halloran's pub near his apartment building. The original O'Halloran was long dead, and now his son Pat ran the place, though he too was old and gray. He was wiping up a spilled drink on the counter when Stone came in.

The place was dim as usual and nearly dead. A man in a trench coat sipping a Manhattan at the bar, a couple in a far booth chatting over martinis, two guys at the end of the bar watching a late night rerun of last night's *Tonight Show* on the TV affixed to the wall (Branford somewhere off camera), a woman at another table wearing a collection of sweaters on top of one another as if she were a Russian matryoshka doll. That was it, that and the familiar smell of cigars that were illegal to smoke inside but that Pat smoked in the back room anyway.

Stone took a seat next to the man in the trench coat. Pat tossed the rag in the sink and put a glass in front of him. "Roland Stone, what can I do you for?"

"You can start by using my real name."

"Now where's the fun in that, I says." His fake Irish accent had hints of Brooklynese in it, which never made any sense to Stone since the bartender spent all his time here in the Upper West Side. "Name your poison, oh King Wesley of the Quaff."

"I've had a shitstorm of a day, so pretty much anything you pour in that glass will slide down just right."

"Bushmills it is then."

Pat filled Stone's glass halfway, dropped some ice cubes in it. Stone picked it up and swirled it, took a sip, glanced at the TV. Jay Leno was doing headlines, and everyone in the bar seemed to care but him. Pat leaned over and tapped his finger on the bar. "Had the television on for the happy hour crowd. Said to myself, let's see what ol' Roland has for us tonight. I flip to your station and lo and behold you've turned into a lass. A fine lass at that, no lying, but a lass nevertheless. Next thing I know you're standing in some corner talking about some mutt that had baby kittens or some shit and I says to myself, he'll be in for a tall one tonight."

"Laughable," Stone replied, breathing out of wall of whiskey, "I know. Dumb broad from Louisiana stole my job, shook her titties for the boss."

"Fine titties at that."

"You're not helping."

"You want to tell O'Halloran all about it, do ya?"

"Not really."

"Oh come on, son, titties like that shouldn't go undiscussed. That's a crime, that is."

It was then that the man in the trench coat decided to join their conversation. Without taking his eyes off the TV, he said, "Must be good for ratings."

Instinct told Stone to politely tell the man to screw his mother, but something in the back of his mind stopped him just short of executing that goal. The voice—Stone knew that voice. Oh God, did Stone know that voice. His third bad thing had arrived.

"As if my day hasn't been shitty enough. What the hell are you doing here?"

Doug Hardwood spun around in his bar stool, his Rolex catching the green Guinness advertising sign behind the bar and reflecting tiny stars across the counter top.

"I live here now."

What the hell did he mean by that? "What the hell do you mean by that?" Hey, between the Crown Royal and the Bushmills he was pretty much in a one track frame of mind.

"The neighborhood," Hardwood said. "Just got a new place two blocks over."

"Where?"

"The Howitzer building."

The Howitzer was fairly new, definitely upscale. A two-room apartment was going for around six grand a month. All the amenities a rich codger could ask for, including half naked massage therapists that made room calls.

"So why are you here, at my bar?"

"Come now, Stone, let's eschew the machismo. We're colleagues, not schoolyard rabble. Mr. O'Halloran liked that my money was green,

I liked the convenience of this place. It pays to get out and meet the public, provides them with a sense of trust when I deliver the news. Besides, I didn't know you had a stake on the place."

Pat cleared his throat, sixty years of gravel mixing in his larynx. "I want a good clean fight, both of ya. No hitting below the belt, and no biting."

"Sorry, Pat," Stone said, taking another swig of the whiskey. He looked back at Hardwood. "You came up today is all. Kind of why I'm being replaced by tits."

"Be fair, son, those tits are sculpted by the ghost of Michelangelo himself."

"Again, Pat, not helping."

Pat took the hint and went to check on his other customers. The sweater lady was nodding off at her table. He poured her another and stuck it under her nose.

"It's an admirable game, is it not?" Hardwood said.

"What's that?"

"Our business. What I'm assuming is the reason behind your ire. We try so hard to maintain objectivity, to appeal on an almost paternal and/or professorial level. Can't cheer when a baby is rescued from a burning building, can't sneer when a serial rapist makes parole. It's the news, we just report it. So why do they watch me over you, or you over me? Same news in the end. But you throw an attractive woman in the mix…"

"We've got fucking pink bunnies now."

"I saw." Hardwood motioned for Pat to refill his glass. The old Irishman obliged him. Stone followed suit, beginning on what was probably his second quart of whiskey for the night. "Problem is," Hardwood continued, "one can't truly be objective when one is dependent on the ratings. So while it's the same story on your network as on mine, it's the flair that ultimately wins. Snappy headlines and hackneyed sign-offs are no match for the allure of a female anchor."

Is he trying to piss me off, Stone thought, or does he believe his own bullshit?

Stone downed the Bushmills, snapped his fingers for Pat, who was laughing at some idiotic stunt Leno was doing. Goddamned Marsalis was still off-screen.

"So let me ask you this, Hardwood." He was sure he was teetering on the bar stool now. "You made anchor quick as a senator sleeps with his aides. You stole the show on the Winslow murder case. What sort of spin did you put on it? What was your flair?"

The old newscaster leaned in close, put a hand on Stone's shoulder the way Cheese always did, whispered in his ear. "Roland—"

"Wesley."

"I'd prefer we stay on a professional level. Roland, before the news can make us appealing, we have to make the news appealing."

With that, he put a fifty on the bar for Pat, pulled on his leather gloves and silk scarf, slowly and methodically took a Nat Sherman out of his sterling silver cigarette case, said, "Past my bedtime, see you around," and left the bar.

On the TV, fucking Marsalis was still nowhere in sight.

CHAPTER 4

Doug Hardwood stepped out into the frigid New York City night and pulled his coat tight around his throat. At his age, fighting a cold involved more than a day in bed and some chewable vitamins; his immune system was not what it used to be, and it simply wouldn't do to be absent from work with a fever, not with this new blonde-haired bitch riding the anchor desk over at WWTF.

Her presence had stunned everyone at WYNN, but perhaps none as much as himself. Why now, he wondered. What were they getting at? Did they see his age for what it really was? Were they staging a ratings coup based on some notion that he was near retirement?

They were sorely wrong, if that was the case.

He wasn't going anywhere.

Still, it concerned him. Attractive women always had the potential to draw an audience, both male and female…if they were good enough.

The other networks hadn't dared put anyone worth real money up against him in over two years. Oh sure, they'd tried here and there, but the results never varied. In the end, they failed, whether from sheer insipidness or lack of brain cells, and the viewers always came back to what they trusted.

The father figure. The pedant. Him.

Hardwood was number one, it's just the way things were, and trying to change it was like trying to change the weather. The public demanded him (if the viewership numbers had anything to say about it) and these other yahoos always went home with their tails between their legs. There'd been so many: Brad Forge, the chiseled Yale grad WKPA brought in last year, with his open collared shirts and spiky hair. He looked good but he stumbled over words with more than two syllables. Gone. Jack Brown, an older man who wore bow ties. He was well spoken, but made no bones about his love of sci fi movies. The other media labeled him a geek. Gone. Dan Proud, who might have made a go at it, if it wasn't for the sex scandal. Gone. There were more, too many to count.

He turned the corner and saw the Howitzer Building loom magnificent in front of him, the holiday lights adorning it like jewels on a gigantic scepter. It wasn't that he'd needed to move, could have stayed in his old place, but the Howitzer had been big news since its units went on the market, and when you were on television, where you lived was as important as what you wore.

"Southern accent," he said to himself, sorting out the pros and cons of this new Mason woman in his head. Never in all his time reporting the news in New York had there been an anchor with a southern accent. It was so daring and out of sorts with the paradigm of Big Apple media that it was borderline brilliant. It was exotic and alluring, and that spelled competition with a capital C. Add to that her movie star looks, brains and quick wit, and for the first time in a long time, Hardwood realized he was going to have to work harder than ever to stay number one in his time slots.

But then, Hardwood knew about hard work. And he knew about what made a man a symbol of trust and respect, because he *was* such a symbol.

The Winslow case.

No, he thought, it wouldn't do to ponder the past right now, not until he knew all sides of the issue. If this Mason woman was the future, then he needed to concentrate on shutting down her operation, he needed to stay focused on the here and now.

But his subconscious decided to run with this line of thought anyway.

The Winslow case. Mason. Ponder it, Doug, you know about hard work. You know what this city loves.

He shook his head.

Maybe. But that was over. He'd promised himself. What is past is prologue, no use letting it affect him right now.

When he'd arrived in New York City fresh from college, the first thing he'd noticed was the overwhelming sense of solidarity among the natives. New Yorkers would fight and kill each other in the streets of Times Square over a subway token, but fucked be the person in California or Utah who made a comment about New Yorkers being classless, rude animals. When that happened, New Yorkers became an army unlike any other in the world, a band of brothers that would die in a heartbeat to save each other. New Yorkers protected their own.

Which is why Doug Hardwood had lied at his first interview, so many years ago, when the former director of KWBG asked him where he'd grown up. A small town in Ohio would never have done, but Hell's Kitchen was music to the station director's ears. A local. That's what they wanted, that's what they all wanted.

Truth was, he'd never been to Hell's Kitchen, still avoided it now when it was at all possible.

"Good evening, Mr. Hardwood," the doorman said as Hardwood arrived at the Howitzer. The doorman opened one side of the glass double doors, letting out the heat from inside.

"Evening, Louis," Hardwood replied, walking up the steps toward the lobby.

"Nice job tonight, sir. The five o'clock news, I had it on at home."

"Thanks, Louis."

"Anything you need before you retire for the night?"

"No, thank you."

"I could have the bar bring up a hot cup of tea. It'll warm you up, sir."

Hardwood stopped, turned to the man in the red overcoat. "I'm not as frail as you think, Louis."

"Not at all sir, I merely meant—"

"How old do I look, Louis?"

"Sir?"

"It's a simple question. Do I look like I'm too old to be out this late in the cold? Do you expect me to bitch about my arthritis when the snow falls? I'm a big deal in this town, Louis, and it would take naught but a simple call to have you working on a garbage barge by morning. Don't think for a second I don't have the power to."

"Sir, I didn't mean—"

Hardwood raised his hand and shushed him. "Forget it, Louis. I'm sorry, I'm merely displacing anger and tension at you for something you know nothing about. I guess I really am an old codger in some respects. My sincere apologies."

If there was one thing Hardwood knew about New York City doormen, it was that they were the eyes and ears of the people. It was more than common for the media to grease the palms of doormen who might overhear conversations among prominent citizens—it was practically taught in journalism classes. They knew when to talk about what they heard, and when to keep quiet about it.

Hardwood slipped him a twenty. Better to keep this incident quiet, especially in light of recent events with WWTF. It wouldn't do for people to know he was upset. Tentatively, Louis took the money, unsure of whether or not he was being tested.

"Go on," Hardwood said. "No tricks. You deserve it."

The doorman put it in his pocket and thanked him.

"So," Hardwood continued. "You watched my news cast, you say?"

"Yes, sir. Every night, the five o'clock. I'd watch the ten, but well…"

"You're here, opening doors. I understand. You didn't happen to flip channels, did you?"

Louis' eyes went a bit wide.

Hardwood had seen this type of look many times on the faces of interviewees recounting traumatic experiences. Like a shark attack victim reflecting on what it was like to suddenly find himself staring down through the waters at a large fish with razor sharp teeth swimming up toward him at bullet-like speed.

"I may have switched channels...for a moment...during a commercial."

"And what did you think of her?" Hardwood asked, sure he could hear John Williams' *Jaws* score playing in the distance.

"She's, well, she's beautiful."

"Ah. I see."

Despite the subzero temperatures, Louis seemed to be sweating. "I flipped back as soon as the commercials were done, I swear."

"Relax, Louis, relax. I'm not upset. I know, I saw her too, she's stunning. Damnit. And I am getting old, no doubt about it."

"Yeah, but you know, this city still loves you. You helped catch the Winslow murderer."

"Yes, I did, didn't I?"

"That counts for a lot around here. You're still number one, sir. 'Doug Hardwood, the most trusted name in news.' If I could be so bold, sir, I tell my friends I work at your building and they all want to know what you're like."

"And what do you tell them?"

Hardwood could almost see the man replaying the exchange of money over in his head.

"That you're as refined in person are you are on television."

"Good answer, Louis. But, still, I'm no set of ample breasts."

Hardwood looked through the glass doors into the lobby where a fire was crackling near the front desk. Richard, the night clerk, was busy reading a magazine and sipping a cup of tea. From the look of it, it was some kind of men's magazine, possibly *Maxim* or *Stuff* or something of that ilk. On the cover, a half naked woman was blowing a kiss to the camera.

So it was true. In the end it all came back to attractive women. If a hot woman was selling a bag of ice, Eskimos would line up to buy it.

"You know what? I think I'll go for a walk, Louis. I'll see you in a bit."

"Yes, sir."

With that, Hardwood stepped away from the doors and walked toward the moon.

In his mind, he replayed the Winslow murders over and over, remembering how they'd remained front page news for months, remembering how the killer had sent notes and photos to Hardwood and how he'd shown them to the public on air, despite the station's stern warning that it was just an invitation to trouble. Remembering how he'd gone from being just another newscaster to the number one newscaster in all of New York City. Remembering how the ratings had shot through the roof. Remembering how he'd cracked the code in the killer's notes when the police couldn't, and the ratings he'd gotten from that—beyond anything WYNN could have ever hoped for. Remembering, also, how he'd felt no remorse when the police shot and killed Daniel Reading, the so-called Winslow Murderer, after he, Doug Hardwood, had tipped them to the man's whereabouts live on television.

If WWTF and this southern bitch thought they were going to push him from his rightfully earned number one spot, they had another thing coming.

Something deep inside him, something he'd buried years ago, was awakening.

CHAPTER 5.

Stone's apartment building was four blocks away from the bar. It wasn't the Howitzer by any means, but it was classy and cost a pretty penny. Six months ago he'd have balked at such high rent, but making anchor, and the divorce, had prompted him to take a chance.

But he didn't feel like going home just yet.

Bushmills was pumping through his veins like gas, revving him up and pitching him down the sidewalks among dirt-covered snow banks. The Upper West Side was quiet, just the clicking of bare tree limbs in the wind. For a minute he closed his eyes and imagined giant beetles skittering around inside a box. Clickety click click.

For some reason he always felt better walking down a tree-lined street in Manhattan; the crime and bums and drugs and grotesque mistreatment of one human being to another, the stories he'd been reporting on for almost five years now, it all seemed to disappear in the presence of those trees.

The Howitzer building still had Christmas lights on it even though it was almost February. Wearing a red overcoat to match his winter-tender cheeks, the doorman asked Stone if he was expected. When Stone didn't answer, the doorman offered to get him a cab. Finally the doorman resorted to a simple, "Sir?"

"Doug Hardwood lives here," Stone said.

"Yes, sir. Are you his friend? Wait a minute, don't I know you? Are you part of his news team?"

"Son," Stone slurred, breathing whiskey into the doorman's eyes, "take down the damn lights."

"The Christmas lights, sir?"

Cold air bit into his face as he shuffled off, ignoring the cockeyed stare of the doorman. Will he tell Hardwood I came by, Stone wondered.

Mr. Hardwood, your friend came by last night.
Which friend?
I dunno, stank of booze and cheap coffee.
Ah yes, Roland Stone, got replaced by a bunny. Fine man.

He drifted down a side street, headed toward the FDR. Under the orange street lamps, the dirty snow banks looked like bruised tits rising out of the ground. Images of Mason's cleavage assaulted him, which wasn't necessarily a bad thing, nice rack like that, but it defeated the purpose of getting drunk to forget how he was less important than curves and a flamboyant rodent. He crossed into a small community park, cut across it and came out in front of a boarded-up building. It wasn't dilapidated or anything, just being renovated. He stood and looked at the funny scribbles some taggers had spray painted on the boards, bunch of nonsense he couldn't make out but that could mean life or death to rival gang members. Two bicycle cops came by, looked him over but kept on pedaling. Then he was alone.

"Tricia Mason," he spoke out loud, "pair of tits with a southern drawl. How do you top that?"

You top it by taking a piss on the side of a building, he decided. Before he could unzip his pants, though, he heard a low wheeze. The wheeze was followed by a cough and a gurgle. As a reporter, he'd done his fair share of stories about the homeless; not a winter went by that a handful didn't die outside in the blistering cold. Some of them just chose to sleep on the sidewalk instead of in the shelters, don't ask why.

"Hope you got some whiskey there, pal," he said quietly to himself. "Your insides are gonna freeze up. Dying from exposure can't be much fun, out here, alone, just me listening to you…"

Something about the fact he was the only one around suddenly struck him as serendipitous. Blame it on the booze, but there was a palpable sense that he was meant to help this person. Maybe he could save him, this bum, make it a feel-good story, feed him and clean him up, bring the guy on the air and have him tell his tale. Have him tell New York City how Roland Stone saved him from imminent death. Roland Stone, rock star news anchor.

Yeah, why the fuck not?

He found a loose board on the side of the building, pushed it aside and entered. The ground floor was gutted, covered in dirt, nothing but girders here and there with loose wires dangling around them, and cinderblocks stacked about on tarps. It was pitch black and stingingly cold. He followed the wheezing around a giant pyramid of cinderblocks, tried to separate one shadow from the next. It didn't matter, though, because after two steps he kicked soft flesh and almost pitched forward to the ground, regaining his balance only by waving his arms wildly. Whoever was on the ground let out a feeble grunt, but other than that, didn't seem to mind being kicked in the ribs.

"Hello?" Stone asked.

No answer, just slow wheezing.

Bending down, he flipped open his cell phone and aimed the display light near his feet. The weather-cracked face of an old man swam into view, his bushy beard painted aqua blue from the LED screen.

"You okay?" he asked.

No reply.

Not only no reply though, nothing. No breathing, no wheezing, no signs of life of any sort. Dead?

Just to be sure, Stone reached down and shook the guy, gave him a slight backhand to the cheek. Still nothing, other than the sudden stench of feces. The smell was heinous to the point Stone leaned over and fought to keep his dinner down.

Oh shit, Stone thought, did I kill a bum? He could see the headline now: ROCK STAR NEWS ANCHOR MURDERS TRANSIENT, TELLS NEWS AT RIKERS. No, no it couldn't have been him. He barely hit the guy, just a light slap. No, it was hypothermia; it had to be.

Saliva pooled at the corners of his mouth at the thought of throwing up. Wiping his mouth off with his sleeve, he thought, NEWS ANCHOR PUKES ON BUM, STORY AT ELEVEN. When you worked in this business, headlines became your nightmares.

He managed to keep his insides from turning out, but really, didn't think the guy would mind being puked on anyway. Whoever found him would guess it was a result of alcohol and sleeping outside in winter.

Wait a minute, Stone thought, I've found him. What the Hell do I do now?

First, he walked back around the cinderblock pyramid to escape the aroma of shit. Then he dialed 911, or at least started to. He stopped before the third digit, stood there thinking. He shook his head to clear it, but a new thought kept popping back up, a buoyant turd that wouldn't stay flushed. The thought was this: what if I can use his death to my benefit, make it a juicy story, an exclusive? Hell, I was gonna use him anyway, right? And when life hands you lemons, you make lemonade. He could turn this into something equally compelling—a rescue story.

No. No, he couldn't. That was crazy. He just couldn't.

Or could he?

Oh God, he was drunk, and worse, he was a thinking drunk.

Somehow, standing in the freezing cold with his whisky breath forming clouds before him, it seemed to make perfect sense.

Slowly, hesitantly, he drifted back to the bum, opened his phone on the dead man's face again. Bending down and holding his breath, he took off a glove and put the back of a frozen finger against the bum's dirty aqua blue neck and felt for a pulse. There wasn't one. He wiped his finger in the dirt, put the glove back on, and sat and stared at the dead man's blue face. The bum was caked in dirt, wearing a black ski cap and several layers of clothing, some puffy ski gloves he'd either found or stolen.

Stone thought of Mason and her lovely tits. Those tits would win an Emmy. He thought of Doug Hardwood, and how the city had been glued to the screen during the Winslow murders. Everyday Hardwood had revealed some new tidbit, some insight into the case, something he'd learned from a secret source or piece of mail he'd received. The bastard ultimately helped catch the murderer, if you can call going down in a hail of police issue .45s being caught.

"Murder." Stone said it aloud, let it roll around his tongue. "That could work. People love serial killers."

I mean, the guy is already dead, he thought. Anything I do at this point is just decoration. And if it made Cheese's dick hard, well, he'd be stupid not to take advantage of this opportunity.

He was not going to be the shit on Hardwood's shoes, or Tricia Mason's, or his ex-wife's, or anyone's. He was going to wow this town, be the biggest thing since Edward R. Murrow, come hell or high water. Just you watch! Murder. A top story.

Need a signature, he thought, something that will stand out. Something the public will eat up. Maybe I can write a satanic message on the walls, he thought. Nah, that was boring. He could strip the man naked and lay the clothes out next to him. Too weird. Probably the simplest thing to do was carve something into him. Hell, the guy was dead, it's not like he'd scream. Couldn't be much different than carving a steak—had to be similar. And the guy probably didn't have a family. It's either that or Stone's Moans, he reminded himself. Do it now while you're drunk, now before you chicken out.

Standing up, he flashed the phone around the work site, saw some scrap metal lying on the floor. He chose a long flat strip, like a ruler, and swung it through the air like a swordsman, listened to it whir. This'll work, he thought.

Once again standing over the dead bum, his cell phone tinting the scene a moldy hue, Stone put the edge of the strip against the bum's forehead, and considered the best way to create a serial killer.

Gacy, Bundy, Dahmer, Manson, all the notable ones flashed through his mind. But unless he was going to dress as a clown, rape the cadaver, then eat it, most of them weren't going to do him any good. Manson, though…Manson got him thinking about things. Manson became a leader—granted, a leader of wingnuts, but a leader nonetheless. Manson still had fans. Hell, there were women who still wanted to marry the crazy SOB. But the thing about Manson that Stone always found interesting, the thing that really made him a leader, was that he was so out of his head, so nonsensical, you almost assumed he really was a genius and you were just too dumb to figure him out. You almost tried to find the hidden meaning in his ramblings. In the end, of course, he was just the wingnut king. Still, it got Stone thinking.

How far gone in Crazy Land do you have to go—or appear to go—before people see you as something special?

Stone started carving.

The body bled, he gagged, but he was quick about it.

When he was done, he ambled home, a bloody souvenir in his pocket, skirting wide of the Howitzer Building, and crashed down in front of his computer. Chauncey, his mongrel, walked over and laydown nearby, went to sleep.

Watching the dog dream, he came to the realization that what he'd done tonight could so easily remain a secret if he too just went into the bedroom and put his head down, closed his eyes. But then what? When he woke up in the morning, would he once again be the same old failed newscaster, the same old divorcee? The same old nobody?

C'mon, Stone, he told himself, you took a chance tonight, you know where it can get you. You just need to follow through. Do it right and you'll put Cheese and Hardwood in their places. You'll get the respect you deserve.

"Just do it already."

Keeping his leather gloves on, he grabbed a sheet of paper and typed up a bit of wingnut nonsense, found a padded envelope, slapped a stamp on it (moistened under the faucet, not with his tongue), dropped the souvenir inside, and took the letter outside. There was a mailbox on the corner, but someone might see him. He needed some way to get it mailed from another location, someway he wouldn't be seen.

A passing bum caught his eye—for a second Stone thought it was the ghost of his recent news project, but it turned out to be a she—and he paid her ten dollars to drop the envelope in the mail down in the Lower East Side. He told her he was from the planet Golox and would grant her untold riches if she followed the order. She bowed to him, called him the Goloxian Supreme Chancellor, and took off running.

If she followed through, good. If she didn't, even better.

As the temperature continued to drop well below freezing, Stone went to bed and slept soundly.

CHAPTER 6.

Opening his eyes Stone thought, why is the room upside down? Oh wait, I'm upside down. Rolling over, he righted himself on the edge of the bed and waited for his brain to catch up. When it did, the pain was quick and brutal. Whiskey was personified by a prize pugilist, at least in Stone's world. And it was a mean son of a bitch. Gripping his head to hold his brains in, he hobbled into the shower and struggled to wake up.

The hot water helped, but it contributed to his tired state of mind at the same time. When last night's activities started to come back to him he found himself too relaxed to give a shit.

I'm going crazy, he thought, wondering if he could pray to the shower gods to take him somewhere he couldn't think or speak or see. Take him back to six months ago, when he had a wife and a promising job and a conscience.

Mason was in the lobby when he arrived at WWTF, her skirt higher than yesterday, her tits somehow rounder. Several employees, including the women, were drooling in her wake. "Hiya, darlin'," she said to him, a great big smile on her moist red lips. "y'all wanna take the elevator up with me? I got me some items I wanna bounce off you, editorial ideas for your segment."

"Sure," he replied. A strange voice hurt his head, and after a few seconds he recognized it as his own.

"Look like something the cat dragged in. Rough night, darling?"

"Don't know. Can't remember."

When the elevator doors opened, a large pink bunny walked out and flipped Stone off, said, "Outta my way, shithead, before I stomp you." He, it, stormed by and went to wherever large pink bunnies go.

"New friend?" Mason asked.

"Me and bunnies, like bleach and ammonia."

In the elevator, she handed over some printouts from local community websites; certain passages were highlighted for Stone to read.

"This one here is about a squat downtown," she said. "All the inhabitants pulled together and started selling art out of it. They want to make it a store but the city won't let them."

"Is the art good?"

"I don't know, darlin', I haven't seen the price list. But it'll appeal to the liberals."

New York is an artist's Mecca, and if there's one thing they'll get their stoned asses off the couch for, Stone thought, it's a censorship battle. It was a good lead.

"Yeah," he replied, suddenly reminded of a story. "I covered this exhibit once. This lady put a gasmask over her head and covered her naked body in ice cream. Then she had this rhesus monkey in a tiny NASA suit—"

The elevator door opened. "We can discuss it later," Mason said, inadvertently batting her eyelashes at him. "I need to speak to Charles first." She took off down the hall to Cheese's office, her ass swishing back and forth ever so slightly.

Charles? She was on a real name basis with him?

Stone walked to his office, tossed the printouts in the garbage, fell in his chair and dialed up his voicemail. Nothing. The computer was still on from last night, so he checked his email. A few press releases, some spam about penis enlargements, an email from Cheese saying he wanted to talk ASAP. Leaning back in the chair he thought, tonight's top story: PENIS ENLARGEMENTS, A GROWING INDUSTRY. He liked that, made a note on a post-it and stuck it to the computer.

The phone intercom buzzed. He hit the speakerphone button. "Stone."

"Stone, it's me." It was Cheese. "I've got Mason here in my office. The Board has been calling all morning. They loved the bit last night. Sales is raving as well. Stone's Moans is perfect for us, and you're perfect for it."

"Good thing my name is Stone, huh?"

"I want you to come up with something hot for the segment today, something that'll create a stir. Tricia said she gave you some leads. Get on them and make them shine."

"Cheese, the segment is crap. Don't tell me I'm stuck with it for good."

"Well, let's see, you could do a segment on unemployment, in-depth research if you get my drift."

Mason…Pastore…whatever her name was now, was laughing in the background, a light snickering that was somehow alluring. Stone said, "I believe that's illegal."

"What's illegal is that this sexy face isn't on a billboard somewhere."

Stone rubbed his chin. "Well, I wouldn't say I'm sexy, I just stay out of the sun and—"

"Duncan!"

From somewhere in the room: "Yes, sir?"

"Get Mason's pouter up on the side of the building. Put her on busses and taxis. Today, Goddammit! Stone, I expect your piece to give me an erection today. Can you do that?"

He looked at the post-it on the computer. "I think I can manage something."

Stone hung up and dialed his ex, deciding he would take out his angst on her, save his job. She was out of breath when she picked up.

"Hello?"

"Who're you boning?"

"Wesley, what the hell do you want?"

At least someone still used his real name, thank God.

"Sounds like you're having a good time."

"It was fun until the Sherpas showed up, then it just got weird."

"You'd know."

"And you wouldn't."

"Yeah, well, some of us don't just fuck the first thing that goes moo."

"You were gone morning till night, hon, what'd you expect? Shit, I'm not rehashing this now, either you have a point for this call or I go back to my workout. I'm counting to three…one…two—"

"Did you get the alimony check?"

"Yes. And it's been cashed. Why, do you need it back? Out of money? Thought the hookers in the village worked for compliments."

"They raised their price to a cup of coffee."

"I left you some coffee."

"You want to go to dinner tonight?"

"Good-bye, Wesley."

"Fine. You know, all that money still won't fix the blackness inside you."

"Maybe you could do a piece on spurned housewives for your Stone's Moans piece."

She started giggling so he hung up the phone. Bitch. He gave her everything she asked for—an apartment, clothing, vacations—and she goes and fucks some young, vacuous model and that entitled her to half his life. How was that fair? She was heartless. Still, she'd watched the show so what did that mean?

Aw fuck it, he thought, and put his head down and drifted off.

A red-headed production assistant woke him at three o'clock, said something about the editorial meeting was on and why wasn't he answering the phone.

The meeting was halfway done when he got there, wiping crusted sleep from his eyes. Nobody seemed to mind that he was completely disheveled. Darrell Lock, the assignment editor, was rattling off something about a high school that was getting sued for royalties over some play they were producing.

"Stone," Cheese said, "Nice of you to join us. You look over those leads. Anything worthwhile?"

"Absolutely. Good stuff. But nothing I can do tonight on short notice. What'd I miss?"

Nice save, Stone.

A skinny guy with bad hair stood up. "We have a piece ready to go about a woman downtown that just adopted quadruplets."

"Who's this yahoo?" Stone asked, pointing at the man. The guy looked like he'd lost a fight with a Flowbee.

"I'm Ron, the new producer."

"Well produce me a cup of I-give-a-shit. That story sucks."

"It's that or the art squat story," Cheese said. "We're cuing up tapes now so flip a coin quick."

Stone sighed. "Yeah fine, show me the tape of the crazy lady and her brats. We'll follow up in six months after she's in the loony bin. Now that'll be a story."

Everyone was staring at him now. His lack of conviction to Stone's Moans was clearly on his sleeve.

For the rest of the meeting he just stared at Mason's chest while Cheese went on about needing better leads. A good ten minutes was devoted to which public appearances Mason would be putting in, and what she should wear, and whether or not she should get highlights.

Investigative stuff, Stone thought. Real nail-biting television.

Then it was prep time for the newscast.

He hit make-up and had the staff clean him up, fix his bed head, cover the dark circles under his eyes. Mason sat two seats down, Cheese circling her like a hawk above a dead jackrabbit. "I'm thinking you go short-sleeved," he told her.

"Charles, please, we're not trying to Foxify the station."

"Could get us a quarter share in ratings by next month. Hell, maybe you're right. No, I'm right. All this change is the kick in the ass we've needed. I mean, look at this set. How do you feel about it? I think it looks like shit. This is 1997 right here." He swept his hand around the set. "We need the 2000s. We need updated and sleek. What's that fucking term where you put your shit where it affects your Kafka?"

"Chakra," Stone said. "Feng Shui."

"Right. Duncan!"

"Yes, Cheese."

"Get me a book on Feng Shui."

"Feng Shui's out, Charles," Mason said, "interior design is back in. It's not the same thing."

Cheese was daydreaming. The kind of daydreaming a madman does when he tells you he's going to blow up the moon. "Yeah, interior design. Like how WYNN has those big potted plants now near their desk. You see them? They look good, homey. Look, you get me another point today, Mason, I'll let you pick the designer."

"Delicious, sweetie, I know the perfect designer, works with fruit rinds."

"Fruit rinds, now that's a new twist," Cheese said. "Maybe even a story. I'll get Duncan on it. See Stone, listen to Mason and you'll learn a thing or two. Get connected with the here and now. Okay, let's move, we're on in fifteen."

Tricia was at her best as soon as the red light came on the camera. Somehow, her lips got moister, her breasts ballooned, her eyes spoke of endless nights of debauchery. Damn, she was good. She finished her outro to the piece on the MTA and then bantered with Stone before the commercial.

"Roland, do you remember when subway fare was only fifty cents? Seems like just the other day."

No, thought Stone, and neither do you being from the South. But he had to reply and he couldn't think of anything. It was unscripted dialogue. Watching from just off camera, Cheese was trying to kill him with his eyebrows. First thing Stone thought of was: "Fifty cents won't even get you directions from a prostitute these days."

Utter silence. Tricia brought them into commercial break. Cheese was in Stone's face immediately, heat breathing out of his flared nostrils. "That was fucking brilliant, you dumbass. Jesus Christ, and you want anchor back? Get your head straight, do your piece and stop making my asshole jump up my back."

Claymore Swift had his head in his hands. He shook it back and forth and sighed.

It was at this point one of the production assistants rushed up with an envelope and pressed it into Stone's hands.

"Mr. Stone, this just came for you. The mailroom said it smelled funny and thought it might be food. They didn't want to wait."

"The hell is that?" Cheese asked.

Stone turned the envelope over in his hand. He didn't know what to feel. It's not that he'd forgotten last night, but he sort of hoped the bum he'd paid to deliver this would have used it to wipe her ass. Instead, here it was, looking just the way he'd left it. His ticket not only back toward an anchor position, but fame. Or hell. He opened it, took out the note, and read it aloud.

"Roland Stone, last night I began work on a project of life-altering proportions. Not my life, mind you, but the lives of all New Yorkers. For it is written that someday the meek shall inherit the Earth, and I am here to tell you that that time is now. These moans are real. No longer will the pigs and sheep follow the corral to the slaughterhouse, no longer will they lay down and bleat while you cut them to bits. The turds of the city will be cleansed, the criminals both lauded and exterminated. When the cycle of sorting is complete, the kings will walk among the heads of the warmongers. Enclosed you will find a token from the first lucky soul, a disillusioned fiend stuck in limbo."

He tilted the envelope and out fell a sticky white marble. An eye. The bum's eye. He feigned disgust and let it fall to the floor.

"Jesus, is that real?" Cheese asked. He was shocked, but Stone could see the gears in the director's head spinning fast. He continued reading.

"Though he is little to blame for the tyranny you and your allies perpetuate, he was nevertheless like a candy wrapper blowing in the wind. Useless to all sides. I have freed him to a better wastebasket. Please announce my warnings on your news show, and I mean you and only you. Failure will only result in a stronger work ethic on my part. Let all the devils of the city, and the world, know what awaits them. In the meantime, you will find the owner of this token in an abandoned building. He carries the rest of this message."

He looked up at everyone, their wide, expecting eyes staring back. "It gives an address," he said.

Cheese threw his arm over Stone's shoulder, said, "Walk with me." Together, they walked back to the anchor desk, and Cheese straightened Stone's tie for him.

"Listen here, Stone, when that little red light comes on, we're cutting to you. This is good breaking news. Take your time with it, maybe ad lib an opinion. Wait, what's your opinion?"

Not the first time Stone had been asked for his thoughts on something, but a rarity nonetheless. "The people deserve to know," he said.

"People will eat a plate of dog shit you tell them it's monkfish and charge them four hundred dollars for it. Fuck what they deserve to know, focus on what they want to hear. Got me?"

"Got you."

"Good, so we're going to throw up the breaking news graphic, you read the letter, and we'll call the cops after. If they give us shit, fuck 'em. You don't hand over a story like this no matter what they threaten. You know what this means?"

He thought, an anchor position?

"It means," Cheese continued, "Barney the dinosaur could go ape shit and beat his kiddy cohorts live, he still wouldn't pull the viewers away from us. People love serial killers. Fucking phones will be off the hook the next twenty-four hours. Advertisers, the public, the works. You play this up and we'll be on page one of *The Times*. You all set?"

Tricia Mason, still at the anchor desk, was watching intently while make-up fixed the one out-of-place hair on her head. Stone looked her up and down. Could she feel how Cheese's dick was suddenly pointed away from her and at him? Oh, he liked this.

"Everything okay?" she asked while manually lifting her tits a bit higher. Those two melons practically had a make-up artist of their own. Pat O'Halloran was probably mixing his drinks with a hard-on.

He nodded, smiled. "Everything's perfect. Let's do this."

CHAPTER 7.

When the red light flashed, Tricia Mason read the teleprompter, a bit confused but she went with it. She was a pro, acted sympathetic even. In the monitor, Stone saw the Breaking News graphic appear in flashing red, and, you guessed it, some designer font dripping blood. If it had been a story about diet pills the station would have been flashing images of Auschwitz. Cheese—the man was the devil, and as such he got results. Stone took a deep breath, and then it was his time to shine.

"Ladies and gentlemen," he began, real serious and confident. He stood straighter than he'd stood in years. You'd think Cheese had shoved a tent pole straight up his ass and propped him there. Slowly, methodically, he read the note, pausing for dramatic effect just like Cheese liked. They cut in a shot of the eye, now on a white board, a black bar over most of it, then back to him again as he explained how it came to him. Across the room, he could see producers and assistants suddenly answering their cell phones as if a mysterious ring tone was on the loose; the excitement was already beginning.

The monitor showed the camera zooming in on him, and he took full advantage of it. "Rest assured ladies and gentlemen, I will keep you informed of this story as best I can. Lock your doors and report any suspicious activity to your local police. Back to you, Tricia."

Across the room, Cheese was practically tap dancing. He dropped something on the floor, some piece of paper, and Duncan Willis scooped it up like a Yankee making a diving catch. He realized it was trash and tossed it down again. What a prick.

Mason and Swift were chatting, transitioning to the weather report, and Stone could see he was no longer needed. Cheese motioned him over and they walked into the control room. Tricia's tits decorated the monitor screens; cameramen are voyeurs by nature and if you give them an inch…

"Nice job, Stone," Cheese said. "Let's hope this nutcase keeps you on his VIP list."

"Excuse me."

"You know what I mean. You keep getting letters, this could be something big."

"Big enough to get me back at the desk?"

"Let's not jump the gun. First off—Duncan, if you don't get off my heels I'm gonna display your address on Stone's next segment."

"Sorry. I was just—"

"Cops are gonna be here in a second, Stone."

"Cops?" Just saying it brought on the sweats. What if they found him out? Suddenly this whole plan felt extraordinarily stupid.

"We don't have to call them first, but we don't want the public to think we're screwing things up either. I was you, I'd make a photocopy of that letter. They're going to take it."

"Cops?"

"Pay attention, time is short and we have a lot of work to do. We need to get cameras out to the victim's location stat."

Cheese was ahead of him already, thinking like the boss he was. Stone handed the letter to Duncan, motioned for him to take care of it. He hesitated, but when Cheese turned and looked at him he took off like a cockroach caught in a spotlight. Stone was about to steer the conversation back toward his old anchor position, when the now familiar red-headed production assistant appeared from nowhere.

"Um, Mr. Stone. Mr. Cheese…I mean, Cheese…I mean—"

"Spit it out, kid," Cheese barked. "Time is money and you're costing me."

"Sorry, sir. There's something you should see."

The young assistant led them over to the television screens monitoring the competition. Doug Hardwood was at his anchor desk, looking serious and presidential. The kind of look that demanded attention and exuded trust all at once. If Stone didn't know Hardwood was such a megalomaniac, he'd shave his head and walk backwards if instructed by the man. The guy knew how to find a lens.

The graphics box over his right shoulder had a body outline on it. Inside the outline were the words CASANOVA CARVER STRIKES. It was written in some goofy comic book horror font, with drips of blood running down it. It looked better than what Stone had had behind him just minutes ago.

"Turn it up," Cheese said.

The PA turned it up and stepped away. Hardwood's voice grew audible but it sounded like the bit was almost over. "...Police have no information at this time, other than to tell us the victim's heart was indeed cut out. They are looking for her relatives."

"What does he mean by that?" Stone asked. "What the hell is going on?"

Cheese shushed him as the report continued. Looking slightly grief-stricken, Hardwood held up a letter.

"Concerned viewers, I have no idea why this man chose me to confess his slaying to. Surely I am no patriarch, nor absolver of any sort. But for whatever reason, this person sees me as Hermes, messenger of a self-proclaimed deity. To rip the heart from any human being is to rip out not only an organ, but all the love therein."

Sweet Jesus, play up the drama Hardwood.

"Had I been quicker, maybe...well, I thought it was just a junk email. I had no idea the pictures would arrive later, that we'd find her exactly where the email said she'd be. For this I apologize. We are all the wiser now. I pledge to keep you informed, as it is what you deserve, and I will do my best to help the authorities however I can. When we return from commercial, we'll see how a single father of ten is making a difference this season."

The control room was silent. If a mouse were to fart it would be a sonic boom. Cheese slicked his hair back. Not that it needed it; the Concord's nose was less streamlined than Cheese's hair. Though actually, now that Stone noticed it, there was a loose strand in the back, and every time he rubbed it down it popped back up. He'd never seen Cheese's hair do that before. It was so…unnatural.

"Duncan!"

"Yes, sir." Duncan appeared like a ghost out of thin air, the photocopied letter in his hand.

"What's this Carver bullshit?"

"No idea, sir."

"Well find out."

"Yes, sir." And off he went like a Dickens character promised two farthings if he came back with a turkey.

"Stone."

"Yeah, Cheese."

"Looks like you're not the only anchor who got a love letter from this nut tonight. The guy must have hit all the news stations. Hey you, kid, was this on any of the other stations?"

"No, Cheese, I mean sir, I mean—"

"No one else got a letter?"

"Not that I know of."

Cheese looked at Stone, seemed to relax just a bit. "So you and Hardwood have an admirer. Shit. There goes our exclusivity."

"Actually, Cheese," Stone began. "I don't think…"

"Don't think what? Get to it already."

That's when Tricia Mason walked in, all business. She pushed aside the PA and got in Stone's face. Her breath smelled like cinnamon and mint.

"I don't know if I should be pissed y'all stole the show or kiss you rotten for doing it so well."

"Do I get to choose?" he asked.

She wasn't listening anymore. She stood next to Cheese and rubbed his arm and every one in the room adjusted their pants. "We need to get on this right away. There's a better angle here if we can find it. Tomorrow, I play the reporter, dig for some dirt, and y'all, Stone, y'all learn all you can about this kind of thing. Profile him and get a picture in people's heads. Is he going to strike again? Where? How? What's his reason? But don't make it up. Find someone official who can back up our thoughts. We banter, we open up lines of thought. Get the viewers involved. We do a piece on self defense to hold their attention."

"You wear a lower cut dress?" Stone teased.

"Sex and violence do go together like grits and butter."

"Hold up," Cheese interrupted. "Stone, what were you going to say before?"

"Nothing. Just that I don't think it's the same killer."

"What's the same killer?" Mason asked. "What are you talking about?"

Cheese filled her in about Hardwood's report. When he was done, Duncan returned and shook his head to mean he hadn't learned anything new. Mason grabbed the letter out of Stone's hand. "There's no mention of ripping out a heart here."

"I know," Stone said. "It's a different guy."

"What? You sure? How—"

"Trust me."

"Two guys?" Cheese said. "Hold on, my head is fucking spinning. How can there be two guys? What are the odds on that? Seriously."

"Exactly what I'm wondering."

"Doesn't matter," Mason piped in. "Our killer is better than Hardwood's."

"Why's that?"

"Because we're going to make him better."

Cheese looked at her like he wanted to lick her neck down to the bone. Mason was just his ticket, thought the same way he did. Ratings equals money equals power. If Cheese was Citizen Kane, she was his Rosebud. And if Hardwood had a killer, she was going to conjure up Lucifer himself for WWTF.

Together, they left the control room and disappeared. Stone waited for the police to arrive. To leave would be too suspicious, and besides…he had to know what the hell was going on.

CHAPTER 8

Detective Ramon Garcia took Stone's statement and secured the letter in an evidence bag, said he'd be in touch. He was a tall, skinny man who spent the entire interview sucking on a Tic-Tac and rubbing the back of his neck as if he'd slept in a knot. When he ran out of questions, he handed over his card and told Stone to call if he thought of anything.

As the detective was walking out he said, "Kind of funny two crazies send two letters to two newsmen on the same night telling where their victims are."

"Yes," Stone replied, "But New York City gets all kinds."

"Yeah, that's true. You better believe it. Well, at least we have this dog hair to go on."

Stone's eyes didn't flinch, though they wanted to burst out of his head. "Dog hair?"

"Yeah, this one. See. It was in the envelope the letter came in. Looks like a short hair, brown, starting to get some gray in it. Funny how even dogs go gray."

Leaning in close to inspect the hair in the detective's rubber-gloved palm, Stone recognized it as Chauncey's. "Oh, that's from me."

"From you?"

"Yeah, my dog. His hair gets all over my clothes. Probably fell in when I opened the envelope."

Garcia's eyes walked over Stone's blazer, his pants, his shoes. Because Stone kept his suits shut up in the closet, and he used a lint remover before he went on air, there wasn't a dog hair anywhere on him. "I don't see any hair on you," Garcia said, studying the air between them, judging the distance. "You knew this was your dog's that quick? From over there?"

"Well, it looks like my dog's is all. I just assumed…"

"Mind if I keep it anyway?"

"Well…um…I guess not."

"Thanks. We'll be in touch."

What the hell have I gotten myself into, thought Stone, as he headed to O'Halloran's to try and stop the nervous shaking that had taken hold of him since the interview. Blindsided by a goddamn dog hair, how was that for luck? Finding fingerprints or weapons near a dead body, apparently that sort of evidence was too boring for the boys in blue to look for. But drop a dog hair in their hands and look out, the case was going to get cracked and promotions were going to be handed out. How could he have been so stupid?

The familiar stench of cigar greeted him as usual, but this time he found something else unsavory inside. Hardwood was at the bar drinking red wine, a few of the locals hovering around him bugging him about something, no doubt the Casanova Carver news. Furious, Stone slammed his fist down on the bar top and watched as everyone cleared away.

"Stone," Hardwood said, gallantly as always.

"You stole my story. How'd you do it?"

"It is quite a coincidence isn't it? Two news anchors...excuse me, two newsmen receiving letters on the same night confessing heinous crimes. What are the odds? Unless it's the same killer and he sent letters to all the media. It's perplexing."

"It's not the same guy and you know it."

"Do I? You seem rather perturbed for someone who got as much attention tonight as you did. How many calls have you gotten so far?"

"*The Times* and *Post* called my cell while I was walking here, I told them no dice, it's my story. I haven't checked my machine at work yet."

"And yet you're angry with me. It's not my fault some deranged soul—or souls as you propose—chose the same day to send us letters. Hell, I get letters all the time from people. Sometimes, yes, even the ramblings of lunatics."

"But you never read them on the air."

"This one struck me as urgent."

"Bullshit, it struck you as a golden opportunity to steal back an audience that was glued to my report. What, someone in your office saw my report and you cut to commercial so you could dig through your mailbag real quick?"

Pat came over and put a glass of whiskey on the counter for Stone.

"I took a guess, I did. Dewars on the rocks. And perhaps for it being on the house you could disclose some juicy details about your new story for ol' Pat. Like Mr. Hardwood here did."

The drink didn't steady Stone's nerves as much as he'd hoped, but it helped. After it settled in his gut, he glared at Hardwood. The sonofabitch would use a story to get any small amount of attention he could, be it a wink or a blowjob. Getting attention was his livelihood.

"Only a minor detail," Hardwood said, reassuringly. "Something so that Pat here can impress the ladies."

"Aye, it's the talk of the town tonight and Ol' Patty got the goods. I'll sell a few black and tans at the promise of inside news, I tell ya. So give me what you got, oh Wesley."

It was nice to hear his own name again, and so he bit his lip and thought about the possibilities. It didn't matter what the letter actually said, he decided, if he made something up now it would come true soon enough. But he decided against it on the notion that if Pat knew something before the cops did it wouldn't take a brain surgeon to connect the dots.

"Sorry, Pat. What you heard is what I know."

"Ol' Hardwood here confessed that the Casanova Carver named his victim John Donor. Get it?"

"Not really. I thought it was a girl."

"Ah yes," said Hardwood, "but don't we say mankind when referring to both genders? The killer sees the species, not the sex. I left the name out of the report on purpose. Gives me something to use if I ever track him down. If he knows it's really me, maybe I'll get an exclusive interview."

"Yeah, well, maybe I will too."

"By all means. Such is the freedom of the press. To repeat and reform until every angle has been squeezed."

Stone paid Pat and waited until the bartender left before he spoke again. A group of men walked in and sat down at the table nearby so he spoke low, the first buzz of the night catching up to him.

"Something's fishy here."

"Oh, please. Sending letters to the media is the oldest trick in the book. The Zodiac killer, the Unabomber. They all send their deranged musings to us. It's in the serial killer's handbook or something. It's amusing but terribly trite."

It was then that Hardwood reached for his drink and Stone noticed the cuts on his forearm. They were fresh, the result of something thin and sharp. He'd seen cuts like that before during stories he'd covered, usually on rape victims but more often on the attackers themselves. It never failed that an attacker using a knife cut himself.

"Hurt yourself?" he asked.

"Oh, these lacerations? I was hanging a mirror last night and it shattered when I misjudged the hammer. Shame too, it was an antique from my relatives in Portugal."

Now, what happened next, as Stone sat back slowly and felt his chest tighten, was sort of like emerging from the mental fog that surrounds a dream. Everything became clear real quick.

"You sonofa…Hardwood, you killed that girl."

"You're drunk."

"First drink of the night, not even done with it. You did, you killed her. You sick bastard. Killed her for the story. Sonofabitch. You, the great and successful Doug Hardwood, killed her and made up The Casanova Carver."

From the TV at the end of the bar, there came a riotous burst of canned laughter. The bar patrons followed suit, as did O'Halloran. Stone looked up and saw Branford Marsalis beaming, pointing at Jay Leno as if he'd just one-upped the big-chinned host.

Slowly, calculatingly, Hardwood spun in his barstool and got in Stone's personal space until their noses were practically touching.

"Funny you should bring it up, my sleepy-eyed competitor. I know where you were last night…Roland. I know about the bum in the building and what you did to him. Care to have a conversation about it?"

Inside Stone's head a loud voice shouted, what!? How the hell did Hardwood know about his trip to the construction site? There hadn't been a soul around last night, not even a stray cat looking for a frozen mouse.

His heart beat faster, the backs of his hands started itching. Sweat from his armpits began running down his sides, cold and uncomfortable. The poker face he was trying desperately to maintain was becoming ever more transparent as the seconds ticked off.

"Surprised?" Hardwood asked.

"I was home all night."

"Please, Stone, ixnay on the eyelays. The simple truth is that as I returned home last night, Louis—he's my doorman—got my blood boiling and so I went for a walk. I must have walked two blocks when I turned back and saw you talking to Louis. You must have just missed me. Curious as to what could be bothering you at such an hour, I followed you to the FDR—"

"It wasn't me."

"It was. And knowing as I do that you don't live out that way, I kept after you and watched, somewhat mystified I admit, as you discovered your sleeping corpse. What came next was merely vaudevillian in comparison to what I think you were trying to do, but nonetheless shocked me. Look me in the eye and tell me I'm lying."

Stone looked in his eye, saw three decades worth of interviewing criminals and politicians and knew he couldn't lie his way out of this one. "Vaudevillian?"

"Vaudevillian. It means—"

"I know what it means. So then what, you figured you wouldn't be outdone and went off and gutted some poor girl?"

"Unlike yourself, Stone, I do not need to mimic other anchors to get my stories. Let's just say there was something in the air"

"What are you getting at?"

"Do you find it amusing when two movies come out with the same plot, and yet the directors swear they never heard of each other?"

"You're losing me."

"Think about it. Movies take many months to produce, which means they were begun at around the same time. See, some spiritualists believe that ideas exist in an ether, and seep out into people's minds all at once, and that's why people on opposite sides of the world have the same idea at the same time."

"Wait, you're telling me you *set out* to kill someone last night? Because that's not what I did. I didn't kill anyone. I'm calling the cops."

"Will you now."

"Why shouldn't I?" From his pocket, Stone pulled out his trusted miniature tape recorder and showed it to Hardwood. It was something he'd learn long ago in the news business—always be prepared for an interview. He always carried it in his pocket just in case. "Should I play it back? It's been recording since I walked in."

Hardwood smiled, picked up his glass and finished off the wine. From his pocket, he removed a similar tape recorder which was also recording. "Such is the business," he said. He put the recorder back in his pocket, stood, and motioned for Stone to follow him. "This place is rather, well, filled past the point of comfort. At least for our garrulous dialogue. Let's walk."

Stone took a long pull on the Dewars, put the glass back on the bar. Pat saw them getting up and waved a friendly goodbye as they headed out the door. Neither noticed.

On the street, the bitter cold was like a nail gun to the cheeks. Stone pulled his overcoat's collar up and around his neck. "Get on with it," he said.

Walking, Hardwood started playing hardball.

"Stone—"

"Wesley. It's Wesley Farques."

"Fine, Wesley. Who picked Stone, anyway?"

"Cheese did. He picks all the anchor names. I don't know who the fuck is who in this business anymore. We're not obligated to make it legal, thank God."

"Well, Wesley, Stone, whatever, before you go to the police with anything, let me ask you some questions. When you were carving up your story last night, did you think to take your shoes off?"

"If I was even where you claim I was, what difference would it make?"

"Only that the police surely have a shoe size in their records by now. And seeing as how it hasn't snowed since two days ago, they probably have the shoe pattern too."

Stone looked down at his shoes. They were size 10s, a cheap knockoff of Maglis he'd purchased at Macy's. They did in fact have a tread pattern on the bottom.

"Big deal, lots of people wear these shoes, Hardwood."

"Well, did you think to pick up any hairs that may have fallen off your head? What about prints? You were pretty drunk, did you take your gloves off at all? Did you know you've got a small bloodstain on the bottom of your coat, right here?"

Hardwood bent down and pointed to a rust-colored dot on the tail of Stone's tan overcoat. Dark as it was outside, it was plain as day.

"What the…?" Stone replied.

"Probably just something you sat in, but you can never be too sure. That, basically, is my point. Are you sure you got away clean with your midnight endeavor, or are you relying on being an upstanding citizen, and I admit, a minor local celebrity, to keep you out of the detectives' minds?"

He stood in the frigid cold, now trembling with a newfound heat, a heat that radiated from a second wave of nervousness. The son of a bitch was right. He had been drunk, he had been careless, he had left clues that would lead to him. How could he have been so foolish? "What do you want?" he asked.

"Me, nothing. I don't even know what you're talking about. If you're referring to the fact you wear the same pair of shoes as a million other New Yorkers, or that I cut my hand hanging a mirror, then all I can say is our lives are fairly insipid. Do you know what I mean?"

So that was it, Stone realized, he was making a deal, one closed mouth for another. But the fact still remained, he had desecrated a corpse and Hardwood had…Jesus God…committed murder. The evidence was against him either way, especially if Hardwood testified against him. How could he prove he didn't kill the bum? The older newscaster was smarter; he couldn't help but grant that.

"So tell me, all those exposé stories you're so famous for…you created them?"

"I work hard for my ratings, Stone. Nothing more, nothing less. I expect you do the same, especially since I see you just had a very influential story fall into your lap. What are the odds?"

The New York night was still very much alive with honking horns, firetruck sirens, and yelling pedestrians. People passed by without concern for their conversation. Even if someone had been listening, chances are they would have been too amused by seeing Hardwood in public to even decipher what was being discussed. Stone began to relax, to let the cold seep back into his bones and calm him down.

"I have some work to attend to," Hardwood said, slipping on his imported leather gloves. "Perhaps we can work more closely on these stories another time. Good night."

Stone watched him disappear into the crowds on Third Ave., the old man's silver hair fading into a cloud of cigar smoke from some young punks wearing gold chains. He thought, Jesus, what now? I just let a murderer go free to save my own ass. A murderer who was off to God knew where to do God knew what. A murderer, he reminded himself, who would be gobbling up his audience by tomorrow afternoon.

Above all, he couldn't have that.

CHAPTER 9

Hardwood's three-bedroom, two-bath suite on the 21st floor of the Howitzer Building overlooked the west side of Central Park. During the day, from the windows in the living room, he could look down past the trees and watch joggers on the paths, artists near the bridge drawing charcoal caricatures of lovers on vacation, children throwing snowballs on the fields currently blanketed in a layer of white powder. During the night, he could watch the police patrolling the perimeter of the park, looking for drug dealers and rapists, and spy on horse-drawn carriages taking couples on romantic circles under the streetlamps.

But no matter the time of day, the people always looked small and insignificant—tiny fleas in a flea circus. And looming above them, he felt like God.

It was all so boring.

He turned from the window and went into his home office where his many awards sat on bookshelves alongside his collection of first edition books. The tape recorder he carried with him was resting next to his computer. He turned it on, listened as Stone's voice recounted their earlier conversation.

It couldn't be ignored how strange the coincidence that they both decided to go the route they did in their mutual need to rise above Tricia Mason's existence. While it concerned him on one level, he knew Stone was an amateur who would get himself caught in no time, so there was really nothing to worry about in the long run. When the Press Club Awards rolled around he'd still be accepting the award for Best News Anchor, as usual, and he'd still be number one with the public.

He went through the tape and erased the parts of himself talking, then recorded Stone's admissions onto a second tape. This he sealed in an envelope and placed in his safe. Before closing it, he removed a black gun case, set it on the couch.

Satisfied with that, he got a bottle of wine from the cooler in the kitchen. It was an Australian Syrah he'd been saving for a special occasion, and tonight was certainly unlike others. The digital display on the Wine Cellar 2006—a top pick in last year's *Robb Report*—showed that the inside was a temperate sixty-one degrees, perfect for this particular bottle.

Returning to the study, he took a Cuban Monticello cigar from the humidor on the desk, lit it up, and returned to the window in the living room.

"Ah, Stone," he said, "are you out there now, spilling blood and whispering my name, preparing some distinct marvel for me? I do hope it is worthy of my challenge. If I'm to lose sleep in the coming days, it had better be for a game that tests my skill."

The wine was peppery, with hints of oak and a patina of fruit. He sipped it and let it slide slowly down his throat, taking in the subtle nuances of the vintage. It would go well with prime rib, or perhaps pork loin, especially a dish with the earthy tones of mushrooms. It would be perfect with his favorite dish, veal cubes covered in truffles on top of mushroom risotto. The mere thought of it brought the taste into his mouth. He had not experienced it since the last time he'd seen…Jeremy.

The thought caused him to turn and look at the picture on his desk. A sunny day at Rockaway Beach, his arm around a young man, so much like himself. It was evident from the young man's grimace he did not want to be in the picture. More to the point, Hardwood knew, he did not want to be with Hardwood. The subtleties in his body language made it look like he was about to run out of the frame. It had been—what?—three years since they'd spoken? Right before the Winslow murders began. It was an ache, a void, he'd learned to live with, but for some reason now, he felt the need to call the young man. What if something were to happen to me, he thought, and I perish before having a chance to reconcile? Is Stone stupid enough to come after me?

Swirling the wine, he drew in the smoke from the cigar, which was bold yet smooth, well worth the thirty dollars he'd paid for it on the sly at the smoke shop he frequented down at the Seaport.

A siren wailed somewhere in the distance outside, bringing him back to the present.

"Stone, Stone, Stone, just how ostentatious are you thinking? Is your quarry a public darling? A commoner who will draw sympathy? Or is this more about flair? A wise man once said that it's better to influence than to impress."

Hardwood rose and moved across the room toward his collection of Sinclair Lewis novels, all first editions, including the author's first story, *Hike and the Aeroplane*, written under the pen name Tom Graham. He ran his fingers across the spines of the books, feeling their history and imagination, his wine in one hand, his cigar in his mouth, until he reached the end of the shelf.

There, on the wall, next to an original Cezan, was a painting of two shadows kissing, done by a local artist who called herself Rouge. He'd bought it at an auction a couple of years ago that benefited children living with AIDS, where he'd appeared as a guest speaker. The painting was poorly done, the shadows applied willy-nilly, the perspective grossly out of whack, and would normally have cost about twenty dollars in a local gallery. But he had appeared in *The Times* with it after the auction, talked it up as the greatest piece of art he'd ever bought, making sure to point out its one-of-a-kind value, and knew he could sell it for upwards of a thousand dollars today if he wanted to.

Because he'd made it famous.

So much of fame, he knew, was based on what you could convince the public was a one-of-a-kind element.

Murder was no different. The more unique the killing, the more attention it garnered. If it were legal people would no doubt market it.

Just what was Stone doing out there tonight? What type of killing was he preparing to show the world tomorrow on his show?

Hardwood stared at the painting of the shadows kissing and took another sip of his wine.

"We'll start small," he said. "I'm sure daring pieces will come in due time. But for now, it's just important to get in the game and feel out the opposition."

He found his hunting knife and ski mask in the hall closet. Holding them again was like unearthing a buried memory, one that was not necessarily unwelcome. He placed them with the gun case, then went to the bathroom and removed a spool of thread from his portable sewing kit.

CHAPTER 10

Back at home, Stone sat in his easy chair and pet Chauncey on the head. The dog kept whining for more attention despite his touch. Probably the dog just missed Carlie. She used to let Chauncey sit on her lap sometimes, and Stone was pretty sure the dog liked her better than him but there was no way she was getting it in the divorce. Chauncey was Stone's dog.

"Good boy," he said as he scratched the dog behind the ears. The clock on the wall said 2:45 AM, which may as well be high noon in New York City. He took a few moments to write down the night's events, transcribing the conversation he'd had with Hardwood with a selective memory. No use bringing up any of his own recent accomplishments, especially in light of the purpose of the letter, which was to ensure Hardwood had a proper finger pointed at him should Stone's body be found missing its heart. He sealed it in an envelope and placed it in the basket near the door so he wouldn't forget to mail it in the morning. It was addressed it to his lawyer, with instructions not to be opened it unless something happened to him. Yes, very Hitchcockian to say the least. Sue me, he thought.

Next on the agenda was rustling through his closet, looking for an old pair of shoes that were a size too small and caused his toes to damn near bleed. They were under a box of photographs he'd been saving for God only knows what reason. Various pictures from events he'd attended throughout the years. At the MOMA fundraiser with some local philanthropist, with jolly African American weatherman Bud Rawlings at a benefit breakfast back when he'd been a field reporter, with Carlie at some celebrity golf tournament in Jersey that didn't involve celebrities beyond C-list actors. Stuff that meant nothing really, but that fed his ego nevertheless and had moved him up the ladder. After taking the shoes out and setting them on the bed, he went and got an old gym bag. From this, he emptied out the contents—old ties, a folded up *New York Times*, a date book that he'd never written in—and replaced them with the shoes. To be safe he tossed in a pair of jeans, a sweatshirt and a garbage bag.

Chauncey looked up at him with sorrowful eyes—a silent beg for attention. He gave the dog a scratch behind the ears and set its tail wagging.

"This is my story, Chauncey, and there's no way I'm letting anyone else take it over. Too long I've paid my dues to watch some pair of tits take away my promotions. Too long that snob Hardwood has had this city's eyes and ears glued to his every breath. If it's ratings they want, it's ratings they'll get."

But first...some practice.

*

As Hardwood stepped from the elevator into the foyer, he saw Louis open the front door for him. The cold air rushed in and hit him in the face before he made it outside and set his bones aching. He hated to think his age could ever impede him, but reality was reality. Tonight's business would have to be played out carefully, unless he meant to spend the coming weeks with pneumonia.

"Evening, sir," Louis said. "Don't usually catch you out this late."

"Just a late night work meeting, Louis. Nothing I need to be coddled over."

"Of course, sir. I just meant—"

"I know. Just doing your job, Louis, don't worry what a codger like me says this late at night. I'm not happy to be out at this hour is all. My vexation is not directed at you."

"Do you need car service?"

Hardwood almost never took the subway, and only took cabs when he was in an absolute rush—the smell and sickening racecar mentality of many of the cabbies made him nauseas. So car service was a given for him. He'd already called for one.

"No thank you, Louis, I took care of it. In fact, I believe this is my car coming now."

A black Lincoln town car was pulling up in front of the building's door, its tinted windows hiding the driver inside. It pulled to a stop.

"Very good, sir," Louis said.

Hardwood handed the doorman ten dollars, his subtle way of saying there's more where that came from if you keep your nose out of my business.

"Thank you, sir."

"Keep up the good work, Louis. One of these days I'm going to do a story on the real people who make this town work, and you're going to be the first on my list. Goodnight."

"Goodnight, sir. Drive safe."

Hardwood got in the car, smelled the distinct mixture of the car's heating system and freshly Armor All-ed leather wash over him, closed the door and checked out the driver. He was a young Italian man, mid thirties, with greasy black hair combed straight back Dapper Dan style. He wore a pair of sunglasses despite the hour and lack of anything resembling sunlight.

"Are you invoking the spirit of Ray Charles?" Hardwood asked, "or is there a problem concerning ultra violet wavelengths I've yet to hear about? I'm a newsman, you know, I'm fairly certain I'd have heard about it."

The driver took the sunglasses off and remained silent. Hardwood took this as a victory for himself, and decided not to press further. "Tenth and third," he told the driver. "It's a bar called Fredo's."

The driver turned around, revealed a thin black mustache that Zorro would be proud of. "Yeah, sure, I know Fredo's. No sweat."

"You do your people proud."

If the driver caught the insult, he didn't show it. He put the turn signal on and pulled into traffic. "Hang on."

As the driver cut in an out of traffic, Hardwood took the ski mask out of his pocket and played with it. He had never needed one in the past, because he was a thorough worker who planned ahead, making sure his "stories" never got a good look at him. But tonight he had something unique in mind, a true work of art, a one-of-a-kind exhibit that depended on intimacy with his victim; he would need to be up close and personal for this artistic endeavor.

Unlike the amateur painting he'd been looking at earlier, he would apply the shadows properly and take time with the perspective. He would be meticulous, because the beauty was often in the details.

And when the work was done, he would make it famous.

Stuffing the mask back in his pocket, he felt the spool of thread there as well, its needle pinned through the side. It was a red thread, chosen for its theatric tone, though whether the intent of the color would register to the law and the rest of the media was anyone's guess. Television led the world to believe that detectives were damn near deities in their ability to solve crimes, but the truth was they were largely inept. He'd seen the unsolved crimes database on a story a while back…extensive did not begin to describe it. You couldn't pull fingerprints off a pillowcase, and computers could not clean up a grainy security camera photo enough to get a clear image of someone's face.

After several minutes of the driver racing to beat the red lights—a common pattern with drivers in New York, since it was possible to go from one end of Manhattan to the other without hitting a red light if one was fast enough—the car pulled up to Fredo's, a small disco that looked like it still belonged in the '70s. People were standing outside smoking, some of them giving the finger to a police cruiser that was parked nearby. The mayor's closure of one of the city's more popular clubs had upset the children of the night; the cops were awaiting repercussions. Mostly this would involve vandalism and angry blogs, but the potential for more serious statements was always there.

"Let me out here," Hardwood said.

"I can get you closer."

"Here is fine."

Hardwood handed the man two twenties and told him to keep the change.

"Hey, thanks. You need me to pick you up later?"

Hardwood shook his head no, got out, and shut the door.

"Hey, the news is here!" someone yelled. "Look, it's Doug Hardwood! Hey, everybody look!"

This was exactly the reaction he was hoping for. By being seen in one establishment, he essentially had an alibi for being elsewhere. Which was part two of the plan.

He waved to the people, jokingly replied, "Just meeting a friend for a drink. I'm not too old to hang with you cats am I? I can still do the monkey pretty darn good." This got a big laugh, and everyone enthusiastically told him to come in and do it for them. Not very likely, he thought. When celebrities were caught acting stupid in public it ended up on every website from here to Timbuktu. But he laughed with them anyway and made his way to the door, which thankfully did not have a line. The doorman recognized him and asked if he needed a special table. It just proved his point about the power of doormen.

"Just meeting a friend," he replied. The doorman opened the door for him and motioned him to enter.

The interior of the club was dense with smoke, and smelled of cheap incense. Women with tight tops and men with tight jeans sat at small tables around a lighted dance floor, doing their best to look fashionable. The crowd was mostly Italian, probably from Jersey and Long Island, what they called the Bridge and Tunnel crowd. And if anyone couldn't tell this was an Italian hangout from the crowd alone, posters of films by Martin Scorsese, Brian DePalma, and Francis Ford Coppola lined the walls. Le Sheik was playing over the sound system.

People pointed as he made his way to the bar and ordered a scotch, double malted. They didn't have this, so he settled on a Budweiser—swill to himself and anyone with a refined palate. The bartender, a thin Italian boy torn from the pages of a glamour magazine, said, "Hello, Mr. Hardwood," as if they were old friends.

Hardwood lingered on the boy's face for a minute, a twinge of self-loathing rising in his chest. Did he know him? Was this a specter of his past come to haunt him? Couldn't be. The boy was too young to be an old friend. Like the people outside, the boy probably just recognized him from TV.

Still, the boy was...attractive, muscular and well-manicured. The type of man Hardwood had sworn to ignore. And yet, he couldn't look away. Images of the two of them kissing in a fit of debauchery flashed through his mind's eye, tracing hands over one another's abdomens, sliding down toward the heat between their legs. Quickly, he shook his head and squelched the vision. "Ignore it," he told himself, self-loathing and shame overtaking him.

He took the beer and made his way to the rear of the bar, leaned against the wall, and pretended to drink it. Had it been whiskey, he would have savored it, but right now he needed to get on with his plans.

The bathroom was down a long hallway painted black with Christmas lights running along the ceiling, the kind that stayed up all year long. They were hanging up the last time he'd been here as well.

That was a while ago, and even then there'd been a reason for being in such a lowlife place. He'd met someone for a drink, someone who'd only invited him to make it clear he was unwanted. The memory of that hurtful night still burned bright in his mind and he knew it now like his favorite movie. Across the dance floor, he spied the bar where the dialogue had taken place, and watched himself sitting there, listening to words he knew verbatim.

A drink, some brief apologies, the person telling Hardwood he shouldn't call anymore. Then watching as the man left by the front door, never to be seen or heard again.

He blinked his eyes to erase the image, turned and looked down the hallway to the bathroom, remembering how it had ended. Hardwood, number one news anchor in New York City, had slinked out the backdoor that night and cried.

It was the fist time he'd cried in twenty years.

And it was, he decided, the last time he would ever cry.

It wasn't until the next morning that something odd stuck him about leaving by Fredo's back door, which had everything to do with why he was here now: the alarm had not sounded.

There were many reasons why this might have been, but the obvious one was drugs. People who went clubbing did drugs, oftentimes buying from the bartenders or bouncers or even the owners themselves. Special K, cocaine, ecstasy, GHB, party drugs mostly. The back door was an easy way to evict patrons who were passed out or in a K hole or, hell, just plain dying from an overdose.

No one wanted to get shut down by the mayor.

He set the beer on a small table. Passing by the bathrooms, the memory of that painful day fresh in his mind, he pressed against the push bar of the back door and opened it into the small garbage area between Fredo's and the building next door. There was no alarm.

Looking around, he found he was alone, exactly as he'd hoped.

The nearest subway station was a block away, close enough to avoid recognition if he moved quickly. Just to be safe, he kept his head down and his collar drawn. He donned the ski mask like a winter cap and walked to the end of the subway platform, away from the largest group of people, and awaited the train. When it arrived, he sat alone in the rear car, the only other occupant a bum who was passed out and, from the smell of him, probably covered in feces.

The subway took him to the Flatiron District, where he got off and walked east to a small dog park near the edge of the city. There, he found what he was looking for.

A couple sitting on a bench under a tree.

Two men.

Kissing.

*

The cat purred in Stone's arms as he carried it into his apartment. He'd seen it near the dumpster out back numerous times, and a simple "here kitty kitty" had drawn it out of the shadows.

It jumped on the couch and started clawing the cushions. Chauncey came by and stuck his nose against the cat's butt to investigate the mysteries of the feline intestinal tract and got a swat for his troubles. Whimpering, he went and lay near his dog dishes.

From the kitchen, Stone grabbed a knife, came back and sat down next to the cat.

It was hard to ignore the purring and the furry face, which now seemed to be smiling up at him. Its large green eyes were radiant emeralds of content, so peaceful and nonjudgmental. The cat climbed into his lap and curled up, its warmth seeping into Stone's legs.

"Don't do this. C'mon. How can I do…this"—he waved the knife around—"if you're gonna be so affectionate?"

There's your answer, Stone, he thought. You can't. You're a pussy. Hardwood is gonna take your ass to town. And Mason is going to have your job. And Carlie will never stop laughing at you. And—

"Okay, I can do this. I have to do this. I have—Chauncey! Leave the cat's ass alone!"

The cat looked up at him as Chauncey once again lay on the floor. Mowr.

"Yeah. Okay. See, here's the thing, cat. This is just business, okay? Don't take it personal. I'll do it quick. You won't even feel it. I mean, quick across the neck or something. You just go to sleep, okay? But I gotta do it. I gotta…I gotta be strong."

Mowr.

"I know. I don't want to. But this is how it works these days. This is entertainment. So…"

With that, he took a deep breath, thought of Carlie's laugh, and stabbed the blade into the cat's neck. The animal went wild, limbs flailing with ferocity, hissing and rolling over onto itself. "Stay still and I'll finish it!"

Thrusting his hand into the melee of claws and teeth, he found the knife's hilt and yanked it across the animal's head, taking it clean off.

Quick. Easy. Over before he even knew what he was doing. That was the way to do it.

The cat's body fell to the floor, limp and lifeless, just a prop.

Chauncey got up and went into the other room.

Thinking that was a pretty good idea, Stone went into the bathroom and threw up.

Again.

When he was finished, he sat under the sink, rocking back and forth, repeating to himself, "I did it. I did it. Not so bad. I can do more. I can do more."

After a while he stood and looked at himself in the mirror, and though not a religious man by any means, said goodbye to his soul.

CHAPTER 11

"Excuse me?" Hardwood said, standing behind the men on the bench. They were young, perhaps in their twenties, each bundled in a heavy winter coat and thick scarf, their arms around one another as they kissed. Pulling their heads apart, they looked up and studied Hardwood, perhaps to make sure he was safe to talk to, perhaps to make sure he wasn't a gay basher or pervert looking to watch. Mostly because they were being interrupted and just who could it be that had the nerve to bother them?

Their eyes went wide when they saw the ski mask.

"Shit!" the blond one said, bolting up to run. Hardwood grabbed him by the collar and hit him over the head with the gun. Crack! The man fell down moaning.

His compatriot found his legs and took a swing at Hardwood, caught him in the head. But the punch was hesitant, impeded by fear, and Hardwood merely staggered back a bit. A younger man might not have staggered at all, but his age was what is was, and it sent a shock through his frame. Adrenaline rushed to numb the area where the blow connected, and gave rise to a moment of non-lucid anger that passed as quickly as it came, replaced by cold calculation.

He pointed the gun at the young man's face, a gesture the man understood to mean he was invited to throw another punch if he fancied himself faster than a 9mm.

"I didn't see that coming."

"Please, don't shoot."

"You're going to live," Hardwood said. "I promise you. I'm not here to kill you, but if you do that again, I will shoot you in the cock.

Don't think for a minute your boytoy here won't find someone else to fuck him once your coital instrument is gone."

"What...what do you want? Money? Here, here's my wallet. Just take it and leave—"

"Please, don't insult me. If I wanted your wallet would I have announced my presence so casually? I make more money in an hour than you make in a month. No, I want something else."

The blond man was sitting up now, watching his lover staring down the barrel of a gun. "Tim," he said, looking back and forth from his boyfriend to the masked gunman, then to the street to see if possible help was nearby. But they were alone. "Give him whatever he wants. It's not worth dying—"

"He said he don't want our money."

"I don't," Hardwood replied. "I want you two to sit on the bench for me. Like you were."

Hesitantly, the two men sat back down on the bench. Hardwood came around the front of them and squatted down to be eye level with them. He glanced up at the surrounding buildings, many of which had windows looking down into the park. Thankfully, the bench was under a tree, and away from most of the street lights. So long as no one screamed, he should be okay,

"So...so...what do you want?" Tim asked again. "Are you going to hurt us?"

"Only if you yell. Sit quiet and you'll be fine.

"What I want is to maintain the status quo, you see. I want to ensure that my life's work is in no way negated and shoved aside by a buxom blonde with some willowy eyelashes and a tight posterior."

"What business?" the blond asked. "I don't understand."

"Let me tell you a brief story then. It's a fairly common one, one that I'm sure you'll appreciate on some level. Business man works very hard, for many years, at the bottom of the ladder, getting coffee for the boss, pushing papers, what have you. Yes, you know this story. Working hard for the man, getting no respect. But, aha, eventually that hard work pays off and a few years later he is now an integral part of the company. We don't always see this part of the story but it does happen. Only this company, you realize, it's very public, and as such the now-successful businessman must maintain a clean image. America, correct me if I'm wrong, is extremely ignorant, and will not hesitate to hand out stereotypes based on religion, and especially, sexual preference."

The blond was scared, breathing heavily. "Is this because we're gay? Because if so—"

"Let me finish, please." Both men shut their mouths and sat still. When Hardwood was sure he could continue without interruptions, he said, "As I was saying. Stereotypes, in this country, can kill. Now our friendly businessman, the one who slaved his way into a very respectable public job, has a little secret that his family is unaware of. He can't hang out on a park bench like you two. He has to steal his kisses elsewhere. And so he does. But one night, while he's with a special friend, hiding in the shadows as they always do…he's recognized. And not just recognized by anyone, but a powerful politician. Said politician has voiced his concerns in many a speech about the businessman's lifestyle, and is clearly opposed to it. Said politician will not hesitate to bring to light that this businessman—"

"Um, no offense," Tim said, "but it's cold and you're taking a long time. I think we get it. You're gay, you're a politician, and another politician saw you kissing a man."

Such bravado these New Yorkers have, Hardwood thought. "You are very perceptive. I congratulate you. Did you figure it out too, Blondy?"

The blond man nodded, though Hardwood doubted he had figured it out. There was a certain blissful ignorance in the blond man's eyes, the kind of idiocy that makes men think they can outrun bullets. Tim, on the other hand, showed a modicum of deductive reasoning, hence the fight instead of flight response to seeing Hardwood's gun. In this respect he liked Tim, and in this respect, he'd been sure to stay honest with him.

"Good job," Hardwood said. "You're not entirely right but you're close enough."

"Did you…did you kill him?" Tim asked.

Hardwood nodded. "Oh, yes, I killed him."

Killed him and enjoyed it, Hardwood thought. In fact, the only thing that haunted him, after he'd snuck into the upper west side condo that fateful black night and stabbed and butchered Martin Winslow, his wife, and their three daughters, was how if he'd killed the dog too, he could have garnered the attention of the animal rights groups. It was a missed opportunity.

"Jesus," said Tim.

"No, but I try."

"Um…It's okay that you're gay, you know?" The blond said, trying his best to identify with his captor.

"I'm aware of that, thank you," replied Hardwood. "I'm not doing this because I'm gay, or because you're gay. You're just in the right place at the right time. And me, I'm doing it because I've invested too much in my position. See, I did something nefarious, and as chance would have it, it was a bigger benefit to my career than I could ever have dreamed possible. It taught me how to excel in the world. So you see, I've put in a lot of time and energy to get where I am, and nothing, not an ignorant politician or woman with ditzy charm, is going to wrench it from me.

"But, this is all moot. What I really want is for you"—he pointed to Tim—"to say goodbye to this dolt."

"What! But you said you wouldn't kill us!"

"No no no. I said I wouldn't kill you. But your friend has to die for this to work."

"But—"

"Shhh. Don't fret, you'll be remembered. You're the first, after all, since the Casanova Carver made his headlines, so you're going to be famous. I'll see to it. Eventually, I'm going to cover the streets of this city in blood. No one will be safe, especially lovers."

"But—"

Hardwood put the gun to Tim's temple, and shushed him again. With his other hand, he slipped the hunting knife out of his pocket and stabbed at the blond man's neck. The man threw his hands up to protect himself, but Hardwood quickly rapped him on the head with the gun again, momentarily stunning him. Then, apathetically, he ran the blade across the man's throat.

"Don't scream, sir," he said to Tim, whose eyes were out of his skull as his body shook, "or I'll alter the deal."

The blond man leaned back on the bench and gurgled, his lover finally looking away and crying. The gurgling lasted for several minutes, until the blond man's body sat still, steam breathing out of the rip in his neck.

"Now," Hardwood said to Tim, "I want you to kiss him."

"I…but…"

"If you don't I will shoot you. Trust me, you're going to live, but only if you do this one last thing for me."

Crying, shaking, Tim picked up his dead lover's head, and kissed it on the mouth.

Hardwood removed the thread and needle from his pocket.

The hour passed in a worried haze of bloody cat daydreams as Stone thought about the best way to go about executing his plan. Maybe execute wasn't such a good word to use, he thought as he cleaned up the bloodstains left from the cat—which he'd wrapped in a trash bag and deposited back in the dumpster.

Oblivious to his master's dilemma, Chauncey licked Stone's hand and ran in a frantic circle after his tail, something the dog hadn't done since Carlie'd left. It might not have been considered approval of his plans in some people's books, but Stone took it as the dog's way of giving him the green light.

Time to get moving.

First thing he did was don a pair of leather gloves. Your average black jobs, purchased long ago at a Duane Reed. Then he ran a brush through his hair to get rid of any loose strands before slapping a hat on his head.

Before leaving, he slopped a big can of dog food in Chauncey's dish and rubbed the dog's furry chest. He also grabbed the chef's knife from the kitchen and put it in the briefcase with the shoes. He'd have to replace it with a new one tomorrow. He shut off the lights and headed down to the street to catch the next train to Avenue A, making sure to keep a low profile; everything in his life suddenly revolved around not leaving a trail.

On the train he let his mind wander. He thought about what he wanted out of life, about what he was willing to risk, about how much of himself he didn't mind destroying. The crossroads lay ahead somewhere, and figuratively speaking, he was about to sell his soul to the devil in exchange for celebrity and job security. It wasn't exactly the same as exchanging it for some holy talent the way Tommy Johnson did, no, it was better. In America, Stone thought, celebrity is a money generator. Celebrity brings in advertising, brings in the hungry masses just dying to dish out their hard-earned income on some ridiculous possession they could more than do without. Mel Gibson tells you to buy baked beans and the goddamn ozone layer is farted away in weeks. In the end, it would all be money in his pocket so what did he care. In the end, it would put him back behind that anchor desk, probably with an executive producer credit as well.

At Avenue A, he got off the train and hailed a cab.

New York has a lot of desolate areas, if one knows where to look. The industrial parks of Brooklyn, the warehouses of Queens, hell, even parts of the Village get lonely at night. He steered clear of anything near Manhattan and told the cabbie to take him out past Williamsburg. Naturally, the guy pissed and moaned, because for some reason the damn cabbies hate to drive outside the grid. It wasn't until Stone promised him double the tip that he agreed.

Over the Williamsburg Bridge they went, out past the refurbished apartments on Broadway and down to the old Boar's Head truck depot. Stone told the cabbie to head toward the park and he obliged, though he wasn't happy about it. When they hit the park (a loose term for a dirt lot with weeds poking up here and there), Stone said, "My apologies, I meant Morgan Ave." He did this on purpose to frustrate the cabbie, so that the man wouldn't bother writing down the destination in his log or calling it in to his depot, and it worked. With a huff, the cabbie spun the car around and sped toward the renovated lofts. Once there, Stone feigned confusion and pointed the cabbie down more side streets until he finally noticed there wasn't a soul in sight. The surrounding factories were closed, the windows dark. By this point the cabbie was pissed, asked for his money right away. Through the money slot of the partition window, Stone slipped him a fifty dollar bill. The fare was $32.

"All I have," he told him. "Keep it."

The moment weighed on his back like lead. Here indeed was that crossroads he'd been anticipating. One path left to safety and the insulting life he woke up to every morning. The other led to a place of darkness he could never return from. A place where he'd be lauded and loved, at the expense of his soul.

Hello America, how are you? I've come to introduce you to Wesley Farques, otherwise known as Roland Stone, otherwise known as the most trusted face in news.

Stepping out of the cab, he quickly knocked on the cabbie's window. The man rolled it down and yelled, "What you want?"

"Sorry, my watch is dead. See."

Stone showed him the watch on his wrist, which was working fine, but he knew the cabbie couldn't tell in the dark. "I was just wondering if you had the time."

The cabbie leaned out to look at Stone's watch. Stone punched him in the face. The car lurched forward as the cabbie stepped on the gas. Stone dove inside and grabbed the wheel, spun it hard. At the same time he hit the cabbie square in the mouth with his elbow. A loud crack resounded through the car as one of the cabbie's teeth broke out of the jawbone and bounced to the floor. Blood spattered all over Stone's sleeve. "Stay still, will ya?" he heard himself say.

Frantic, the cabbie bit Stone's shoulder, thrashed his head back and forth like a wild animal trying to tear off flesh. Stone screamed and stuck a finger in the cabbie's eye, shoved it in as hard as he could until he heard a pop. The man kicked wildly and threw his arms up to cover his face. The car drifted into a chain link fence that ran the perimeter of a vacant lot and came to rest, Stone still halfway in the car. He dropped back out and scanned his surroundings. Still empty, not a transient in sight. No apartment windows lit up. Checking back inside the car, he noticed the cabbie's head drooping slowly to the side, blood flowing freely out of the man's ruptured eyeball. So he did what anyone would have done: he bent over and threw up.

He was going to have to stop doing that.

It felt like everything came up. If he still had a soul it would be splayed on the ground in a puddle of yellow slime. Standing over the puke, he almost asked if it was worth it. But before he could, he saw himself signing his first book, published by Time Life, of course. He saw his face on the side of every bus in town, and he liked it. Once purged, he opened his gym bag and took out the shoes. Just trying to slip them on was excruciating enough to make him consider not carrying out this part of the plan, his toes mashing together like sardines in a tin. But he forged ahead, and grabbed the cabbie's head and tilted it out toward the street. Within a few seconds a small pool of blood formed on the dirty salt-covered cement, mixing with the puke. He smeared the blood on the bottom off his soles and walked in circles for a minute. The pain in his ankles was blinding.

"Well, Hardwood, let's see you get my audience away from this."

Taking the knife out, Stone placed the blade against the back of the cabbie's ear and began sawing down. There was a distinct crunching sound as the knife cut through the cartilage. Right when it plopped off into his hand, the dead man lurched and coughed. "Jesus Christ!" Stone screamed, jumping backwards. The cabbie was wailing, praying to God, or Allah, or someone named Ahhhh! Stone didn't know what to do so he shouted, "Shut up! Shut up!"

The cabbie grabbed at him with shaking hands as drool dribbled down his mouth and fell to his chest. Stone did the humane thing at that point and slit the man's throat. It wasn't unlike the cat, really. It was pretty easy, all things considered. He didn't exactly like it, mind you, it was just business. At least that's what he told himself. Just business.

The cabbie gurgled for a bit, air escaping from the wound like a fart from a sleeping dog, then became still once more. To make sure he was fully gone, Stone poked him a few times. There was no reaction. He poked him again. "You dead? Hey, you, move if you're alive. C'mon, don't fucking do that again. My heart can't take it."

No response. The guy was gone.

Finally he had a moment to breathe, and leaned against the car sucking in air. Not for too long, he thought, stay focused. Get back to work before someone comes by.

The other ear came off in one slice, now that he was getting the hang of it. Both ears had gold earrings in them, which seemed out of sorts for a Middle Eastern man. But then that's why they came to America, Stone thought, to have those little bits of freedom they couldn't get anywhere else.

He sopped up the blood in his palm and wrote THE KING WALKS on top of the cab. Shit, he thought, I hope they don't think this is an Elvis joke. But even if it was, would that be so bad?

"It's a start," he told himself. He knew Hardwood would be bringing his A-game—as Greely the sports anchor referred to it—to this little challenge, and to really pull ahead with the audience, he needed a shocker. So he stripped the man naked and cut open his lower back. The blood seeped out thick as maple syrup and stinking of sweat. Actually, that was the cabbie; he stank to high heaven.

He steeled himself for the next move, having never done anything so remotely horrific in his life before, even considering the cat. People think cutting a man's throat is horrific, and yes it is, but the knife does the job and all the killer feels is a slick handle and some ache in his triceps. But this…Stone reached inside the open wound, grabbed a handful of wet insides, and yanked as hard as he could. Viscera exploded out onto his pants, hit him in the face, coated his hair. The empty pit of his stomach tried to run up his throat and he hacked and dry heaved so hard he was sure he pulled a muscle in his neck.

Taking up a ropy length of intestine, he cut it in half and pulled both ends out even further till they looked like two long, gray sausages trying to escape from the body. Holy Christ the smell! He thought: is that shit inside there?

It's amazing how big a human's insides are, crammed so tightly in such flimsy packaging. Like man was a suitcase God was packing and just sat on top of it to make it all fit. It was spilling out of the cabbie at an alarming rate, pushing its way to freedom. When both bits of intestine were long enough to reach the cabbie's head, Stone stuck them into the corpse's mouth, all the way down the throat.

Flipping the cabbie onto his back so that the handiwork was easily noticeable, Stone took the kitchen knife and went to work on the chest area.

The man had a lot of chest hair, and to eliminate the problem of it covering Stone's message, he ran the edge of the blade down it sideways and shaved off a patch of fur. He sank the knife into the pectoral muscle and carved CATTLE in the cabbie's chest.

Standing up, he looked over his work. Was it the work of a nutcase? Yeah, it was out there, but mostly because the messages didn't make any sense. It would drive the cops nuts, but better than that, it would turn the viewers into living room Sherlock Holmeses. Every person in the city would be trying to decode these nonsensical clues. Especially after the exclusive report he was going to give on it in a few hours time. Brilliant. He gave himself a mental pat on the back.

He should have kicked himself though, because aside from a clever massacring, he had fucked up the rest of the job. There was more blood and guts on his person than in the corpse. From a nearby road came the sound of cars driving by, and he knew it was only a matter of time before one of them turned this way. He needed to change quickly.

"Okay, Stone, here goes."

As quickly as he could, he tore off the bloody garments and used the dry sections and some snow to wipe off his face and hair. The winter night was harsh enough to sting bare flesh, make it itch on contact. The brief couple of seconds his feet touched the bare ground had him hopping like a kid at a toy store. And with all the shivering he was doing, it was difficult to get the clean clothes and shoes back on without falling over. When he was done, he stuffed the bloody clothes in a plastic bag in the briefcase and rubbed snow on the outside to clean off the few smears of blood it had acquired.

In the car window, he checked to see if he'd missed any spots. A patina of pink coated his face, but in this chill weather, it would easily be mistaken for a winter rouge.

Then, making sure he had a good amount of blood on the soles of his shoes, he trotted toward the subway station, leaving a distinct trail of shoe prints one size too small for him. He caught the L train back toward Union Square. There wasn't anyone in the car with him except a man with his back turned away reading a newspaper, so he took the shoes off. His poor toes uncurled slowly and painfully. He rubbed them while gritting his teeth. The freedom felt nice, so much so he debated leaving his shoes off for the whole ride. But no, if someone happened onto this car they would surely notice a man with no shoes and pink stains on his hands.

From Union Square, he took the 1 Train uptown, thought about his report, about buzzwords and names for his killer. Hardwood had invented the Casanova Carver. It was a good name, it worked on different levels, most cerebrally that it denoted losing a loved one. Hardwood would be a tough obstacle to overcome, at least in the sensationalist arena.

What did his killer have? Well, he cut people up, referred to them as animals. He was anti-establishment for sure. He didn't use a gun which meant he got up close and personal with his victims. The thing with the intestines, now that was interesting. What was he thinking? Maybe there was something in that, the whole make-the-victim-eat-himself theme. How about The Cook? Hmmm, it needed more pizzazz, the kind of thing Tricia Mason would come up with.

Then he had it, The Chef. It had a ring to it, a name he could see on the front page of *The Times*. A graphic appeared in his mind's eye, a fork and cleaver and a chef's hat with the name written on it in blood. He'd have to explain that to the graphics guys at the station, see if they could make it happen. Fucking Cheese would be sucking him off for that one. Yeah. The Chef.

*

When he arrived home, he wrote a note to himself and stuck it and the cabbie's ears in an envelope. He was just about to wet it when, from out of nowhere, Chauncey grabbed it and shook it like a chew toy. "Let go. Now!"

The dog yanked it out of Stone's hand and ran into the bedroom, crawled under the bed. "No. Bad dog." The ears, he realized, the dog wants the ears. Reaching under the bed, he grabbed the envelope away from the dog and gasped when it ripped open and the ears fell out. Chauncey grabbed one and tried to swallow it. "Shit. Bad dog!"

Lunging, he grabbed it and yanked with all his might but the dog wouldn't let go. Engaged in a tug-o-war, they spun around the room, the dog growling, Stone yelling, "Bad dog, bad dog!"

The ear, slick with dog drool, slipped from his hand.

"Sonofa—"

Chauncey fled down the hall to the living room, the ear flapping in his mouth.

Stone had taught Chauncey a few tricks during their time together. The dog could shake, he could sit, but Stone had no idea Chauncey knew how to open the front door. The dog was quick about it too—a paw on the handle, a bit of a yank. He thrust his nose in the crack and opened it wide just as Stone reached him.

Then they were in the building's hallways.

A little game of cat and mouse.

"Gimme that ear, Chauncey. Don't you dare swallow that. Bad dog!"

One of his neighbor's doors opened and an old gray-haired woman stepped out. She was wrinkled from head to toe, with liver spots dotting her face. Her glasses were coke bottle-thick. "What's all the damn noise?"

Chauncey ran between her legs and into her apartment. Stone made the mistake of following the exact path, trying to grab the dog's tail. It was a bad idea.

"Help! Rape!"

"No no no," he said, standing up, placing his hand on her shoulder to calm her down. "I'm just...my dog ran—"

"Fire!"

"Fire?"

"They told us at the senior center to yell fire when a rapist is after you."

"I guess that makes sense."

"Right, because people love a fire. And then they come running and catch you trying to rape me."

"But I'm not—"

"Fire!"

"I'm not raping—"

"Fire! Fire!"

"Okay. Okay. Look, I'm backing up. See, I'm not here to hurt you. I'm backing away."

"You want to crawl up my gown." She raised her nightgown and revealed white thighs stitched with varicose veins. "You want this honeypot but you can't have it. I haven't given this up in five years."

Only five years? Oh gross.

"Fire!"

Stone put his head in his hands. "Jesus, will you just listen to me for a sec?"

People were coming into the hall, many of them in bathrobes and pajamas—one of them had a fire extinguisher. This was ridiculous; if he didn't get Chauncey soon the mutt would eat the ear. He could feel everyone's eyes on him.

"Look, miss…uh…"

"Davis."

"Miss Davis. Didn't you see my dog run under your legs? You must have felt it."

"Sure I did. But I know what you're doing. You use him as an accomplice is all."

"What!"

"Teaching an innocent animal how to take advantage of old

women—it's shameful."

"No…no I don't—"

"I know you," she said, pointing at Stone's face. Her nightgown was still hiked up. "You're that newsman who lost his job and now does that goofy moaning thing. They got that woman now instead to replace you. Drove you to raping, did it? Fire!"

"I didn't lose my job, you bi—"

"Mind your manners, Mr. Rapist. There are witnesses here now. If you want this honeypot now you're gonna have to wrestle it away from me, only I don't think you can fight everybody off."

This was a battle he couldn't win, not with everyone watching. "You're right, Miss Davis. You got me. I was going to have my way with you, but, well, you're too tough for me. I'll just be getting my dog and leaving. Can I do that?"

"You'll be back. They always come back for this." She pointed to her crotch.

Chauncey suddenly appeared between her legs and came back into the hall. The ear was gone but he was chewing on something. Shoving his hand in the dog's mouth, Stone pulled out the cabbie's earring.

"Is that mine?" Miss Davis asked. "Teach him to filch women's jewelry too?"

"It's mine."

He held out his palm to show her what it was, which Chauncey took as him handing out a biscuit.

The dog jumped up and ate the earring.

"Well, that's great. Now you owe me an earring," the old woman said.

He wanted to tell her that he'd give it to her the second it came out, but instead he just said, "Fine. You win. Goodnight."

As he was leaving, she hollered down the hall, "I'll be waiting for you, you sex monster."

"So is there a fire or isn't there?" the man with the extinguisher asked as he passed by.

"Only in her pants," he replied.

Chauncey ran to his bowl when they got back and slurped up a load of water. "Thanks, buddy. Way to help me out."

The other ear, which Stone retrieved from the bedroom, had a bite mark in it now. Not that you could really tell it was a dog bite, but still, it could probably be traced. Not to mention the dog's saliva was all over it. It would need to be scrubbed clean. At least the earring was still in this one.

Chauncey padded into the room and looked up with sad eyes. "Bad dog. Go lay down."

The dog slinked off into the other room, scorned but secretly happy nonetheless.

Okay, okay, Stone thought, I'll just wash it off, mail it nice and clean. What did it matter if he sent in one ear or two? They'd still figure out who it belonged to after he gave them the location of the body.

On his way to the bathroom to clean it, his cell phone rang. It was Duncan Willis, and he was virtually panting. "Stone?"

"What do you want?"

"I've got Cheese here, he wants to talk to you."

Stone checked his watch. It was close to four o'clock in the morning, but when Cheese came on the phone he sounded spry as a spaniel. His voice was sharp and clear.

"Stone, baby, did you hear?"

"Hear what?"

"Just came in over the wire, there's been another slaying out in Brooklyn. Same MO, carved the guy up and wrote some shit in his chest. Only this time the guy made the victim eat his own insides. Christ, the genius of it."

Stone stood motionless, listening to the city noises outside, frantically going over everything in his mind. Did he check for trace evidence? Did he drop any hairs? Had anyone seen him? What did Cheese mean "genius?"

Chauncey appeared and burped. Stone smelled ear. At least in his mind.

"Stone? You there?"

"Yeah, Cheese, I'm here."

"Good. Get your ass out of bed and get down to the lobby. I'm having the night crew pick you up. I want you out there to report live. We're going to cut in to programming."

"I…uh…I'm kind of tired. Send a field reporter."

"No way. You became the lead on this story when you got that letter. Speaking of which, I called the studio to see if a new one came but it didn't. Maybe tomorrow, though I'm sure New York's finest will be there waiting for it, the bastards. Regardless, after you shoot your roll tonight, I want you at the station working on developing this story. Mason is going to meet you in the AM, give it some life. She has some names for this creep, too. Genius stuff."

"I already came up with—"

But the phone went dead. Looking at the display, all he saw was Duncan Willis' phone number. What a prick.

CHAPTER 12

Twenty minutes later Stone was back standing by the corpse of the cabbie while police buzzed about like beetles near a fresh turd. Detective Garcia was there, and he approached with a cup of coffee in his hand.

"They got me out of bed for this shit," he said.

"Yeah, me too."

"You look like it. Dark circles under your eyes. Remind me of myself. My eyes been dark for so fucking long I can't remember what the glare of the sun feels like. My wife has all this goopy shit she tells me to rub on them. Just makes my face smell like chalk. Who're these guys, your crew?"

Behind Stone, a skinny cameraman fresh from film school stood next to an overweight gaffer from the union. They were working on a shot angle. "Yeah," he replied.

Garcia leaned in close, exhaled coffee into Stone's eyes. "You get another letter about this one?"

"Not yet, no."

"We had trace check the last letter you gave us. Nothing much there."

Secretly, relief flooded through Stone.

"Except for the finger print."

"Print?" The relief took a hike, and welcomed in panic.

"Yeah. Can you believe it? Man, the equipment they use these days. It ain't like the TV makes it out to be, but it's pretty cool anyway."

"And the print?"

"Belongs to one Janice Holloway. A bum."

"Bum?"

"Yeah, you know, homeless. She got pinched years ago stealing some liquor from a bodega. Only problem is, we have no idea where to find her. Put the word out to some people with the same lifestyle, but we ain't found her. Don't think we will either. From what we gather she don't have many friends."

"Not if she's killing bums." Stone faked a chuckle, which did nothing to relax his heartbeat

"Well, that there, that's the thing. I don't think she's our killer. Nah, bums don't carve people up and write those kinds of letters. Bums steal jackets and socks and shit, but generally that's where it ends. No, clean cut white guys with good jobs carve people up. I think she was paid to mail the letter, to get her prints on it. She's a red herring. Which is what weirds me out about this case."

Stone swallowed. "What's that?"

"Just, why would this nutball kill a bum, tell us it was for the bum's own good, then use another bum to deliver the letter? If he hates bums so much and all."

Garcia had a point, one that Stone couldn't shed light on. It did make little sense when you thought about it. But then again, the less sense it made the better off he'd be when it came to leading the authorities astray.

"Maybe he's like Dracula, you know, kills some people but then uses others for his own devices. Puts him in control. Isn't that what these guys are after anyway—power?"

"Yeah, our head doctor said the same. I dunno though, twenty years I been chasing these freaks and one thing I've learned in all that time, these guys are particular. If they don't like bums, they don't like bums. It ain't like the movies, all weird cryptic messages and clues and shit. Sometimes it is, but mostly not. Usually they just cut the vic up, bury him, move on to the next one. But this...this is some weird shit. Soon as the city hears about this fucking carnival it's gonna be vigilante city out here. So you mind how you report this, if not for me then for your own good."

"I'll do my best."

"I'm sure." The sarcasm in Garcia's voice was thick.

"Excuse me, detective, my guys are ready, I've got to shoot my piece."

"You stay behind this yellow tape, I don't care what footage you get. You step over it I'm tossing you in jail and taking the camera. Got me?"

"Sure. I got you."

A young officer ran up behind Garcia and handed him a piece of paper. Garcia read it and then rolled his eyes. "You gotta be fucking kidding me. Another one?"

"Just found them a few minutes ago," the young cop said. "Paramedics are on the way."

A news van from WTLB was pulling up, trying to push past some uniformed officers controlling traffic. A blonde women, young and thin and wearing an expression of self-assurance, leaned out of the window and yelled, "Either I do a story on a cut up cabbie or I do one on the city suppressing the press. Got me?" It was Jennifer Forge, whose real name Stone was currently at a loss for. Not that it mattered, WTLB was less important than PBS news. The cop waved them through.

Stone could see Garcia was not so much upset as exhausted by all the media and uniforms hovering around. "Bad news?" he asked.

"Can you believe this shit? I got another vic across town. And that guy is even worse than our cannibal cabbie here."

"How so?"

"Well, for starters, he's alive, but he's sewed up to another person."

"I don't get it."

"Just what it says here. Body found sewn to Caucasian man. The live guy's nose is smashed to shit and his lips are sewn to the dead guy's lips. So, basically, he's breathing through the dead guy, who has a big hole in his chest where his heart used to be and…Jesus H. Christ, what the fuck is wrong with these maniacs? It's like all of a sudden I got two killers trying to outdo each other or something."

Stone wasn't listening, he was feeling rage well up inside him. Hardwood, that bastard, how did he think of such a grotesque angle? Keeping someone alive, and forcing them to breath through a corpse. Shit, it was masterful. Of course everyone would be glued to that developing story, rooting for—or against (let's not forget it's New York)—the living man. There was no doubt in his mind Hardwood already had field reporters there covering it.

From somewhere nearby he heard Forge say, "Okay, guys, just got word the Casanova Carver struck too. Got a live one at that scene so shoot what you can here in thirty seconds and we'll do A roll at the Carver site. Move, time is money!"

Just to be sure it was indeed Hardwood's story, Stone climbed inside the news van and turned on the TV. Sure enough, there was a reporter from WYNN on the scene. Police lights and curious onlookers filled the background. The victims were off to one side, several feet back, surrounded by EMTs and other medical professionals. A viewer wouldn't see the extent of the situation, but the gasps and frantic rushing about of the rescuers made it clear things were tense.

"Look at that," Stone said to the cameraman.

"What, the reporter?"

"Yeah, look at his hair." The reporter's hair was held in place with some heavy duty hair product; the wind was really whipping about, but nary a strand blew loose. "That's some good shaping, gotta find out where he gets it done and make an appointment."

"Hey, Stone," Garcia leaned into the van and drummed his hand against the corrugated floor, "you get a letter for this, don't touch it. I want it undisturbed."

"Can't promise you…press and all."

"Oh, come on, Stone, don't get on my shit list. You seem like a nice guy. I'd hate to have to shoot you." Something in Garcia's playful tone felt too serious to laugh about; behind the joke was a mild threat. "I'm just kidding you, Stone."

"Yeah, I knew that."

"I won't shoot you, but I will make sure you get any ticket I can give you. J-walking, drunk in public, you burp too loud I'll get you on noise violations. Got me?"

"Yeah," he replied. The cameraman gave him the hands-in the-air okay-let's-go-I'm-freezing sign. Clearing his throat, he took up his position and waited for the signal from the news room. When it came, he responded: "A disturbing scene at what appears to be another slaying by the man who, just yesterday, sent a letter to the attention of WWTF. A man I call The Chef, after seeing the heinous way he disposed of one hard-working cabbie tonight. Ladies and gentlemen, I must warn you what you are about to see is quite graphic."

CHAPTER 13

As the sun came up, Stone put on another pot of Folgers, reminded once again of how Carlie had taken him for a ride. He spent a half hour before work scrubbing a severed ear free of dog spit with a less than enthusiastic attitude. Also, a new letter was in order considering the world knew of the body already. After he wrote it, and the ear was clean, he sealed them once again in a padded envelope and paid the nearest bum he could find ten dollars (with the promise of riches from the planet Golox to follow) to deliver it to the office by noon—he wore a sun hat, pulled a scarf over his nose and mouth, and covered his eyes with large sunglasses. He looked like a mental patient, but better safe than sorry. The bum agreed—word of Goloxian riches was getting around.

Doing it this way was going to have to change. But, for now, he had no other way to get the letter there without bringing it in himself and dumping it in the mail. But everyone was watching the mail. Cheese probably had x-ray machines set up to scan each envelope that came into the building. Having it delivered was easier. At least this time.

By 10:30 that morning Stone was a zombie. He could barely keep his eyes open as he entered WWTF, and if it weren't for all the kudos he was getting for the live coverage earlier, he may have fallen straight on the hall carpet and zonked out right there. Tricia Mason practically had her tongue in his ear, licking and smacking her lips as she spoke. "That report was hot, sug. The Chef, I love it, great name. I want to add a little wowie spice to it though. Let's go with the Tri-State Chef. Bigger scare, more people glued to the set to see if they're safe. Here, have some of this coffee, you smell like cow pie."

The coffee went down easily, though he barely tasted it.

He stopped in front of Cheese's office. Inside he could hear the director's sharp voice shouting out dictation. "No, you have failed Tri-Sate Chef, we will not pander to your idle threats, we will not bow before such useless violence, we will not...read that first part back to me again."

Duncan's voice: "We are not cattle but free roaming stallions, we are—"

"No no, not that part, the part about the bloodhounds of truth."

"There's nothing about bloodhounds."

"Really? Could have sworn I said bloodhounds."

"Let me see...lizards of liberty, flies on the wall of purity, two leather straps and some PVC piping—"

"No no, that was for something else, personal stuff. Okay, fuck it. Make it lions of responsibility, or better yet, satyrs of justice."

"Isn't a satyr a bad thing?"

"Nobody knows what the fuck a satyr is anymore, Duncan, get with the times."

Finally, Stone knocked and opened the door.

"Stone," Cheese said, throwing his arm over Stone's shoulder. "Hell of a report. Good name too. But Mason came up with some—what did she call it, Duncan?"

"Wowie spice," Stone offered.

"Aha! So she already spoke to you. Fantastic. I suppose you know we got a letter for you too, just came this morning. Another bum. Ran away screaming about ruling some planet. Cops are looking for him. Anyway, listen to this:

Dear Mr. Stone,

Your pitiful attempt to name me and pigeonhole my methods only reinforces my notion that you and your viewers are victims of a carbon-copied society in need of fresh blood. Your uninspired Hollywood paradigms only convince me to kill more people faster. Blah blah blah," Cheese concluded. He dropped the paper on his desk and then said, "So the killer hates the name, fucking loathes it. Could this be any more perfect?"

"I—"

"Shut up for a second. Here's where we're going with this. We want you to keep pissing him off, tell him you won't change the name. I want him to get so angry he calls the station, or better yet, shows up here waving a machine gun. I'm working on material for you right now."

"Wait. You want to make the insane serial killer angry? He might kill more people."

"No shit, Watson. You've seen Hardwood's killer. That nutball is inventive. We lost last night's live coverage halfway through, everybody switched over to watch some guy lip-locked with his dead friend. Brutal, but fucking-A if it wasn't ratings heaven for WYNN. But not to worry, our guy is still good, he just needs some encouragement. Like I said, we're gonna make him a star. So piss him off some and make it quick."

Oh man, Stone had to laugh. Cheese was eating this up like it was a prize boxing match on Pay-Per-View. Shouldn't be any reason not to be back at the anchor desk now, he thought. Right? One way to find out.

"I want to report it from the desk," he said.

"Not yet. This Casanova Carver has style, unlike our Chef. If this refusal to change his name doesn't set him off and get him bringing his—what does Greely call it, his A-game?—if he doesn't do that, then we're covering the Casanova Carver, and I'll need Mason on that."

"What!? You're kidding me. This guy is writing to me, and only me out of the whole damn city. We've got the market."

"Market shmarket, either he shapes up after this, or we go with the Casanova Carver. Shit, we don't have to give him coverage. Ratings, remember. They equal sponsors equals paychecks equals you get the point. But look, for now, this guy wants your thoughts, so I want you in your own arena. Mason is doing the initial report. Came dressed for it too. Talk about low cut dress, man oh man, you can see all the way to Miami. Duncan!"

"Yes, sir."

"Get out of here, you're making me nervous."

"But…"

"Now."

"Yes, sir." Duncan slinked out like a bad dog.

"Okay," Cheese continued. "I've taken the liberty of changing the story a bit."

"Changing the story?" Stone asked, taken by surprise. Hell, why did he go through the trouble of killing the guy if Cheese was just gonna change the story?

"Thirty years I've been in this business, Stone, I know what I'm doing. First off, the whole cabbie eating his own insides was good, but not enough. This is the 2000s; I've seen enough people eating intestines on *Fear Factor* to last me a lifetime. And the ear…please. Been there, done that. Wait, did I mention the ear?"

"No."

"Oh. There was an ear. Doesn't matter. You seen one severed ear you've seen 'em all. Cops already picked it up. Where was I?"

"Changing the story."

"Right. Tricia is going to report that the station got a call from the guy who says he's The Chef, says he has a collection of human remains from unidentified victims in his cellar. He's planning on putting these remains in local foodstuffs around town."

"That's—"

"Brilliant, I know."

Actually, Stone was going to say it wasn't really plausible. Not to mention grossly unethical. But Cheese was right, an audience will believe what you tell them. "I like it," he said. "But what happens when this guy comes after you for lying about him?"

"He won't. I'm in charge, I'm the director, I make the decisions about what airs. He knows that...I hope. Point is, he's supposed to be controlling you, not being controlled by you. He'll fight back, sure, but only with you. And that's a good thing for us."

If The Chef was real, Stone thought, Cheese would be putting him in harm's way. Hell, Cheese'd be delivering him to the guy's front step. But again, that's why Cheese was the boss.

"Oh, I scheduled you for interviews with *The Times*, *The Post*, and *Time-Out*. Don't give too much away, but let them know we're holding back, and that at some point we'll reveal all our secrets. Hook the audience like a fish."

Stone threw his hands up in protest. "I don't want to do interviews. This is my story, I'll report it."

"You're doing them or I terminate your contract. It's free press, puts the station on the map. Besides, Hardwood did one late last night and got it on page 1 of *The Times*' entertainment section."

Cheese went to his desk and picked up the day's edition of *The New York Times*, flipped to the page in question. He showed it to Stone. The headline read: CASANOVA CARVER FEARS GRIP CITY. And underneath it, a subhead: FROM WINSLOW TO CASANOVA CARVER, ANCHORMAN DOUG HARDWOOD IS THE SERIAL KILLER'S BEST AND WORST FRIEND.

"Does it mention The Chef?" Stone asked.

"Briefly, at the end. Not much though. That's why we need the press. The interviews are scheduled for lunch time. Make The Chef a star or call Hardwood and see if you can butter him up for tidbits. It's one or the other."

Walking back to his office, Stone couldn't get Hardwood's work out of his head. A big photo in the paper, half the city in his lap. At this point he could charge a college's tuition just to speak at one. Hardwood had done a book on the Winslow murders', a small run from a small publisher, but Stone knew he'd do one on the Casanova Carver too. These days, everybody got a book. All you had to do was sleep with a rock star, flash your tits online, and slur your words for a video on *Access Hollywood* and you'd sell better than Hemingway.

At his desk, Stone pulled open the drawer and took out his flask, realized how cliché it all was, and put it back.

The phone buzzed. He hit the speaker phone function.

"Stone here."

"Mr. Stone, there's a Detective Garcia here to see you."

Ah shit. "Tell him I'm busy."

Just then the door opened and Garcia walked in. He grabbed the only other chair in the office and pulled it up in front of the desk. Over the phone intercom the receptionist said, "Strange. I can't find him. I think he left. If he comes back I'll tell him you're not in today."

Smiling at Garcia, he replied into the phone, "Don't hurt yourself," and hung up.

"She's a cutie," Garcia said. He took out a Tic-Tac and tossed it in his mouth. "You want one?"

"No, I'm good."

"Just came from Hardwood's office. Boy, you guys don't do nearly as much work as I thought you did. Far as I can tell, most of the time is spent working on your hair."

"They have naked news anchors in other countries. Image sells."

"Well yeah," he shifted in the chair, "you could tell me the government was instituting mandatory body cavity searches on everyone's birthday, so long as a hot co-ed delivered the news. That new one you got, Mason, she's a looker. But hair and tits, it's not the same thing. Where was I?"

"Hardwood."

"Oh yeah, Hardwood. We're tracing his emails, trying to get a lock on this Carver psycho—"

Stone's heart leapt. "You found something?"

"What? No, nothing. Well, maybe something. Police business though, I can't tell you."

"I'm the press."

"Then talk to our press agent. She'll let you know if it's okay. As for you though, we picked up the letter this morning, as you know. Left you the photocopy, as you know. Also found the bum who was paid to deliver it, as you didn't know, but now you do."

His heart slammed into his Adam's apple. He was busted, finished, going to fry in the state pen. Suddenly he had visions of leaping over his desk, strangling Garcia, rushing to Hardwood's office, kicking his teeth down his throat and suffocating him in his own blood. Then an Uzi in his hand, Carlie riddled with holes, a Times Square massacre, the last bullet in his own head.

Come back to Earth, Stone, come on back. Calm down.

"That's great," he said, conscious of every pore on his body suddenly glistening with sweat.

"Not for you," Garcia said.

"Why's that?" Throat dry. Gulping. Back to thoughts of the UZI. Wait for it...wait for it...

"Well, turns out the shmoe doesn't remember the guy, this Chef as you call him, who gave him the letter. Oh, he remembered to deliver it for some space money. But his brain is Swiss cheese. Too much booze and drugs. It's all selective memory now. Money, sure, address, yep, face, fuck no. But, we have the area, uptown, Westside. Near where you live in fact. We got footprints too from the scene. Very sloppy work if you ask me. Almost like the guy wanted us to find the footprints. I mean, he could have easily covered them over with the snow, but he didn't. Anyway, I figured you could use that in your report, but like I said, it don't mean much which is bad for your report."

Calming down now. Imaginary Uzi going back in its hiding place.

"Not that bad. Everything helps. We want to catch this guy."

"Do you now? If we catch him you lose your spotlight. How's that going by the way, all this new-found celebrity?"

"I wouldn't call it celebrity. Besides, people already know me, it's nothing new. I was an anchor just last week, people saw me every day."

"That's right. I imagine it's hard to go from an anchor position to hovering off-screen, but what do I know about show business."

"Show business?"

"I mean the news."

Stone had no response to that, just sat still. The intercom buzzed so he answered it. It was the receptionist. "Mr. Stone, I think I saw that detective walk to the elevator. I think you're in the clear."

"Thank you." He smiled at Garcia and hung up. "No hard feelings," he said, motioning to the phone, "I just didn't want to agree to any gag order before I did my report. But that's not what you wanted anyway…"

"Do you want police protection? Might be a good idea."

Won't get much work done with a gun and a badge always at my side, Stone thought. "No, I'm okay. If I get iffy about walking alone, I'll give you a call."

Garcia stood up, buttoned up his coat. "When the lab reports come back, if there's anything the public should know, I'll give you a call."

"I heard there was an ear in the envelope, can I use that?"

"Sure. Sure you can. In fact the letter came for you, so I can't really stop you using it unless I want liberal America suing me for some Freedom of Press bullshit. Anything else, call our press agent. I'm headed out to conduct some interviews, see if anyone saw anything. Take care, Wesley."

Calling him by his real name, that was a nice touch. Just a little way of letting him know they'd been checking up on him.

"Is that all you wanted?" Stone asked.

"No, I want to interview you when you're free."

"I got interviews lined up with local papers."

"Yeah, but I have different questions. Soon, okay? Gotta run."

Garcia walked out and left him alone in the office, sweat running down his underarms. He wondered what the police had found in Hardwood's emails, though knowing Hardwood like he did, it had to be some kind of red herring.

He put in a call to the police press agent, a woman named Dana Brown, asked her if any info they had was okay to report. She told him they were sitting on some things and they'd get back to him if necessary. Shit, he thought, what were they hiding? Did any of it point to him?

He hung up and leaned back, thought about what he was going to tell the papers. He certainly wasn't going to give anything away. This was his story, his killer, his ticket to the big time. From the hallway, he could hear Duncan Willis patronizing some poor production assistant about the quality of the coffee. You get shit on enough you're bound to try and displace it onto someone else.

What a prick.

CHAPTER 14

Despite the incident in the park taking a bit longer than he'd hoped, Hardwood made it to work around 10:00, which was on par with his daily schedule. There was a time, long ago, when only four hours of sleep would have slowed him down, but 40 years of nightly news work had long since acclimated him to operating on minimal sleep. He'd woken up with hints of black circles around his eyes, but some concealer had cleared that up (Hardwood, like many television personalities, had his own assortment of make-ups and creams at home). There should be no reason anyone would suspect him of doing anything untoward the previous evening.

The news director, Harold Boomer, swept by him at the elevator and asked to meet with him in a half hour, to go over some things before the production meeting. He was wearing a yellow tie with a red shirt, looking more like an advertisement for McDonalds than an important member of the media. Which, when one looked at Boomer's performance record, was only the tip of the iceberg for how much of an idiot he really was. His last bright idea had been to do a five-piece series on the city's cracking sidewalks. Everybody was tripping and falling and pretty pissed off about it, was his take. The viewers' take was that just about anything on any other channel—including reruns of *Saved By The Bell* and *Golden Girls*—had more entertainment value than old cement. That week proved to be a ratings nightmare for WYNN, and they'd lost two advertisers in the process.

At the end of the last report of that series, Hardwood had stormed over to Boomer, and in front of the entire crew, swore that if Boomer ever orchestrated another fiasco like that again, he'd call Corporate and tell them to put Boomer in the mailroom. Nobody in the room doubted who Corporate would side with.

Needless to say the man was a poor choice for director, as far as Hardwood was concerned, but the job was too encompassing for Hardwood himself to take on, so he lived with it. Begrudgingly.

"Good morning, Mr. Hardwood," Gina, the receptionist, said as he passed by her desk. He nodded hello to her. "The phones have been ringing off the hook for you," she continued. "This whole Casanova Carver thing, it's crazy, it has everyone going bonkers. Look, they just keep calling!" She pressed some buttons on the phone and put whoever was calling through to the studio's main voice mail. "I'm taking the liberty of screening the calls and only putting the legitimate ones—at least the ones that seem legitimate—through to your voice mail. What should I—"

"Thank you, Gina, just keep doing as you're doing. And be careful, sometimes it's the ones that sound the sanest that are the craziest."

He passed by Boomer's office, not even bothering to look in, and continued on down the hall toward his own office. On the walls, pictures of himself with notable persons provided a timeline of his commitment to the studio: him with a young Robert De Niro, Ed Koch, David Letterman, Dave Winfield, Frank Sinatra, the cast of Cats, among others. More journalistic snapshots from various moments in the field complemented them: a young Hardwood in front of a burning building, at the zoo as a lion cub was taking its first breath, in a helicopter hovering above a riot, in a subway station where bodies lay covered in bloody sheets.

"Good morning, Mr. Hardwood," a spry intern chirped on her way to deliver files somewhere. He didn't know her name or when she'd started working here, but again, he nodded.

"Top o' the morning to you, Mr. Hardwood." It was Jamaal, one of the producers, one of the more intelligent members of the team who, sadly, did not speak out enough.

"Same to you," Hardwood replied. "Jamaal?"

"Yeah, Mr. Hardwood?"

"I'm going to need someone to bounce my copy off of later. Will you be around?"

"You've got it. I want to bounce some things off you myself. I've got some ideas for some stories. How does three o'clock sound?"

"You're a credit to the station."

"Thanks, man. But until that idiot Boomer is fired I don't think anyone besides you is gonna take me very seriously."

"Want me to kill him?"

"Ha! Yeah. That would be a blessing. Okay, see you later."

Jamaal scurried off to complete whatever task he was doing. Hardwood admired the man's temerity, his eagerness to learn and educate himself. He'd never asked Jamaal's background, but he knew the man grew up in Chicago, perhaps in the ghetto, perhaps not. Whatever the catalyst, something in the man's life had assured him that only the educated survive.

Hardwood agreed. If only his own spawn could have learned that early on.

Turning the corner to his office, a group of administrative assistants saw him coming and parted like the Red Sea, each one offering a morning salutation as he walked by. One of them, a young girl with a houndstooth skirt, looked somewhat star-struck, and instead of words emitted a tiny squeak. This amused him for some reason, as if it was the squeak of his celebrity machine powering up.

The in-box near his door was overflowing with various papers and files. Many of these would be scheduling materials, he knew, and many more would be story leads: press releases, ideas from the production team, headlines from the AP wire. A hallmark card was stuck in the middle of it all, looking completely out of place. He took it out and read the name on the return address, failed to recognize it, and opened it up. As he suspected, it was fan mail. Generally, fan mail got weeded through by interns in order to discard the ones that were just ramblings from lunatics complaining about the city, and cull the more important ones, which were then placed in the mailboxes near reception. Someone had let this one slip through:

DEAR MR. HARDWOOD. I LOVE WATCHING YOU ON THE NEWS EVERY NIGHT. I AM A LONELY WOMAN AND YOU MAKE ME FEEL LIKE SOMEONE OUT THERE CARES. YOU ARE AN ANGEL AMONG BEASTS IN THIS HORRID CITY, SO OVERRUN WITH DEBAUCHERY AND SIN. I WOULD LOVE TO INVITE YOU TO DINNER FOR STEAK AND WINE. HERE IS MY PHONE NUMBER. I LOVE YOU. YOURS IN CHRIST, AGNUS WILLOBY.

He tore it in half, entered his office, and tossed it in the waste basket near his desk.

Women. He had enough problems with women right now, especially that Tricia Mason.

Opening the blinds, he let the afternoon sun in through the floor-to-ceiling windows, dousing the room in brilliant natural light. Up here on the twelfth floor, much like at his apartment, he could look out over the city and marvel at how all the little people scurried about, so busy yet so insignificant.

He hit the play button on his phone's voice mail.

"Hello, Mr. Hardwood, this is detective Ramon Garcia. I'd like to talk to you when you have a moment, about this whole business with the Casanova Carver. I'm gonna need to see those emails you talked about. I'll be over your way in about fifteen twenty minutes…maybe we could chat real quick. Just some minor questions, routine stuff. Gimme a call."

Hardwood wrote down the number and played the next message. The voice belonged to Lionel Proud, New York City's most liberal radio host.

"Doug, hi, Lionel Proud. Been a while since we spoke. Remember, last year at the Press Club Awards? Anyway, look, my team and I…we're putting together a story on these recent killings. Fucked up shit, and you're right in the middle of it. Jesus, just like the Winslow case, huh? Anyway, look, I thought maybe you could extend me a courtesy with this story, and hell, I could even get you on the air. That's up to you, of course. Not like you need it. It's going to be a five-part series—"

Hardwood erased the message. No more five-part series.

He went through his email and found the message Detective Garcia was looking for and flagged it. He also clicked on the new one he'd sent himself last night, describing the process by which he'd sewn two lovers—one dead, one wishing he were dead—together in the small dog park.

He printed it out and strode back through the throng of administrative assistants in the hall, inviting himself into Boomer's office.

"Here, we need a graphic of this," he said, placing the printout on the director's desk.

"New email? What's it say?"

"Bunch of nonsense. Confesses to the lip-locked couple last night. Says gays shouldn't exist, says love is a product of government conditioning, bunch of other stuff. I'm no profiler, but he mentions things he said to the couple we didn't air on the show…I'm sure it's authentic."

Boomer looked up from reading the printout. "Fuck me. Doug, I'm getting you police protection."

"I don't need protection, Boomer. That's not why he's writing to me. He wants the attention; he wants me to get it for him. That's what I'm doing. He's not taking it for granted. Not yet anyway. Besides, it's my story and I'm not letting it go. I told the public I'd keep them updated and I'm honoring my word."

"And if he kills you and finds another anchor?"

"Please. Professionalism is in decline in this business. This…misanthrope…whoever he is, chose me for my merits. Another anchor would blunder it, make a mockery of it, and he knows it. Besides, with Roland Stone and that blonde belle at WWTF dealing with their own story, he's got nowhere else to turn that would get him as large an audience."

"I don't care. This isn't some game, you know. It's not safe. We lose you and we lose—"

"What, your ratings, your advertisers? Boomer, you think in complications, not solutions. The truth is that he's created a paradox. Kill me and no other anchor will deal with him, they'll be too afraid. Kill me, and he loses his conduit to the masses. He realizes this."

"Boy, you could have fooled me?"

"About what?" Hardwood asked.

"You sound a hell of a lot like a profiler."

"Just a perception, Boomer. I'm not proposing truths. You don't have to believe me."

"Yeah, well, regardless, if the other anchors refuse, at least they'll be alive. Why you're choosing to tie yourself this—"

"If I'm found on the Hudson's trash barge with my heart cut out, it'll be the greatest thing that ever happened to this station. Were I so inclined to augment the net worth of my shares in this company, I'd tell him how and when to do it. But then, I'm sure heaven is more boring than my current confines at this network's anchor desk."

"Fine." Boomer sighed, used to losing battles with Hardwood. Secretly, the man knew who was in charge, same as everyone at the station did. "Fine. Do whatever you need to do. I'm following up your five o'clock report with a story on bulimia in the pre-schools. Got a new field reporter—saucy little Latino girl, hot stuff, hotter than that Tricia Mason anyway—she's taping now. You're free to add your own intro."

"Pre-schools?"

"They start young."

"I seriously doubt you'll find attribution for it, but it's honestly the first good idea you've had in a while."

"There're some skinny kids these days, and new parents love learning about what their children do behind their backs. Did you know my daughter told me she's already tried pot?"

"She's seventeen, if I remember correctly."

"That's right," said Boomer, awaiting whatever snide remark Hardwood was going to deliver to him.

"Don't be such a sheltered putz, Boomer. She, like all seventeen year olds, has a superiority complex...in her mind she's sure she knows much more than you. She's probably robbed a bank, filmed a porno, and stolen a car by this point."

"Oh, it's worse than that."

"How so?"

"I think she's getting involved in politics. It breaks a parent's heart..."

"You'll survive. Take Jeremy…" Hardwood stopped, shocked that he'd let himself slip up, shocked that he'd given into a memory he'd locked away long ago. Thankfully, Boomer decided not to pursue it. After a few seconds, he came back to Earth, pointed to the printout on Boomer's desk. "Anyway, just have graphics make up something nice for this letter. Something very…how do I describe it…German."

"German?"

"Yes. Oh, and there's a detective coming by soon. He'll want to subpoena my email records. Call our sorry excuse for a lawyer and have him block it."

"If I can. Don't forget the Patriot Act."

"We're press, Boomer. Don't forget that."

CHAPTER 15

Hardwood made Detective Garcia wait in the reception area until the morning production meeting was over. There, he met him with an amicable demeanor, shook his hand, and invited him back to his office. On the way, the detective studied the photos that lined the hallway, remarking about some of the more notable celebrities. In particular, he seemed interested in the one with the dead bodies in the subway.

"Subway killings of seventy-four," Hardwood said, satisfying the policeman's silent curiosity. "You remember? I was the first reporter on the scene, heard it on the scanner and realized my cameraman and I were only a block away. We arrived before the metro police, which says nothing for their reliability."

"My first time around dead bodies," the detective said, "I scared myself because, you know, I was more fascinated than afraid. A couple drug dealers, heads all bashed in with a hammer. Brains everywhere, like gray scrambled eggs. I kept staring at the eyes, you know, like, waiting to see if they'd blink. They were so dry, they looked fake. And I just kept staring. I got back to the precinct and I told my captain there was something wrong with me. He laughed, said me being fascinated…that's what made me normal. Scary how humans react to this shit, huh?"

"I guess I just look at it as a job," replied Hardwood.

"Good way of looking at it, I know. I do the same. You see a lot of this kind of stuff?

"Firsthand? No, not for many years. But I see my fair share of footage. Car crashes, murders, war-torn countries sending each other messages. It's always gruesome, sometimes visceral, but always just a job to me."

"Do you miss it, seeing it all firsthand?"

"Sometimes," said Hardwood. "The salad days were far more exciting, yet far less lucrative in the monetary sense—field reporters don't do endorsements, or speaking engagements, or sell books. Not to mention I didn't have to engage myself in the quote unquote corporate bullshit I tolerate these days. Sometimes I think it would have been easier to stay a field reporter."

"So you miss it…the dead bodies?"

Hardwood smiled, nodded his head. "Ah, I see. I missed your point. You're interrogating me."

Garcia chuckled. "Sorry, my job. More of a habit these days than anything else."

"Then allow me to speak openly. I have no morbid fascination with the Casanova Carver, and am not following his instructions because I fancy myself some kind of Renfield."

"That's Dracula, huh? That book big with newscasters?"

"I wouldn't know. Why?"

"No reason."

"Yes, well, vampires aside, my involvement in this current affair is purely professional, nothing more. The Casanova Carver wrote to me, for whatever reason, and the public demands to know what he's saying. America has a morbid curiosity, as we already concluded. I have a responsibility to them and this station to report on the killings."

"Uh-huh. But what concerns me, really, is the call I got from your lawyer right before I got here. He said I can't see the emails. Talk about stopping me dead in my tracks. Can't see the emails? Whoa, I haven't had that kind of resistance from the press in a long, long time. Now why would he say that?"

"I'm sure I don't know," Hardwood said, his face unreadable.

"All I can think is—since I can't stop you from reporting on it anyway—all I can think is, maybe you want to protect him for some reason. Or maybe you want to keep me from catching him, so your station stays morbidly infatuating."

"Come now—"

"Or maybe, really, I'm just grasping at straws."

The two men stared at each other in the hall, a game of mental chess beginning, until an intern tried to pass by them and said, "Excuse me." Both men stepped apart and let the intern pass.

"I don't decide who gets to do what around here," Hardwood finally said. "That's the director's job."

"And that would be…hold on…" The detective flipped through a small pad. "Ah, here, Harold Boomer. Hell of a last name. Well, I'll ask him when I'm on my way out. I'd love to hear his reason. Could be he's just protecting you, which is understandable. How are you anyway?

Do you want me to have some badges follow you around, just to be safe?"

"I'm quite all right, thank you."

"You're a brave man, Mr. Hardwood. It's strange to me is all." Garcia put the pad back in his pocket.

"Because?"

"Because most people don't trust killers. In my experience, only the people who meet a killer face to face and make a judgment call based on talking to them…they're the ones who make educated decisions to not be afraid. Yet this guy contacted you last night right after offing someone and you rush a reporter out to the spot he was last at. Didn't it concern you he might still be there?"

"Not really. We take risks in this business."

"I guess so. Gotta get the story, right?"

Hardwood gave a slight nod. "The bottom line."

"Did your reporter notice anyone strange?"

"You'll have to ask him."

"Oh, I will. It just seems…you know…strange. Like you had this guy's word he wouldn't be waiting in the shadows for your co-worker."

"There's been no contact between the two of us beyond his emails. I promise."

"Hey, no sweat, I believe you. Okay then, I guess I'm going to go arrest Boomer. Take care of yourself."

Detective Garcia turned and made his way back toward the station director's office. He was almost there when Hardwood caught up with him, put a hand on his shoulder and stopped him.

"Detective Garcia…Detective Garcia…might I inquire as to the charges against Boomer."

"I figured you would. Aiding and abetting a murderer. Want a Tic-Tac?"

"No. And how so?"

"Eh, police secrets, you wouldn't be interested. To be honest, I don't even know if I can make it stick…but he's making my life hard blocking these emails and I'm as fun as the next guy…I can play games too."

"This sounds spiteful."

"It's like this: the spirit of the law lets you guys protect a source. I get that. But when the source is an imminent threat to the public, well, then we've got new laws—"

"The Patriot Act. It's governmental tyranny."

"You say tomato, I say jail time. Boomer might look good with 'hate' and 'love' tattooed on his knuckles. They still use guitar strings, you know. I hear it hurts like a bitch. Unless you want to maybe give me a quick look at the emails."

In no way was Hardwood intimidated by the detective's threats, but then he didn't want any conservative judges subpoenaing more than just emails should it come to that. In the end, blocking access to the emails was more of a bluff than anything else, just to see if it was possible, to see what was safe and what wasn't. Somehow he was sure he'd lose the gamble. He could lie and say he'd erased the emails, but he'd done a report on identity thieves a few years back and knew the police could retrieve whatever he deleted. Unless he smashed the hard drive and bought a brand new computer—which would look just a tad suspicious—he was going to have to rely on subterfuge.

Thankfully, the Blackberry he'd purchased from underground hackers, from which he'd sent the emails, was unregistered and safely hidden. Yes, good journalists had their sources, and those sources had sources, and if you went far enough down the list you could find what you were looking for. With enough money, nobody asked questions. The black market wasn't fat because of loose lips.

"Sure, Detective Garcia, right this way."

In Hardwood's office, the detective scrolled through the station's email server, found the two emails in question, read them over carefully, and forwarded them to an email address Hardwood did not recognize. He made a call to his precinct immediately afterward and spoke to a computer technician.

"Okay, call me right back," the detective said, hanging up after a brief conversation. Then to Hardwood: "Thanks. I'll be outta here in a minute, as soon as he calls back."

"And he was?"

"Guy named Jorge. I call him Hal. He hates it."

"Hal, as in Hal nine-thousand?"

"Can't put much past you."

"I admire the classics, be it film or literature. Actually, I've experienced both in this case. Arthur C. Clark was a favorite of mine back in college. Sadly, the genre has progressed into a mockery of itself. Literature is a dead art, which explains the simplistic mental state of the world today."

"Wouldn't know, I don't read much."

"Just *Dracula?*"

"Nah, saw the movie. Gary Oldman was good. My wife reads them romance novels, though. Can't get enough of 'em. Look stupid to me."

"He must be a computer technician."

"Hal? Best on the force. I think the technical term is nerd, but don't quote me."

The cop stood up from the desk and moved to the shelves on the far wall, where Hardwood kept many of his awards. He popped another Tic-Tac in his mouth and read the awards methodically, picking up some of the smaller trophies and reading the tiny print on the bases.

"You have a lot of fans."

"People like who they can trust. I make sure they can trust me."

"Yeah, people love me and my colleagues too. Love us like lesbians love a sweaty nutsack. It don't pay to be a cop in this fucking city, let me tell you. What's this one?"

"On occasion I do some work with World War II veterans. It's a passion of mine, making sure they're not forgotten. They gave me an award a few years ago."

"Oh yeah, my Padre fought in the war. Came to New York about '39. Worked on a boat the whole time, though, didn't see any action. And what's this?" The detective picked up a small statue and turned it in the sunlight. "You break some furniture?"

"No, it's a sculpture."

"What, like art? I don't much get art."

"Yes, art," Hardwood replied, taking the cherry wood sculpture of what looked like an upside-down pitchfork from the detective's hand and placing it back on the shelf. "It's expensive, thank you."

The detective's cell phone rang. Answering it, he moved back to Hardwood's computer and stared at the email messages while someone—arguably Hal—spoke.

Hardwood could feel his chest tighten. Not knowing what Hal knew was killing him. How easy it would be to smash the sculpture down on the detective's head and break the man's skull, if only he didn't feel so ill at the thought of ruining good art.

The detective kept saying "yeah" and "sure" and "okay" as he looked over the emails. Finally, he hung up and straightened his tie.

"Find something?" Hardwood asked.

"Well, yes and no. Hal says he can work with what I sent him. Says it's really just a matter of working backwards to find the source. IP addresses, rerouted channels, something about a free email account and a wiped mac address. I don't know this shit…I gotta take his word.

So listen, thanks for meeting with me. I have to run, got a bunch more interviews to do today. It was an honor meeting you in person, you know?"

"It was nice meeting you as well," Hardwood replied.

"Don't forget, if you need police protection you just call me. Hang on, I got a card here somewhere." Garcia reached into his pocket and withdrew a business card. "Here. And tell Boomer I said hi."

Hardwood took the card, waited for the detective to leave, and sat down to read the emails again. What had the detective found? Had he even found anything or was he just putting on a show?

It was driving him mad.

Forget it, he thought, he was sure he'd been thorough. If there was one thing he knew how to do, one thing he was experienced at, it was covering his tracks. Refocusing his efforts towards work, he deleted a bunch of spam mails for penis enlargements and began writing his five o'clock segment.

CHAPTER 16.

When one o'clock rolled around, Stone got a phone call from *The Post*, a no-nonsense woman asking questions about The Chef. Was he scared, and was he holding back info, and could they come get an exclusive photo of him? No, no, and yes he told her.

"Has he mentioned why he chose you as a contact?" she asked.

"No, he hasn't. I've had fans for a while now, ever since I was anchor. He probably watched me night after night. People sometimes personalize their celebrities, like they're friends with them. They eat dinner with them every night, they go to bed with them, they drive and listen to their music. Some people don't get that the celebrity has no idea who they are, that they're just a number on a sales tracking sheet. But then again, who knows."

She hummed an agreement and continued. "Do you think the Casanova Carver and The Chef are the same person?"

"Well, the cops say no. Different methods, different implements. Personally, I think the Chef is a trickier killer. The Casanova Carver takes hearts, sure, but that doesn't leave him much else to do—"

"What do you mean? He sewed his last victims together."

"I know, I know, but listen. His signature is that he takes hearts. To do that, well, it limits you. It pigeon holes you. You can't change your MO half way through your spree and start taking eyeballs, people will think you can't make up your mind. But the Chef, he's shown us in just two killings that he's going to up the ante every time and that's frightening."

"I'd say they both upped their ante. Why is the Chef's method any worse?"

"I just...the Casanova Carver just doesn't, he's not—"

"I hope you don't mind me saying this, Mr. Stone, but it sounds like you're trying to glamorize The Chef for some reason. Maybe for your audience?"

Shit, she was right. What was he doing! He was trying to bash Hardwood in the news. Stupid, stupid. "No," he replied, "not at all. I just haven't slept much and, well, I hope we catch this guy soon. The streets aren't safe while he's out there. While they're both out there."

"Is there anything in the letters you haven't read on the air? Are you going to read the new one tonight?"

He pulled the photocopy out of his pocket and looked at it. She must have heard about it from the police. It had a couple curse words in it. He'd have to remember to keep it cleaner next time. "No, I haven't left anything out, and yes I'll read it tonight in full. Why, are you going to run it if I don't? Jump my gun?"

"No, we haven't seen it yet, but there's nothing that says we can't when and if we do. Are you purposefully keeping it to yourself?"

"What? No, just—"

"In your professional opinion, what does this guy want?"

"I think he wants…I think he's tired of people passing him over based on looks and wowie sauce, and now he's playing their game."

"What was that? Wowie what?"

"Nothing. I just mean, I think he's disgusted with life. He's a sick person, obviously. I have to go now."

"Wait, are you afraid?"

Every time he'd looked in the damn mirror the past couple of days he'd seen a man who'd lost his humanity. Was he afraid? Shit, he didn't know what was worse, that he had killed and felt no remorse, or that he might not be doing a good enough job of it to get his anchor position back and bury Hardwood in the ratings. No, he wasn't afraid, he was out of his mind. "Not really," he told her. "Right now, I'm his conduit. When I stop getting letters, when he has no need for me anymore, then I'll worry. And you know what, you'll be the first to know. I have to go now."

"But—"

He hung up the phone and buzzed the receptionist, told her to tell the other newspapers he wasn't doing anymore interviews today. Pulling up his contact list on the computer, he dialed Hardwood's office number. It took a few minutes for him to get on the phone.

"Stone," Hardwood said, "you haven't called me here in…well, ever I suppose. To what do I owe the honor?"

"What are you doing?"

"I'm writing copy for the five o'clock segment—"

"That's not what I mean. What do you get out of any of this? You're already the number one anchor in the city. Why take more?"

"I'm sorry, I still have no idea—"

"Last night! What the hell was that!"

"If you're referring to the fact I was reporting on the Casanova Carver's latest work before anyone else, it is because I received an email from the killer only moments after it happened. And you? How was your night?"

"You know…you're a…"

"Yes?"

Stone sighed. "I lost viewers to you."

"Yes, well, work is work. Please don't take it personally. Your team is quite gifted and honed, if not a little superfluous in its presentation. It's like I said last year as keynote speaker of the Press Awards: just as objectivity in the newsroom is a conscious effort, and therefore, by nature, not really objective, so too is the method by which it is relayed a meticulous effort at reservation, which by nature, exudes pomposity."

"Yeah, yeah, I get it. We're salesmen who pretend to not be salesmen. I've heard it all before. I used to hear it everyday in my college communication classes. I don't need you laying it on too, especially when I know a thing or two about your ethics. I get it."

"Then relax, Stone. I can't help that I'm the more trusted salesman. Deal with it or move on. It doesn't behoove you to bother me at work about it. And on that note I really must be getting back to—"

"What did they find in your email?"

Hardwood grunted. "No idea, they won't tell me. You either, I see."

There was a pause. Neither of them spoke. Finally, Hardwood

said, "Wesley, Stone, whatever moniker you ascribe to yourself this week, I do have to get back to work, so if there's nothing else—"

Stone hung up on him.

Doug Hardwood had been around a long, long time, well before Stone got into the business. Pictures still existed of him with the likes of Richard Nixon and Lyndon Johnson, present at the country's most notable milestones. Of course, there was that whole Winslow Murder Case that raised him to popularity on a national level for a short while.

To exist in this business for that long, Stone knew, you've got to sell yourself. You are, essentially, a product, not unlike a can of soda. There are important factors to consider, such as image, name, slogan, what you endorse, and all of these break down into subcategories. Image: are you clean cut, rustic, European, casual or formal? Slogan: AKA the sign off, which Stone devised on his own after two full college-ruled notebooks were filled with the kinds of one-liners people's grandfathers thought were funny during Eisenhower's term. Endorsements: ascribed mostly to national media gigs; as long as they aren't overtly right wing or overtly left wing, pretty much anything that brings in money and viewers is okay. But perhaps none are as important as the name. The name is what people remember. It doesn't matter how good you look or how polished your sign off is, if your name doesn't lodge itself in the public's conscience, you might as well take up haunting mansions—you're forgotten as soon as the television goes off.

There were literally thousands of newscasters in the country, Stone knew—not including the rising crop of online news correspondents. Within the business, it was fairly easy to learn people's real names; in fact some people couldn't wait to shout it out.

Theories existed as to what Doug Hardwood's real name was. Some of them made sense, but Stone was sure they were untrue.

Leanne Bonita, formally Brenda Grautpferzich, who did the morning traffic report at WLLL (fifth in the rankings for many years now, but that's what you got for being an affiliate of CW) had heard that Hardwood was servicing a congresswoman back in the day and that it was she who came up with the name. But then, there were rumors about Hardwood's sexual orientation that would say otherwise. As far as Stone was concerned, Hardwood's sexual orientation, while it might be worth knowing—knowledge is power, kids—was the least of his concerns.

The true etymology of Doug Hardwood's name, as far as he could tell, was this: his parents gave it to him.

Some people were just born gifted, born to be a household name, born to succeed. The argument then was: did Doug Hardwood make his name, or did the name make him?

Stone could spread this theory if he really wanted to, but odds were most people wouldn't even believe him. Hardwood's origins were more attractive as a myth.

Still, he could be wrong.

*

On the air he read The Chef's letter, careful to speak each sentence as if it were the stanza of a magical chant.

DEAR MR. STONE,

YOUR PITIFUL ATTEMPT TO NAME ME AND PIGEONHOLE MY METHODS ONLY REINFORCES MY NOTION THAT YOU AND YOUR VIEWERS ARE VICTIMS OF A CARBON-COPIED SOCIETY IN

NEED OF FRESH BLOOD. YOUR UNINSPIRED HOLLYWOOD PARADIGMS ONLY CONVINCE ME TO KILL MORE PEOPLE FASTER. I WILL MAKE MY VICTIMS SUFFER LONGER AND HARDER THAN EVER BEFORE. WHERE ONCE I WAS DETERMINED TO FREE THEM, I AM NOW FORCED TO PURIFY THEM AS WELL. THE SOUL IS A SPONGE THAT ABSORBS THE SINS OF EARTH'S SOCIETIES, BUT LIKE ALL SPONGES, IT CAN BE PURGED WITH A LONG HARD SQUEEZE—LIKE SHIT (Stone said "stuff" instead) FROM AN INTESTINE. EXPECT MY CONTRIBUTION TO THIS CITY TO BE JUST THAT, SHIT (again, "stuff") UNTIL SUCH TIME AS I DETERMINE THE CITY TO BE ABSOLVED. READ THIS ON THE AIR OR MORE WILL SUFFER THE CONSEQUENCES OF YOUR INACTION.

After that, he read Cheese's response. The graphics guys had done up the chef hat logo with the bloody font like he wanted. It was good stuff.

Tricia Mason did a report on the body parts being put in food, though she covered her integrity by saying the information came from a dubious source and that they were only mentioning it as a safety measure.

Swift had his head in his hands again.

At the end of the newscast, Cheese called the sales department and checked the numbers. They were up again, but were still lagging behind Hardwood's station. Stone got filled in and learned that Hardwood read his own email, and then cut to exclusive information detailing how the Casanova Carver was choosing his victims. Apparently there were clues in the emails that pointed toward various sections of town.

Sonofabitch. He'd lied about the email.

Clues that were obviously planted for the police, that would now make them look inept considering a news anchor "decoded" them and broke them on television. Hardwood was slick, and he'd scored another point. What's more, it would get the police off his back, since they would be in whatever part of the city he wanted them to be in while he was somewhere else doing God only knew what to his next victim.

Stone considered blowing the whistle on him, but knew he couldn't. Considering Hardwood had an ample amount of information to load his own cannons with, for now, they were in this race together. Enemies, but allies.

CHAPTER 17

The next afternoon, Boomer stuck his head in Hardwood's office, said, "My daughter just got suspended from school for fighting. I gotta go pick her up. Take care of things while I'm gone?"

As if that's any different from how it normally works, thought Hardwood as he nodded. Flustered, Boomer took off, leaving him to wonder about his own offspring. Perhaps it was time to bury the hatchet and talk to Jeremy. As much as his job fulfilled him these days, he still hadn't figured out how to fill that particular void in his heart, and it was killing him that he couldn't get control of the situation. Maybe now, when he was knee deep in danger, the bastard might hear him out. After all, if he could win the public's trust, he should be able to win it from his own flesh and blood. Before he could change his mind, he grabbed his jacket and walked out of the building.

Donovan's was a popular restaurant in SoHo that specialized in seafood. Even if you didn't eat fish, the wine list alone was worth the visit; it was the most impressive in the city, with the exception of

Gertrude's. Hardwood's favorite dish in the city just so happened to be a signature at Donovan's as well: veal cubes covered in truffles on top of mushroom risotto; it was delectable.

What he remembered of it anyway; he hadn't had it in years.

Currently, the lunch crowd would be leaving and the restaurant would be setting up for dinner guests, a change-over period that would leave the place fairly empty. With luck, the chefs would also be having a few minutes of downtime as they waited for some of the night's staples to heat up. Talk time would be scant once he got there, but he only needed a few minutes to speak his piece.

If nothing else, if he was asked to leave, at least only a select few would see him.

The car service met him at the front door of the WYNN studio, where he stood bundled in his wool overcoat and black leather gloves. A searing cold wind tore his breath away before it had time to freeze in front of him. Someone from the corporate office stood next to him smoking a cigar, the smoke wafting in his face.

"Is that Cuban Seed Habano leaf?" Hardwood asked, recognizing the rare scent.

The man took the pipe out of his mouth and looked Hardwood up and down. If the man recognized him, he didn't show it.

"Mmmm. It is. You're a smoker?"

"Off and on. It tapers in the colder months. I've had Habano before, and I've never forgotten the taste. Very rich flavor. I thought it was under an embargo right now?"

"Nothing's under embargo in New York City."

Both men chuckled. Hardwood removed a Nat Sherman from his silver cigarette case and lit it up. "Not nearly as good as what you've got, but it'll do. Might I inquire as to where you bought it?"

The man shook his head, as if to say, you wouldn't understand. "I buy it from a fellow in my smoking club—"

"Smoking club?"

"Mmmm. Yes."

"The one near St. Patrick's?"

"Mmmm. No. Private membership."

"Really? Sounds fascinating. How do I join?"

Again, the man shook his head, a clear dismissal. Who was this man, Hardwood wondered. Was he from the parent company? WYNN was, in actuality, owned by a firm that specialized in building battleships. "Sorry, I can't tell you. You have to be invited in, you see."

"Ah. A bit like the Freemasons, yes?"

"Mmmm. A bit. A bit. But…Oh look, my ride is here. Good day."

Hardwood stepped in front of the man, blocking his access to the arriving limo and doing his best not to look antagonistic. "I'm sorry, but…I don't suppose, you might at least tell me who is in the club? I have many friends in this city…perhaps I know somebody who could vouch for me."

The man, clearly unhappy to still be in the cold, stepped around Hardwood and said, "The club is for refined individuals only, not for people who invade the personal space of others. I'm sorry. Good day."

He got in the limo and it took off. The arresting scent of Habano leaf dissipated into the air.

Well, that was rude, thought Hardwood, suddenly aware of just how cold he was. And strange as well. A private smoking club in the city and he had never been invited to join? Everybody who was anybody in this town knew he was a cigar aficionado. Who was keeping it a secret from him, and why?

It was worth investigating. But he'd have to do it later if he intended to get to Donovan's before the dinner crowd started spilling in.

He got into the black Cutlass that was waiting for him, and gave the driver the restaurant's address. "Hurry, I'm trying to beat the crowd."

"Yes, sir."

It took only a few minutes to get to Donovan's. As he suspected, the interior was mostly empty. The smell of cleaning agents mixing with scented candles hung heavy in the air. A couple businessmen sat at the bar drinking martinis, most likely awaiting the happy hour. The bartender was elsewhere, probably in the back room counting the liquor bottles. At the far end of the dining room, the hostess was helping the waiters set up the tables. Aside from the two men at the bar, who were trying to figure out why Hardwood looked familiar to them, nobody saw him enter.

The doors to the kitchen were beyond the bar, and from the other side of them came the sounds of pots and pans clanging, and voices shouting. He recognized one of the voices immediately, and felt reality sink into his skin. This was going to be more than trying.

On the other side of the doors...

It had been years since he'd seen the man on the other side of those doors. Years since that night at Fredo's, when half of his heart had been ripped out. Years since he'd found himself so vulnerable.

Hurry up, he told himself, before the men at the bar put two and two together and bug you for an autograph.

Head low, he strode to the doors and pushed them open. Having failed to look through the porthole before he did, he had no idea that someone was at that moment walking by holding a large bread knife. The door slammed into the man's hand and drove the knife up into his neck.

"Ahh!"

"Oh dear," Hardwood said, quickly stepping over the man who

was now sprawled on the ground. He was wearing a white apron, a button down shirt with the sleeves rolled up exposing the tattoos on his forearms—two lightning bolts and an eagle. A trickle of blood ran from the man's neck and made its way to Hardwood's Bruno Maglis. He stepped away to avoid soiling his shoes, and bent down to offer a hand.

The man waved it away without looking at him.

"I'm so sorry," Hardwood said. "It doesn't look to be deep. I don't think you need stitches. Here..." Hardwood retrieved the knife, which had slid across the floor, and returned it to the man, who was now sitting up. "Oh," he said, realizing who the man was.

Pressing his palm against the cut, the man stared at Hardwood with the intense disgust a woman might show a rapist. "Dad?"

"Hi, Jeremy."

"You're not welcome here."

"I want to talk to you."

"Were you planning on doing it before or after you decapitated me?"

"I said I was sorry."

Jeremy stood up and tossed the bread knife into the nearest sink. Two of the other chefs stood nearby for support, but Jeremy told them to get back to work. "You didn't get any blood on your shoes, did you?"

"No, I stepped over—"

"Sarcasm, Dad. Your reflexes are slowing."

"I suppose I deserve that. Look, son—"

"Don't call me that."

"Can we talk? I promise I won't be but a moment."

"Jose!"

A young Mexican boy appeared from the back room where the dishwasher was running.

"Si?"

"Clean up this blood. Use gloves, it's got bad DNA in it." Jeremy turned back to his father. "I'm busy, I don't have time to talk to you."

"Don't have time or don't want to?"

"I'm not one of your investigative reports, Dad. Don't patronize me. Like I said, I'm busy. But for the sake of being honest, no, I don't want to talk to you either." Under his breath he continued, "It's enough I gotta deal with all these wetbacks, I don't need you here making it worse."

Hardwood raised his voice. "I think I'm in danger."

There are some silences people hope will speak volumes. The kinds of silences that resonate deep in the bones, and put import on situations. Silences that can crush eons-old grudges and erase histories of war. Hardwood prayed this was such a silence.

But it wasn't.

"Good," said Jeremy, finally. "I don't care."

"Please, Jeremy."

The young man spun on Hardwood and got in his face like a boxer intimidating his opponent. Hardwood didn't flinch, not even when his son's nose touched his own.

"I told you not to contact me. I don't want you in my life. I'm happy without you."

"Then you should be happy that I'm in danger. But I don't plan on leaving you alone until I speak to you. Don't forget who I am…I'd have no problem doing a report on the unsanitary conditions of this establishment you worked so hard to become a prominent partner of."

"Huh. Too late. Besides I don't believe you. You never repeat an op-ed piece if you can help it."

Hardwood nodded; it was true. "Five minutes."

"No."

"I'll come back every day until—"

Without saying a word, Jeremy flung open the kitchen doors and stormed off toward the bar, running his hands through his hair like a man on the verge of a breakdown. Hardwood followed him out of the kitchen and watched him silently as he kicked the business men out. "Out. We're closed. Come back in a half hour. A drink on the house when you return. C'mon."

Confused but clearly intent on getting a free drink, the men downed their liquor and left the restaurant. When they were gone, Jeremy went behind the bar and poured two scotches into snifters and handed one to Hardwood. "All right, Dad, talk."

"Have you seen the news?"

"Yeah. I see you have a new friend likes to cut people up. You're a fucking beacon to the freaks of this city. You always have been. So what?"

"You watch me?"

"Nope. But it's written on the fucking clouds right now, kind of hard to miss."

"He's going to kill me."

"Like I said—"

"What did I do to you?"

Jeremy finished his drink in one swig and poured another, not bothering to offer any to Hardwood. "What you did? You're kidding, right? Jesus, I don't know, only caused Mom to leave when she found a stack of pictures of you and another man sucking dick."

Hardwood looked around, saw some of the waiters watching and hoped they were out of earshot. "Not so loud."

"Why, Dad? If the city finds out you're gay they gonna fire you? Jesus, you're ego is unreal."

"What would you have me do? I cherished your mother like she was the Mona Lisa herself. It was her tenacity and unrequited pathos—"

"Stop! Just stop. Shit. Listen to you. Don't you ever stop talking down to people? Can't you just use normal words? It's so fucking condescending the way you talk."

"Should I dumb myself down—"

"No, but ease up on the pretense please. Talking to you is like watching a foreign film about stamp collecting."

The scotch was helping Hardwood, both warming him up and inhibiting his fear of furthering the conversation. "Your mother left for other reasons, too."

"Name one."

"You."

"Whatever."

"It's true. Your mind got warped."

"It ain't warped, it just looks that way to you because you're the one who's warped. The pictures proved that."

"Still, I wasn't only reason she left."

"What do you want me to do about it, Dad?"

"I want you to forgive me."

"No way. You fucked up my childhood, and then went and got famous, and when I needed help—"

"Help? All you ever wanted was money. I can only guess for what."

"To help start this restaurant."

"To help fund a homophobic, racist cult. I've seen the propaganda you and your friends distribute."

"Distributed. I don't do that shit anymore. I barely have time to breathe trying to run the kitchen here."

"And how's business?"

Jeremy slammed his snifter on the bar, drawing the attention of the hostess who was stacking menus at the greeting station. "It was great until your report on health code violations."

"That again? I found rodent feces in my food. You put it there on purpose. You made your own bed with that one."

"Well good. You got me back. Gold star for you."

"Such insolence. How does your staff—"

"Shut it. Look, you don't like me, and I don't like you, so if there's nothing more to say, get your faggot ass out of my establishment. I'm not forgiving you, and if they find you dead, tell them to have someone else claim the body. I don't want it. This is the second time I've told you to get out of my life. Get. Out."

Jeremy stepped out from behind the bar and went back into the kitchen, leaving Hardwood staring into his scotch. If there were answers at the bottom of the glass, he couldn't find them.

"Mr. Hardwood, something I can do for you?" The hostess had snuck up behind him, menus in her hand, looking embarrassed that she had seen the exchange between father and son. "It's just...I'm a big fan. I didn't know you and Jeremy..."

"Jeremy who? I don't know a Jeremy."

"But...your son is—"

"My son died years ago."

Hardwood excused himself and hailed a cab in front of the restaurant, took it back to the studio, all the while kicking himself for even trying to reconnect.

Jeremy was truly dead to him.

CHAPTER 18

On Sunday, Stone cried in the bathroom, yelling at the scruffy reflection in the mirror. Images of the cabbie's face swirled around him, accosting him, until he filled the sink with icy water and dunked his head in it. Underwater, he heard his own voice: You liked it. And that's okay. You liked it and you're good at it. You're going to be so fucking famous they'll carve your face on the moon. You need to get out there and keep at it. Now!

He wrenched his head up, splashing water all over the mirror. "No!"

When the shaking subsided, he dialed Carlie's number but hung up before she answered. She wouldn't calm him down; she'd just piss him off. It wasn't until Chauncey came in and licked his hand that he was able to relax. He decided to lay low until he could come up with an awe-inspiring scene of destruction worthy of The Chef's new creed. A taxi driver eating his own entrails would simply not cut it anymore.

Just thinking about it felt surreal. Killing was not like a nine to five job, there were no prerequisites for getting the work, and job security only depended on how well you knew what you're doing. It would be the perfect job in a perfect world—vacations whenever you wanted them, no co-workers driving you crazy one cubicle over with a radio playing gansta rap, no bosses jumping down your throat for being five minutes late, no working overtime on salary. In fact, killing could be lucrative, almost commission-based, if you planned correctly. A few fat cats with cash on their persons, a few grand dames with diamond jewelry, and you're in the riches. The more you kill, the more you make.

...in a perfect world.

The weekend anchors were on tonight, so he had the night off. Tricia Mason wanted to get together with him and discuss work, and since he was beyond horny—his last sexual escapade occurring back when being charged four dollars for a coffee would have resulted in a homicide—he jumped at the chance to grab a drink with her. O'Halloren's was out of the question, unless he wanted to run the risk of her and Hardwood getting friendly, or Pat trying to lure her into the back room to show her his shillelagh. The best bet was to grab a cab and head downtown to one of the hundreds of little bars and pubs that catered to the in-crowd.

At 10:45 she buzzed his apartment and he let her in. When she entered, she threw her leather jacket on the couch, rubbing her upper arms in an attempt to warm up. "Lord, it's cold," she said. "How long does it take to heat up 'round here?"

"What month is it?"

She laughed. "February."

"Not long now, like August or so."

"I believe it."

She was dressed in a low cut cashmere sweater, and when she gave a slight shiver her tits swayed back and forth like ocean buoys. Stone nearly got an erection. Chauncey rushed up to her and sniffed her crotch, and though Stone was instantly embarrassed, she was good-natured about it.

"Oh, what a cute doggie." She pat the mutt on the head. "I heard y'all had a dog. You look like one of those dog guys to me."

"Dog guys? Chauncey get down."

"Oh, you know. Guys who buy into the whole 'man's best friend' thing. Nothing wrong with it, mind you. Back home every boy I know has a dog. Call 'em hounds down there. It's charming, but I'll tell y'all, women ain't so keen on being second fiddle to an animal that drinks from the toilet."

The way she referred to men as boys concerned him. It was patronizing, and yet matronly, like she'd take care of a man, even though she thought he was an idiot. She had a hell of a body, but it was her domineering charm that no doubt turned her lovers into slaves. Stone wondered at all the 'boys' she had seduced as part of her career advancement. Or had she even had to sleep with them? Her voice was soothing and fun, she was always smiling, and her knack for making people feel like they were the only one who mattered was a better weapon than what was between her legs.

"Well," he said, grabbing Chauncey and pulling him back, "Chauncey and I are partners, huh, boy? But he knows when to give me space."

"Boys do need their space," she said, looking around the apartment. "You must have been living here for a while."

"Why's that?" Had she not heard about his divorce?

"Because I just moved here and even on my salary the only thing I can afford is a one bedroom the size of a commode."

"I figured you to make some good money, new lead anchor contract and all."

"Oh, honey, I do, but New York rent is beyond the realm of unfair, it's ri-fucking-diculous."

Stone paused. "I figured we could head downtown and get a drink," he said. "I know a little place with good jazz. We can discuss how to play out this serial killer thing."

"I'd love to, but I don't want to go back out in the cold yet. Can we just work here for a bit? That is, unless you have nothing to drink."

"Yeah, sure. I have wine and rum and…um… I think I still have some whiskey."

"Red wine?"

"Naturally. I hate white wine."

"Me too. Pour me a big glass."

As he drifted into the kitchen, she began to talk work, light stuff about how much she enjoyed the station. Through the open archway he could see her looking at pictures on the walls. Most of them were of his ex; he'd put them up in a fit of self pity, had never taken them down. Maybe there was more to it than that.

"It would be nice if this Chef had your home address," she said, cutting to the point. "That way you could get the letters and not worry about people in the office leaking information. Would you consider giving it out?"

"I'd rather not," he said, twisting the cork out of the bottle of merlot. He thought, should I care that she just suggested giving my home address to a psychotic killer? Chauncey heard him making noise in the kitchen and came and sat next to him, under the impression a can of food was being opened for him. "But I agree we should establish a better means of communication. Maybe an email address."

"No," she said, moving to the bookcase and inspecting his collection of biographies. "He wouldn't trust it and besides, that's how the Casanova Carver operates. We'd be asking him to copy someone else's MO. Phone would be best. If we could get an on-air call—"

"The cops would be on our ass in minutes." Not to mention, unless he became an expert ventriloquist overnight they were shit out of luck anyway.

"True, but don't forget, sugar, we're the press, we can spin the police's failure to catch this guy any way we want and there's nothing they can do about it."

He poured the two glasses of wine and met her at the couch. She took her glass, swirled it, and took a sip. "Mmm," she hummed as she swallowed a gulp. She licked her lips and sat on the couch.

"You do know how to get people's attention," he said, and then just to make sure she didn't think he was referring to anything sexual, he added, "I mean about the police, that is." He sat down next to her.

"I get what I want, but I'm not cheap. This story could put us into the number-one slot. Kills me that that senior citizen Hardwood got a letter from another serial killer as well. I swear, it's like he planned it. Or did you?" She chuckled.

"I didn't plan it." Not really he didn't, it just sort of happened in a drunken fugue. "But hey, at least I'm not stuck on that Stone's Moans bullshit."

She looked him over rather critically. Her glare was powerful, demanding, freezing him in place. "I know you don't like that I took your spot at the anchor desk. I'm not dense."

"It, uh, it hasn't been easy."

"Because I'm a woman?"

"No, because it was my seat. I know this town and I worked hard to get its respect. I worked my ass off to get that anchor position. Then you waltz in, not only take my spot but dictate my new position. Hell, you're not even from New York."

"Please, we may as well argue semantics, honey. Fact is, I was the number one anchor in Louisiana for three years straight. And I did that by taking charge and making hard decisions about what we aired. Trust me, in a couple of months you'll thank your lucky stars you have Stone's Moans."

"Oh right, it had nothing to do with your looks." He regretted saying it as soon as it left his mouth. But then again, the truth was the truth.

"I know what y'all men think of me. Y'all think I'm a piece of ass. Well you know what, sugar, it's true. But I'm a smart piece of ass. I know you resent me, but I also know you think my ideas are good, and

I know you're a little bit afraid of me, too."

"True, you're confident and that can be disconcerting to some men. And true, some of your ideas are okay. Not Stone's Moan's, I still hate that, but you've got a way with delivering the news. It's captivating. At least Cheese thinks so."

"I also know you'd love to fuck me. But I'm not going to let that happen yet."

Stone swallowed, a little uneasy. "Yet?"

"Until such time as I see its benefits, that is."

Not only had she turned him down, but she was making him feel powerless.

They stared at each other, at a loss for words. The clock over the television clicked away the seconds. Outside, car horns honked in the distance, and some hoodlum yelled at someone else whose "bitch ass needed a good slap."

"Anyway," she said, putting her empty glass on the coffee table. "Let's get back to The Chef. How do we get him on the phone?"

"I don't know," he replied. He needed to get her off the phone idea. "I suppose we tell him to call the office. But we'll have to do it on air, and then the police will know about it and tap the lines. The Chef'll probably figure that out as well and tell us to fuck off."

"You're probably right. Let's look at this another way. We want him on the phone to grab the viewers, but that's not viable. But we still need viewers. We haven't done the ol' compare and contrast yet, you know, see how he rates to past killers in the area. I personally find it very trite, but it might grab some attention. The other logical slant is to find us a serial killer expert and do some sort of special report."

"Who do we get?"

"I'm not finished, sugar. Sit tight and listen. I'm playing with the idea he's in a cult, and maybe tied to the Casanova Carver. We could do that."

"What? I don't think—"

"Hush. If they're both in a cult, well, now we're talking about something bigger, something grandiose, and the audience will eat that up. Think of Heaven's Gate, and the Waco fiasco. Those were lead stories for months. I think a cult story will work. Hardwood hasn't made that connection yet."

"Because it's not true."

She finished her wine and handed back the empty glass. "Truth ain't what the people want. They want to feel something after a long day at work. They want to know there's a world out there that's strange and beautiful and more interesting than scanning rolls of toilet paper at the supermarket eight hours a day. Besides, do you know for a fact it ain't true?"

"Well, no," he replied. "I just don't think it's the case."

"We don't know what the case is, do we? And since we're left to conjecture, sug, we can take some liberties with our assumptions. I think the next Stone's Moans should be about former cults in the area. What do you say?"

He didn't know what to say. Cults? If done correctly, it could tie in, though it annoyed him she wanted to lump him and Hardwood together. If both killers ended up on an even playing field, and both Hardwood and he reported on it, Hardwood would get the audience hands down. It'd be like sticking Brad Pitt and a flatulent donkey in a singles bar and telling them the first one to get a woman's phone number wins. It would be no contest.

"I'm not sure. I don't think it's a great idea."

"Tell you what, I'll run it by Cheese and see what he thinks."

You do that, thought Stone, go to the boss and shake your moneymaker. It's what you do.

She reached out and touched his hand. Her soft fingers played on his wrist, her thumb rubbing the back of his knuckles. "How about some more wine?" she said.

In the kitchen, as he poured her another glass, he realized just how annoyed he was at the whole situation. Hardwood was continually besting him even when he wasn't trying to. How did he end up so far in Hardwood's shadow? He needed to take The Chef to a new level, new heights of shock. If he wanted viewers, if he wanted the anchor desk back, he needed the viewers to demand him.

When he handed her the glass of wine, she stretched back on the couch, her tits pushing forward like trains pulling into a station. She took a sip of the wine and smiled. "When did you decide you wanted to be a newsman?" she asked.

"I didn't. I actually wanted to be a piano player."

"Get out." She giggled.

"I took lessons as a kid but I wasn't any good. When I was in high school, I got a job at a smalltime radio station as office help. I made friends with the DJ and we talked about piano and stuff. He let me help with the news once in a while, kind of as a joke." Jesus, he thought, even then he was only part of the news so long as it was a novelty act. "Anyway, that's when I got bit by the bug."

"And then you got your degree in Communications. Interesting. I always knew I wanted to be behind an anchor desk, ever since I was a little girl, swinging on the tire swing out back near the garden. I'd run into the house and report on everything I saw, including my neighbors cussing at each other, and my older brother lighting off fireworks with Red Hawkins down the road—Red later went to jail for grand theft auto so I always knew I should keep an eye on him. Momma said I was the biggest gossip around, but still she asked me for the goods every night over dinner. It got me attention."

"It still does."

"You could say that." She sat up, looked at her watch, and invoked Vivian Leigh. "Why, I do think I'm getting a bit tipsy. I should get going."

"I thought we were gonna hit the clubs?"

"The wine has done me in, sug."

"Want me to hail you a cab?"

"That's all right, I can manage. Let's get in early tomorrow and build this cult story, maybe find an expert. Can you be in by nine?"

"Nine it is."

"And let's hope we get another letter."

They wouldn't, Stone knew, but maybe that could work to their advantage.

When she closed the door, Stone sat alone with Chauncey and thought about his next move. No matter what, he wasn't going to let Hardwood saturate the spotlight. He wasn't some novelty act.

He was The Chef.

Right?

CHAPTER 19

When Mason got home, she poured herself some more wine and took a steno pad from the desk in her bedroom. For some reason she was always more creative right before bed.

The past few days had been a whirlwind of activity, and she'd not had time to formally put her thoughts together on what was happening. Getting thrust in the middle of a serial killer tug-o-war had not been a prospect anywhere on her to-do list. But far be it from her character to ignore opportunity's knock. She needed to make a list of what was important, what was undiscovered, and how it could all benefit her nightly reports. The last thing she needed was Cheese repositioning her and making Stone the sole reporter on the story.

She sat at the kitchen table and scribbled the killers' names at the top of the pad. She drew a line between them, separating each into its own column, and tried to remember the details of each. The Chef and the Casanova Carver were just names to her at the moment; in order to exploit them, she had to find out what they could offer.

"Okay," she said aloud. "The Chef. Kills a bum in the Upper West Side and a cabbie in Brooklyn, delivers his messages in envelopes." She wrote all this in the Chef's column. "The Casanova Carver. Kills a girl in the Upper East Side and a gay couple in a dog park, uses the internet to deliver his mail." Again, she jotted this down. But that's as far as she got, nothing else would come to her.

Rising from the table, she emptied the wine bottle into her glass and thought aloud. "Bums and cabbies, well they don't get much respect from anyone. Could be The Chef feels neglected. The girl and the gay couple, that feels sexual somehow. Shit. So...what? The Casanova Carver has penis problems? Actually...I can use that." In the Casanova Carver's column she wrote IMPOTENT? THE CONNECTION BETWEEN ERECTILE DYSFUNCTION AND VIOLENCE.

Leaning back, she tapped the pen on the table and thought, that could be a hell of a story. But was it plausible?

Picking up the phone, she dialed Cheese on his cell, knowing if there was one man who could identify sex traits it was him.

"Mason? Calling me for a late night rendezvous, you sexy thing. What can I do for you?"

"The Casanova Carver has a sexual identity problem, I'm pretty sure. I want to turn that to an advantage for The Chef. I need ideas."

"Off the top of my head, I have nothing. How do you know he has—"

"Call it women's intuition."

"I don't know. Sounds good on paper, but might not fly on screen."

"Want to come over and discuss it?"

"Sure, I'm outside your door."

There was a knock on the door that sent shivers down Mason's spine. She dropped the phone and stepped cautiously to the door. Sure enough, when she looked through the peephole, Cheese was standing in the hallway waving back at her. She opened the door.

"You have a teleporter in your house?" she asked.

"Nope. I was on my way here to see if you wanted to…work." He held up a small vial and shook it.

"What's that?"

"Inspiration. It helps me focus."

"Not since my college days—"

"It'll come back to you. You don't have any candles, do you? I've got an idea."

The rational part of her mind told her to run, but the part that knew Cheese was a path to further fame caused her to grab him by the collar and yank him inside like a rag doll.

Ten minutes later, Cheese was tied to the kitchen table as Mason dripped candlewax on his testicles. The sweat this brought to his forehead was a testament to the pain, but the smile on his face said that that was the point.

"If he does have a sexual identity problem," Cheese said, "we could make it a week long report and tie it into online predators, Asian slave trades, all types of stuff."

Dressed in a baby blue bikini that was a bit too small, Mason moaned. "Gives him motivation. People aren't as fascinated by average people with everyday problems, even if they are butchering people."

"Which makes our guy plain nuts, and therefore—"

"Therefore more interesting. Not to mention if the Casanova Carver does have a sexual identity issue, the cops probably have leads already. They might catch him."

"Which leaves us The Chef. Of course we can't say he's nuts, his words have to do it for him. The people need to sense it."

"But he needs more than just mumbo jumbo on a page," Tricia said, taking the candle and playing it around near his asshole. She slapped him in the face and cooed to him. "We need to create a mythos for him, spin his words into something larger and more sinister. Could be he's part of a larger cult."

"Ooh I like that. Cults are like conspiracies, you dig deeper and deeper for meaning that isn't there."

Perfect, she thought. She knew the cult angle was gold. "It'll stay with viewers, even if The Chef himself disappears. Even if the Casanova Carver gets bolder."

"You're a smart cookie, Tricia. Hop on my cock and tell me I'm a bad boy for wearing mommy's underwear."

She slapped him again and dripped wax onto the head of his penis, pretty sure that if this conversation had any credibility, Cheese could very well be the killer. She'd never seen a man with so many sexual deviance issues. "Cults are better than a sex crime, sug. While we dig to the bottom of this cult angle, we make sure the people know the Casanova Carver is just a man confused by his sexuality, build up The Chef as the true danger. It's a winning move. You try to bite my nipple again, hon, and I'll stick the lit end in your ass."

"Oh, Daddy like."

"Pay attention, Cheese."

Cheese shook his head and said, "Okay, yeah, I can probably find a therapist who will confirm the sex thing. What did Stone say?"

Mason grabbed Cheese's cock and thrust it inside her. Both of them moaned, Mason throwing her head back and Cheese shaking his head side to side on the table. The moment lasted a second or two before Mason got off of him, a sinister Cheshire-cat smile bearing down at her living toy.

"More," Cheese breathed.

"Not yet. Soon. But first, promise me I stay on this story no matter what happens to Stone."

"Yeah, yeah, sure."

"I said promise. I want to hear the words, Cheese."

Cheese's erection was rock solid now, the veins so full of blood Mason thought the ugly little thing might burst all over her kitchen. "I promise," he said at last. "Jesus Christ just do something to me now!"

"That's my boy," she said. "You're all my boys."

Picking up the compact mirror from the table beside her, she licked the remainder of the cocaine off the glass and shoved her tongue in Cheese's mouth. As she played across his own tongue, she could taste hints of spaghetti sauce—which was almost enough to make her lose her drive. But then, she'd been in enough intimate situations that had nothing to do with attraction…at least not for her. She could keep the ruse up a little longer, spaghetti sauce or not.

"Ready for more?" she asked.

Her boss nodded vigorously, desperately trying to thrust his hips toward her vagina. With the amphetamine coursing through her, and the thought of her face on the side of the Empire State Building, she grabbed Cheese's penis and squeezed it hard. She dripped more candle wax onto his scrotum, thrust him inside of herself, slapped him in the face, shoved the candle stick in his ass, and said, "Hot southern bitch fucks the shit out of New York City bigshot—report at…mmm…now."

CHAPTER 20

The problem with secret clubs is that eventually somebody talks. Somebody brags, or tells a loved one, or just lets it slip in front of others that they belong to a hush-hush society which, incidentally, meets at such-and-such a location at such-and-such a time and, by the way, don't tell anyone I told you.

Because of this, Hardwood always found conspiracy theories about the American government to be wildly entertaining. That anyone would believe men in black suits were hiding spaceships in the dessert, or that some offshoot of the fabled Illuminati was running the White House from a bunker in Florida, was laughable. The White House could no more keep secret an affair between two lowly aides, or what the president had for breakfast, than maintain an ongoing puppet regime.

Which is why Hardwood knew he could find this secret cigar club if he asked enough people. It's not that he needed to find it, it was more that the meeting with his son had left him with a sense of defeat he'd been carrying around inside. The cigar situation only made it worse. How could he, Doug Hardwood, go on knowing that two people had brushed him off so effortlessly? He needed to set things right.

As he was leaving for work Monday morning, Hardwood slipped a one hundred dollar bill into Louis' hand. "Morning, Louis."

"Mr. Hardwood."

"I've never asked, but do you have children?"

"I do, sir. A girl, Dominique, five years old."

"Getting ready for school? She must be excited."

"Yes, sir, she talks excitedly about getting homework. For some reason she thinks it's mature." He chuckled.

"Adorable. You mind if I ask where you live? The station receives plenty of supplies for children and I thought perhaps I'd have some mailed to your home. A gift, from me."

""That would be great. She could use some new supplies."

"My pleasure."

Louis rattled off his address and Stone made a mental note. "Got it."

"They grow so fast," Louis continued. "My wife and I are at the mall all the time buying new clothes for her."

"Yes, before you know it they're on their own, forgetting all about you." Hardwood pulled another hundred from his wallet, handed it to the doorman. For the briefest second, Louis' eyes appeared to bulge. "Very generous, sir. Thank you very much."

"No need. Just giving some credit where credit is due. I prefer to lead a private life and you've helped me maintain that. Much in the way Jeeves was always the confidant and friend of Bertie Wooster first, and his employee second. Jeeves, of course, was well taken care of for his…ah…discretion and diplomacy."

"Yes, sir."

"I'm looking for a new smoking club. One that doesn't let any old riff-raff in, one that has strict entry regulations. Privacy, I've found, is all too exploited these days. You wouldn't happen to know of such a club, would you?"

"Sir?"

"Come now, Louis. Are we dancing? It's cold and I have to meet with Boomer before lunch. You know Boomer? My director? The man makes lobotomy patients look like MIT engineers. If I don't get there soon, he's likely to turn the station into a free range chicken farm, or something equally idiotic. So, about that club..."

As if being watched through sniper scopes by men in the surrounding buildings, Louis looked around slyly and finally said, "I hear the Gates club is—"

"I'm a member of the Gates Club, Louis. Half the city is a member of the Gates club. If I wanted to fraternize with insipid bankers and dog-wagging politicians I'd pay it a visit. But I'm looking for something a little more elite. There's a cigar club in this city that has not approached me for membership and I want to know who runs it. Rest assured, if you tell me, your secret is safe with me. Now, here's another hundred...the location of the club please."

Paranoia was visible in Louis' eyes, his head still swiveling to look for cigar spies. Taking the money from Hardwood, Louis bent close and whispered, "I'm not supposed to tell, you understand."

"Louis, I think I've figured that out."

"All right. But if they find out—"

"Louis. They're cigar smokers, not the mafia. Nothing will happen. Either tell me or I shall rescind my offering."

Reluctantly, Louis cupped his hand around his mouth and whispered an address in Hardwood's ear. When he was done he stood straight and resumed his careful watch for sharpshooters who, as far as Hardwood could tell, were the type of people you hired to kill mercenaries, tyrannical dictators, and the occasional doorman who ratted out cigar cliques.

"Thank you, Louis."

Work went by quickly, focused as he was on writing his Casanova Carver story in response to Stone's interviews in the papers. The articles had been rife with lies and speculation, and he'd be damned if Stone was going to slander his alter ego in yellow rags like *The Post*.

Unfortunately, he wouldn't have the early morning to undertake his task at the cigar club, which meant sneaking out after the promo tapings and being very diligent. The address Louis had given him was, thankfully, not far away, but would still require at least an hour's worth of time to get to, make his statement at, and leave.

As he left his office, he found Boomer escorting a group of nuns around the station. They were promoting an event at the church to benefit their anti-drug program. "There will be free brownies and cookies and all sorts of snacks," he overheard them telling one of the mailroom boys with bloodshot eyes, long hair, and a shirt that had the slogan MARY JANE 4:20, written on it like a bible passage. "Free cookies? Nice. Can't abide drugs," the boy replied.

"Boomer?" Hardwood said, gently pulling the man away from the sisters. "I have to scoot out for a little while.

"Now? We're taping in two hours. The script is shit and needs rewriting. I've got Marion trying to get us a live feed from Los Angeles for that whole Michael Jackson fiasco and it's falling apart. I need—"

"I saw nothing on the wire about Jackson."

"Because nothing's happened. That's the problem. I've had Marion staked outside that goddamn ranch for a month and Wacko hasn't even looked out the window. How the hell am I supposed to get dirt on him if he won't shave a lion or marry a lawn chair or something?"

"And this is important why?"

"Hardwood, when you and Stone go on tonight, doing your respective reports, they're going to follow it up with a bit on cults. I have inside info on this. And I don't have any cult members to put on! Jackson's as close to cult weirdness as I can get right now."

"We discussed this in the meeting," said Hardwood, giving the one-minute finger to the nuns, who had exhausted their conversation with the mail boy about whether or not Jesus could beat the Xbox game Halo on master level without dying. "We will follow it up with home safety installations. We're getting B-roll now."

Boomer, evidently not impressed with home security in the face of a potential baby-dangling/kid-touching/hair-igniting/monkey-loving/mutant-bone-purchasing goldmine, shook his head and massaged his brow in frustration. "Not good enough. If I'm going up against cults, I need a ratings grabber. I either want my own cult members, or I want something equally as good. I want Jackson to do something stupid. I need these ratings. We're not as far ahead as we used to be. Not nearly."

Having heard enough of Boomer's nonsense, Hardwood checked his watch and decided to get on with his business before it was too late. He knew full well he could stand there for hours arguing with Boomer, which he'd done many times in the past, the only result of which would be a splitting headache and a strong desire to fry the man's head in a wok. He'd be better off arguing political science with a slice of pizza. "Home security, Boomer. That's my final decision."

"It ain't your decision. It's mine."

"On paper, yes. But if you don't do it, I'm making calls. And get Marion away from Michael Jackson's house. His antics aren't news, they're stale attempts to stay in the spotlight. I've got some friends to meet now. I'll see you in a bit."

Boomer motioned for the nuns to follow him and pushed past Hardwood toward the lounge. "Yeah, well, watch out for anyone that looks like they might cut you up," he said as he drifted down the hall, "friends included. You're still a target. You don't come back for the evening segment, ten bucks says Mazda pulls their advertising and

Sales crawls up my ass. I hate Sales."

The smoking club was hidden above a jewelry store in the West Village. Entry to the club was granted by way of a narrow staircase accessed behind the sales counter in the store, where a tiny man with white hair inspected diamonds for flaws under a jeweler's loop. Hardwood introduced himself and told the jeweler he'd been invited to the club as a guest, and asked if he could pass by and take the stairs. Recognizing the ruse at once, the tiny man blocked the way, picked up a phone next to the stairs, and spoke to someone in a whisper.

"Please," the man said, hanging up the receiver, "Wait one moment. Someone wishes to talk to you."

Ah, good, thought Hardwood, finally someone will acknowledge my stature and endorse me for membership. If so, perhaps I can change my reasons for visiting. If not...

There were a few minutes of uncomfortable silence—the jeweler scrutinizing Hardwood as if he were a cloudy gemstone—before a stocky balding man in a three-piece suit appeared at the bottom of the stairs holding a cigar.

Hardwood recognized him at once as the man he'd met in front of the news station last week. He looked vexed, to say the least, upon finding Hardwood staring back at him.

"Mr. Hardwood, you found us."

"I may sit at an anchor desk these days, but I'm still a news reporter. And a popular one I might add, which leads me to question who your *Dramatis Personae* includes if even I'm not respected enough to join. Surely someone up there knows me."

"Respect has little to do with it. Excuse us, Horace," he said to the little man, who was watching the exchange intently, "give us a minute alone?" The little man shrugged, took a cigar out of his pocket, and went on up the stairs.

Hardwood nodded toward the empty spot where the man had been standing. "Let me guess. He's an honorary member, just has to keep his mouth closed."

"It's a fair trade. We don't want just anyone to show up here."

"So if respect has little to do with it, might I ask what the requirements to join are?"

"I told you, you have to be invited."

"And nobody up there will invite me?"

"You have to be invited first. You can't just show up and hope to know somebody."

The conversation, now going in circles, was beginning to bore Hardwood, who was doing his best to look unfazed by the man's insinuations. "Anyone can be invited? What if they're loud-mouthed imbeciles? Or drug dealers? Or—"

"Power, Mr. Hardwood. Do I need to spell it out? They must have power. I won't deny that you have…a modicum of power in this city. We all remember the Winslow case. But it's not power. Winslow, now he had real power. He didn't tell the news, he made it."

If you only knew, thought Hardwood. "He was also a gay basher."

"Doesn't matter if he ate newborn babies. When you need things done, policies changed, you need people who can produce." The man sucked on the cigar and blew a plume of smoke toward the ceiling.

"So that's what this club is about. Lobbying."

"Lobbying is for do-gooders, Mr. Hardwood. If we want something done, we don't run around getting signatures. We just make it happen."

Out of nowhere, Hardwood found himself laughing uncontrollably. He hadn't laughed this hard in years, not since Boomer had been promoted to director. "Please, Mr.…whatever your name is…you're not running the government from a room above a jewelry shop. This is not a conspiracy, it's barely even a cult."

"A cult?"

"Long story."

"Well, you're right, we're not a cult."

"Oh, you're a kind of cult. A cult of fanatics."

"We have means—"

"No you don't. You may have figured out a way to get Cuban tobacco delivered in bulk, but that's no coup. Hell, I could manage that with enough phone calls. You're deluded fools with money."

"You're free to think as you want," said the man, again sucking on his cigar. "But you haven't been invited, and now I'm asking you to leave. And don't think about mentioning this on your program. We wouldn't want to have to show you how powerful we can be."

Whether the man's threats were sincere or hollow, Hardwood realized the conversation had exerted itself. It looked like he would have to carry out his initial plans after all, which was just as well. A quick check of the ceiling revealed two small cameras hidden behind tiny mirrors, one clearly pointed at the front counter, the other more than likely a wide angle that took in the showroom. The tapes would need to be found and destroyed before he left. But first things first.

"Do you know why you all hang out together up there, acting like you're protecting something precious?" Hardwood asked, slowly removing his gun from his jacket pocket.

The cigar hit the ground with a barely audible plop as the man watched the weapon come to bear on his forehead.

"Do you know?" Hardwood asked again, stepping forward and putting the gun against the man's nose.

The man could do nothing but shake his head ever so slightly, his eyes crossed and focused on the gun's barrel. Hardwood pressed the gun harder, bending the man's nose down until it turned red.

"I'll tell you why. Listen closely. Because your money can't buy you everything, and that kills you. You want power you can't truly have. But here's what you didn't know, and what I know all to well in my line of business—people are fascinated by silly groups like yours. You're not serving your needs, your serving theirs. Cults, secret societies, glorified boys' clubs. Everybody knows they're going to implode at some point, if for no other reason than the real people who run this country will not risk the chance that one group might proliferate and encourage others. And when they do, when they go down in a hail of bullets or poisoned Kool-Aid, or just simple apathy, we secretly thank our lucky stars that we have a real government, inept or not. We laugh at you, and turn it into a movie of the week."

"I...I don't...please don't shoot. You can join the club."

"I don't want to join your stupid club. Don't you understand what I'm saying?"

"N...no."

"You formed your little club because it allowed you to govern yourselves. Allowed you to choose who got to live in your world. But it's not real power. The real men with power are sitting in offices over at NBC and CBS and FOX cutting deals with the CEOs of major corporations, arguing over time slots for thirty-second commercials. Are you following me?"

The man, now sweating, shook his head.

"Power is not having money, it's the ability to take it from people. To take it from them without them knowing they're even giving it away, giving it away willingly. That's power. This...club...is a tree fort in the woods."

On the floor, the cigar was smoking, burning a hole in the rug. Hardwood bent down and picked it up, stuck it in his mouth and took a pull on it. "Habano leaf," he said. "Where do you really get it?"

"Bill—"

"What?"

"Bill Murphy. He owns the Lexus Dealership on 45th street. He goes to Cuba and buys it, they never check him at customs because he wears an oxygen tube."

"Ah. Smart. Well, any last words?"

"But…I thought you said…just a tree fort. I mean, yeah, okay, you're right."

"I know. But you forgot the other part of what I said. People love to watch these groups go down. You're not really a cult, but I can still make it work for my eleven o'clock."

Before the man could respond, Hardwood drew his hunting knife from where it was strapped under his jacket, and drove it into the man's eye, cut around it and plopped it out. A deafening scream filled the room as the man fell to the ground, blood pooling on the floor around his head. Taking another pull on the cigar, Hardwood stepped on the man's throat and crushed his larynx. He ashed into the man's eye socket and ascended the stairs to the club.

Outside on the street, a passing bum heard the faint screams, thought Goloxian aliens were trying to steal his brain, and ran away yelling a protective charm that sounded a lot like Mary Had a Little Lamb with the names changed.

CHAPTER 21

The Stone's Moans piece that night was indeed on cults, both their history in the state and their resurgence of late. It was a far cry from the bullshit kittens and puppies Stone had reported on not long ago, and he was beginning to think it wasn't such a bad gig after all. But then again, it was no anchor desk.

Truth was, he had no idea if cults were resurging, but he had an expert, Dr. Paul Montgomery from Columbia University, who testified that yes, the city was awash with religious and anarchistic zealots who wanted nothing more than to smother human flesh on their rye toast every morning.

They sat opposite each other in new leather chairs Cheese had bought just yesterday. They had fruit rind patterns on them.

"These types of personalities," Montgomery said, adjusting his bow tie, "are led to believe by their leaders that they are a part of a gestalt, a singularity made up of smaller parts, that cannot operate without each part being present and in working order. Christians, Jews, Muslims, and most other secular organizations, do not experience this—the religion continues with or without its members—and therefore are unconcerned, within a tolerable degree anyway, whether or not fellow worshippers adhere to guidelines. But to the cultist, the gestalt is not only the sect, but also the society it exists within. He or she, the cultist that is, is driven to eliminate those parts of the organism that might slow it or degenerate it. Sort of like a cancer, if you will. The Chef and the Casanova Carver, who in my opinion belong to a new order of extremists, quite possibly Luddites, consider themselves the white blood cells of our society. They will not stop until they have rid that which they consider the disease. I can say with assertion that more of their kind will arise in the near future. It's all in my book, *The Mindset of the Programmer*, available from Warner Books."

"Thank you for your thoughts, professor," Stone told him. The book plug was part of the deal of getting him on on such short notice. It was crude, but then so was most of what he was doing at this point. Montgomery had already signed a copy over to the station before the newscast began. Would Stone read it? Did he care about a cult leader's personality? He guessed he did. He could use all the help he could get at this point, and orchestrators of mass suicides and Hollywood murder sprees, he could only assume, knew a bit more about being a high profile killer than he did.

Mason stole another minute of air time and asked if the Casanova Carver and The Chef were working together.

"Stone," she asked impromptu, "does the professor believe the two are in touch with each other?"

He relayed the question to his guest.

"It's my belief" the professor answered, "that they have absolutely no idea how to get in touch with each other."

Mason fired off another question, and Stone couldn't help but feel she was going to take over the interview: "Are we talking multiple organizations here?"

Again, he relayed her question, and the professor answered, "We'll be seeing more of these cults springing up soon. Just as video games breed violent children, cults breed entire violent cultures. The loyalties of the killers lie with their respective cults, because that's what created them. But I can't say if it's the same cult or different ones. Again, I have to think if it was the same cult they'd be in touch...and like I said..."

Stone thanked him and took them out of the segment a second time, already removing the Telex from his ear so Mason wouldn't get any ideas and start asking more questions.

Near the control room Cheese stood with Duncan Willis. He folded his arms and motioned Stone over with his head.

Stone grabbed a bottle of water from the craft service table and approached him as Mason turned back to Camera One. Duncan gave him a dirty look as he edged him out of the way.

"Nice job, Stone," Cheese said. "I liked the angle. Didn't care for that walking tub and his JC Penny tie, but I'd say you planted a productive seed of hysteria tonight. Good job."

"Yeah," said Duncan, "Good job."

"I heard you and Mason got together the other night," Cheese said matter-of-factly.

"We did," he replied. "Just work, nothing big. In fact it was her idea—the whole thing about the cults."

"I know. And you were angry I put her at the desk. You know, she put Louisiana on the map."

"So I hear."

They both looked at Mason, both smiling for different reasons. She was laughing with Swift, who seemed rather stiff, as if he had an erection under the desk.

"Next," she said, turning back to the camera, "police are still questioning witnesses of a grisly scene in the West Village, where officials believe the Casanova Carver struck again. We'll have details after these commercials."

Cheese smiled and straightened himself. Behind him, Duncan followed suit. What a prick. "Tell me she doesn't make murder sexy as hell," he said. "I knew she was what the shareholders wanted. Just look at that smile, Stone. That's a million dollar smile."

Stone's head swam with ire as he watched Cheese leering. This was supposed to be working in his favor; he was supposed to be back at the anchor desk. What was it going to take to get Cheese to see that he was the better man for the job? The Chef wrote to him, not her. How much motivation did he need to exude? He'd already killed two people. Well, technically only one. But he was putting his life on the line for this. He was past the point of no return and still, he was just a sidekick.

"Stone?" Cheese was tapping his shoulder. How long had he been doing it? "Stone?"

"Sorry. What?"

"Back to you and Mason—I'd rather you let her and me work out the lead segments from now on."

"But why? I used to—"

"Because I said so," Cheese snapped.

Stone was taken aback.

"Because I need you to establish contact with The Chef," Cheese continued, smiling now. "He came to you, right? So figure out a way to get him to contact you. While you're at it, do the same for the Casanova Carver."

"Then what, you give the story to Mason?"

"She's lead anchor. You're supposed to work off her."

"But—"

"Hush. She's back."

Stone closed his mouth, watching Duncan eye him like a jealous lover. It occurred to him then that Cheese wasn't so concerned about focusing on exclusives as he just didn't want anyone hanging around Mason. Had he actually slept with her Sunday night Cheese probably would've fired him, Chef or not.

Professionalism dictated he deal with it and not let it bother him, but he was feeling ganged-up on. All he could really do was repeat to himself that soon all these corporate whores would be begging him to take anchor, begging for a chance to ride his coattails to fame and fortune.

CHAPTER 22

"A grisly scene above a jewelry store in the West Village," Hardwood reported during the eleven o'clock report, "where a multiple homicide has been uncovered. Authorities are not releasing details of the murders just yet, but have alluded to possible mutilation of some of the victims. Alana Gomez is live at the scene. Alana?"

The newscast cut to a young Latino girl outside the jewelry shop, fingering the Telex in her ear. Behind her, police officers rushed in and out of the building, barking orders at lookieloos to stand clear of the scene. Strobing red and blue lights played across the building's façade as another sheet-covered body was brought out on a stretcher.

"Thank you, Doug," the young girl replied when she heard Hardwood's voice come through the ear piece. "Indeed it is a grisly scene here at Hirsch Jewelers, where the investigation continues. Police are saying there are at least fifteen bodies inside, all of whom have been mutilated with some form of sharp instrument. We don't know the names of all the victims yet, but we do know that one of them is Horace Hirsch, who owned the jewelry store for the last thirty years, and another is that of David Porter, board chairman of Logman Industries."

"Are the police pointing toward any suspects?"

"Reports are varied at this point, but there is talk that the hearts are indeed missing, suggesting that this is the work of the infamous Casanova Carver. As you can see behind me, both local and federal authorities are trying to figure out the specifics of this tragedy. It appears the security tapes have been taken."

"Federal?"

"Yes, Doug, some of the victims were from New Jersey, constituting a killing across state lines. For WYNN news, I'm Alana Gomez."

The scene cut back to Hardwood, who was nodding in understanding, playing up his concern for the camera. Obviously, this was the young girl Boomer had hired to combat the introduction of Tricia Mason at WWTF. But where Mason had a sense of class and charm to balance out her raw sexuality, Alana looked more like a teenage porn star strung out on heroin. Her cleavage was ample and exposed, her Botoxed lips slick with gloss, her short skirt revealing tight, tanned thighs like table legs. Sure, she had the lingo down, but you might get crabs from listening to her.

"Thank you, Alana," Hardwood said, holding a printout in his hand. "For those of you just tuning in, I received an email from the Casanova Carver several hours ago, listing fifteen names to be found in the address above Hirsch Jewelers. One of them is in fact David Porter. Other names include Jonathan Frank, import entrepreneur, and Ben Harold, of Harold and Finn Brokerage. As is the killer's MO, the email came with instructions to report the crime on the air, ensuring the proper recognition in exchange for fewer future deaths.

"The email has been turned over to the police, and we will keep you informed as we learn more."

Offset, Boomer was mouthing the word "cult" to Hardwood, his way of saying hurry up and get to the meat of the story before we lose viewers. While he felt no need to oblige Boomer's instructions, he knew it was his best chance of staying ahead of Stone.

"The fifteen men found above Hirsch Jewelers are raising concern for another reason. All fifteen men were successful and prominent businessmen, and all of them major campaign financiers for the Republican and Democratic parties. But just what were these fifteen influential men doing in the small room above the jewelry store at the same time?

"WYNN has received information that the men were part of a secret society intent on fostering trade in illegal goods and services. Papers found at the scene mention the names of infamous drug lords and black market traders. Neither tips have been confirmed by police, however WYNN has learned that each man recently received large sums of money deposited into Swiss bank accounts. The police are investigating.

"When we return from commercial, a special report on elite secret societies in New York's history, from the Freemasons to the Eleventh Brotherhood. Just who does have the real power in this city?"

They cut to commercial, and Hardwood motioned for the make-up girl to come refresh him. He smiled, proud of the way he'd spun the last part of the report. The papers found on the scene had been a unique stroke of luck. Truly, the members of the smoking club had delusions of grandeur, thought they could win favors with men who had nefarious connections. Chances were, though, it was just a ruse to make them look "tough." When he'd spun on them with his knife, they'd screamed like girls.

Boomer came down from the control booth and leaned over the anchor desk, took off his headset. "Fucking brilliant. Fucking-A brilliant. What are the odds, huh? Just what were all those guys doing there? I want to marry this Casanova Carver. He practically handed us a win for tonight. I bet Charles and that bonehead Stone are sucking their thumbs right now. Man, what a stroke of luck. I told you, didn't I? I told you we needed to beat them at their own game. And you wanted to do home security systems. Bah! Is that the same suit you had on this morning?"

"No. And yes, Boomer, you deserve a pat on the back. This was much better." Hardwood's sarcasm was as thick as mud, but Boomer wasn't listening to anyone but himself, which, Hardwood thought, was par for the course.

"Tell you this, too," Boomer continued. "If we ever get to talk to this Carver guy, I'm thanking him. Hell, I'm gonna buy him flowers."

"So does that mean I no longer have to hear you insist I get a bodyguard?"

"Look, the fucker's still a nutball, don't get me wrong. But hey, if he can keep handing us stories like this—"

From the control room, someone shouted out the thirty second warning until the newscast commenced, and Hardwood shooed the makeup girl away. Boomer put his headset back on and said, "Okay, when we get back, you do your thing, talk this up, make the people love it. You saw the script, right?"

"I took the liberty of editing it. Somehow, I find it egregious to say the Red Angels are a shadowy society of superheros. They're a disorganized band of grown men playing GI Joe."

"I wouldn't say that to their faces."

"I know someone who would."

"What's that?"

The man in the control booth began counting down from ten…nine…eight.

Boomer backed off and took up his spot behind the monitors once more, already forgetting the slip of Hardwood's tongue as he ordered his men around. As the red lights came on on top of the cameras, Hardwood went into his report on secret societies, discussing ideas such as the control of information, buying votes in Congress, and yes, even puppet regimes.

When the show was done, he retired to his office with aplomb where he viewed a tape of Stone's report on cults. The expert they'd hired was a dolt in every sense of the word, though the report was well-constructed and just dumb enough to enrapt anyone with a hint of gullibility. He could only hope his double-edged report—both the story on the slaying at the cigar shop and the bit on secret societies—would outdo Stone and Mason.

Mason, he thought, turning off the tape and looking out the window toward the nearby skyscrapers. Mason was still an element he hadn't worked out. It was one thing for Stone to work alone, and garner notoriety through his endeavors, but as it appeared Mason was getting her hand in the works more and more, she could prove an even bigger problem down the line.

Bearing thought on this, Hardwood decided to touch base with his opponent, if for no other reason than to gauge the man's spirits and acumen. The phone rang for several moments, six times to be exact, before Hardwood gave up. Stone was either celebrating his night's triumph, or chewing on the discovery of what had happened at the jewelry store. Hardwood wanted to know the numbers, but was eager to get a good nights' sleep for once, and so opted to gather his coat and turn off the lights to the office…

…when the phone rang.

"Hello?" he answered.

"Doug. It's me."

"I just rang you."

"Yeah. I was listening to Cheese shout about killing you."

"Kill me? I dare say you're not serious?"

"No, not really, just angry ranting. How'd you know about our angle tonight?"

"Honestly?"

"No, Douchebag, lie to me."

"You're testy. You know people slip up when they let emotion get the better of them."

"Listen, Confucius, when I want a lecture on self-control I'll call my wife."

"You mean ex-wife."

"I wish. When that bitch gets under your skin she never leaves, despite what the courts say. She's like herpes."

"I wouldn't know."

"How'd you know about our angle!?"

Hearing Stone's anger was music to Hardwood's ears, and he sat back down at his desk and for the first time in a long time, put his feet up. "Honestly, I don't know. Were I to hazard a guess, I'd say it was merely serendipitous."

"Oh yeah, just like the first time you copied me, right? That was serendipshit too."

"Are you drunk?"

"Are there bugs in my office? Did you bug my office?"

"Roland—"

"Wesley!"

"You should really just stick with one name."

"Cheese won't let me."

"Stone…I swear to you I don't know how Boomer gets his information, nor do I care. Truthfully, I had an entirely different report scheduled for tonight, but happened upon an opportunity I could not pass up. You should really relax about it all, I'm playing fair."

"Fair? Fair! Are you watching the same events I'm watching?"

"You're sounding a bit desperate now."

There was a long pause, and Hardwood could hear the distinct sound of a flask top being unscrewed, followed by a gulping noise. "Why did you call me, Hardwood?"

"Honestly?"

"No! Why would I—"

"Sorry. Yes, I called to see how you're faring. If you want to cut it all out, step aside and concede defeat, I will be happy to give you the credit you deserve and put an end to all this—"

"Oh no, no fucking way, no no no. This ain't over."

"Then when does it end?"

"When I get what's coming to me. When I get back the respect I had before this all began."

"You had respect?"

"Fuck you, Hardwood."

"Very well."

"Good."

"Want to get a drink?"

"What? No," Stone replied.

"Just being friendly."

"I'm already drunk. I'm going home to bed."

"Then I bid you goodnight," Hardwood said, a second before Stone hung up the phone on his end without saying goodbye.

Gathering up his briefcase and jacket once more, Hardwood locked up his office and left the building. On the way home he couldn't help but muse out loud to himself: "You're losing your marbles, Stone. Let's not do something stupid."

When he arrived at the Howitzer, he found Louis in his normal rigid position outside the door. There was a new look in the man's eyes, something reserved and yet enlightened. Of course, Hardwood thought, the man had heard the news about the cigar shop massacre.

"Evening, Louis."

"Mr. Hardwood."

Hardwood let the next few seconds pass in silence, merely watching Louis for signs of betrayal. If the man was afraid, or looking to be a hero of some sort, he wasn't showing it. It all comes back to money with his kind, Hardwood thought. It can buy information, and it can buy silence. And in this case, it may have just bought an ally. Only time would tell.

To be sure, he added: "Everything all right? The wife and daughter doing okay?"

Suddenly Louis was unable to maintain eye contact. He looked at his feet and answered. "They're very good, sir. Very happy."

"Fantastic. I haven't forgotten about sending those gifts over. They should arrive in a day or two." He let the words hang between them, then repeated Louis' address just to clarify that he had it right. Louis caught the nefarious intent behind it, nodded. Finally, he said, "Goodnight, Louis."

"Goodnight, sir."

Hardwood entered the building and rode the elevator to his apartment.

CHAPTER 23

By the end of the week, Hardwood was once again ahead in the ratings. News of the jewelry store massacre was everywhere. Annoyance had Stone pacing his office, wondering just what he was supposed to do to get Cheese to see his potential. Fact is, he wasn't as smart as Hardwood, he wasn't as attractive as Mason, and he wasn't about to kiss ass like Duncan.

He picked up the phone and dialed the numbers he equated with the Devil. She picked up on the second ring, out of breath as usual. "What the hell do you want?" she asked.

"Hi, Sunshine. The station wants me to interview you about your Guinness world record, the one about bitchiest—"

"Wesley, do I need to call the cops?"

"I dunno, do they respond to hissing?"

"Don't call me again."

"Hold on, I'm just playing. Did you watch my segment?"

"No, I watched WYNN."

"Hardwood! You watched that asshole?"

She was still breathing heavily. And was that a man's voice he heard? "Yeah, I watched Doug Hardwood. You're not my husband anymore, Wesley. I don't need to watch you."

"But I'm being stalked by The Chef."

"I know. How does it feel?"

"What's that supposed to mean?"

"Jesus, Wesley, I'm busy. Is there a point to this?"

Was there a point to this? Not really, he realized. He was just pissed off and figured if he was going to be in a bad mood then so was the bitch who still took half his paycheck. He worked hard to get the money he was making, and even that went to someone else.

"Come get dinner with me," he said. He said it so fast he stunned himself.

"You're kidding."

"Apparently not."

"Wesley, I told you last time—"

"I have something important to tell you, Carlie, and I can't say it on the phone. Please, just one dinner, then I'll leave you alone."

Her breathing became rapid, more labored. "Is there someone there?" he asked.

"Hold on," she said. There was an audible thump as the phone fell to the floor. A series of grunts and screams followed, both man and woman, that seemed to last forever. He didn't know what made him angrier, that she was fucking someone while she was on the phone with him, or that she had never screamed like that when they were married.

As he waited for her to stop, he checked his email. All he had was some spam mail for a porn site. He clicked on the link and was rewarded with drunk co-eds doing things with beer bottles he didn't know was possible. Between the pictures on the screen and the noises from the phone, he was starting to get an erection. Getting a boner while your ex-wife gets slammed can't be healthy, he realized, and shouted for her. "Hello? Hello!"

She picked the receiver back up. "What do you need to tell me?" she rasped. "I'm not going to dinner with you."

"Who's there?"

"None of your business. Tell me what you need to tell me or I'm hanging up."

"I…uh…I'm not paying you alimony anymore."

"Fine. I'll have my lawyer call you. Bye."

"Wait! I mean," he added quickly, "I've come into some money. Endorsement deals and all that. I'm willing to give you half, we're talking hundreds of thousands up front, if you agree to a few things."

"What things?" Then, to her bedmate, "Hold on, honey, I'm still on the phone."

"Going again, huh? Don't you ever stop?"

"Yes, well, unlike you, some people can go the distance."

"Kind of easy when your vagina—"

"What things, Wesley!?"

Calm down, he told himself. No sense getting upset because she had another man in bed. That was old hat by now, and he was used to it. "I'll tell you at dinner. Tonight, at Gertrude's."

"You can't get a seat at Gertrude's on this short notice. Even you."

"You'd be surprised, sweetie. I'm Roland Stone, The Chef's confidant. People want the inside scoop."

"Which you don't have. All you have is a crazy letter or two ranting and raving about nonsense. This is New York, Wesley, do you think we care about some antisocial nutball who kills a cabbie?"

"I'll get us a table. Just meet me there, okay?"

She sighed, whoever was with her grunting in pleasure once again. Stone wanted to kill the sonofabitch. "Okay," she said. "I'll meet you there in two hours. But if this is bullshit, I really am going to call my lawyer and the police. Goodbye."

She hung up.

Well, that was easy, he thought, except for the whole part about getting a table at Gertrude's on such short notice. But he knew someone who could. That someone was Doug Hardwood. His fifteen years behind the desk had afforded him carte blanch at almost every eatery in Manhattan. Rumor in the news world was that he'd had Cher removed from a table he requested, that she'd been escorted out right by Hardwood and given him the finger. Stone was fully aware that threatening him for such a favor was going to have repercussions he'd regret. But perhaps he could make a deal. He dialed Hardwood's number.

"Hi, Doug," he said.

"Is it Wesley or Stone?" Hardwood asked. "I forget."

"Stone, please."

"So we're friendly again?"

"Sure. Sorry about the other night. Just business, you know."

"Good, then what can I do for you, friend? I was just on my way out."

"First let me commend you on your work," he said, sucking up as best he could. "Very imaginative."

There was a long pause. Then, "I'll assume you were talking about my newscast the other night. Since anything else would be...unwise to discuss over wires."

"Yes, of course. That's what I meant. You were very imaginative when you picked...your segments."

"Thank you. Some segments just catch my fancy and I can't wait to...play them out. I'd return the sentiment if not for the fact you seem to have had a...slow week."

All they needed now was to speak pig latin, wear decoder rings, and give themselves code names and they'd be bona fide secret agents, thought Stone. Although he guessed they already had the code names. "I need a favor," he said.

"In this world favors come via generosity or price. I have neither to offer so my reply to your rather presumptuous command is sure to disappoint you. But I admit I'm curious."

"Um...yeah...anyway...I need a table at Gertrude's."

"And what have I to fear should I respond in the negative?"

"Nothing. Just that you might need my help someday. I know we're competitors now, but I always repay a favor. And I can't imagine there's anyone else who'd be willing to, say, corroborate that you were out to dinner with a colleague should someone bother to ask about dates and times."

"And this for a seat at Gertrude's?"

"No strings attached," Stone assured him.

There was another long pause. Hardwood was playing mental chess, deducing his next move in regards to how it favored his future. If he took Stone up on the offer he would lose a pawn and Stone would lose something more important—a bishop.

It was a piece Stone was willing to lose at the moment, a sacrifice for a greater gain. He clicked back to the porn website as he waited, tried to read the labels on the beer bottles that were half submerged in—

"Okay, Stone, I'll get you a table. But I'm holding you to our pact."

"Gotcha."

"How does nine o'clock sound?"

"Sounds like a deal."

*

He arrived at Gertrude's at 8:45 to discover that a table by the window was set and being held for him. Hardwood was worth his word after all. The restaurant was dimly lit, a pianist playing soft music near the back wall, candles and fresh flowers on the tables providing a soothing aroma throughout. The tinkle of crystal champagne flutes and murmuring patrons filled out the atmosphere.

He had no idea what he was doing. For months since the divorce he'd been bitter enough to not dwell on what he'd lost. After all, he got the dog. But the truth had always lurked under the surface like a stingray: he loved Carlie—loved her and hated her, and even deeper, hated that he was so obsessed with it. And like the pain that accompanies stepping on such a creature, whenever he had a mind to think of her, his insides hurt. It was stupid, really. After all, it was he who discovered she'd been cheating, and it was he who filed for divorce. But, rationalization makes anything seem okay, and he wanted to believe she had cared, that she still cared. When he thought about it, everybody had urges to be with other people, even married couples. Maybe he should have let her have some fun and responded in kind. Sex was just sex, when you got down to it.

But when she walked into Gertrude's with a well-toned, younger man on her arm, he quickly changed his tune. Fuck the bitch. Fuck her long, and fuck her hard, and may she not be breathing at the end of it.

"Hey, sweetie. You look good," he said, kissing her on the cheek where he felt the coldness of a thousand dead souls. She was pure evil.

"I can't believe it, you got a table."

"I told you I was popular. Who's the…who's this?"

She motioned to the man, who looked more like a boy to Stone. "This is Javier. He's just dropping me off, don't worry."

"Who's worried?"

"Mr. Stone," the man—boy—said, extending his hand. "I'm a big fan."

Did he stress the word big, Stone wondered. Was that a jab at his penis size? What had Carlie been telling this guy? He shook the guy's hand and smiled. "Thanks." And he added in his head, you fucking prick.

"I mean it, I respect you. That's gotta be dangerous being on The Chef's mailing list," Boy-man said. "How much longer you give him before the cops catch him?"

Okay, he was fairly certain Boy-man stressed the word longer. Suddenly he needed a drink of something harsh. "I have no idea," he said. "He's pretty well endowed."

Both Carlie and Javier gave him a funny look.

"I mean at what he does," he said. "He seems pretty skilled with a knife."

"That's not what the paper said. They said the job looked rushed."

"Yeah, well, the paper can take a fucking leap—"

"Will there be three tonight?" a waiter asked, appearing behind them with a wine list. Stone hadn't seen the waiter approach, and not wanting to cause the scene he was headed toward, he calmed himself.

"Just two. Thanks. And can you bring a bottle of Chianti?" He turned to Carlie. "I remember it was your favorite."

"Too bad you got nothing else right," she said.

The waiter nodded and left, but not before giving a look that said if he was putting up with relationship shit tonight somebody was tipping well.

"I'm starving," Stone said. "Let's see what's on the menu."

Carlie kissed Javier hard on the mouth and patted his ass as he turned and left. Stone recorded his face for The Chef's file of prospects.

Linguini and mussels and pan-seared sea bass filled out their order when the waiter returned. It was a prix fixe menu and the prices were not listed, which meant, Stone knew, he was going to pay out the ass. As civilly as he could, he engaged Carlie in small talk until the food came. Mostly, she wanted to know how the dog was, and whether he was feeding him and taking him for walks. She never missed an opportunity to make him feel like less of a man.

To balance the scales, he asked her if she was keeping the old apartment in good shape, the one he'd spent every weekend renovating.

"So tell me about the money," she said, sipping the Chianti. "How many figures are we talking about?"

He had forgotten all about the ruse. There were no endorsements, there had been no commercial interest in him outside of the papers wanting interviews.

"What are you promoting and why involve me?" she asked.

"It's…um…a book deal about my life."

It would be easy to get an exclusive interview with The Chef for a book, but publishers would probably want verification that it was indeed the killer's own words and not something he made up. One and the same, of course. And even if they didn't buy it, dubious content always worked to a writer's advantage. As a reporter he'd seen the gleam in the public's eye when someone reportedly witnessed a UFO or a ghost. Believers wanted desperately to believe, and skeptics wanted desperately to debunk, which meant both demographics bought the kind of books that discussed such nonsense. The same was true for serial killers. Throw in some handwritten notes from The Chef and both sides would slap down hard earned cash for a chance to confirm or negate their authenticity.

As he dwelled on it, he realized it wasn't such a bad idea after all.

"One hundred thousand, plus percentages of any movie or television deals. Within in a few years you could be looking at millions."

"Books don't make millions."

"What about *Harry Potter?*"

"That's not a book. That's an exercise in brainwashing."

"I met with an agent and he promises six figures."

"And what am I supposed to agree to do to get it?"

There were a hundred things he wanted her to do, like jump off a bridge, or stick her head in an oven, or sleep with him again…and then stick her head in an oven.

But he said nothing, just looked at her.

The silence set her off: "Jesus Christ, is there a point to this?"

"If I give you a fair share of the profits, enough to sustain you for a long time, will you knock off the alimony?"

"You're nuts. I'm supposed to agree to let you stop paying me over some gamble? This is what I came to dinner for? I don't think so. When the book comes out, then I'll have my lawyers call you."

"Fine." Somehow, he now felt content. Her anger didn't matter anymore. In the end, he had only wanted to have dinner with her and he could mark that off as a success. Call it a moral victory. "Your loss.

You'll get nothing from the book."

"I'm not dumb, you know. You lured me here for some personal reason. What, to try and get me back? I told you before, we're done."

"We could try."

"Wesley."

"C'mon."

"This is bullshit."

"I'm just saying—"

"If there's nothing else—"

"Wait. C'mon. Sit and have dinner. The food's good and I'm paying. What's it cost you to eat it?"

"It's costing me my blood pressure." Reluctantly, she sat back down, picked up her fork again and began eating. She didn't speak or even look at him, just concentrated on her food.

"How are you doing?" he asked for the second time that night.

"I told you, I'm doing fine."

"Good, good. Aren't you even a bit concerned The Chef thinks I'm his pal?"

"Look, Wes, you know I care. But we're done. I can't keep telling you I care because you keep taking it the wrong way. So to answer all your questions: Yes, I care, yes, I'll be sad if he kills you—which would be your own damn fault by the way for obliging him and not protecting yourself—and no, I won't lose any sleep in the meantime."

"What if he kills Javier?"

"I seriously doubt that's going to happen."

"Oh, I don't know, it could happen."

"Will not."

"You don't know."

"The Chef stays to the shadows and Javier is afraid of the dark. I doubt they'll meet. The Casanova Carver, now him I'm worried about.

He kills people right out in the open. They say he can climb the sides of buildings."

"What?! Where'd you hear that?"

"*The Post.*"

"*The Post*? Look, he's not Spider-man, he's just a freak with a bit of prior experience."

"What do you mean, 'prior experience?'"

"Nothing. Forget it."

"Do you have inside information—"

"No. I only know what the public knows. I know he can't climb buildings."

"Says you. Either way, he scares me."

He sat silent for a moment while the piano player cracked his knuckles and started into a new tune. "Do you miss me?" he asked.

"Shit, Wesley, I'm not doing this. You need to move on."

"I thought I was what you wanted. I have money, I'm successful—"

"You're a news anchor. I don't know that that's success. I know a lot of people who can enunciate well and have good teeth, doesn't make them Man of the Year. Plus that Stone's Moans thing is pretty dumb. It reminds me of Gene Shallot's movie reviews."

"Must you always make me feel like—"

"Yes. You lied to get me here. I'm not happy. And since I'm done eating, I'm going to leave."

She threw her napkin on the table and started collecting her things.

Frustration and a desire to sleep with her gave way to good old anger, and numerous slurs began making their way from his brain to his lips. As she was putting on her coat, as he was about to blurt out something utterly rude, a man at the next table said, "Carlie? Oh snap, is that you?"

With a tilt of her head, she studied the man's face, then dropped her eyes down to his groin. A smile spread across her face. "Maverick?"

Maverick? Maverick! Oh, come on, Stone screamed inside his head. Who the hell was this guy? Only Maverick he knew was the Tom Cruise character from *Top Gun*, and he'd heard both actor and character were gay. This guy was in his early thirties, okay looks, a stylish sport coat and tie, but certainly nothing made of money. The woman he was sitting with, however, was a different story.

Petite and blonde, she wore a red dinner dress sporting a knockoff logo of Guillermo Torres, a hot new designer whose items were worth the price of a small sedan. She had the kind of thick lips that give men hard-ons, and the large eyes of a Japanese cartoon character. Studying her in the candlelight, Stone realized he'd seen her somewhere before.

"Maverick?" the blonde girl asked her date. "You told me your name was Clarence."

"It is, baby, they just call me Maverick because I look like Tom Cruise."

Somebody shoot me.

"Carlie, you look super," Maverick said.

"I do," she replied. "And you're as dashing as ever."

"Whatcha doing here?"

"I'm having dinner with someone."

She said 'someone,' Stone realized, not friend. She was good like that, managing to put him down without overtly making herself look like a bitch. She had evil genius qualities, enough to be the bad guy in a Bond film. Bond would lose against her.

The guy looked at him, studied him for a second, and then seemed to catch on to who he was. "Yo, Roland Stone," he said. "What up?"

Finally, a fan, he thought. A chance to show Carlie just how appreciated he was. If he played it right, maybe he could get the guy to ask for an autograph, show her that he was more than good teeth, that he was an integral part of the community. He reached out a hand and they shook.

"You watch him?" Carlie asked the man.

"Watch him? You could say that. We roll with the same outfit now, we're co-workers."

What the hell was he talking about? Stone had never seen this man before in his life. Maybe the guy was in the IATSE union, one of the gaffers. They always got shuffled around from studio to studio. Usually they spent twenty minutes fixing the lights and two hours gabbing over coffee.

"Yeah," Maverick continued, "you know. I do the kids segment in the morning now. Cheese hired me."

"Wait," Stone said. "You're the pink bunny?"

"Yeah, that's me, Bradley Bunny, right after the food segment. You pulled my ears that one time."

"What?" Carlie asked.

"Don't worry," Maverick said, looking from Carlie to Stone. "I ain't mad. Not anymore. Shit happens. Getting fired brings out the worst in all of us."

"I wasn't fired." Stone balled his hand into a fist. He couldn't believe this. Carlie knew the bunny that had fired him. And if she knew a man, it most likely meant she knew him carnally. An image of a big, pink bunny fucking his ex-wife sprang up in his mind's eye. *His carrot's much bigger than yours, Wesley,* she said in the reverie. He blinked to clear the image from his head, but found he couldn't fight the tenseness in his jaw. *So big and orange and tasty. Not like your little withered veggie.*

I'm gonna kill him. I'm gonna kill him.

Maverick turned to Carlie. "So you know Roland Stone, huh?"

"Unfortunately," she answered. "He's my ex-husband."

"Well, hey, Roland, lemme tell you. This woman got all the right moves. But I guess you'd know that." He laughed.

Carlie smiled at this. The blonde woman, however, was not thrilled. She scowled, and that's when Stone realized who she was. Her name was Mindy Muffin. Not her real name of course—who had a real name anymore on television? She did a kids show on the public broadcasting network, taught simple math and reading and such. Basically, she ripped off *Sesame Street* and passed it off as her own material. Seeing her next to Maverick, Stone had to roll his eyes; apparently people who dressed up like idiots for a living gravitated toward one another. Can't say as they didn't make a good living though, considering where they were eating. Were they really more popular than him?

"I know about her moves," Stone replied. "I've been there."

"You know nothing of my moves, Wesley."

"Ex-wife," Maverick said. "Shit, I didn't even know you were married, Carlie."

"No longer, thank God. And before you start in, Wesley, we weren't when I met Maverick."

"That's such a relief," he said as sardonically as possible. "For a second there I questioned your loyalty."

She ignored the comment. "Anyway, Maverick, it's nice seeing you again. I was just leaving. Give me a call and we'll catch up sometime."

"Yeah, girl, all right."

With that, Carlie left.

Miss Muffin got up and left the table in a huff, disappeared into the ladies room. Stone wondered if she'd even return to the table, or if she'd come out of the bathroom and walk by with her head held high, exit the restaurant, and use the experience for a puppet skit on her show in the morning.

"Man," Maverick said, looking after Miss Muffin, "women are crazy. I figured if I got this one liquored up, I could get her to get freaky with me tonight, wear that milkmaid outfit she wears on her show. You ever fucked a milkmaid, Stone?"

"No." He wanted to kill the guy right now.

"Me neither. But I like it exotic. That's why I been hanging 'round Tricia Mason at work. I'm not sleeping till I get her in bed. You just know she gonna pull out some weird shit, like maybe throw a saddle on me and ride me around the bedroom. Cowgirls like horses, that's the truth."

"She's from Louisiana, not Texas."

"Same thing. Say, you hear anything from that killer guy who hollered at you?"

"Not yet."

"That's some fucked up shit, right there. You must be pretty scared."

"Not really."

"For real, dog?"

"For real. Dog."

Maverick took a long gulp of his beer, wiped his arm across his mouth. "Well, I would be. A little bit anyway. Not like Doug Hardwood must be though. Shit. You believe that? The Casanova Carver been going nuts lately. That motherfucker is a bona fide one-man death squad, if you know what I'm saying. Do you get Hardwood's newsletter? It's on his website. You should get it. He's got some good theories on who this guy is."

"I couldn't begin to imagine."

Miss Muffin came back to the table, her eyeliner a bit smeared, her face flushed. Her eyes were glazed over and even in the dim light Stone could see that her pupils were dilated, the telltale sign of an opiate user. Heroin, he guessed, she must have just snorted it in the bathroom. He was going to make a comment about it as it related to teaching children, but then he thought, fuck it, it's not like kids even watch her show. It was up against *Reading Rainbow* or some shit and it just regurgitated what Big Bird taught the week before anyway. Hell, you'd think the heroin would help her come up with some original material for once.

He said, "Maverick, you look as much like Tom Cruise as I look like Jiminy Cricket. And trust me, Mason doesn't want anything to do with you. If we were somewhere else, I'd hurt you."

"What? Yo, man, why you being so cold and shit?"

"Because you disturbed my dinner."

"Whatever, man. Fuck you. Duncan is right, you're a dick."

Picking up his fork, Stone cut into the sea bass and pretended it was made of pink felt. The overwhelming fury welling up in him made it hard to focus on anything. Everywhere he went, it was Casanova Carver this and Casanova Carver that, Hardwood this and Hardwood that. He was tired of it, tired of looking over his shoulder to see if the cops were coming and still not getting ahead. He was tired of putting himself in a position of high risk with no reward. At that moment, he knew that the only way to beat Hardwood at his game, the only way to raise himself and his creations above everything else, was to throw caution to the wind and outdo Hardwood on such a level that it would shatter the news world.

And what the hell was Duncan saying behind his back?

That prick.

CHAPTER 24

By one in the morning, Stone was sitting in a drunken stupor on a bus stop bench one block from the Howitzer Building, mumbling curse words to himself and doing his best to feel his toes. It was a game he played whenever he was blitzed, seeing if he could control certain body parts without using his hands. As usual, no part of his body wanted to respond in a timely manner to commands sent from his brain. He was beginning to slide off the bench like a glob of melting ice cream.

And all the while he couldn't get the night's reports off his mind.

Who did Hardwood think he was? As if the old bastard could just steal Stone's angles, his ideas, his thunder, and not expect him to take serious issue with it. If he could figure out a way into that damn building, past that gorilla of a doorman, chances were he'd cheat on their unspoken rules of fair play and be done with it.

But then, that would be the stupidest thing he could do. No doubt Hardwood would have a contingency plan in place for just such an occurrence, maybe a hidden camera in his apartment, or some type of booby trap that involved a sharp implement carving his heart out. Stone wouldn't put it past the bastard to put his ticker on the five o'clock segment and eulogize him like a hero, just so that the whole city would watch WYNN instead of WWTF.

The man was a genius.

And he was soused. Time to go home and forget this spying shit. As he rose from the bench, a voice came from behind him:

"Leaving? You know, you can see better from across the street."

Turning—if throwing your arms wildly to the side and letting them spin you around can be called turning—he came face to face with Detective Garcia, who was holding his requisite cup of coffee in one hand and a cigarette in the other.

"Didn't know you smoked," Stone said, his arms now hanging limply at his sides in an effort to look composed and sober.

"Yeah, well, the wife don't let me do it at home, you know how it is. I usually tell her I gotta work late, which is just an excuse for me to get out and smoke this in peace. Otherwise it's nag this and nag that. Marriage, they don't tell you how fun it is when you're younger, you know. Should come with a warning label or something."

"If you really want to smoke in peace you could always just divorce her. I don't see marriage as anything but a jail sentence anyhow. I'm divorced and I'm still serving it."

Garcia raised the cigarette in a mock salute and took a couple puffs, all the while staring up at the Howitzer Building. "Expensive place to live."

"Yeah, so I hear."

"You know anybody lives there?"

"In there?"

"Yeah, up there. Place is new, I hear some celebs got condos up there before it was even finished. Doesn't Johnny Depp live there? Maybe it's someone else. Who am I thinking of? On television all the time."

"Are you following me?"

The cop started chuckling, and a sly smile appeared on his face, the kind that said he'd been found out but that he appreciated Stone's cunning for doing it. "No, I'm not following you. I was…in the neighborhood. You guys always spy on your competition?"

"What, you mean Hardwood?"

The detective didn't answer, just stood waiting for the inevitable answer.

"I wasn't spying," he said. "I was just…um…"

"Hey, you know what, I don't need to know, you're not breaking any rules. In this city, you can't help but look up at apartment buildings."

"And you, you're spying?" Stone asked.

"Maybe."

"Maybe?"

"Actually, I've been pulling double shifts, you know. Half the force is. We got two blood-crazed losers running around at night cutting people up. You should have seen what I saw at the jewelry shop. It's nuts. I figure, better I'm on the street than at home watching reruns of *Taxi*."

"And getting bitched at for smoking."

"And getting bitched at for smoking," Garcia repeated in agreement.

So was that it, Stone wondered. Was the cop sending him a message, letting him know he was on the street during the witching hours, hoping to catch him red-handed? What was he really doing at The Howitzer? The reporter in him couldn't back down.

"And you happened by the building where Hardwood lives? Just a coincidence?"

Pulling out a small notebook from his pocket, Garcia read from it and asked, "You ever meet a David Porter?"

"You mean the guy at the jewelry shop, the guy the Casanova Carver murdered?"

"Yeah, that guy. You ever meet him?"

"No. Why would I have?"

"Well, as VP of Logman Industries, whose sister company was Brown Communications—"

"They own some magazines."

"Right, they do. One of them is *Smoke Shop Magazine*. Did you also know that Brown Communications entered into a deal with Jack Halloway—"

"The VP of WYNN?"

"Jeez, talk to you I never get to finish a sentence."

Stone didn't know where this was all headed, but he knew it had to have a purpose and it was making him sweat.

Garcia pitched his cigarette butt into the street, set his empty coffee cup on the bench, and took some Tic-Tacs out of his pocket. "Want a Tic-Tac?" he asked.

Stone shook his head, no.

"You're right," the detective continued, "Halloway is VP of WYNN. Turns out Porter was visiting WYNN not long ago."

Every ounce of Stone's being urged him to blurt out Hardwood's name in connection with the Casanova Carver's massacre of Porter and his buddies at the jewelry store, but he forced it back. After all, if he implicated Hardwood, he'd implicate himself. He was pissed, granted, and that was something he couldn't fight, but he knew he'd get over it in a day or two. No point having a knee-jerk reaction here.

"And?" he asked.

"And," Garcia replied, "I wanted to see if Hardwood might have seen him, seen anyone he was with. You know, these killers, when they make contact with a messenger—like you—they sometimes like to stay within viewing distance."

Thinking someone might be watching him sent a shiver down his spine, until he remembered it was he who was the killer. Good old alcohol fucking with him again.

"Good to know," he said.

"Yeah, well, I figured maybe the killer might be watching Hardwood's place." This last he said without taking his eyes off of

Stone, a Tic-Tac swishing around inside his mouth, clicking like the hammer being pulled back on a gun.

"What, you don't think I'm—"

Garcia laughed. "No, not you. I doubt you'd be that dumb even if you were a serial killer—you're not a serial killer are you?"

"I killed a few spiders last summer."

"I'll send forensics to get specifics. No, all I'm saying is, Hardwood might be in harm's way, so I figured if someone was watching him, he might be on the street, like you are. But like I said, he wouldn't be in the open…like you are. Unless he wanted me to think he was just an insignificant drunk guy…like you are right now. Drunk, anyway."

Garcia was definitely messing with his mind, and doing it well enough he couldn't follow the logic of it. He was too drunk to follow the bouncing ball on anything, really, even a children's song. Call it paranoia, but he swore the detective was waiting for him to trip up. Best thing to do, he decided, was clam up and go get some shut-eye.

"I think I'm gonna go home," he said.

"Want me to call a black and white for you? Remember what I said about these guys lurking nearby."

"No thanks, I'm not far away."

"Suit yourself; I can't make you do anything."

"Not unless we're married."

"Ain't that the truth. All right, but stay under the streetlights and don't feel childish if you feel the need to bolt. Better safe than sorry."

"Thanks, coach."

"I'll be in touch. I got more questions for you, but I don't want to ask them when you've been drinking—could complicate things. Oh hey, you know the doorman's name there?"

Garcia pointed to the large doorman Stone had accosted not too long ago about the Christmas lights—which, by the way, were still fucking on!

"No. Sorry."

"Yeah. No sweat. I think I'm gonna chat him up and see if he's seen anyone skulking around the area."

"Goodnight, detective."

"Be safe."

CHAPTER 25

Stone was quickly learning a lesson about lies: trying to cover up one with another is an intellectual challenge worthy of game show status. You'd better be able to think on your feet if you're going to avoid exposure. You could tell the truth, and blow your cover, but let's be realistic about things. Nobody tells the truth when another lie is sufficient to buy a chunk of time.

In the morning, Stone's lie, his creation, resulted in a gaggle of nut jobs banging on the WWTF office doors. Each one swore he was The Chef, and each looked crazier than the previous. One even had a dead owl on his head. How that made sense was beyond anyone's guess.

The first one had the station personnel sweating, because nobody had any idea what The Chef actually looked like, and the guy played the part well. His antisocial ranting matched Stone's letters to a tee. He wore a black trench coat, ratty hooded sweatshirt underneath, jeans with Bible quotes written on them in shoe polish. His salt and pepper beard was a bushy mess that grew down to his chest, and he pulled on it as he yelled. Hell, he almost had Stone convinced.

The cops showed up and tackled him like, well, like cops jumping on a crazy person. Cheese ordered every available camera outside to capture the poor shmoe getting squashed by New York's finest. It was quite a scuffle, but then any man crazy enough to spell Jesus with a Z was going to give his all against oppressors.

They dragged him away in a cruiser, his beaten face mashed up against the window for all the cameras to see. Cheese was elated, predicted a 20 point jump in the ratings. But his fire was extinguished when another yahoo came running out from behind a parked truck, covered in blood, screaming that he was here to make the world pay for its sins. He had a fork in one hand and a meat cleaver in the other. He too had a scruffy beard, which led Stone to conclude that crazy people only had enough memory to retain equinox dates, zodiac signs and psalms from the Bible. All other important information, such as grooming techniques, teeth-cleaning methods, and the importance of clean underwear went in one ear and out the other.

The cops came back and beat his ass as well.

It went like that for a few hours.

Yeah. Hours.

Detective Garcia showed up a little later and waited inside the lobby, some boys in blue beside him, and every time one of these charlatans made it past the cruisers outside, he offered them a Tic-Tac. It confused them long enough for the cops to tackle them.

By the end of the day six Chefs were sitting in a jail cell downtown arguing their individual authenticities. Garcia told the precinct captain to keep the ones that might prove threatening and let the others go, sans any weapons. There were, as an aside, no Casanova Carver copycats in the cells. If that wasn't a reason for Stone to pat himself on the back, nothing was.

Regardless of the ruse being exposed early on, Cheese kept filming throughout the day, and Mason later decided they could use the copycat angle as a lead-in story, give viewers something to chew on. They'd chew alright, Stone thought, chew their lower lips off with worry. The city was going to jump every time it saw a bum talking to God, or a businessman with a facial tic, wondering who was going to pull out a knife and go to town on the nearest person. But she was right, it would grab viewers, and viewers equaled advertising equaled bigger pay. The phrase was like the answer to some long lost question no one asked. By spreading alarm, they'd create a fear that would need to be quelled. Everybody would turn to the news for reassurance that the police and local officials were doing all they could to solve the problem. Such was the business. Reel 'em in and keep 'em hungry.

Mason, Cheese, Stone, Swift…the most trusted names in news.

CHAPTER 26

Despite the number of Chef impersonators that made the news, the jewelry store massacre was making even more headlines now than had last week. Cheese was getting pissed, spent days arguing about marketing strategies. "We need angles, people. We need to hit every demographic." Despite the fact that Garcia was lurking in the shadows, Stone knew he had to get back in the game.

An idea hit him as he was walking Chauncey in Central Park in the early morning. They stopped so Chauncey could pee in the snow next to an old man sitting on a bench. The old man glared at them and kicked his foot at the dog, missing by an inch.

"Hey, don't kick my dog, you jackass."

The old man stood up as fast as his decrepit bones would allow, flipped the bird, and walked away. Unperturbed as Chauncey was, Stone still bent down and gave him a pat on the behind for reassurance. In doing so, he remembered a story he had done on a group of thugs out in Brooklyn that ran a dog-fighting operation. It was because of his investigation that they dissolved their little gambling business. This pissed off the police who already knew about it and were gearing up to make a bust. Stone got the story, superficial as it was, and the cops got nothing.

It was a bright moment in his early career that caused Cheese to remark, "I'm gonna keep my eye on you." It also got him put on the police shit list for a while.

Chauncey led Stone down one of the winding park roads toward a baseball field, but stopped before they got there to sniff a tree. After careful consideration the dog decided that, yes, this tree needed his personal touch. As the dog squatted to relieve its bowels, Stone pulled a baggie from his coat pocket. Curbing Chauncey was not something he was particularly fond of, but in light of his new fame he wasn't going to just leave it and risk someone seeing him walk away.

"C'mon, buddy, hurry up, it's getting cold. That shit's gonna freeze before you get it all out. Push harder."

Chauncey looked up at him with a sad stare that said, sorry master, but you try taking a shit through a frozen asshole and see how fast you go.

"Cute dog."

Stone spun around, nearly yanking Chauncey from his business. "Detective Garcia? What are you doing here?"

The detective was carrying a cup of coffee. "It's Central Park on a Saturday, even I have to get out and take a walk once in a while. I got some bad veins in my knees and my doc said I gotta exercise every once in a while or they'll clog up, you know."

Bullshit, thought Stone. Something else was going on, but what? "Pretty cold out to just be walking around, even with bad knees. You should get a gym membership."

"Eh, I got a gym at the precinct if I want it, but it ain't the same. This is outdoors, fresh air…girls jogging. Sure they're bundled up, but they're still out here. Loco."

"That's New York for you."

"What? Crazy?"

"Yeah. Jogging in the snow, what else can you call it?"

"Seems to be a theme these days. How you holding up? You give any more thought to some protection?"

"I'm good. Like I said, I don't think he wants me."

"What's your dog's name?"

Stone looked at Chauncey, who was still squatting and giving it his all, a look of sheer embarrassment on his furry face. Despite this being the nature of dogs, Stone was starting to feel a bit bad.

"Chauncey."

Garcia pointed to his head, as if he to say he'd just made a mental note. "Right. The dog hair. Looks like a match. At least, from what I remember. How long you had him?"

"Got him when he was a pup. Well, my ex got him, but she wasn't much for taking care of him so she let me have him when…" He wasn't about to discuss his personal life with the detective. Not now anyway. Turning back, he saw that Chauncey was done with his business and was giving it a sniff for good measure.

Placing the baggie over his hand, he scooped up the mess and flipped the bag over, trapping it inside. He almost had it back in his pocket, to be thrown out at the nearest trash can, when Garcia stepped closer and pointed at it.

"Hold up. Can I see that?"

Stone held out the bag, just to be sure. "What? This?"

"Yeah. You mind?"

"You want to see my dog's shit?"

"Believe me, Mr. Stone, I've asked for weirder. I'm a cop."

Something didn't feel right to Stone. Why would the cop want to see Chauncey's excrement? What was he missing here? Before he handed the bag over to the cop, he instinctively turned it over and tried to see what the cop was after.

Sure enough, there was something small and gold in the mess.

An earring. Oh shit. Why now after all this time! What kind of fucked up intestines did the dog have?

"I should throw it out," he said, trying to find an excuse to get rid of it.

"Lemme see," Garcia replied. He reached out and took the baggie, turned it over in his hand. "Right there," he said, pointing at the earring. "Looks like jewelry. Yours?"

"No idea. The dog's like a vacuum cleaner, if it looks anything like food he'll eat it. Probably belongs to my ex."

"How long she been gone?"

"Few months now."

"She didn't notice she'd left it behind?"

The son of a bitch is interrogating me, Stone realized. Perhaps his best bet was to just stay quiet, feign ignorance. It's not like the cop could arrest him because he had a dog that shit jewelry. "I don't know. Who knows where the dog found it. Does it matter?"

"Maybe. That cabbie we found in Brooklyn, he was missing his ears. Remember? We got one in the envelope addressed to you. It had an earring like this."

Sweat was starting to run down Stone's back. This was not good.

A blonde woman in a wool hat and gloves jogged by and smiled at

Chauncey. The dog started to take off after her, pulling Stone sideways. "Looks like Chauncey wants to keep going."

"So no idea whose earring this is?"

There was, in fact, one person who might corroborate that Chauncey had found the earring somewhere else, if she was senile enough to do so. It was worth a shot. "Yeah, you know, now that I think of it, Chauncey got loose not long ago and ran into my neighbor's apartment. She's a little nutty, but I remember her saying something about him getting her jewelry. I thought she was seeing things, but I bet that's where it came from."

"You got a name for this woman?"

"Miss...uh...Davis. I think."

"Davis. Okay, I'll give her a ring, see if she wants it back."

"You gonna keep the whole bag worth?"

"I don't really want to reach in there right now so I'll take it to the lab and have my buddy George take it out all nicey nice. He loves it when I give him stuff like this. Makes his day. Unless of course, you need the...rest of it...for some reason."

"Um...no. No. You keep it. I'll get more later, I'm sure." Chauncey barked an affirmative. "Listen, I gotta run. I'll see you around."

Garcia gave a little wave and walked off toward the opposite side of the park.

With Chauncey dragging him in the direction of the blonde jogger, Stone couldn't help but curse his bad luck. "Thanks, Chauncey." The dog sped up, damn near pulling him to the ground in its wake. "You can't just eat the fucking dog food I buy you, you have to eat pieces of gold? Jesus."

*

When he got back to the apartment he poured some wet food in Chauncey's bowl and switched on the home computer. His mind kept coming back to the dog-fighting ring. It was the type of underground operation that drew lots of people to a tight space. And police were the last people you'd find there. That many people all crammed in tight, all in some basement or warehouse in no man's land, he couldn't help but think he could take advantage of that somehow.

Animal Rights people were a crazy enough faction that they'd probably build a statue of him if he did something about it. In this game, he needed all the support he could get.

His desktop folders were a collection of old leads he'd never followed up on, or that had fizzled out into nothing, but he was fairly sure he still had some info on the dog fighting ring. Lucky for him, he learned early in the business to stay organized, file everything away. You never knew when a bit of info would come into play.

He found the necessary information a couple of minutes later including a list of addresses and names where the gambling had gone down. One of the names was a man named Juju, as in Bad Juju. A voodoo kind of guy who lived up in the Bronx. He didn't actually know voodoo, barely knew simple math he did so many drugs, but his lack of teeth and dirty dreadlocks worked well for the name, and when you ran in dog-fighting circles, image went a long way.

Juju had been Stone's informant for the story. In exchange for twenty dollars, he would provide the location of each week's fight. He often told more, stuff Stone didn't even need or want to know, such as where to find underage prostitutes, where to get untraceable guns, where the bodies of some high ranking gang members were buried. Of course, Juju also said that for fifty dollars he would explain where the aliens were living. Something about White Castle hiring lizard men. Stone chalked up the rest of his secrets to too many speedballs.

Juju wasn't all there.

But his dog leads had been, and so Stone wrote his number and address down and switched the computer off.

In the cab, he read the morning's paper. The Chef and Casanova Carver news confirmed the police were still looking for the killers. He wondered what Hardwood had up his sleeve. He wondered just exactly what Hardwood's motives were. If he was already the number one anchor in the city, how scared of Stone could he be? Or was it just a grab for more power? Power begat power, or so they said. Like drugs, you always wanted more. He took out his cell phone, called Carlie and left her a message: "Hey, it's me, just wanted to tell you when we used to have sex I thought of someone else."

There. Power.

The Bronx is not as bad as most people believe, Stone was thinking as he took the subway uptown. (Constantly switching modes of transportation was a hassle but better than ending up in jail if he was being followed). It was sliding into a more mixed demographic as rents skyrocketed, though it did have its bad pockets. Ramshackle buildings with beggars out front, gangbangers and dopers talking another language on the stoops. None of it a real language, more like made up nonsense with a lexicon so rich you needed a translator half the time. If you were the wrong person in the wrong place, it could cost you. But, like most of New York City, daylight was tea time, people were amiable for the most part. Everyone was out at work or sleeping, unable to cause too much trouble.

Rancid paper products and dirty bits of trash whipped around his feet as he came up from the subway and made his way to Juju's apartment building. Despite the sunshine, the day was bitterly cold, and he pulled his collar together to keep the wind off his chest. People were out, everybody bundled up. Some kids were playing dodgeball with a tennis ball. The manhole covers were giving off plumes of steam from the subway.

He had called ahead to see if Juju was home, not realizing till after he'd dialed that Juju may not even have a phone anymore. Hell, he could be dead.

But he wasn't dead and his phone still worked. When you need your drugs you need a way to call for them, right? He buzzed Stone into the apartment building, a crumbling cement structure with unintelligible gang tags on the façade. Stone was out of place and the collection of hard stares from the people on the stoop meant they either thought he was a cop, or severely lost.

Climbing the stairs to the third floor, he noticed what looked like a puddle of piss on one of the landings. It was disconcerting to say the least. There were some dark brown stains on the walls as well, possibly chocolate, feces, or dried blood. He chose to ignore it as he rapped on Juju's door.

A dark shadow moved behind the peephole, checking things out. Stone held up a twenty dollar bill and the door opened.

"Well sheeit! Talk about the white devil."

"Hi, Juju."

"Get in here man, 'fore someone sees you and slices me up for being on five-O's payroll."

"Too late. I got the evil eye from everyone downstairs already. I think they think I'm a cop. You might need to move."

"You serious?"

"Always."

"Eh, fuck 'em. Motherfuckers step to me they're gonna get blasted, know what I'm saying?"

"Yeah, sure."

Smiling, Juju snatched the money from Stone's hand, waved him into the apartment.

There wasn't much to see: a ratty couch, a large television he could only guess was stolen, a floor lamp with a dark red shade, some porn magazines on a scratched up coffee table. A mirror sat in the middle of the table, a dusty white film on it. On the seat of the couch was an ashtray with a lit cigarette in it. The floor was covered with dirty clothes and old take-out food containers. The view from his only window looked out at the backside of the adjacent apartment complex, and by tilting your head just a bit you could see into the neighbor's window. The blinds were drawn, but it felt too close for Stone, like he should speak softly.

"Nice place," he said.

"Man, fuck you. I know it ain't shit, but I been here for over five years and the rent is controlled. Government can't take it from me. Government can't take shit. Dumb motherfuckers. Take a seat."

"That's okay, I'll stand."

"Suit yourself. You want a hit of this?"

Juju held up the cigarette from the ashtray. It was a fake, a ceramic knockoff that was packed with marijuana, or something else mind-altering. He sucked in a hit to show how good it was, shook his head and coughed. His dreads swooshed back and forth.

Stone shook his head no. "I need to know where the new dog rings are." He had mentioned this on the phone, but who knew what Juju had forgotten since thirty minutes ago.

"Dog rings, dog rings. They ain't so easy to break into no more. You can't just walk in and lay down a bet. Motherfuckers will shoot you on sight. 'Specially you dress like that. Know what I'm saying?"

"I'm not concerned about me. Can you just tell me where they are?"

"Well, it's not that easy—"

"You said you knew."

"I do," Juju replied, taking another hit of the fake cigarette. "I do. But there's more to it than that. There's codes and shit you gotta know, or you won't even get near the building. There's people you gotta know too, vouchers."

"Can you vouch for me?"

"Shit. Are you…are you serious? Man, I ain't vouching for you. Soon as you run your story I'm a dead man."

"It doesn't matter. Just give me the address. I'll do the rest."

Juju's look became increasingly circumspect, like he thought Stone might be an alien come to brainwash him. Some youths walked by in the hallway outside, talking loud about how so-and-so needed to get "jacked." They might have said it because they knew Stone was in the apartment, they might have been referring to a rival gang member. Who knew, but tensions went up a notch. Stone scanned the room for possible weapons, saw a golf club leaning near the door, obviously for reasons of protection.

"Tell you what," Juju said, "give me twenty dollars and I'll point you in the right direction."

"I just gave you twenty. You used to be cheaper."

"C'mon, motherfucker, you gotta factor in inflation. Prices have risen since we last talked. Hell, you was a nobody reporter then. Now you're a bigshot. Everybody is talking about you. Say, what's going on with that Casanova Carver stuff?"

"You mean The Chef."

"Oh yeah, him too. You got any idea who he is? I seen he sent you letters. Are there funny symbols and clues and shit in them? I'm good with code breaking. You see the paper? There was a big article in the newspaper—"

"You read the newspaper?"

"Nah, but I take the bus, and the guy in front of me had it, and I seen it was about the Casanova Carver. He's got big plans. I can tell. Know what I'm saying?"

Jesus, Stone thought, was that true? Was Hardwood going to go bigger than the jewelry store massacre?

"So where's he going to strike next?" he asked.

"Shit. Couldn't tell ya. But it's gonna be a big deal, I promise ya. Big big deal."

"All right," he said, annoyed that time was being wasted. "Forget the Casanova Carver. Here's another twenty. Who do I see about getting into the dog rings?"

Juju took the money and wadded it down into his pocket, all the while sucking on the fake cigarette pipe. A cloud plumed from his nose when he exhaled, like an angry bull in an old Bugs Bunny cartoon. Leaning into Stone's ear, dreadlocks resting across both their shoulders, he whispered a name.

CHAPTER 27

Hardwood had not slept well since seeing Jeremy. Stress dreams plagued him, always ending with Hardwood begging for his son's acceptance. Of course, it never came. His stomach began to suffer from gastro problems. He drank Pepto like it was water. Still, it did little to ease the frustration that was slowly growing inside him. Why had he even bothered to try and talk to the boy? He knew it was going to end the way it did. Jeremy had made it clear to him all through his teenage years, and especially at their meeting at Fredo's, that he had washed his hands of him.

Still, a father has a hard time abandoning his son regardless of how stubborn the son can be. He was, in the end, still the man that had given Jeremy the genes that made him what he was. Jeremy was intelligent, good looking, and had a strong work ethic. And that all came from Hardwood. It was hard to let that go.

Boomer caught him at the door and asked where he was going. "We've got to go over these stories before the newscast," he said. "You can't go out right now."

"I'll be back shortly."

"You don't look good. I think this whole situation is getting to be too much for you. I can't afford to have you on the verge of a nervous breakdown here."

"Relax, Boomer. I'm just going to see…"

"Who?"

It was not his character to be melodramatic, but Hardwood sighed none the less. "I'm going to see Jeremy."

Boomer's silence said it all. It was no secret Hardwood and his son didn't get along, though no one was stupid enough to ever broach the subject. It was obvious that if he was going to see his son, something important was going on.

Boomer's tight face seemed to sadden a bit. "Okay. Just be back in an hour. We really need to get this work done."

"You do the station proud, Boomer." Hardwood made no attempt to hide his patronizing tone.

Jeremy's schedule was fairly consistent, so chances were he was at the gym. Last Hardwood knew, he frequented the Crunch down in SoHo, a place known more as a cruise bar than an actual exercise location. That it was close to Jeremy's restaurant obviously beat out the boy's prejudices.

When he arrived, a slender girl wearing sunglasses stopped him at the desk and asked if he had a membership. Before he could answer, she realized who he was and apologized, asked if he was there to do a story.

"Of course," he told her. "But I prefer to check it out by myself, if that's okay?"

She said it shouldn't be a problem, and then asked for his autograph.

"On the way out," he told her, and entered the main area of the gym. Machines lined the large glass windows that looked out at the cobble-stoned street where people window shopped. The gym was designed so that the best looking members could strut their stuff to all the passersby, as if to say that anyone who worked out here would end up looking like an Adonis.

Several heads turned and followed him as he entered. Of course, in his three piece suit, he stuck out like a sore thumb. A young man with chiseled good looks and a washboard stomach smiled at him as he made his way to the free weight room. Hardwood almost smiled back, but then remembered why he was here. That is, remembered the moments in his past that had led him to lose his son. His attraction for the man turned to hatred, and he looked away.

Sure enough, he found Jeremy in the weight room. From the looks of it, he was done lifting, and was toweling sweat off his head. When he saw Hardwood, he threw the towel down and scowled.

"What, you come here to find a boyfriend? Wrong place. You want to go to the Crunch in the West Village."

"I thought we could try again."

"Sorry. I spoke my piece. Look out, I have to shower. If you try to sneak peeks of the guys in there and get yourself in trouble I'm not helping."

"Must you always be vulgar?"

"Must you always be a loser?"

From behind Jeremy, one of the body builders noticed the exchange and said, "Mr. Hardwood? You gonna join?"

"Not today, I'm afraid. I'm just here to talk to…an acquaintance."

The body builder, whose dark skin and Latin-American accent spoke of a possible Brazilian heritage, hoisted a set of dumbbells over his head. "I could spot you. What can you bench?"

"Hey, fuckstain," Jeremy put in, "he said no, let it drop."

"How 'bout I drop these on your head, little man."

Jeremy was half the man's size, but was clearly of the mind that showing no fear meant you had none. Hardwood knew different, having seen enough forced bravado in victims' eyes to know that in this type of situation, Jeremy was a goner. Still, he was curious to see how far his son would go.

"Go ahead and try it, nig…" Jeremy cut himself off, aware that half a dozen other men in the room were African American. He was clearly outnumbered.

"Go ahead, say it." The large man put the dumbbells down and got in Jeremy's face. "Go ahead, call me that word. See what happens."

"Pardon me, sir," Hardwood interjected, placing a hand on the man's chest to break them apart. He couldn't help but notice how tight the man's muscles were, and again, how it enticed him. "I'm not denying your right to pummel this man at a time of your choosing, but right now I need to talk to him. Can he take a rain check on the beating?"

The large Brazilian man looked Jeremy up and down, and finally went back to his weights. "Get him out of here before I kill him," he said.

You don't have it in you, Hardwood thought.

"Come on, Jeremy."

"Fuck off. I'm taking a shower."

"Then I'll wait for you outside."

It was nearly a half hour before Jeremy appeared outside the gym. Boomer would be pissed at Hardwood for coming back late, but the man had little power anyway so he'd just have to deal with it.

Jeremy, now dressed in khaki pants and a bulky flight jacket, slung his bag over his shoulder and headed for the subway station.

"You can't keep showing up to bug me...Dad. Take a fucking hint."

"I thought maybe we could talk about your mother."

"You thought wrong."

"I think it would do us good to get it out in the open. Maybe you'd give me a chance to explain myself. You have to understand how embarrassing it is for me."

"Embarrassing for you? Please. Your dad's not supposed to be the one wearing a dress during your upbringing."

"I've never worn a dress in my life."

"Semantics."

They walked in silence for a few steps.

"Would you really have fought that man in there?" Hardwood asked.

"Sure. I put your face on him. I would have won."

"Your racism will get you in trouble some day."

"So will drugs, drinking, smoking, and gambling. We chose our vices. You sure as fuck chose yours."

Could he tell Jeremy that his anger was partially his, Hardwood's, fault? Perhaps it was better to let it lie idle inside the boy instead. If he mentioned his own anger's influence, even on a genetic level, Jeremy would just have another reason to hate him.

They made a left at the corner and continued on toward Houston Street. Smoke from a nearby peanut cart caught Hardwood's nose and gave him a moment of hunger pangs, even though he couldn't stand the peanuts.

"I can't just let you go," Hardwood said. "In the few years we haven't spoken, I've never let go of the hope we could solve this."

"Then you're setting yourself up for a fall. Unless you're going to bring back Mom and fix my childhood, I don't see much help for you. Try a shrink."

"If I met you alone in a dark alley, and handed you a gun, would you kill me?"

Jeremy stopped walking, looked Hardwood up and down. "I don't know what the hell that's supposed to mean, but truthfully…no. You're already in hell, and I like to watch you suffer."

"I don't feel like I'm in hell."

"Oh, yeah." Jeremy studied the crowd around them. He yelled, "No, Doug Hardwood, I'm not going to suck you off on the train. Stop bothering me. If you want to be gay, there are easier ways than paying me to do it. Go to a bathhouse for God sake. Just leave me alone."

The crowd stopped and stared. Some were unsure if it was a joke or not, but others were weighing the possibility Hardwood was actually soliciting this young man.

"A joke," Hardwood said to the crowd. "Please, ignore my friend."

Laughing, Jeremy made his way down the subway station, swiped his transit card through the reader, and took a seat on the bench along the track. Hardwood followed him down and sat beside him.

"That was amusing."

"I'll do that every time you come near me. Think you can handle it?"

The train was just a stop away, its light visible down the dark tunnel.

"Do you remember when you were in grade school, and we went to the museum because you wanted to see the dinosaur exhibit?"

"Oh, you mean the one day you didn't go to work or off to fag out with someone."

"That's my favorite memory of you. It all went downhill after that."

"Thanks to you."

"I'm tired of the hurt this brings me."

"Boohoo. You know the only reason I don't tell the world what you really are? Because it's too embarrassing for me. So don't think me keeping your secret means anything more than that."

The train pulled into the stop and the doors opened. Throngs of people pushed off and headed up the stairs. Jeremy rose from the bench and got into the train. Through the doors, Hardwood asked, "Are you really my enemy?"

"If you like."

"Son, you don't want to be my enemy."

"Dad…" Jeremy held up his middle finger as the doors closed, and the train sped out of the station.

CHAPTER 28

First thing Stone did when he left Juju's was buy a wig and some glasses. He sure as shit wasn't going to get into a dog fighting ring if they knew who he really was. Not after what he'd done to the last one so many years ago.

The wig and glasses looked ridiculous, but then, so long as he acted as nervous as a white guy would be at a dog fighting ring, they'd probably just peg him as a man with a gambling problem.

Juju's contact was a small, fat, Latino man named Tomas who blinked rapidly. It cost Stone another forty dollars just to get in to see him at his office out in Astoria. Office in this case meant a shithole of an apartment that smelled of rotting Indian food. He sat at a small card table in a dirty living room, smoking a cigar, wearing a heavy winter football jacket, the colors of which no doubt represented the colors of a local gang. On either side of him, two Mr. Universe contenders looked at Stone the way gorillas look at bananas.

The procedure was simpler than Juju made it sound, though definitely cautious: Stone gave Tomas the money, and in return Tomas made a mental note of Stone's face and gave him a code word: lollipop.

*

The dog fight was a few blocks away. It seemed that the theme for the night was to move from one dingy hole-in-the-wall to another, and this place was no exception. Covered in graffiti, reeking of old booze and piss, and patrolled by thugs in football jackets with obvious bulges in their waistbands.

If the strange lights coming from the basement windows didn't cue you in that something was amiss, the sheer volume of lowlife traffic going into the building would. Stone knew scumbag Puerto Ricans and Dominicans didn't usually hang out together, at least not in urbanized locales. Gangbangers and shady Korean bodega owners didn't hang out either. Unless there was a dog fight on, in which case it was a melting pot of animal cruelty proliferators.

Stone gave the code word to "security" and they reluctantly let him pass. It was evident from their hesitation that they didn't trust him, but his money was as green as anyone's and they were probably under orders not to stir things up. He headed to the basement, repeating lollipop to anyone who gave him a funny look. He had the wig on again, and the glasses, and no one seemed to realize who he was.

The basement was two levels deep, and it was in this sub-basement that the fight was about to commence. It was a scene out of a horror movie. A low-watt bulb hanging from a dirty wooden beam, all races of men circling a large earthen floor, sweat stinking up the air. A man at a chalkboard was taking bets as people waved their money in the air like soldiers on a train waving goodbye to their lovers.

Stone made himself small, stayed behind people's backs, and moused over to a secluded spot by a large drain pipe.

On either end of the room, cages sat covered with dirty blankets, presumably so the dogs inside couldn't see each other, so they would go berserk when they did. The air was filled with constant growls and barking.

It took a few minutes for all the bets to get placed, and then the wranglers lifted the blankets off the cages. Inside were the meanest pit bulls Stone had ever seen, salivating and baring their razor sharp teeth. These were the kind of animals that you had nightmares about as a kid. Stone thought of Chauncey, and how the man in the park had kicked at him, the look in Chauncey's face as he tried to make sense of what was going on.

These dogs made him want to cry. They had been tortured and twisted into the beasts they were now. It wasn't their fault, and it didn't take a rocket scientist to notice the fear in their eyes. The scene did nothing but illustrate the ungodly power man has over every other species. And for what, some money? A thrill?

Yet, they were beyond dangerous, and had to be put down lest they unleash their savagery on some small girl or boy in the area. He hated to do it, but he had little choice but to make them casualties of this night's events.

The crowd cheered as the doors of the cages were opened. The two dogs raced at each other across the dirt floor and cracked teeth into teeth, bits of canine flesh flying into the air, blood raining to the ground. Between the horrific growls and agonizing yelps came cries of encouragement from the crowd.

The bloodthirsty maniacs. The dregs. The scum of society.

He would feel no remorse at this. He almost wanted to do it regardless of what it would do for The Chef. But then again, The Chef needed this. He pulled the wig off, thought of the press this would generate, thought of Hardwood, thought of the poor dogs, thought of the smile on Cheese's face.

He grabbed the paring knife taped to the inside of his jacket.

Moved over to one of the security guards. Saw the gun sticking out of his waistband. Rammed the knife in the man's throat. Snatched the gun. Shot the light. People shouted, scattered, became confused. The gun popped again, flashed in the dark. A body fell with a wet thud.

Chaos ensued, people rushing for the exit, trampling each other, yanking on a door that was blocked by a body. Stone backed against the wall, crouched low and made himself small, waited for an opportunity. Fired again. Moved to a new spot. Found a rhythm: Bang. Run. Crouch. Bang. Run. Crouch.

Someone fired back and hit flesh. Not Stone's, someone else's. More guns fired, the guards shooting in a panic, dropping people to the ground. Gunpowder permeated the dank air.

In a groove now, Stone circled the perimeter of the basement, letting fear and confusion work its magic. His heart slammed in his chest. Another body fell next to him. He reached inside its jacket and found what he expected to find: a gun. Where there were criminals there would be weapons. Again, he fired, moved. Again. Again. Sometimes slashing out with the knife. Sometimes throwing an elbow or knee. It was impossible to see anyone in the dark, but the dogs seemed to be getting the hang of it. Their jaws snapped and sank into the flesh of whoever crossed their paths. This was turning out to be easier than he'd expected. A natural feeling. No fear now, just anticipation. No wonder people started riots; they became their own monster, and you could just sit back and watch it destroy itself.

A traffic jam was still blocking the door. Everyone seemed to be trying to open it. All bunched together now. Like shooting fish in a barrel, Stone thought.

He listened, aimed with his ears, fired.

The dogs weren't the only ones yelping.

CHAPTER 29

Two mornings later the letter arrived at the office. A runner brought it to Stone's desk. Cheese stormed in, the way kings used to enter their court: brows furrowed, head held high, walking just faster than the average person. A man who had plenty of business to do and little time to do it in. Duncan was on his heels. Mason was there too, playing queen to Cheese's king; the news had spread before Stone could get the damned envelope open. Others filed in, the crew, the administrative staff, all eager to be the first to hear what The Chef had to say. Stone looked the letter over and read it to them.

As he described the grisly scene that awaited the police in Queens, their faces twisted in disgust. But when he remarked on how exclusive a story it would be, they were all smiles.

"You're riding shotgun with Mason on this," Cheese said, the whites of his teeth as bright as new-fallen snow, his black pearl cufflinks shining like raven eyes. "This is huge, this is big, this is the motherload."

Mason slipped through the crowd and put her arm on Cheese's shoulder. "We've got to hold this back from the police. Not even the AP gets this till we're finished. I should run out and get a new blouse, and Stone here needs a haircut. He looks like shit."

You spend the night getting these kinds of ratings and see how you feel in the morning, he thought.

Cheese patted her on the ass, and yes, Stone was envious. "Duncan!"

"Yeah, Cheese." Duncan looked like he had high hopes for whatever was coming. Stone was willing to bet the opposite.

"Get the network on the phone for me. We're gonna cut into the 11:00 schedule for a Breaking News Report. Do it now. Then take care of this ASAP." Cheese handed him a dry cleaning chit. Duncan's smiled turned upside down, and inside Stone laughed. "And on the way back stop and get me a salad from Herzog's."

"Yeah, Cheese. I'll tell them to cut into *The View*, that way—"

"Don't say shit! Just get the network on the phone for me and I'll take care of it. Fucking Barbara Walters will have me killed if word gets out beforehand."

Duncan was good at remaining dignified while being demeaned, as if he actually believed he was useful. He looked at Stone with a smug smile and did his best to turn his errand into something important. "Excuse me, Stone, I have to call the network."

He swept out of the room with his head held high, trying to mimic Cheese. What a prick.

"Okay everybody, let's get this fucking show on the road," Cheese shouted. "I want whatever van is closest to get over there now and get me B-roll. Hurry, before the cops shut it down!" People filed out of the office, chattering like squirrels as they rushed back to their desks in the pen. No doubt some of them would leak this out on the Internet; but it didn't matter, they'd be going live before it made any real rounds.

Cheese, Stone and Mason stayed behind, and Mason sat on Stone's desk. Her ass was the best paperweight he'd ever seen.

"You good to go on this, sugar?" she asked Stone.

"I want the lead in."

"Negative," Cheese said. "Mason leads in, then we go to you. Either way," he smiled, nodded, "you're back at the desk so buck up."

Hallelujah! thought Stone, but he decided to play it cool.

"We're going to need a special report for the five o'clock spot," Stone said. "Viewers are gonna be itching for more and I think we should dedicate the entire thirty minutes to it."

"Can't, some of the stories we're running have sister companies that bought ad space. Got to run them. But we can do a long ten minutes at the start. Hot damn! I can feel the shares going up already. I don't know why this maniac picked you Stone, but I'm glad he did.

Casanova Carver be damned, I knew our guy would do us proud. See, I knew if you pissed him off he'd respond."

As Cheese walked out of the room, Mason leaned over and whispered in Stone's ear, "Play this right, and we might just be the number one anchor team in the state soon. Next stop could be the network."

In the back of his mind, that almost sounded like a threat, but Stone couldn't be sure.

He could see down her shirt as she leaned over, could see the black lace bra she was wearing. It was filled out very nicely. God, he still hated her, but if she wasn't threatening him, and was serious about the network, well then, she had him worked up for two reasons.

*

They were going live at 11:00am, cutting into the mid-morning talk shows. Word was, as they sat getting their hair and makeup done, the camera crew already had footage. They said it was one of the most disturbing things they'd ever seen. They said the station would need filters to show it. Pride flowed through Stone's veins. It was back.

Somebody from the station called the police, since it would be very bad business to hide things from them for too long. The last thing they wanted was the public thinking they were stopping the boys in blue from finding this nutjob. But they held off calling until a script was done and the footage cued. Sure, they knew they'd have to answer for that, but the cops and the media had been playing Hatfields and McCoys for so long that actually getting cited for obstructing an investigation now would require more paperwork than they were willing to bother with. What's more, the police needed the media—

needed Stone—and they knew it.

Mason had indeed sent someone out to find her a blouse with a long sloping neckline. And Stone had someone trim up his hair and pluck his eyebrows. Together they looked good; they looked like a team.

Being back at the anchor desk felt like coming home from the worst vacation he'd ever been on. Power coursed through him, the knowledge that all eyes were on him. Well, they were probably on Mason's tits. But he was right there alongside them. That had to count for something.

When the camera's red light came on, he felt a bulge in his pants.

"Good morning," Mason said, her head cocked ever so slightly to show how serious this report would be. Off camera, Cheese had his arms folded, his eyes locked on her. His suit was pinstriped, not a line bent. Duncan arrived with a salad and Cheese waved him away, not wanting to be bothered. Mason Continued: "We interrupt your regularly scheduled program to bring you a special report…"

What the people of New York City heard for the next fifteen minutes was what The Chef had done to the participants of a dog fighting ring out in Queens. As Mason described the setting, Stone watched the crews' jaws drop in astonishment.

Twenty-seven people had been butchered, dismembered, mutilated, and maimed. But there had been actually thirty-one people present, and so the rest of the story was what really got people talking.

The four remaining people were forced (at gunpoint, though only Stone knew that) to eat the scattered body parts. Not just eat them, but eat them until they died of suffocation. Hanging from each mouth was a collection of fingers and bones and hair and eyes and what have you.

In the center of the ring, beside two dead dogs with bullets in their heads (quick merciful kills) a collection of heads, legs, and arms spelled out the word: SINS

Extreme did not begin to describe the amount of gore that covered the floor of that sub-basement. If this didn't get viewers buzzing, he didn't know what would. He could tell just by the expressions of the people around him that this was the worst thing they'd heard of in their lifetime. On the monitor, the tape showed the bloody scene, diffused with a filter. This was going to put WWTF in the number one slot, no doubt about it.

When Mason was done reciting the script on the teleprompter, she told the viewers the station had a letter, and turned to Stone as the light on the Camera Three came on.

"Good afternoon," he said to the viewers. For flair he added, "A horrific scene in Queens. But the story is not finished. I hold in my hand the latest letter from the man who we now know as The Chef:

DEAR ROLAND STONE,

I WARNED YOU THAT I WOULD TURN YOUR MOCKERY INTO A CLEANSING BLOODBATH. THE FILTH THAT LAY IN THE BASEMENT IN QUEENS HAS BEEN SHOWN THE TRUE DARKNESS OF THEIR VILE LIVES. BY INGESTING THEIR OWN HUBRIS, THEY HAVE TASTED THE SINS OF THEIR WAYS, AS WELL AS THE SINS OF THEIR BROTHERS. A HUMAN RACE THAT REFUSES TO ACCEPT ITS OWN SICKNESS. YOU AND YOUR MEDIA HAVE UNLEASHED ME UPON THE WORLD. BECAUSE OF YOU, THIS CITY WILL RUN RED. AND NO, I DO NOT ATTEND PATHETIC CULT MEETINGS WITH AMATEURISH COPYCATS. I AM THE REAL CURE TO THE REAL DISEASE. CALL ME BY WHATEVER MONIKER YOU WISH, BUT DON'T CRY WHEN I FORCE THE SINS OF THIS CITY DOWN ITS OWN THROAT. THE WAR HAS BEGUN."

He turned back to Mason and paused for effect. (A pause is very important in the news. It builds anticipation, it builds drama, and it also gives the pauser time to get ahead on the teleprompter. Some newscasters will practice their pause-face in the mirror for hours, toying with every nuance: lip tautness, eyebrow-raising ability, head tilt. Stone discovered his one night while brushing his teeth in the bathroom, thinking about whether or not he liked scallions in his tuna fish sandwiches. Looked up and saw himself in the mirror and thought, damn, something pensive is going on there. Stayed like that for the next hour, getting it just right. Still didn't know if he liked scallions in his tuna fish or not, but when he paused on air now, people noticed.) For the first time, he thought he saw a glimmer of fear in her eye. For all her prior enthusiasm toward The Chef, suddenly it seemed she was weighing the consequences of her participation. He felt bad, but only a little. After all, she'd chosen to play her cards this way.

It's not like he had plans to kill her, anyway. Not yet, not unless there was a point to it. And he was back at the anchor desk, even if it was as part of a team.

For all the blood that was on his hands, his life was turning around. If it wasn't for Hardwood still trying to steal the ratings out from under him, he might consider it game over.

"Tricia."

Mason glanced at him, the fear in her eyes now replaced by stoic professionalism.

"Scary words, Roland," she said. Then, to the camera: "Police are investigating the scene, but are keeping all media back until further notice. We will keep you updated as reports come in. We now return you to your regularly scheduled programming."

When the cameras turned off, Cheese came over, and for the first time since this all began, asked if Stone was okay. "I think we should get you police protection," he said. It would be nice to think that Cheese actually cared about him for a minute, but his next statement put it all in perspective. "If we lose you, he might send his letters somewhere else."

"It's fine," Stone said. "I don't think he's coming after me."

"Just think about it." Cheese clapped his hands. "Okay, good job everyone. Let's wait and see what happens. Sales will be calling soon. Damn I feel alive. You know how long it's been since we've cut into daily programming?"

"We're talking possible national headlines here," Mason piped in. "I want to get PR on the line. We should go cross-country with this, get satellite subscribers interested."

Cheese nodded his agreement. "Duncan!"

Duncan appeared out of nowhere, a clipboard in his hand. "Yeah, Cheese."

"Get the network on the phone again, set up a meeting for me. We're going to do what I got into this business to do."

"What's that?" Stone asked.

"What do you think," Cheese replied, smoothing back his silken hair. "Get paid."

CHAPTER 30

Get paid was what they got.

Cheese met with Corporate and they agreed to restructure the ad rates. Even those current clients who weren't locked in for more than three months had their contracts amended. Buying a thirty-second spot during reports on The Chef now cost triple what most stations would charge.

And what's more, it was eaten up in no time. National advertisers like Gillette Razor and Maybelline Cosmetics bought space, as did the local companies that could afford it.

The morning after the breaking news report, *The Times* ran a front page article on The Chef's massacre. It mentioned Stone's history and speculated as to why The Chef was using him. He was not the first reporter to become a messenger for a serial killer, and the paper listed a handful of other reporters, both national and international, who'd found themselves in similar situations. A few of them ended up in body bags.

Detective Garcia was quoted as saying that the police were working on multiple leads, though he couldn't divulge details yet.

The picture they ran was newsworthy in itself, since *The Times* was pretty restrained when it came to blood and gore. They ran a shot of the basement, blacking out the more stomach-turning portions of it. What it did was cause readers to use their imaginations. What was behind the black bars? Why was only half of this body shown? What happened to the other half of that one?

CNN Headline News, which had mentioned both the Casanova Carver and The Chef as minor stories just days ago, now placed them in their first ten minutes of air time. Their website ran a banner ad for it: NEW YORK MURDER SPREE.

And yes, the ratings books had come in. WWTF was number one. Eat your heart out Hardwood…pun intended.

A day later, two college girls recognized Stone at lunch and wanted an autograph. They told him he was the talk of their campus and asked if he was going to do a speaking engagement. He heard "spanking engagement" and replied, "Tell you what, if you're gonna be there I can guarantee it." Couldn't wait to call Carlie and lay that one on her. She wasn't the only one who could get young tail anymore.

He figured he would celebrate with a bit of whiskey at O'Halloran's that night, perhaps even buy a round for everyone. Perhaps not. More for him.

When he walked in, all heads turned and watched him as if a starting pitcher for the Yankees had entered. There were long stares, some frantic whispers, and then the yells began. "Hey, Stone, who's The Chef?" "Hey, Stone, does he send you the body parts?" "Hey, Stone, need a bodyguard?" As he made his way to the bar, hands clapped him on the shoulders, rooting for him, telling him he had a courageous set of balls.

Pat shouted over the din, "Let 'im through, you bastards. Give the man some room." He plunked a highball glass on the bar in front of Stone, pulled a bottle of Bushmills off the shelf. "This first one is on the house, lad."

"Thanks, Pat."

"That was some bloody scene. Old Pat's getting a bit worried about you. You sure you shouldn't be laying low now?"

"I'm fine, Pat. This psycho isn't going to come after me. We've got a…kinship."

"Do you now? Well lay it on old Pat, and spare no details. What aren't you all reporting on that tube? What secrets you keeping?"

Other patrons were leaning in close, eager to hear inside information. He toyed with the idea of making up a juicy inside tidbit, but decided to win them over with traditional bullshit instead. "The people know everything we know. We wouldn't dare keep you in the dark." A big smile now. "We're here for the people."

"Atta boy," Pat said. "Roland Stone, everyone, a true man of the people. Cheers!" He took a shot of the Bushmills, and the other patrons shouted and threw back their drinks. For the first time in a while, Stone was feeling good about himself.

On the TV behind the bar, Jay Leno and Branford Marsalis were dressed in mock Sumo wrestler outfits. Branford had Leno pinned on the ground and was smiling his friendly, wide smile.

He took a big gulp of the Bushmills, felt his insides warm as it coated his stomach. Elsewhere in the bar, people returned to their conversations. A few eyes continued to dart his way. He wondered if Mason felt this way when she went out; he wondered if Hardwood felt this way as well. Respected, trusted, envied, like the movie heroes of Hollywood's golden era: Bogart, Wayne, Grant. Real larger-than-life personalities, not pretty boys from some reality show, just men of true grit.

He felt like one of them. And it felt good. It felt empowering. He wanted to jump on the bar and shout, "Bring me the head of Douglas Hardwood! Go, my minions!"

And then Hardwood walked in. All stares lifted off Stone and floated over to the door, followed Hardwood as he passed by and sat two stools down at the bar.

Pat wasted no time sliding a drink in front of the older newscaster and saying, "Well dear me. Seems we've got two of the city's most wanted men in here tonight. Mr. Hardwood, I do hope your week was filled with less ado than Mr. Stone's over there."

Hardwood turned to Stone. The seat between them was empty. "Stone."

"Doug."

"I saw your special report. Breaking into programming. Risky move."

"Put us in number one."

"I can imagine. A scene like that, images such as they were, it'd be hard to pull your eyes from the screen. Our vulnerabilities are our most scrutinized attributes."

"I guess."

"It's not the blood that fascinates the viewer so much as how the blood was drawn, and the wonder of whether it could happen to them. That's what attracts them. Like moth to flame, right?"

"Yeah, it was horrific news," he said, not sure where Hardwood was going with this. "The Chef took a lot of time setting that scene. It was pretty magnificent in a morbid sort of way. People needed to know."

"And the animal cruelty angle—you're aware PETA designed an ad using a silhouette of what is arguably The Chef? The madman has supporters now, if you can believe it. Lucky for you. Viewers tend to believe that the station with the first report is the most professional. As if somehow, timeliness equals godliness. But then, all of that is jejune in comparison to the statement he made with such an abundant slaying."

"Abundant? I suppose. I see it as more of an example of his work ethic. Obviously he means business."

"Yes, well, I agree. And apparently it warranted a haircut and a low cut shirt for your counterpart."

"Whatever works, Hardwood. You know that."

The old man nodded. "Yes, I do."

"Anyway, it's out on the AP wire now. We're not flying solo with it. It's everywhere."

"I know. We reported on it—I reported on it."

Stone drank more whiskey, noticing for the first time a darkness deep in Hardwood's eyes. An anger that seemed out of place. The kind that bullies feel when they realize the entire schoolyard has banded against them and won't take it anymore. The man hadn't banked on him accomplishing such an extreme act, and it had put him in his place.

"Am I to assume that Stone's Moans has succumbed to the laws of entropy?" Hardwood asked.

"It's on hold for now, yeah."

"And you're back at the anchor desk?"

Hardwood was not his usual condescending, pedantic self tonight. He was simply pissed. Had he never lost the number one slot before? Ever? As far back as Stone could recall, since he'd started in the business, Hardwood had been synonymous with The Big Apple.

"Co-anchor," he told him. "Mason still leads off. But—"

"She's got them nice titties," Pat said, replenishing Stone's drink. "They should have their own show. If I was in charge I'd have them on every channel, I would. Channel one, a big titty. Channel two, another big titty. Left titty on one channel, right on the other. If you got cable, you get to see them bouncing around all naked. Damn fine, damn fine." He raised the bottle in the air and shouted, "To Tricia Mason's titties!"

The patrons, the men anyway, echoed the sentiment: "Tricia Mason's titties!"

Maybe it wasn't such a bad idea to bring her here for a drink after all. When people saw them together they'd sure as shit envy him the way married men envy porn stars.

Pat lit up a cigar and disappeared into the back room.

"What's this about, Hardwood?" Stone asked.

Hardwood took a pull on his drink, straightened his cuffs. "That detective came by again. He subpoenaed my computer, wants to see if there's anything else in my emails."

Stone slid over to the empty stool, closed the gap between them. He spoke low and frank, tired of the charade. "Well, how good are you with a computer?"

"As good as the next man."

"You think they'll trace anything back to you?"

"No. My emails come from a secure wireless source."

"You don't have anything about me on there, do you?"

"About you?"

"Yeah, you know, notes and shit. You got anything like that on there?"

"The only thing they'll find are a bunch of penis enlargement emails."

"Good. Because if anything comes back to me..."

"I'm not worried. Not about that. What I'm worried about is what you think you're doing."

"What do you mean?"

"I have to admit, Stone, I didn't take you for someone who could last in the big leagues. I assumed you'd have settled for the initial burst of fame, the newspaper interviews, the recognition on the street. The way a child is content with a small toy today rather than a big toy tomorrow. Immediate satisfaction."

"Then you don't know me very well. The only thing I know these days is that my life is bound to keep getting worse. So fuck the small toys. If I don't get the big one I'll never have anything that lasts."

"I figured you were too green to stick it out, figured you'd get scared and call yourself off."

"Number one, Hardwood. When I want something I go for it."

"Bullshit," the older newscaster shouted, loud enough that a few heads turned. "Bullshit. You were sinking like a torpedoed sub, racing toward disgrace. Hubris pushed you into this. Fear of obscurity." He regained his composure, took a drink. "And you're excelling. I commend you, but I'm warning you as well."

"Warning me? About what?"

"If it's a game you want, a game you will get." He turned to Stone, and for the first time that night, made no bones as to why he was at O'Halloran's. "You cannot beat me. I rule the airwaves in this town, and I will not be made a fool of."

"If you go to the police, so do I."

"Oh, I have no intention of reporting you. In fact, I'm looking forward to the challenge. To watching you accept defeat at my hands."

They stared at each other long and hard. Pat returned from the back room and busied himself replenishing the drinks of the few patrons at the bar. On the television, Branford was back with the band while Leno humored a man who collected funny shaped fruits. Hardwood extended his hand, a gesture as old and familiar as time itself.

"May the better man win," he said.

"Good luck," Stone replied.

They finished their drinks at opposite ends of the bar and left.

CHAPTER 31

It was rare that Hardwood had trouble sleeping, but as the clock struck two in the morning, he was tossing like a sock in a dryer. Frustrated, and finally giving in to the fact he wasn't going to beat his anxiety, he rolled over and turned on his bedside lamp. On the nightstand sat the evening's paper, Stone's face smack on page one staring back at him, smug as hell.

Damn that Stone, the boy was making waves.

His kills were admirable, his ingenuity top rate. The dog ring slayings were the talk of the city.

The problem, as far as Hardwood could tell, was that he'd given Stone an easy way to keep outdoing him. For every man or couple or group of people Hardwood killed, Stone could simply add one more, or two more. The equation was pretty simple to figure out. Stone was going to wait for Hardwood to make a move, and then top it however he could. Hardwood, in return, would be forced to continue the same game, topping Stone, all of which, he finally realized, was doing naught but creating a vicious circle. Eventually, one of them would strike a powerful enough blow that the other would be unable to top it. In theory, if they didn't nip this cycle in the bud, one of them would have to start a nuclear war.

Hardwood rubbed his chin. It was easy enough to tack on one number to any kill, and call it a better job. It would be better to deliver a blow that was significant, not because of numbers, but because of prominence.

He had to kill somebody important.

Just like the Winslow case.

"Bah," he said, taking his reading glasses off the nightstand and flipping through the paper. "Idiotic of me not to deduce this sooner. Idiotic."

The front page story continued onto page four, where Stone once again took a jab at the Casanova Carver, saying the killer was predictable and would be caught in no time. Hardwood had already read the article twice tonight, and clearly it was part of the reason he was having trouble sleeping. The underlying intent of the article, of course, was to anger Hardwood in hopes he'd make a hasty mistake. But it wouldn't work.

Oh yes, Stone, thought Hardwood, try and goad me all you want, it won't matter. I'm going to change the game here, give you some real pause, and it's you who will be forced to second guess yourself if you want to sustain. First place might seem within reach for you now, but let's see how strong your resolve is to reach out and actually grab it when it means even greater risk.

Throwing back the covers, Hardwood got out of bed and moved to his bureau. From the top drawer he removed a crinkled envelop that had RETURN TO SENDER stamped on it. Under the stamp, scribbled in pen, were the words NO MORE. The envelope itself was still sealed, still had Hardwood's handwriting on the outside.

Breaking the seal and opening it up, he took out the birthday card that sat inside. A picture of an attractive girl wearing nothing but an apron and a chef hat stared back at him. He read the joke inside, regret and sadness rising in his heart: "It's your birthday, here's a hot dish for you." Such a dumb card, the kind of thing guys like Jeremy seemed to like. But Jeremy hadn't even bothered to look at it, just sent it back without a thought.

Few, if any, pains Hardwood had ever felt were even close to what he felt the day he got the card back in the mail. Just five days after he'd sent it, two days after his son's birthday. After the night at Fredo's.

His son. His "dead" son.

Despite the card coming back, Jeremy had bothered to write the hurtful note on the outside, confirming that the address Hardwood sent it to was correct. His son lived just north of Houston, not far from The Johnny Rockets diner.

Checking the clock again, he made a mental calculation of how quickly he could get downtown, and how much sleep he'd get before having to make an appearance at the office. Thirty minutes down, thirty back, some time talking to Jeremy. If he worked quickly, he'd still get a couple hours of shut eye, which would be enough to operate on, so long as he slept soundly the following night.

"Okay, Jeremy," he said, "it's time to talk man to man."

Grabbing his gloves, donning his slacks and a heavy sweater, and throwing on his winter accessories—gun secured on the inside of his jacket—he rushed down to the lobby and had Louis get him a cab.

"Cab?" Louis asked.

"Yes, cab, Louis. Last minute meeting. No time to call the car service."

Despite the truth that New York never slept, the cabs were easier to catch at night, especially in Manhattan. Louis had one hailed in record time, and opened the door for Hardwood when it pulled up. The doorman's face wore an expression somewhere between concern and curiosity, which did not bode well for the future of the game being played. How much longer before those lips sank this ship?

Louis shut the door and the cab sped away.

The building where Jeremy lived did not have a doorman; the only way to get in was to be buzzed in by a tenant. Hunched over from the chill night air, hugging himself for warmth, Hardwood scanned the mailbox names until he found Jeremy's—Jeremy Christy.

Christy.

It had been a long time since he'd even thought of that name. It was Jeremy's mother's name, her maiden name, back before she swallowed a bottle of Percocet, back before she found the stack of pictures that destroyed their family.

Hardwood pressed the button next to Jeremy's name and waited for a response. When no one answered, he tried again, holding it down a little longer. Maybe Jeremy wasn't home? Maybe he—

"Yo, relax, I was in the can," came Jeremy's voice, "who's this?"

Hardwood had hoped he would still be up. Some chefs worked late, but Jeremy was an executive chef now, and usually left before his kitchen closed. It was possible he'd already be in bed. But his voice sounded fresh and awake.

"Answer or fuck off."

Hardwood checked the street around him. Some punk kids were smoking at the end of the block, being purposefully boisterous. A cab was turning a corner on the adjacent block, picking up a couple of girls walking home from a club. When the punks saw the girls they shouted some rude comments. The rest of the street was bare.

"It's me, Jeremy."

"Oh shit. What do you want?"

"I didn't get to finish talking to you at the gym."

"Yeah you did. I ended it. See this? See what I'm doing?"

"No."

"It's a middle finger. Just like before. Remember. It means it's over. Now go away."

"Please, Jeremy, I want to make it up to you. Everything I did. I want to help you."

"Help me with what? I don't need your help. Why don't you get—"

"Just listen. I...I want to put your place on the news, I want to spotlight it. Can't get better free advertising than that, right? I'm number one in the city, Jeremy, it'll help you."

"And what do I have to do for you. Pretend I like you?"

"No, not at all. All you have to do is give me five minutes of your time. Tonight."

"How'd you find me?"

"I'm the news, Jeremy—"

"Bullshit. You pay someone?"

Hardwood debated telling him the truth, about the card, but thought better of it. "No. No. I've just known for a while is all. I didn't know if you'd still be here…I took a chance. Just five minutes tonight. Then I put you on the program, and if you get nothing out of it—"

"I won't."

"Jeremy, please, what's five minutes? Hear my idea, and if you hate it, I'll leave."

"And you'll come back. So what, I need to move now?"

"No. I promise you I won't come back. You know my word is good."

"Your word, or Doug Hardwood's word?"

"They're the same thing."

"Jesus, you really have gone bonkers. Fuck." There was a long sigh, then, "Okay, here's the deal. You put me on Thursday night after *CSI* and I—"

"We don't do cooking segments at night. They go on the five o'clock report, to coincide with dinner."

"Okay then, good night."

"Wait! I'll make it happen. Okay. Sure, Thursday night."

What did it matter anyway, he thought, it was all a lie.

To Hardwood's amazement, the door buzzed and he went inside.

The door to Jeremy's apartment on the third floor was ajar when Hardwood got there, light spilling out onto the gray rug in the hall. Before he could knock, the door opened and Jeremy motioned him inside. He was dressed in a white t-shirt and black shorts. He'd gotten a new tattoo since Hardwood had last seen him at the gym, a vulgar image of a naked woman on all fours.

The walls were covered with posters of rock bands and John Belushi movies, like a college dorm room from the seventies. A large plasma tv playing a DVD of some comedy took up most of the living room, a leather recliner in front of it with a beer in the armrest cup holder. The scent of fresh shit lingered from the nearby bathroom.

Through the open bedroom door in the hall, Hardwood could see the edge of a Nazi flag.

"Thought you didn't have time for that stuff anymore?" he said, pointing.

Jeremy moved to the bedroom and closed the door. "I don't, it's just a fond memory is all. So you can really get me on after *CSI*?"

"Probably," Hardwood said, taking a seat at the small kitchen table. Looking around, he found it was the one room in the apartment that was immaculate. The refrigerator had a computer screen built into the door. The stove had four compartments and took up a large portion of the wall. Above the stove, a multi-tiered spice rack held an impressive collection. On the counter near the microwave, a set of heavy duty stainless steel knives reflected the light from the living room. A framed portrait of *Le Chat Noir* hung above the table, upon which sat a bottle of wine. "If I can find an angle for it," he continued, still looking around the kitchen.

"I know you, Dad, all you've got is angles. Make it happen."

"You use my sayings, did you know that?"

"All right already! So what! Jesus, speak your piece and get going. I'm missing my movie here. If you're gonna tell me you're in trouble again, get on with it."

"Did you know why I said that?"

"No, Dumbledore, enlighten me."

"Because I think The Chef is going to kill me."

Jeremy started to retort but stopped short. "Wait…The Chef? But I thought—"

"Yes. The Chef. The killer bothering Roland Stone."

"Well, shit, now I'm intrigued. So what's he want with you? He want you to stop talking to the Carver guy?"

"I think, eventually, he might kill me because I'm better than he is, and he'll get desperate."

"What do you mean better than he is? Better at what?"

"Reading an audience."

"Huh?"

Tears rushed from Hardwood's eyes, fell to the tabletop like tiny jewels. Through saran-wrap vision, he looked his son, his already-dead-to-him son, up and down and asked himself where he'd gone wrong in raising him. He remembered when Jeremy started hanging around with a bad crowd in high school, but had figured it was a phase. Hell, he was already at the anchor desk then, and he wasn't about to risk losing it because Jeremy was spray painting swastikas on Jewish delis. Was it wrong to want to ensure his career, to provide for his family? Was it wrong to want more money and power? Why hadn't Jeremy just snapped out of it like he'd hoped?

Judging by the hate tattoos on Jeremy's arm, chances were the gun in his pocket wouldn't frightening him, so Hardwood moved to the knives and drew out the largest one.

"Reading an audience," he repeated. "I know what they want."

"What's that got to do with—"

"It's always got to be bigger and better. If not bigger, then certainly better. Audiences get bored easily, see. Right now I'm doing this by numbers. And it's getting hard. It all quantity, not quality. I'm sure of it now. I've got to take this to the next level. It's the only way to win."

"Win what? Am I gonna be on after *CSI* or not? Put my knife back."

Hardwood walked toward Jeremy and ran his thumb down the blade, felt the finely-honed edge even through his latest pair of leather gloves. Tears were falling steadily down his cheeks. "Do you really hate me, son?"

Fear trickled into Jeremy's eyes, Hardwood noticed. But not

because there was a knife pointed at him—because Jeremy thought his father was going to hug him. "Yeah, Dad," he said, "I hate you."

"Well, at least you'll mean something to me in death."

The knife came up quick and caught Jeremy in the gut. At the same time, Hardwood lifted the bottle of wine off the table and brought it down over Jeremy's head.

*

The death of Hardwood's son was front page news for weeks. It was the first time one of the killers had gone after someone close to their messengers. It was the first time they'd killed someone of mild importance. Both Garcia and Boomer urged Hardwood to get protection, but he refused (he'd seen a suspicious looking man walking nearby the other day, so there was chance he was being tailed already anyway). When he gave his son's eulogy live on television, everyone in the city was glued to their sets. It was a record viewership. Outwardly Hardwood cried; inside he wasn't sure what he felt. All he knew was that it was a brilliant career move.

CHAPTER 32

Over the next two months, the snow in New York City melted. It didn't disappear altogether, but the myriad charcoal snow banks, erected sometime in January by lumbering snowplows, began to diminish like soufflés sinking.

As April rolled around, slush still covered the streets, but it had thinned to the consistency of dishwater rather than gravy. New Yorkers continued to scurry about in overcoats, gloves, scarves and wool hats, but they moved a bit quicker, no longer hindered by the freezing power of urban winter wind.

The smell of oncoming spring was in the air, a rainy time for the Big Apple. Even though temperatures would not rise significantly for at least another month, people were emerging from their cocoons. That is, the people who dared to emerge.

Aside from changes in the weather, far more important occurrences took place over those two months. A restaurant in Brooklyn was opened one morning to find its tables had been adorned with new centerpieces: human hearts. A subway car was found decorated with entrails. A ten foot tall doll, made up entirely of human skin and filled with human hair, fell from the lighting rig of a Broadway show, landing on former child actor Barry Williams, who was in the middle of butchering poor Richard III's kingdom-for-a-horse soliloquy. Someone had placed wasps' nests in the toilets of the men's room at the Tavern on the Green, and locked in three patrons—they were found bloated and oozing venom. The Strand Bookstore unknowingly sold a variety of books that, once opened, rewarded their readers with dried aortas.

And that was just the small stuff.

A pipe bomb rocked a nightclub in Chelsea, leaving a mess of dead drug dealers that took the city two days to sort through. Someone had chained together the doors of an apartment complex in Spanish Harlem—a known crack house with a reputation for giving freebies to recovered addicts—and set fire to it. A harbor cruise sank near the Statue of Liberty. A lion from the Central Park Zoo had been found roaming around the Javits Center, bits and pieces of flesh dangling from its teeth. Somebody took control of the scoreboard in Madison Square Garden and flashed the body counts racked up by both The Chef and the Casanova Carver; it happened during the middle of the Ice Capades, right as the actor playing Peter Pan was decapitated by an almost invisible piece of wire.

The snow was melting, rain was coming, people were out and about. But they were scared shitless. Hardwood and Stone were everywhere. Shadows. Lurking. Getting better at their craft with each passing day. The game was indeed on.

They were on the covers of magazines, including *Time*, *Newsweek*, *Entertainment Weekly*, and *People*. Calls came in from their respective parent networks offering money for movie deals. Book publishers called (at least Carlie couldn't call Stone a liar) and wanted them to write their own accounts of what was going on.

Logos appeared on t-shirts and book bags. Internet sites numbered in the thousands. Cheese had even set one up for Stone, linked to the station's site. Emails poured in by the minute. Some of them wanted inside information, some of them claimed to have inside information, and some of them claimed to be from The Chef. Stone wrote a few statements and posted them on the site, happy to appease his rising fanbase.

Everywhere you looked, especially on television, someone was profiling the Casanova Carver and The Chef.

Hardwood was starting to show signs of fatigue. He reluctantly took a night off work, replaced by field anchor Linda Templeton—Stone had met her once at an awards ceremony; she was tall and thin, real name something like Kitowicz. His eyes were turning black from lack of sleep, and his skin looked pasty. Of course, after applying a layer of make-up, you'd never know he'd been out until dawn on so many nights getting his stories. But then, only Stone knew the truth.

As for Stone, he was eroding just the same. Too many nights in the shadows, awash in blood, adrenaline surging through his body.

The game was intense. Both men fluctuated between first and second in the ratings. If Stone killed ten, Hardwood killed twenty, if Stone crashed a bus, Hardwood derailed a subway train. It got so that the legends of the killers were bigger than they could handle. Neither knew when it would end.

One thing was for sure, Stone knew, it wasn't going to end until one of them was satisfied with their place in the media hierarchy and backed off. The fundamental truth to power is that there's always more. He and Hardwood were feasting on it. It was more than the celebrity, it was the respect, the trusting looks they got from citizens on the street. To the public, they were two men staring death in the face, and doing it to keep the city informed. Call it sacrifice, call it bravery, call it whatever you wanted, it wasn't hurting anyone.

Except the unlucky ones who crossed their paths at the wrong time.

Cheese had officially seated Stone back at the anchor desk for good, in between Mason and Swift. Stone's Moans was as dead as Hardwood's son. Mason still led off, but he got to do all the actual reporting on The Chef. He read from the killer's letters, and sometimes showed little souvenirs to prove he wasn't lying.

Stone and Mason gelled. He still resented her for taking his spotlight, but he saw the rapport they had, and it turned out she'd always been right: they were good together.

Detective Garcia was pulling his hair out. Police presence in the five Burroughs had increased tenfold. The FBI was lurking around as well, threatening to shut Garcia's investigation down, though that was off the record. Funny thing about that, though, was that Garcia told

Stone and Hardwood. Perhaps he was afraid the Feds would steal his thunder; he had become a minor celebrity himself. Almost nightly he appeared on some news program, or did phone interviews with radio stations. Stone just knew the detective was going to pop out a book when and if he caught the killers.

All of this was what New York City experienced from February to April.

Fear and balanced news.

At some point, probably when he fell asleep smack in the middle of a newscast, Stone realized it was becoming too much. He needed a break.

It was a quiet Sunday afternoon, while sitting at his desk at home, Chauncey by his feet, that Stone called Hardwood on his personal line. The phone was picked up after a few rings.

"Hello."

"Doug, it's me."

"Stone."

"Meet me?"

Hardwood paused, perhaps listening for clicks like Stone was. They were both pretty sure their homes were wired, especially with the FBI involved. "I suppose I could. How about The Gables?"

"Sounds good. See you in an hour."

The Gables was their code word for a tiny bar in the Seaport called Fidel's. It was dark, and served South American imported wine. The real Gables was up on 87th street, a lifetime away in New York City.

Before he left, Stone called his lawyer, intending to check on the package he'd mailed so long ago. Maybe if things went okay, there'd be no need for it anymore. He wasn't in, so Stone left a message with the secretary and asked for a return call as soon as possible.

At Fidel's, they grabbed a booth in the back, ordered some Chilean Syrah, and Stone voiced his concerns.

"You're tired, Doug, I can see it."

"You are none the better for your opposition. You are the personification of fatigue."

"We need a break."

"I believe I'm ahead right now. How do I know this isn't a ploy?"

"Because, I'm paying you back for seating me at Gertrude's. I told you I would. It's time for a guaranteed vacation."

"So what, we each jaunt off to Jamaica for a week?"

"I don't know. But if we keep going at this rate we're going to get sloppy."

Outside on the street, two cabbies were yelling at each other in a foreign language peppered with bits of English, something about someone cutting someone off. They were, however, well versed in American Sign Language, at least as it pertained to obscenities. Hardwood chuckled as he watched them.

"Roland, perhaps you're right. Look at these two fools out there, upset over a lane of road. There are madmen walking the city's streets, painting the walls with blood, and still people persist to squabble over the innocuous. It's hard to strike fear into the hearts of the already damned."

"Is that what you're trying to do, strike fear in people?"

"I'm trying to be the best at my job that I can be. My point is—"

"Your point is, if we let emotions get the best of us, we're going to end up losing control. Like I said."

"Like those two. Yes."

Across the street, the two cabbies were now taking swings at each other. A beat cop came running up, caught an elbow in the jaw and dropped to the ground like a sack of laundry. Immediately, the two cabbies stopped fighting. They glanced at the dazed cop, at each other, the cop again, and then hopped in their cabs. The one in back waved the one in front on, and they drove off together, united by a common crime.

Stone knew Hardwood had caught the parallelism, could see the smile on his face.

"Okay, time off," Hardwood said. "But first, a good deed from a respected newscaster."

He excused himself from the table, walked across the street, and bent down over the cop. He asked the cop a question—the cop shook his head no—then he slipped an arm under the man' shoulder and helped him stand. The cop rubbed his head and spoke into his shoulder radio. Before Hardwood could leave, the cop asked him for his autograph.

Stone laughed.

CHAPTER 33

Mid-April meant the Press Club Awards, this year held at the W Hotel in Union Square. The best and the brightest in the field of journalism would be present, as well as various other celebrities just on hand to make Page 6.

Hardwood and Stone were each up for Anchor of the Year, as was Mason, which kind of pissed Stone off. But then, she had drawn in viewers like never before and had appeared at more functions around town than most people even knew existed. One could almost consider it campaigning.

A new category had been added to the usual roster of awards, something that hadn't happened since the World Trade Towers fell in 2001: best coverage of New York's tag team killers. It was sort of a moot point though, since every other category made mention of The Chef and Casanova Carver as well, from op-ed to current affairs to arts and entertainment, national news, local news, sports, special interest, features—D: all of the above.

As Chauncey tried to lift up the toilet seat to get a drink, Stone slipped on his tux, which was seeing the outside of his closet for the first time in six months, having only come out for a mayoral event he'd covered. It was still clean and pressed. When he buttoned it up, it felt looser than before. The mirror showed him what he suspected: he'd lost weight. Who said serial killing didn't have its benefits? Sadly, his face was gaunt, his eyes black, his hair thinning.

From the bathroom came the sounds of a thirsty animal drinking the champagne of the canine world, and for some reason it reminded Stone he still needed a date.

Everyone would be waiting for Hardwood and him to arrive, and he certainly didn't want to show up alone. He phoned Carlie, hoping that she might be over their past differences, but she didn't answer. Probably fucking the doorman of her building. Or the doorman of another building.

Or just a doorknob somewhere, the bitch.

His shoulders slumped when he hung up the phone. He knew she probably would have said no anyway, but for some reason it bugged him. The pit of his stomach grew tighter, acid reflux seemed imminent. Why, he wondered. Why, after all this time, was he still concerned with her?

He didn't know many women these days, especially with the amount of time he devoted to work and extracurricular activities. Hell, most of the women he did meet these days he ended up killing, and that wasn't really helping him get any dates.

Mason was going with Cheese, everyone knew that. They said they wanted to represent the station, come across as strong business partners, but he knew they played "assassinate the cooter" late at night. He'd smelled the sex stains on the couch in Cheese's office. Swift was married to a luscious woman that should be in film. Duncan was reportedly bringing one of the interns, and Stone could only assume he'd fed her a line about how he was second in charge, which was only true when referring to taking up space in Cheese's office (the first being a prized Tiffany lamp).

Stone racked his brain for someone who wouldn't only want to spend time with him, but would be so grateful he might actually get laid. Someone who wanted to mingle with the media. Someone who was in the media business, but not respected.

Miss Muffin.

He called Duncan and got Bunny Man's phone number, gave him a call. The guy wanted to know why he should help. Stone told him if he didn't he would have Cheese change his character to a clown. Kids hate clowns; he'd be out on his ass in a week.

Reluctantly, the Maverick gave up her number, but not before adding that she was more trouble than she was worth. Stone didn't care; she was attractive and hungry for exposure. She'd be the perfect arm candy.

He called her, and over the blaring techno music in the background, she said yes.

He ordered a limo and picked her up at her place two hours later. She wore a tight dress with a low cut back. She looked good, the way aspiring actresses always do. He noticed her pupils were dilated, and that she was blinking rapidly.

Cocaine.

As long as he didn't end up babysitting he could deal with it.

When this was all over, she'd make a great story, he realized. Just what is Miss Muffin teaching your children? Report at eleven.

"Do you really know Bud Rawlings?" she asked as they turned into traffic. "I like when he talks to the people on the street with the signs. He's so jolly. That's a funny word. Jolly." She giggled.

"Sure I know him. I even bought his cookbook."

"Oh, I don't read, it hurts my eyes. I don't see the point in it really. Every book that's any good is made into a movie. Even the not so good ones. So, really, if you think about it—is Katie Couric gonna be there?"

"If she is, I'll introduce you." So long as you don't talk, he thought to himself.

"She has great hair. I don't normally like short hair but…come to think of it, even a lot of the straight to DVD movies come from books."

"If you say so."

She squeezed his knee, leaned in close. "I couldn't believe it when I picked up the phone and found out it was you. I mean, the night I met you, I was kind of in a bad mood. And you, well, I didn't know who you were. I know now, of course. Everybody knows who you are now. Which makes me have to ask, this is safe, right? Like, this creepy killer guy isn't stalking you, is he? I had a stalker once, when I first started doing the Miss Muffin show. At first he was just this guy I'd see around. Then he started giving me roses and chocolate. But I had a boyfriend at the time so I turned him down for a date. He kept coming around after that, leaving strange things for me. A picture of me made of macaroni, a comb with a clump of my hair in it, a photo of a tattoo that looked like me naked. He got into my building and left his dirty underwear on my door. I had a friend beat him up, and he quit coming around."

"Boy," he said, suddenly wondering if Bunny Man might have actually been trying to help him, "you sure do talk."

"Sorry, I took some...I had something to drink, to unwind. It makes me a bit—"

"Speedy?"

"I was going to say nervous."

"I think speedy is better. By the way, you've got some... drink...around your nose."

She looked out the window and wiped the white powder from under her nose. Stone's eyes fell down to her chest, which was supple and firm, and from what he could tell, still natural. Shit, he was horny. He checked his watch, saw they were on track to be fashionably late, and leaned back.

Through the window, he watched Manhattan's skyscrapers whoosh by. They loomed overhead like giant tombstones, too tall to see the tops of even if he craned his neck. When he'd first come to New York City, he used to look out cab windows and try to see their tops. Now, he barely noticed they were there. Big didn't necessarily mean important, and important didn't necessarily mean big.

Importance, at least from his standpoint, depended on reaction.

Miss Muffin turned back to him and asked, "Is Matt Lauer going to be there?"

*

The ballroom of the hotel was spacious and atmospherically lit, like someone had rubbed mustard on all the light bulbs. Everything felt sepia-toned, dim. Close to one hundred tables were laid out with lush floral centerpieces, origami napkins, red and white wines, and the evening's program at each seat. As Stone had suspected, WWTF's table was up front, close to the stage, right next to WYNN's. But no one was seated yet.

The room buzzed with the white noise of idle chit-chat, colleagues playing the networking game, the how-have-you-been and loved-your-piece bullshit that everyone sees through yet complains about if they don't hear. Black tuxedos stretched clear across the room, a penguin convention that Stone was contributing to. Evening gowns sparkled, jewelry shimmered, hairdos were painstakingly sculpted. Light jazz drifted from the PA speakers near the stage, accompanied by the clinking of wine glasses and ruffling of paper as people thumbed through the night's program.

A few police officers were standing over near the back of the stage. It was unclear whether they were there to keep the peace, or protect Stone and Hardwood from any unannounced guests.

Stone found Cheese and Mason hobnobbing with Bud Rawlings. Cheese had donned a tuxedo with sterling silver accessories from Tiffany's. Mason was wearing Nicole Miller, a diamond pendant resting in her cleavage. Her blonde hair was long and straight, curled under her chin, her lips brick red and glossy. Everyone was eyeballing her like she was the reincarnation of Marilyn Monroe. Seizing the opportunity to impress Miss Cocaine Head, Stone edged into their little circle and announced himself.

"Hello, everyone."

There were cheerful hellos all around. Mason leaned over and kissed his cheek, told him he looked ravishing and who the hell was the girl at his side with the runny nose. Cheese said, "Here he is, the man of the hour."

Rawlings was thinner than Stone remembered, and everyone who passed by him made a point to stop and stare, proving yet again that being big had nothing to do with importance. He must have lost 40 pounds since Stone had seen him last. Was he spilling blood too? Only on his backyard grill, Stone thought, extending his hand.

"Bud, long time."

"How are ya, Wes?"

"Roland."

"Sorry. Roland. I forgot you'd made the switch. How are you holding up? Any word on your penpal crackpot killer?"

"Just what everyone else knows, that he's still out there and still crazy."

"Well, I must say you've handled it very professionally. I'd have probably locked myself in a closet and chewed my fingers to the bone."

"And you on a diet and all, sug," Mason said.

Everyone laughed.

"This is...um..." Stone had no idea what Muffin's first name was. She ignored the faux pas and introduced herself.

"Danielle Swayback. Pleased to meet you."

"Danielle here has a show on PBS," Stone said. "You may have seen it, the...um..."

"Happy Time with Miss Muffin," she said.

"Oh sure," Rawlings replied.

"Love it," Mason said.

"Whatever works," Cheese put in.

Stone knew instantly none of them had ever seen it. Miss Muffin believed every word though, and looked ready to faint from the sudden ego boost.

"So, Roland," Rawlings continued, "we were just discussing the Senator's take on the new FCC codes. He says he's going to fight for looser regulations, which might be beneficial for your media coverage."

"I didn't think he cared."

"Oh, he cares, at least tonight. If he were at church I'm sure he'd be singing a different tune. He's right over there, talking to Doug Hardwood."

Stone glanced across the room, saw the two of them talking animatedly. Hardwood looked good, less pale then when they'd last talked; the time off had benefited him. He and the senator were laughing and nodding, like two friends catching up on old times.

A thought struck Stone then, almost like stumbling over a gold brick. The senator was important. Visions of the senator's mutilated body swam into view in his mind's eye, visions of the press awards halted by the discovery of his remains. And he, Roland Stone, in the right place at the right time, finding the man, hearing his last words.

Could it be done? Hell, it had to be done. It was important, it was quality, reactions would be magnanimous. People would shit bricks.

Someone tapped him on the shoulder. He turned back, found Miss Muffin staring back. "Mr. Rawlings was talking to you. Are you okay?"

"What? Oh, yes, sorry. What was that, Bud?"

"I asked if you've tried my new recipe for tuna salad. I put it in the last book, but I can give it to you."

Mason and Cheese rolled their eyes in unison and stepped away. Once Rawlings got going on his recipes it was like a science fiction nerd discussing *Star Wars*. You either nodded politely and felt your life drain away, or you made up a lie and ran like the wind. Rawlings was an okay guy, and most of his food talk was business anyway, but he would go on forever if unchecked. Stone wanted to get away for a minute and see where the senator was sitting.

"…you put the pickles in first, not last…"

He squeezed Muffin's ass and eased her forward. She didn't seem to notice, her gaze locked on Rawlings' face, happy for the attention. He didn't know what she thought Rawlings was going to do for her, save for making her hungry.

"...mayo to spread evenly. And skip stringy cheese, go for edam..."

Stone pretended to wave to someone and excused himself. Rawlings didn't seem to mind, what with the drug queen caught in his grasp.

Getting across the room was a bit of a hassle. The waiters had come out and were distributing dinner rolls, and most people were still up and about. Hardwood was still chatting with the senator, which hopefully meant Stone could get an introduction.

He weaseled his way into their personal space, acted as if he'd happened upon them by accident. "Hardwood," he said, extending a hand, "almost didn't see you there. You look good."

"Roland." Hardwood responded, his eyes narrowing slightly in an effort to find hidden intentions. He looked at the senator, back to Stone. "I was just talking to Senator Mills here about the latest security bill on the ballot. Seems one of the points involves teachers learning self defense. We were discussing my interviewing him about its possible effects. You're not here to steal the story from me are you?"

Hardwood laughed, making a joke out of it, though Stone knew he was serious.

"Not at all," Stone said. "But it's an interesting point. Maybe the whole city should learn self defense what with these two killers on the loose."

"Senator Mills, Roland Stone." Hardwood delighted in the introduction, if for no other reason than to let it be known he was already a long time friend of the man. But then, an introduction was what

Stone had been hoping for.

"Of course," the senator replied, making Stone feel a bit taller than Hardwood would like him to be. "I've followed your reports. And between you and me, I don't think these killers are going to be causing trouble too much longer."

"No?"

"No. I've gotten word from some higher ups that they have the suspects nailed down, and are just waiting for them to make a move."

"I do hope we get some sort of nod," Hardwood said. "Nothing to upset the capture, of course, but as two men thrust into the middle of this dire mess, it'd be nice to know in advance as it suits our obligations to the public."

The Senator ran his hands through his hair, smiled at someone at a nearby table. "I would assume," he said, returning his attention to them, "that the police will be informing you two first. In fact, one of my contacts at the FBI mentioned he might call you. He seemed to think there was a bit of Stockholm going on, but I told him he was nuts. I reminded him of your help on the Winslow case, Doug. Of course, who can tell how they're going to play it out? Personally, I think it should end in a shootout…if you catch my drift."

"The public does love video of a public execution," Hardwood said. "Vigilante mindsets are ingrained in even the most judicial Americans, quelled though they may be."

The Senator nodded and continued: "Precisely. That way, I don't get slammed with hate mail from little Billy and Susie's mother complaining about some bullshit legal loophole that lets these two creeps off. Shoot first, celebrate later. Works for me."

"In other words," Stone added, "successful and justified, and Senator Mills can worry about truly important stately matters such as re-election."

"Call it what you will, Stone, I call it a job well done. Two killers dead, two news reporters with grade-A footage to end their nightmares with. Off the record, of course."

"Of course."

"It looks like the awards are about to begin," Stone said.

They all shook hands and took their seats. Stone waited until the senator took his, noting the man's proximity to him.

CHAPTER 34

At the table, the lot of them drank wine with gusto and applauded as reporters routinely walked to the stage to accept their certificates. The clinking of silverware permeated the room as each recipient gave a little thank you speech. All the while whispers floated on the air like trees rustling nearby.

Winning stories ranged from exposes on fiscal corruption to real estate coverage to manipulative rants on the severity of declining senior citizen aid. Some of it Stone had read or heard, some of it was new to him. All of it was boring as shit. The entire affair was making him catatonic.

He spent most of the time staring at Miss Muffin's lips, now a bright ruby red from the generous amounts of wine she was heartily consuming. Her hand found his shoulder more than once, a sign he took as meaning she was good to go.

But that would come later.

When he wasn't staring at her chest, he was watching Senator Mills, who was sitting with his daughter, occasionally whispering in her ear and smiling, putting on a show for a room full of glorified paparazzi. On the other side of him sat a large man in a suit, presumably a bodyguard, but he seemed more intent on the food that what his ward was doing. Stone wondered if the senator's assurances of the killers' impending capture were true, or if he was blowing smoke up everyone's ass in an effort to plant seeds of good fortune he wanted the media to relay to the public. Either way, Stone couldn't shake the idea that Miller was a means to best Hardwood in their little game. Kill the Senator at the Press Club awards, and The Chef would go from shadowy serial killer to a serial killer with balls the size of King Kong's.

The real question was, was he desperate and gutsy enough to try it, right here, right now in the lions den?

He wasn't, but The Chef was.

And so he sat and stared and dreamed of rolling in Mills' blood before going home and slamming Miss Muffin like an animal. If only that bodyguard would get lost, if only Mills' daughter would get up and go mingle. If only he could get the senator alone.

Unlike other occasions, getting this story would require skill and luck beyond anything he'd been able to muster so far. Speed would also be essential, as only the quickest jab with a knife, a prison-style shivving, would get him the prize. Too many people around to get fancy with it.

Miss Muffin leaned over and whispered something in his ear but he shoved her head away gracefully. She didn't seem to mind. "Don't bug me," he said. Across the table, Cheese looked at him enviously. Mason gave him a look that either meant she was turned on or disgusted; he couldn't tell.

He slipped back into planning mode, checked out the exits in the ballroom. There were two on either side of the stage, and the large doors that opened up into the hotel's hallway. If only he could get

Mills in the hall, he thought.

Then, wouldn't you know, opportunity came, and sooner than he'd expected. As they rolled a Spielberg-worthy montage of his and Hardwood's work, the senator excused himself from the table, drifted over to the banquet hall doors, and passed through them. There was only one reason for Mills to head out the doors at that moment, and that was to hit the bathroom at the end of the hallway.

The bodyguard got up and followed.

"This is boring," Miss Muffin whispered in Stone's ear, her words slurring like somebody hand-spinning a record. "When can we leave? Is Bud Rawlings having an after party? Where's Matt Lauer? And what does voting constituency mean?"

Stone's hand gripped a butter knife hard enough to dance with pain. Oh how he wanted to shove it down her throat and shut her up right now. For a brief second he saw Carlie reflected in her face, and the muscles in his arms damn near reacted.

"Honey," he said, handing her the knife, "play with the shiny silverware. I'll be right back."

He excused himself from the table (some curious faces wondering why he was leaving during his own dedication), walked through the double doors, and headed for the bathroom. The hall was empty except for a woman coming back from the ladies room and a hotel attendant passing by with a trash bag.

The only other person was the bodyguard, standing near the bathroom door, arms folded, eyes watching the hall. Stone nodded as he walked by him, and the bodyguard smiled back, he assumed, remembering him as the guy the Senator had been talking to earlier, or simply knowing him from his recent celebrity.

He opened the bathroom door and went in.

The senator's feet were on display under one of the stalls, pointed out in the position of someone sitting.

He was taking a shit.

There was no one else in the bathroom. Nothing besides the muzak pumping in through the ceiling's speakers. Stone unzipped his pants and took a piss in a nearby urinal, listening to the guttural strainings of a man in need of Exlax.

While he was shaking himself off, the bathroom door opened…

…and Hardwood walked in. "What are you doing here?" he asked.

"Taking a leak," Stone replied. "You?"

Hardwood glanced at the Senator's feet. "He's mine," he whispered.

"No way. I was here first."

"First? Stone, I had him claimed in the banquet hall. You didn't really think I was interested in his security bill, did you?"

"You didn't stick a flag in him either. I got in here first, Hardwood."

"I assumed we were adhering to gentleman's rules."

"What is this, a fox hunt?"

"If you like."

They glared at each other for a moment, neither one of them willing to budge. Stone knew Hardwood well enough to know the man would wait until one of them fell asleep if need be. Behind them, in the stall, the Senator groaned and farted.

"Tell you what," Stone said. "When he comes out we'll see which one he comes to first."

"He's not a dog. He won't come running like Lassie."

"Then whoever gets the first blow in has him."

"Nonsense, Stone. You're younger and stronger than me. I maintain that he's mine—"

"Is not."

"Is too."

"Is not."

"This is rather childish."

"Fine, then how about flipping a coin?"

The Senator flushed the toilet, began cleaning himself. The bathroom door opened and Bud Rawlings waltzed in.

"Hey, guys!"

"Oh shit," Stone said.

"Perfect," Hardwood replied.

"Good chicken, huh?" Rawlings said, checking his tie in the mirror. "Not like mine. I use lemon butter. That's the secret to good chicken. Pepper and lemon and you marinate it over night. Sometimes I add some capers, but the thing about capers is that they can overpower the lemon."

Hardwood and Stone exchanged glances, as if to ask, should they take him out as well?

Behind them, the senator appeared at the sink, nodded to them. "Rawlings, Hardwood, Stone. The gang's all here."

"Hey there, Senator," Rawlings said. "Didn't know you were in here. Was it the chicken? It's not sitting too well with me either. I have trouble with spicy foods. Goes through me like fish through water. You all finished in there?"

The Senator looked at the stall, looked back at Rawlings. "Tear her up." Both men chuckled. Rawlings disappeared into the stall, sat down on the toilet.

The senator gazed into the mirror and began fixing his lapels.

Hardwood leaned into Stone's ear and whispered, "Fine, we'll do it together."

"But Rawlings."

"Casualties."

"But I like Rawlings."

"The man is a useless icon for an America obsessed with making asses out of themselves on television, holding up their signs like animals in a zoo. I'm sorry but the Casanova Carver takes this one."

Hardwood reached into the inside of his jacket, pulled out a pair of leather gloves and a small knife.

Instinctively, Stone turned on all the faucets. The Senator cocked an eyebrow, wondering what he was doing. "You feeling okay?"

Stone didn't get to answer him.

Hardwood grabbed the Senator's head, pulled it back, and ran the blade across the man's neck. The skin snapped and pulled apart, blood shot out onto the sink. The senator's eyes rolled back into his head and he gurgled in shock and surprise, his arms jumping to his neck. Hardwood put him in a headlock and covered his mouth with his hand.

"Who's cutting the cheese out there?" Rawlings laughed. "That sounded wet."

The Senator kicked out and connected with the cabinets beneath the sink. The sound echoed off the walls. He kicked again and hit the stall Rawlings was occupying.

"Hey, guys! Knock it off and let a man do his thing. This chicken burns coming out."

Hardwood's eyes were wild. Stone had never seen him work before. There was joy in his face, the elation of a man given into primal instinct. Stone didn't look, but he was willing to bet Hardwood had an erection, he was that excited. Hardwood took his other hand and shoved it in the Senator's torn neck and yanked the wound wider. The senator's blood erupted out and coated the floor. Some spatter shot into Hardwood's mouth and he licked it, though Stone couldn't tell if he meant to do it.

"That's it," Hardwood cooed, "Daddy's here. Everything's going to be just fine."

Daddy? Oh man, Hardwood had issues Stone had never suspected.

Before the senator could struggle enough to alert his bodyguard, Stone grabbed a marble soap dish off the counter, faked a whooping cough, and beat him in the head with it.

Cough!

Crack! The sound filled the bathroom. Involuntarily, Mills' leg kicked sideways.

"The hell was that noise?" Rawlings asked.

Coughing again, Stone hit the senator a second time.

Cough!

Crack! Under the skin of the senator's forehead, small bits of skull began sliding around. At the same time, Hardwood stuck him in the chest with the knife, pushing deep to get past the ribs. He stabbed again and again, sometimes in the belly, sometimes up under the ribcage. Blood pooled on the floor and spread out toward the walls. How long before Rawlings noticed it?

Shit and blood do not mix well, and the bathroom suddenly smelled foul enough to attract every fly in the city. Ironically, Stone had grown used to it over the past several months—most of his victims evacuated their bowels while dying—but how long before the bodyguard noticed it?

He brought the soap dish down one final time, breaking it in half over the man's head. The liberated piece bounced off the floor and slid under the stall, stopping at Rawlings' feet.

"What the hell is this?" Rawlings asked. "Hey, guys, everything all right. Guys?"

"Fuck," Stone said, no longer concerned with Rawlings. "This is taking too long."

"What the hell is this? Blood? Hey, guys, what the…"

The soap dish had broken into a shard, like a large shark's tooth. Stone jabbed it in the Senator's eye. The man's cut larynx kept his pleas from reaching Rawlings' ears, but he struggled with all his might and Stone was sure Rawlings could hear it. Gripping it with both hands, he pulled the soapdish shard out and jammed it in the other eye.

"Fuck," he said.

"Do it harder!" Hardwood yelled.

"Fuck."

"You've got to put weight behind it."

"It won't go any further."

"Twist it while you push. Twist it. Not like that—"

"Will you just let me do it my way!"

Rawlings was doing up his belt. "What's going on out there?"

"Let me do it," Hardwood said.

"If you'd stop pressuring me I'll get it done! Jesus, you're like my ex-wife."

"I can see why she left you. You're stubborn."

"And you're pushy."

"I push because I see the potential in you, and if you'd quell your obstinacy you might find yourself illuminated."

"I'm doing it fine, you arrogant prick!"

"You're just going to break it. Watch, gimme, I'll show you." Hardwood grabbed the shard and twisted it. "See."

It drove right into the senator' eye socket. Stone did see. "Went right in."

"Like a drill. It works past the ocular bone."

"Huh…well I'll be."

"Told you. You assume my age makes me weak, but my wisdom is grounded in years of trial and error. Your way would take you all day.

Just twist it."

"You do this a lot?"

"Not really. I've got bad joints. Fighting like this, my arthritis flares up."

"I know a good doctor who—"

The body lurched. Stone twisted the shard and shoved with all his might.

"There you go." Hardwood smiled.

For a moment Stone felt like a problem student who'd just won over the teacher. He felt united with Hardwood, which was not good. Snap out of it, buddy.

The toilet flushed.

"He's almost gone," Hardwood said. "Come on, once more."

Stone forced the soap dish into the senator's socket until a gray ooze flowed out around it. Instantly, the man's arms stopped flailing and his body sagged. Hardwood let him go and the body fell into the sink, bounced off and sprawled on the floor.

Right in front of Rawlings, who was now standing in the open stall doorway.

Rawlings shrieked like a girl.

Shit, thought Stone.

Drawn by the screaming, the bodyguard burst into the room, saw his ward lying dead at the feet of the two newscasters. He reached under his jacket, pulled out a gun. Stone nonchalantly stepped behind Hardwood, using him as a shield.

Rawlings tore past them, slamming into the bodyguard, sending the man spinning into the wall, and bolted out the door.

"Get Rawlings" Hardwood said.

The bodyguard was already rising, doused in sweat from the adrenaline surge. He was on all fours now.

"Stone!"

Stone looked at Hardwood. The old man was stepping over the Senator's body, heading for the wastebasket. He picked it up, then brought it crashing down on the bodyguard's head. The large man fell back to the floor and dropped his gun. "Rawlings," he instructed.

Stone nodded, stepped over the Senator and picked up the gun. It was a .45, an easy gun to fire. He checked the safety, found it off, and opened the door.

"Use this," Hardwood said, tossing a latex glove to him.

"What's this?"

"For the gun shot residue."

"Were you a Boy Scout?"

"Better hurry."

As he was leaving, he glanced over his shoulder and saw Hardwood draw the knife across the bodyguard's neck. Blood spilled onto the tile, mixing with the Senator's.

In the hall, he saw Rawlings making for the Ballroom.

At the far end a staff member turned the corner into the rear wing and disappeared. Everyone else was inside the banquet room.

He aimed. And fired.

CHAPTER 35

Rawlings never made it to the ballroom. His head exploded onto the wall next to the double doors. Like a lump of pudding he slid down the wall and sat on the carpet. Applause erupted from the awards ceremony in the next room.

Stone braced himself for people to come running out at the shot, but no one did. The presentation taking place on the other side of the doors was loud, the laughter riotous; the pop of the gun was drowned out. Sounded like Ben Carrey, *The Times*' humor columnist, was giving a speech. The man was as funny as a hernia, but his geriatric jokes went over well with the over-60 crowd, and the over-60 crowd voted so he wasn't going anywhere anytime soon.

A hand landed on Stone's shoulder and he spun with his finger on the trigger to find Hardwood standing there, his tuxedo impeccably clean. How the…?

"I like him better this way," Hardwood said, glancing down at Rawlings' body. "At least I don't have to hear him prattle on about elderly birthdays anymore."

"You know how many viewers he got from that shit?"

"Exactly my point. The man was annoying."

"I feel bad. We…we killed one of our own."

Hardwood was already opening Rawlings' shirt, exposing the man's chest. He plunged the knife into Rawlings' body and sawed at the ribcage.

"We have to get out of here," Stone said.

"The job's not finished. I'm not going anywhere until I leave my signature."

"What about my signature? What about the senator?"

"He's dead."

"I know. I mean, we never decided who gets credit."

Hardwood reached into Rawlings' chest cavity and began yanking the ribs apart. They snapped and crunched like someone eating celery. When the heart was exposed, he began cutting it out. "The Senator's heart is in my possession already. My quarry. I left his ribs in the toilet if you want them."

In his possession? Where! Stone was livid. The bastard had sent him after Rawlings so he could claim the prize. How could he have been so stupid?

Hardwood was the kind of opponent that would give no quarter to an enemy, no matter how much he could afford to do so. On some level it was admirable, just not the level where Stone was the dupe. The man didn't need both the senator and Rawlings, but he was going to take them because Stone hadn't done so himself. It was some kind of psychotic early bird theory, only he wasn't so much an early bird as he was a bully.

"That's not fair," Stone said. "I killed Mills."

"We both killed him."

"Well, I killed Rawlings, you can't deny that. You're being a hog."

"I suppose. But I didn't see you doing anything and we don't have time to dilly-dally. There's trace evidence all over the bathroom. I suggest you get in there and clean it up. Wipe the gun off and get rid of it. Do something with the glove as well."

"What? You're kidding me? There's no way to get all our trace evidence out of there."

"I didn't say 'our.' I have gloves on and I stood away from the blood splatter."

"There's some on your shirt. Right there. And there."

"I've got an overcoat at the table. I'm not worried about me. But you might want to wipe down anything you touched and change your own shirt. You've got blood all over it. Did you get scratched?"

Stone checked his hands but found no cuts. They were red, but it was just from the senator's struggling. Talk about luck.

Turning and running, he went back into the bathroom and looked at the carnage. Applause sounded again in the distance and he could only hope Carrey was delivering a riveting, hilarious speech that would drone on for another hour. How long before someone came out to use the bathroom?

On the floor, the senator and his bodyguard were sprawled out deader than Rawlings' career. Somehow, the walls had been coated in angular strokes of blood, like something out of the set design of *The Cabinet of Dr. Caligari*. The faucet was still running, so he turned it off. Peeking in the stall, he saw the senator's ribcage in the crapper just like Hardwood said it was. It was floating in the middle of Rawlings' last meal.

The bodyguard's heart was MIA, his chest cavity opened wide, his ribs gaping like jaws. Jesus, Hardwood worked fast. If Stone didn't get down to business, though, he'd end up taking credit for it in prison.

He had maybe one minute tops to get things done, not nearly enough time, but enough to give it the old frantic college try. First, he wiped off the gun and placed it in the bodyguard's hand. Next he wiped down the sink counters and faucets, smeared the footprints around to disguise all the shoe print sizes (Hardwood had already done most of it for him), and checked the senator for any of his own hairs. He didn't find any. He checked himself in the mirror for blood and cursed at how his white shirt had become a red shirt.

When he was done with that, he moved the senator over to the bodyguard. Opening the guard's mouth, he slipped the senator's nose inside, in between the dead man's teeth. "Sloppy job," he said, "but it'll have to do."

With all his might, he stepped down on the guard's head, snapping off the senator's nose. Reversing the process, he snapped off the guard's nose. Two noses sticking out of two mouths, but like he said, it'd have to do.

Just to be safe, he wrote CHEF WAS HERE in the blood on the wall. Hey, sometimes the obvious bird gets the worm.

Lastly, he ran the soles of his shoes under the sink to clean the blood off (he'd have to toss them out as soon as he got home), wiped off the faucet, dropped the latex glove in the toilet—assuming the dirty, bloody water would render it useless as evidence—wiped off the toilet lever, stepped carefully around the gore on the ground and left the bathroom. He made his way to the end of the hall and used the payphone to check his messages at work. A lame alibi but better than nothing.

Hardwood wasn't in the hall when he finished, but Rawlings was, and his heart was gone. What the hell was Hardwood doing with the hearts? More so, how the hell did someone walk around with three human hearts and not stick out like Kobe Bryant at a Klan rally?

Preservation would say Hardwood had left the building, was on a train heading home (the hearts in his pocket?), but then preservation didn't know Hardwood. In fact, it was because Hardwood didn't play the game like most killers that he was still around. The man knew, as Stone now knew, that the best way to avoid suspicion would involve being present in the audience when the bodies were found. He was probably sitting back at the table right now.

Stone slipped back through the double doors into the banquet room. It was still dark, only a single light above the stage spotlighting Carrey as he gave his speech. He was laughing at his own jokes, his glasses sliding down the bridge of his nose as he chuckled. Pushing them back up, he said, "And that's how I ended up in a jail cell with David Bowie and a forty pound uncooked turkey."

The audience stood up and clapped. Someone shouted, "You the man!"

Stone made his way back to his table and sat down next to Miss Muffin once more, noting how she smelled like a vineyard. Cheese leaned over and tapped him on the shoulder. "Where were you?"

"Outside. Making a phone call. What did I miss?"

"Something they should have outlawed with the Inquisition."

"Sounded funny."

"Be thankful you missed it. I think I need therapy now."

You need therapy anyway, Stone thought. "What's next?"

"Carrey is introducing anchor of the year. You've got something red on your shirt. Spill your wine?"

Stone picked up the napkin in front of him and dabbed at his shirt. Sure enough, it came away bloody. Very bloody. "Yeah, I've got a drinking problem." He chuckled. Cheese turned away unamused.

His overcoat was hanging on the chair and he slipped it on, pulled it closed across his chest, buttoned it up until the blood disappeared beneath it. "I'm cold," he said to Miss Muffin, who was throwing a questioning glance his way.

Onstage, Carrey continued: "Which brings me to the reason I'm up here. Every year we honor a person whose outstanding performance and dedication to the craft inspires us all. A person who influences change, who acts as a leader, and most importantly, goes above and beyond the call of duty to provide the best news coverage possible. There were a lot of candidates to choose from this year, and the competition was fierce. Actually they pay me to say that, right?"

Light laughter from the audience. Miff Muffin slapped her knee and drunkenly buried her head in Stone's back.

"I kid," Carrey said, pushing his glasses up again. "I kid. But seriously, in the end, we felt that there was one person who demonstrated these qualities like no one ever has. A person who puts themself on the front line for the news, a person who risked their life for the story, a person who, though not new to the anchor desk, showed us just what dedication means."

Scanning the room, Stone found Hardwood smirking at him from behind a glass of wine. He had his overcoat on and was practically out of his seat already, heading to the stage. Again, Stone marveled at his clean shirt—how the hell did he avoid all that blood? Where were the hearts?

"Ladies and gentleman," Carry said, "please welcome to the stage…"

Me or Hardwood, Stone thought, who is it going to be?

"…Tricia Mason!"

Stone's jaw dropped.

Mason? Were they serious? What had Mason done besides look spectacular in a low cut dress?

Cheese was on his feet in an instant, clapping like his team just won the World Series. The rest of the table jumped up as well, even Miss Muffin, who was still holding the butter knife Stone had given her before he went after the senator.

Across the room, Hardwood put his glass of wine down as his smile shrunk to a sneer. His chest began rising and falling with the breath of a man trying to control his anger. His balled up fist flexed next to his plate, as if squeezing an invisible stress doll. Couldn't blame him, Stone thought, he won every year. And for a man who just got put in his place by a woman from another state, he was taking it better than Stone thought he would.

Mason kissed Cheese, a long one that was hard enough to mash up their noses, and sauntered up to the stage. Whistles and whoops rang out in the crowd as she climbed the stairs, pulling up her dress a bit to reveal her thighs. Stone felt something in his pants bulge. He considered grabbing Miss Muffin and leaving and going home to play hide the salami, turn his anger into a night of demented sex, but he wanted to hear what Mason had to say.

He wanted to know why she deserved his award.

"Well, get a load of this, y'all," she said, looking out over the crowd. The cheering was still going strong, the other tables were standing up now. Mason was all smiles, her perfect white teeth reflecting the light. She waited for the crowd to sit, which took a minute, and then resumed.

"I just can't believe it. I want to thank so many people, but before I do, I just want to say that New York City is the greatest city in the world. The courageous and inspirational stories I hear every day move me in ways I never thought possible. When I first arrived here in the Big Apple, I realized I had my work cut out for me, but I also realized that, like my mother used to say, information comes from many sources, and it all moves the world. She also used to say a burnt plate of grits will unclog yer plumbing, but that's another story. I can't say I'm moving the world, but I'm trying my best. Every day when I come into the WWTF News offices, I say to myself, okay Mason, you're going to make someone's life better today. You're going to warn them about new drugs, about scams and dangers. You're going to show them what's going on overseas, and in the buildings of our leaders. You're going to keep them in the know, so they can make educated decisions about their life and protect themselves, and get ahead. You're going to be their muse.

"And why? Because this great country of ours was founded on the notion that we the people dictate its course of action. We the people are in charge. We are the shareholders and we must be told how our assets are being handled. The news does that. The news keeps it all in check. And I, as your anchor, will fight tooth and nail to bring it to y'all. Fair. Objective. Free of secrets."

The crowd cheered.

The funny thing about Mason's speech, other than it made Stone want to kill the judges on the press club board of directors, was that she was preaching a crock of shit to a room of professionals who spewed the same crock of shit to the public every night for a living. That's what was funny about it. What was scary about it was that he believed she meant it.

Hardwood was staring at his glass of wine, that sneer still visible under his furrowed brow. Other people in the room were looking at him as well, curious what type of reaction the reining champion would have. And maybe Hardwood realized that, because right then he looked up at Mason and clapped with the rest of the crowd. It was decorum, not respect.

Then someone screamed bloody murder.

It came from the hall.

CHAPTER 36.

Garcia was on the scene pretty quick, along with half of New York City's police force. You'd almost think that people would be shocked and want to go home. But this was a press event. Digital cameras came out of jacket pockets like guns from holsters in a free-for-all draw in the old west. Flashbulbs and the whirring mechanics of digital zoom lenses focusing on Rawlings' corpse filled the room. Reporters were on their cell phones in seconds flat, reporting back to their offices in hopes of breaking the story to the public first. (In truth, the websites would deliver this news before the papers or the television stations. It was getting harder and harder to get people to turn away from the Internet and back to print media. But mostly they all still watched the nightly news.) Around Stone, the shouted descriptions of Rawlings' hollowed-out chest damn near drowned out the myriad cracks, pops, and warbles of all the police radios.

"...The Chef got Rawlings..."

"...Casanova Carver at the ceremony..."

"...the Senator in the bathroom. Yes, Senator Mills!"

"There's blood everywhere! It's horrible! I've got great shots!"

Finally, Garcia grabbed a bullhorn and shouted over the crowd, "Okay! Enough! No more photos, no more cell phones, no more nothing! I don't care if you're press. Right now, this is a crime scene, and it's still illegal to tamper with it. Got me? I want everyone to back up and stay put. I'm also going to need your cameras."

Some people actually stopped talking photos.

But not many.

"You're kidding, right?" came a voice from the crowd.

"No I'm not," replied Garcia. "For all I know whoever did this is still here."

Someone else chimed in, "Oh please. The front and back doors are open. And so are the windows. We're in a hotel, not the Orient Express. What, are you going to go room to room and wake up every guest?"

"Maybe."

"Whoever did it is long gone and we've all got a story to report! We're not giving you our film!"

The crowd was becoming an angry mob. Garcia's shoulders fell.

Reluctantly, he said, "Okay. Damnit. But I'm roping this off so you need to move. I want everyone to go back in the ballroom. I need to talk to each and every one of you."

Which he did for about thirty minutes until the Secret Service and FBI showed up and began to fight and bicker about jurisdiction, ruining everything. Garcia threw his hands in the air and went to talk to the staff, who'd been rounded up in another room. Once it was evident everyone present had a reason to be there, Garcia, the Feds and the Secret Service took down names and released everyone.

***

Leaving, as Stone suspected, wasn't as easy as it sounded. Cheese, Duncan, Mason, Swift, Miss Muffin and he pushed past the crowd toward the front entrance, one part of a massive throng of reporters and media professionals willing to trample their grandmothers to get to this story. Cheese was on his phone with someone at the studio, telling them to get the writers on top of things. Miss Muffin was crying on Stone's arm, but he almost thought it was from the drugs more than the bloody body in the far hall. She was blubbering, "He was such a good man. He told me he liked my show. He liked my show!"

Mason came up beside them, said, "Stone, honey, are you taking note of who's here? Do you see anybody who looks out of sorts?"

"How do I know? There's a hell of a lot of people here. The Chef probably ducked out a back door or something. Hell, could've walked in and out the lobby door, it's not like they're monitored."

"It just gets my goat that it happened under our noses. We could have gotten exclusive footage of him and y'all together."

No she couldn't have, not unless he split himself down the middle with a big cleaver.

"The police have a list now," he replied, "we'll get it from them. Maybe."

Hardwood wasn't anywhere in the crowd, and for some reason that didn't sit well with Stone, perhaps because the man had been faking admiration for Mason last time he was around, and the faking was to cover up some serious anger. Stone also wondered if Hardwood still had the hearts? And what the investigators had asked him.

Where was he?

The cop at the door stopped him, put a hand out to prevent him walking through. "ID, and hurry it up...Oh, Mr. Stone, I didn't know it was you. I totally love your reports."

"Thank you."

"But I need your ID before I can let you out. We're double checking, just to be safe."

Stone reached inside his back pocket and pulled out his wallet. In doing so, his collar popped out and Miss Muffin, her head still on his shoulder, noticed a dollop of blood on it. "You've got wine on you."

The cop nodded "Yup, that's gonna stain. Use Tide, my wife swears by it."

Stone quickly pushed the collar back into his overcoat. Beads of sweat popped out on his forehead. His scrotum shriveled. Under his coat he could feel the brunt of the senator's blood sticking to his chest. So far no one had asked him to take his coat off, but the anticipation of it was making him crazy.

"It smelled funny," Miss Muffin said, her words thick and slow like syrup.

"You did that, honey," he told her, all the while smiling at the cop. "Remember? You had a bit much to drink tonight. Lots of excitement. You bumped my hand when I was taking a drink. Remember?" Say yes, bitch, or I'm killing you right here.

"I did? Um...oh yeah." She smiled, remembering something that never happened.

He said to the cop, "It's all right, I'll make sure she gets home in one piece."

The cop's eyes focused on Miss Muffin. "Looks like she had more than wine. Eyes are dilated like saucers. You have a little something on the side tonight, miss?"

She giggled, tried to stick her hand on Stone's shirt and play with the blood but he stopped her. Stupid doped-up cunt was going to get him the electric chair.

"Just get her home, okay? My chief sees me letting her go around like that he'll rip my nuts off and keep 'em in his office so he can kick 'em once a day."

"Sure thing. I appreciate it." Stone gave the cop his ID. The cop didn't even check to see if it was him before running it into a portable scanner. He'd seen similar scanners used by cigarette companies in bars, exchanging free packs of cigarettes for drivers' licenses so they could get demographic information and addresses to send their direct mail pieces to. "Hey, you think I could get a signature?" he asked.

"Anything for New York's finest." Stone signed the officer's notepad and left.

Outside, Cheese said, "Listen up. This is big news. We got three dead bodies killed under our noses, one of which is a senator, another a celebrity. This is the first time since Hardwood's son that these guys have whacked persons of notoriety, so this needs to be handled with care."

"We couldn't have asked for a better fiasco," Mason piped in. "We've already got The Chef in our pocket, and I think he's reaching out to us. This was a message delivered for the press. If we could just get a phone interview—"

"Unfortunately," Cheese said, "everybody and their grandmother is here, so there's no use running around like headless chickens tonight. I called ahead and woke up Dorey, and the mailroom is on alert for a letter. Stone, if you get something before we do, call me right away. I don't care how late it is. And everybody get in early to figure out how we're going to run with this."

Everyone agreed. Cheese and Mason left together in a black limo that Cheese had rented. Swift and his wife took a cab back to their midtown condo. Duncan—his date now arm-in-arm with one of the hotel's bartenders—looked at Stone like a lost puppy and finally gave up and walked home alone.

Which left Stone alone calling car service for himself and the methamphetamine princess when someone spun him around. He was expecting Hardwood but found Garcia in his face. "So let me figure this," the detective said. "You and Hardwood are here, your penpal killers show up and off the senator and Bud fucking Rawlings, and neither one of you gets a personal handshake from them? Don't you feel a tad bit insulted? Or is someone not telling me something?"

Pulling his overcoat tight around him, Stone replied. "Detective Garcia, if I'd seen him, I'd give you a description."

"I'd like to think that's true. I'd also like to think that the killers were in the crowd tonight and left some clues. You know how you get DNA from piss?"

"No. No I don't. Can you really?" Oh shit oh shit oh shit…did he remember to flush?

"I have no idea, I'm asking. I'll have to check with the lab boys once trace bags everything up. Be nice if you could huh?"

"It would help, I suppose."

"Yeah. Hi, I'm Detective Garcia." He offered his hand to Miss Muffin. Her jaw chewing on imaginary cud, she shook it forcefully.

"You want a Tic-Tac?" he asked her. She shook her head no and said, "I met Katie Couric tonight. Did you know she's really short and her face is kind of lopsided?"

"No shit?"

"You haven't seen Hardwood by any chance have you?" Stone asked the detective.

"Yeah, he wasn't too happy about your girl Mason winning some award. Seemed pretty unaffected by the gore in there. We had about five people throw up in the lobby, but Hardwood didn't even flinch, didn't even take notice really. Pretty jaded. Almost as if he couldn't care less. Kept mumbling something about Mason didn't deserve the award. What, she win best anchor or something? 'Cause that'd make sense on some level. You guys and your damn awards, I swear. I watch her every night myself, even though my wife calls her a whore, I watch her. I tell my wife, 'whatever, I got no beef with whores,' no offense miss."

Muffin giggled and hiccuped.

"Personally," Garcia went on, "I think he's getting old, you know? Hardwood that is. Old and filled with entitlement."

"Entitlement?"

"Yeah, entitlement. Sometimes I use the big words, too. Can't use them around my wife, she thinks I'm trying to put her down. You know, entitlement. Guy thinks because he's been on the air for twenty years he deserves a free hummer on every corner. That's a metaphor…which I guess is another big word."

"I get it."

"Anyway, like I asked him, I'll ask you again, you sure you didn't see your guy here? I know you don't know his face, but maybe some mannerism came across to you. I worked with nutballs before, and generally when they show up at an event like this, they let someone get a glimpse. It ups the danger in their little game. I have to think he knew you were here. You sure no one made contact with you?"

"Like I said, nothing."

"It's strange is all. Lot of strange things about this case. Lot of randomness about it."

Just then, a tightlipped man sporting a crew cut and a black suit came over and said something to Garcia. The large bulge under his jacket spoke of a shoulder-holstered weapon. He regarded Stone with as much interest as a tree does an airplane. Which was weird when he thought about it, because Senator Mills had mentioned the Feds had a lead, and he figured it was him.

Guess not.

The Fed and Garcia went back inside, pointing at spots on the floor and checking things on a notepad. People were still filing out of the building in a panic, but news vans were showing up with more media, balancing the flow of things.

Taking out his cell phone—which he couldn't look at now without seeing a dead bum's face—he dialed Hardwood's cell. Nobody picked up, so he left him a message. It was in the realm of: hey there, pal, you left before I could say bye, it was nice working with you, if you touch one hair on her head the whole deal is off, take care.

Hardwood would know to whom he was referring.

He accompanied Miss Muffin back to her place. She gave him head in the back of the car on the way home. It was the first sexual encounter he'd had in a long time, and it didn't last very long. Her mouth was warm and soft and she used her hand like a real pro. Part of him wanted to propose to her, and part of him wanted to cut her brain out and boil it for almost giving him away.

She passed out as they were climbing the stairs to her apartment, so he left her lying in the hallway—it was a fairly safe building and he had to think she'd slept in worse places. Some of the blood from his shirt was smeared on her forehead so he took off a sock, wiped the blood off with it, then stuffed it back in his pocket. Lying there, she looked like discarded garbage. For all the bullshit Carlie had given him as a wife, he couldn't imagine marrying this train wreck.

The night blurred into another car service ride and passing buildings. Too high to see and not interesting enough to try to anyway. The reality of the past couple hours seemed to grow out of his intestines and spread throughout his entire body, until finally he was laughing so hard tears were running down his face. The driver must have thought he was crazy.

The driver couldn't have been more right.

Later, after he'd burned the shirt in his bathtub, he lay in bed watching the sun rise. He felt invincible.

CHAPTER 37

You never saw so many front pages, websites and news reports with dead bodies on them. It was like the Kennedy assassination all over again. You couldn't wipe your ass without the toilet paper having the senator's or Bud Rawlings' bloated visages on it. People were going nuts over it. Half the country was crying, the other half was putting the dead men's faces on T-shirts and selling them on Ebay.

The news of Senator Mills' and Bud Rawlings' deaths brought out not just more Feds—some of them had to be accountants or computer science specialists, Stone figured, because it was doubtful the FBI could spare so many agents to one location—but vigilantes as well. Times Square was overrun with New York's Red Angels, and bounty hunters from as far north as Maine were practically camping in the streets, their trench coats covering their rifles only on a mechanical level. New York had become a police state overnight. Armed guards at the subway stops, snipers on rooftops, undercover agents in the bars and nightclubs.

The gangs were on the move as well, congregating in subway stations with switchblades and pistols, staring down anyone who looked like a troublemaker.

Which of course, in New York City, is everyone.

On every telephone pole and in every shop window hung the same wanted poster printed by the *New York Post*. It was a sketch of two silhouettes, one captioned the Casanova Carver and the other The Chef. The reward for each was $50,000. If you got them both, or provided information that led to both of their whereabouts, you got $150,000. Stone felt like Billy the Kid, honored and insulted all at once. Only $50,000! Who did a guy have to kill around here to get a decent price on his head?

True to his fashion, he wrote a letter, read it on air, and then gave it to the cops. It was the usual nonsense, and this time he included a cryptograph. Fact is, the cryptograph didn't translate to anything, which meant it would keep them busy for a long time. Cops didn't let that out to the press for whatever reason. He'd heard that the Feds had computers that could supposedly crack any code, and he wondered if they'd crack something unintended out of his, something like: THE BLUE BEETLE WEARS FLIP-FLOPS.

People might go nuts buying flip-flops and painting beetles blue.

Stone's office phone didn't stop ringing for days. It rang so incessantly he just unplugged it and turned off his cell. Cheese got wise to the demands for interviews and hired another media liaison—they already had one, Terry Campbell, who got paid to be the in-between on most interview requests for the anchors, but find an anchor who doesn't want to deal with their own press and you'll see a media liaison who doesn't spend their day bored and playing solitaire at their computer. Now they had two of them trying to schedule Stone for interviews with press outlets across the country. He told them only to book him if Hardwood got booked somewhere.

Hardwood never touched Mason after all, at least not yet, and turned up on air the morning after the awards with his own version of the press awards massacre. Stone TiVo'd it.

After the eleven o'clock news a couple days later, he skipped out on O'Halloran's—and murder—and watched it again. Hardwood was up to something, Stone just couldn't figure what.

Hardwood started the report looking very solemn. He was clean shaven, his suit impeccably pressed, a new Rolex watch twinkling as he gesticulated. A small cardboard box sat in front of him. Props? "This morning I received an ominous parcel from persons unknown. Attached to the box was this note," he said, holding up the letter. "I've been instructed not to open the parcel except live on air, lest hostages in the Casanova Carver's possession meet a gruesome end. I've been instructed not to inform the authorities of the package until it has been opened."

His hands trembled as he undid the string around the brown paper lunch bag. He looked genuinely scared, even breaking a sweat. Reaching inside, he pulled out another package wrapped in wax paper, taped with common masking tape. Peeling that off, he unfolded the wax paper to reveal yet another bit of taped-up wax paper. Only this wax paper had brown stains all over it, and from the way Hardwood wrinkled up his nose, it didn't smell like roses.

He paused. A good pause-face, determined and introspective and concerned all at once. Must have taken him days to master it, and again, Stone knew why he'd been the city's lead anchor for so long.

"Concerned viewers," he said into the camera, "I apologize for what you're about to see. Were it not for the lives of unverified hostages, the package before me would not be seen by the public. Children should leave the room."

Then, on live television, he pulled two human hearts out of the wax paper and set them on the anchor desk in front of him. One was Rawlings', the other was Senator Mill's.

Genius. Absolute fucking genius.

Naturally, every TV set in the city belonged to him that day.

"What's he doing, Chauncey? Huh? What's he doing?"

Chauncey got up and went to his dog bowl, completely misunderstanding what his master was asking him. Like most dogs, his translator was stuck on food-ese.

What *was* Hardwood doing? Playing with Bud Rawlings heart on live television, sending himself evidence the day after a big murder. Was he brazen or desperate?

More importantly, what were the cops doing? Stone hadn't heard from Garcia since the night of the awards, and while that made him happy on one level, it scared the shit out of him on another.

He hadn't heard from Hardwood either, but that was probably for the better. The less contact they had right now the better.

"Fuck it," he said to the empty living room.

The days' newspapers were stacked on the counter in the kitchen, some of which he hadn't looked at yet, so he got up and poured Chauncey some food and grabbed them. Leafing through them, he saw The Chef mentioned on just about every front page. Profilers from here to Timbuktu were spouting theories about the killers.

According to a forensic psychologist from Langley, The Chef was angry at his father, whom he'd been molested by. A professor of Criminology in San Diego said the killers were impotent and wet their beds when they were young. A radio host in Chicago, who wrote a book on The Son of Sam, said Stone had a fetish for cartoons. And a profiler with the NYPD said The Casanova Carver was afraid of death, and the Chef was looking for acceptance from someone who didn't love him.

Stone stared at that last sentence for a long time. Because, somewhere down deep, he realized it may have been right. Was he looking for someone's acceptance? The public's? Carlie's? Mason's? Was Hardwood also trying to ensure his place in history before he passed?

It was a scary thought.

To get his mind off it all, he figured he'd surf the net and maybe look at some porn. Miss Muffin's gift to him was still fresh in his mind and his libido was in overdrive. He clicked the computer's mouse to bring it out of sleep mode, and double clicked the Internet Explorer icon. As it was loading, his email dinged, so he opened the program. There was nothing but junk mail. He marveled at the amount of spam he received on a daily basis.

"Look at this shit," he said. Chauncey looked up from his bowl and then went back to eating. "Add ten inches to your penis. Stay harder with free pharmaceuticals. You too can last longer in bed. Why is it that everyone assumes I have problems with my dick?"

If the profilers had anything to say about it, he should be jumping at the chance to stay hard for twelve hours.

He deleted it all and surfed the net for free porn, visiting a few sites that he'd been to before. Your average girl-on-girl action and the like. He got an erection for a few minutes, but when Chauncey came over and rubbed against his knee, he went limp as a wet noodle.

"Get outta here," he told the dog. With downcast eyes, Chauncey slinked away to the kitchen again.

Bored with the lesbo sites, he started clicking on random links. Man, he thought, there's some weird shit on the Internet. People had fetishes he couldn't believe, and not just your average deviant intrigues like bestiality and tranny porn, but some truly spaced-out shit. He followed one link to a site called Ass Cream Sunday, which had women sticking scoops of ice cream up their anuses and then crapping them out into cones and eating them. Another one he found, Blow Dart Jobs, had women shooting tiny darts into guy's penises. And the guys got hard from it!

After looking at all this debauchery—his sexual urges long since deflated at the sight of such weirdness—he began to understand why these sites existed. It was no different than Hardwood and himself; it was all ratings. Because even if you didn't get off by what you were seeing—and seriously, if anyone was getting off from looking at Peeonmycheerios.com they probably were a serial killer—even if you didn't get off, you couldn't help but look. Just like looking at a car crash or a murder scene. The websites knew this, and so to keep people coming back, they had to keep upping the ante. If one site had girls licking watermelons, the next had them shoving them up their asses. It was all business in the end, no pun intended. Dollars, ratings, the same old song and dance.

He was getting tired at this point, driven more by curiosity than sexual urges. Maybe one more site.

"Holy shit," he said, clicking on Stoogegirls.com, which showed naked women getting fucked by men who looked like the Three Stooges. "Miss Muffin? Where're your morals?" Guess it was true what they said about some girls doing anything to get ahead in show biz, because in front of him a younger Miss Muffin was getting sodomized by two Curly look-alikes.

Suddenly, he was horny again.

He went to the bathroom, did his best Shemp impression, and then went to bed.

CHAPTER 38

Garcia stared at the report on his desk again, flipped through the pictures of the three dead bodies from the press club awards. It didn't make any fucking sense. Why would the killers off two prominent persons and not make contact with their messengers? Not even give them a glimpse? If you had balls enough to pull off a murder spree like that, you had balls enough to show your face to the press, even if you were wearing a disguise.

The two killers were so far outside the box it was like they had no idea what they were doing.

Then there were Hardwood and Stone, who had acted kind of relaxed for two guys finding out their serial-killing buddies were in the building working together. They should have scanned the crowd for a glimpse of them, they should have been afraid, they should have cared a whole lot more.

Working together. There was that too. Killers didn't work together, especially not two guys trying to outdo each other. If these guys were engaged in some kind of competition, why would they suddenly go Dutch on the most prominent slaying of their careers?

Unless they didn't know they were each going to be there. But then why not kill each other? Why not take out the competition? Were they friends of some sort?

It didn't make any sense.

"Garcia."

He looked up from the picture of a bloodied Bud Rawlings, found George Thompson from forensics standing near his desk. "George, you lost?"

"Figured I'd deliver this in person. Feds are reading all the emails, anyway, and I don't need to give them an excuse to patronize us." He tossed an envelope on Garcia's desk

"Must be good news." He opened the envelope and took out the paper inside, read it over, and sighed. "Yup, real good news." The sarcasm in his voice was evident. "Shit. This is getting tiring."

"We can't make heads or tails out of all the bloody footprints in the hall outside the bathroom. Too many people stomped through it looking at the bodies. Not to mention the vomit from the ones who couldn't handle it obscured a lot of it. We've got hairs from at least thirty different people all over the stalls and sink. Hell, it was a bathroom in a hotel, anyone could have used it. No prints on the soap dish. Everything was wiped down. Sorry, Ramon, but we got nothing from the scene. Too many people, and it's a public place so anyone could say they were in there at some point."

Garcia hung his head, ran his hands through his thinning hair.

"You want my advice, Garcia?"

"I'll take what you can give me."

"Back before police work got so scientific, there was a thing called gut. My dad was a cop, my grandfather was a cop, they both told me about going with my gut. I never put much stock in it while I was getting my chemical engineering degree, because you can't use your gut to measure hydrogen bonds. But you know what, both my dad and my grandfather had collars on some bad dudes, and they used their guts to find them. So, if you've got one, now would be the time to use it."

"Yeah, George, I'm trying. And I'm not liking what it's telling me."

CHAPTER 39

Duncan Willis rapped on Stone's office door, entered before he was told to. "Cheese wants you to cover Rawlings' funeral."

Stone closed the *Washington Times* article he was reading online. The Chef and Casanova Carver were now on the FBI's top ten most wanted list, as numbers 3 and 4 (Hardwood being 3, which was infuriating). Bin Laden and another terrorist had the top spots. The heat was coming on thick now, with the president ordering a special forensics task force into New York City to help the police dig something out of all the evidence that had been collected. It was a political thing: catch the killers, get re-elected.

Stone had been chewing that over all morning. In a way, he felt used.

The scene in the hotel bathroom didn't seem like such a bold move anymore. It was one thing that New York's finest hadn't found any evidence linking him to anything, but as soon as the top scientists in the country arrived, it might be a whole different story.

He waved Duncan away. "Why don't you cover it? I'm busy."

"You don't look busy. You look like shit but you don't look busy. Cheese wants you on it. I was you, I'd get going."

"You're not me. I don't jump when Cheese tells me to."

"It's called a work ethic."

"It's called sucking dick."

"I'm reliable. Call it what you will, I'm integral to this station and you hate it. I see how you look at Mason. It must kill you that she relies on me."

"Oh yeah? What has Mason asked you to do lately besides get her a coffee? Face it, Duncan, you're a twerp. A prick. And a stupid prick at that. Here I am telling you to go take care of the taping on your own, show some initiative at the funeral of the year, because frankly I'm exhausted, and you're giving me shit. Fine, lose out. I'll go."

The words sank into Duncan, who stood there trying to find the trap in it all. It kind of made Stone feel good to watch Duncan squirm—he could see why it was so appealing to Cheese. It was a cheap way to lift your own ego.

"Will you tell Cheese?" Duncan asked.

"I said forget it. I'm going."

"But you just said—"

"You missed out. Too bad." Yes, it really was kind of fun to pick on the guy. "If you're done, go get me a coffee."

"Get your own, dickhead. The funeral is at three o'clock. The press has to stay back behind the police tape, but you can bring a camera crew. Do me a favor and walk in front of a bus on your way there."

Duncan spun on his heels and left the office. When he'd made it halfway down the hall Stone heard him yell at an intern to "Get that prick Stone a coffee."

When he was sure he was alone, Stone logged back on to the Internet and looked for more stories about the killings at the hotel. What he found was a breaking news story of a copycat killer in California. Someone who was calling himself the So Cal Cleaver had just attacked CNN's Wes Anderson at a hotel in Los Angeles. Great, thought Stone, here we go again.

At least it would deter some of the FBI; they were required to check out every lead that sounded credible.

Anderson was apparently okay, and told the press he'd have a report within the hour. That was going to be a ratings war with the Rawlings funeral. Anderson was good. Very good.

The phone's intercom beeped. "Stone, honey, are you ready to go?" It was Mason.

"You coming, too?"

"Sugar, everybody's going. It's going to be cutting into programming on a national level. I hope you shaved."

"My face?"

"Don't be fresh. Meet me at the van in ten minutes."

*

A laundry list of celebrities was scheduled to speak at the funeral, including Tom Cruise, Kevin Costner, and former mayor Rudolph Giuliani. Hardwood wasn't interested in hearing any of them talk, he was more concerned with the amount of police presence and whether or not Senator Mills' story about knowing who the killers were was true or not.

More than likely not, he thought, though there was that one cop, Garcia, who was a little hard to read. He still had no idea what had become of the emails the man had copied. Were they being traced? Could they be traced? His black market contact had assured him the Blackberry he was using to send the messages would register an IP address in an entirely different state, and once the cops figured that out, they'd be led on a wild goose chase to several other locations. The service provider was undetectable. Sometimes you had to give it to bored kids.

News vans were pulling in all around the cemetery where Rawlings was to be commemorated. The crowd was thickening by the minute, and pretty soon he'd be elbow to elbow with the other attendees.

He'd gotten here early to avoid the rush and get a good camera angle, only to discover he was about the one-hundredth reporter to arrive. The vans were parked everywhere. Boomer would probably give him hell for not having the best shot, but not too much, not after the spike they'd had showing Rawlings' heart on television.

Which reminded him: Garcia had taken the hearts and said he'd be in touch. But he hadn't called yet. What did that mean?

A van passed close by and beeped, trying to squeeze its way into the maze of other vehicles. It had the letters WWTF painted on the side, which meant it was either Stone or Mason. At least he'd beaten them here—call it a minor victory. The van continued around to the far side of the crowd and was swallowed by the sea of people.

"I need to get a wide shot," the cameraman said, fiddling with his camera's settings. "Can you give me some lens for a minute?"

Hardwood faced the camera and put the microphone up to his mouth. "How's this?"

"Back up a bit, I want to get the statue in the shot."

Hardwood obeyed, taking a step backward toward the small statue of the late morning show host. It had been sculpted a couple of years ago by a fan of the show, but had remained in a closet on the set until now. The sculptor himself had died in a tragic bumper car accident at a fair up north.

"There's good," the cameraman said. "Perfect. Tape that spot."

"It's grass."

"Well, kick a divot out or something. I gotta take a quick shit. Gimme five minutes."

"Splendid," Hardwood replied, "I shall count the seconds until your aromatic return."

"No worries, first speaker don't go on till five after three. If it takes too long I'll rush it."

"Please, not on my account."

The cameraman took off at a sprint, somehow running with his legs together, leaving Hardwood alone among the throng of onlookers.

Not that he was alone, to be sure. Aside from the legions of fans who had taken the day off work to attend, the police and FBI were quite apparent at various intervals, dressed in what they thought was inconspicuous common-folk garb, but in fact made them stand out like sore thumbs. Hardwood wasn't sure who they were trying to fool. Most Rastafarians didn't wear WHAT WOULD JESUS DO T-shirts. Most Yankees fans didn't wear cowboy boots. And he was pretty sure AVOID THE NOID shirts were long out of style.

They covered every entrance to the funeral, sat in cars along the edge of the park, slept on benches, and walked about with dogs like regular Joes out for a stroll.

The crowd noticed them too, and rubbernecked as they walked by, deducing in seconds what their presence meant. The funeral itself would without a doubt take a back seat to the new need to scope out every attendee, file away the ones with shifty eyes for later interrogation. How many innocent people would be reported to the police as suspicious?

Anyone without celebrity, for sure.

What made it worse was that the cops, nonchalant as they were attempting to be, were clearly on edge; they refused to go too far from the procession, expecting something to happen right here at the grave sight, possibly anticipating an attack of some sort. Judging by the way their hands rested on their hips, the vast majority of them had guns under their waistbands.

A small woman in a blue coat—too young to be a bag lady—was practically spinning in circles. Nearby, a white-haired man scanned the fields like a robot with a broken head servo—left, right, left, right, forward, behind, now repeat. The bulge under his jacket spoke of something more than a standard issue glock, maybe one of those rubber bullet rifles.

"The world has gone bat shit, and I'm to blame," he whispered to himself.

Two young men cut a path nearby, confirming his suspicions: "You hear they have sharp shooters here, man?"

"I know. Someone said that The Chef and Casanova Carver are gonna be here. I heard they're even bringing friends."

"Yeah, like a whole shitload of killers are gonna wipe out the crowd. This is going to be insane."

"Shit. Maybe we should just go home and watch this on TV. This is like level red kind of shit."

The two men continued into the crowd, their conversation drowned out by the susurration of the mob. Their paranoia resonated with Hardwood for several minutes, long enough to not even realize that his cameraman had returned.

"Yo, Doug, you ready to do this? I think the first speaker's coming up."

Hardwood smiled. "Change of plans, Gus. Get a shot of the crowd instead, and start taping."

"But Boomer said—"

"Forget what that jackass said. I'm going to give you a much better report. Are we rolling?"

The cameraman checked a light on the power pack, looked through the lens, said, "Yeah, we're going, do your thing."

Looking into the lens as if he were looking into God's own eyes, Hardwood began: "New York City mourns a living legend today, but few eyes are on the ceremony. Most of them are watching the crowd and surrounding locales for signs of the killers. Police presence has been stepped up and a sense of anticipation hangs in the air. Is the crowd here in more danger than they think? Do the police know something we don't? As one attendee put it, 'A simple homemade bomb would be all that's necessary to put an end to Rawlings' funeral, and start an even larger one.' The question on everyone's mind today is not when will the killers strike again, but where. And how big?"

CHAPTER 40

When viewers saw Hardwood's report they stopped giving a shit about what anyone had to say about Rawlings. All they wanted to know was how credible the threat of a large-scale attack from these killers was. Which immediately set Stone's mind racing, wondering how serious Hardwood was about making it all come true.

Mass attack? He wouldn't dare. Would he?

The American public had calmed down quite a bit since the attacks of September 11th. They still got nosy when boarding a plane, profiling anyone that looked Middle Eastern, but for the most part there wasn't anything near the level of fear in the days following that tragic event. And what those days had created, for the media especially, was the notion that the public, when faced with the possibility of a threat, would stay glued to the tube for an indefinite amount of time in an effort to gain a clue about where not to go. The media, of course, hadn't the slightest notion of where such attacks would occur, and though they filled their screens with talking heads supposedly in tune with terrorist manifestoes, the truth was no one had a crystal ball that could foretell the future. And so the public continued to watch and watch and watch, hoping and praying that the next talking head would be the one with the answers.

"How the hell did you not catch on to this?" Cheese yelled, slamming his fist down on the meeting room table. Stone thought he even saw Mason jump a bit. Duncan, who was at the table taking notes, dropped his eyes to his lap in an effort to avoid being singled out for any whipping-boy purposes. "You realize they've been playing that damn paranoid report over and over, and now the other stations are latching on to it, and all of 'em have got numbers better than us. Get out there and find me some people to either refute or corroborate this bullshit or I swear I'm going to have all your asses replaced."

Mason grabbed Stone after the meeting ended and asked if he could speak to her in her office. While he wanted nothing more than to be alone with her in the dark confines of her inner sanctum, he was more interested in what the hell Hardwood had planned. Respectfully declining her offer, he ducked out for a quick lunch and a phone call to the Casanova Carver. Either Hardwood had Stone's number programmed and didn't want to talk, or he was busy. Stone was banking on the former.

This concerned him, as much as the phone call he received on the way back to the office. It was Carlie, and she was pissed off something fierce.

"Hey, babe," he said. "Run out of pink bunnies?"

"You sonofabitch."

"What?"

"What do you mean 'what'?" she said.

"I mean 'what?' It's an interrogative statement. Also a famous catch phrase of one Vinny Barbarino. Remember, we used to watch *Welcome Back Carter* together, until you turned into a slu—"

"Go ahead and say it, I'm recording this conversation for my lawyer."

"Hi, Tom. Your client is a slut. Lemme spell it. S.L.U.T. Also known as a whore, a cumdumpster, a—"

"You gave him my address!"

"Who, your lawyer? Doesn't he have it?"

"Not my Lawyer, you fucking retard, the Casanova Carver! Or the Chef! One of 'em!"

Stone's stomach did a backflip as he walked back into the office, saw Mason waving him over. He waved back that he was busy, one of those, yeah-I-see-you-gimme-ten-minutes kind of waves. She looked as pissed as Carlie sounded, but he wasn't about to put a news segment before this, even if the news segment had everything to do with what Carlie was saying.

"Calm down," he told her, shutting the door of his office, turning away from Mason's vexed glare. "What are you talking about?"

"What am I talking about!? What am I talking about!?"

"Are you repeating this for the court or are you just being difficult? Yes, what are you talking about? Why the hell would I give one of these nutballs your address? Do you think I'm even in contact with them?"

There was a strong huff on the other end, and Stone was pretty sure he heard a man's voice in the background saying something about punching his lights out. Another vapid male model, no doubt. "I woke up last night and there was a man in my apartment, Wesley, and it wasn't Guillermo."

"Guillermo? Do you mail order them from Spain or something?"

"Shut up and listen, dick. I woke up and there was a man here standing over my bed with a knife. He said he was doing you a favor."

Ok, Stone thought, trying to relax, who the hell would do or say that? A copy cat? Someone looking for attention? Or would

Hardwood be so stupid as to go after his estranged wife? What would he gain from it? He had to know that Stone would come after him, that their little deal would be off. It had to be some kind of game, just like the report from Rawlings' funeral. He was up to something but Stone had no idea what.

"Ok, chill out," he said, "I'll call the cops and—"

"I already called them."

"And what did they say?"

"They said they were coming to see you."

Shit. Was she serious? How long ago had she called? Did he have time to get out of the office? "I'll call you back."

He threw open the door and walked into a wall of Garcia. Detective Garcia, that is, who was in the midst of knocking. Instead of rapping on the door, he held up his hand, showed the tiny white pellet that lay in the center of it like a baby tooth. "Tic-Tac?"

"No, thanks. I was just...um...Can I help you?"

Past the detective's shoulder, Stone could see Mason grimacing, as if she sympathized with his predicament. Problem was, he didn't really know what his predicament was, only that Hardwood had gotten any and all attention off himself and on to him—which in Stone's book constituted a near break of the rules—and now the cops were here.

Bingo. There you go. Hardwood wants Garcia focused on me. Why?

"Got a call from your wife," Garcia said, stepping into the office.

"Yeah, she just called me too."

"She's a pleasant woman. Got a real flare with curse words. Can't see why you divorced her."

"Something to do with the CDC and her vagina. I'm foggy on the details."

"You don't say. Well, that would explain the men I met at her place. She told me they were furniture movers."

Men? Plural?

"She told you about her intruder?" Garcia continued.

"Yeah. Said something about a man with a knife? But you know, she's prone to exaggeration so…Was there a knife?"

"Knife. Sure. Had a gun, too. Said you sent him there. Which I don't buy for a second because that would just be stupid. Right? Still, if this is our guy—one of our guys anyway—and he's showing up at your wife's place—"

"Ex-wife."

"Right. The whole CDC thing. You sure you don't want a Tic-Tac?"

"What flavor are they?"

He took the box out of his jacket pocket and read the label. "Winterfresh. Whatever that means. Think it just means mint with some spice added. You gotta look past the ruse with these companies. They cover things up with fancy words and misdirection, but it's all so obvious once you know what to look for. Mint. You want?"

"No. I'm good."

"Where were we?"

"My wife was about to be killed."

"Right, on your instructions. But like I said, that's gotta be BS. So I just figured I'd run down here and get your story and ask, again, do you want protection?"

"You mean I'm not being followed already?"

"We're not the CIA. So do you?"

Stone shook his head, letting it sink in how out of hand this all was. Hardwood was taking their war into personal territory but for what reason he didn't know. Hardwood's latest report had been so high in the ratings everybody else's jobs were on the line. He had to know this. So why was he so power hungry?

"I also wanted to know if you got any letters about the bomb?"

"Bomb?!" Stone heart stopped doing backflips, starting turning itself inside out. "What bomb? What the hell are we talking about? Carlie has a bomb?! Where'd she get—"

Mason barged in the room at this point, pushed her way passed Garcia and brought him up to speed. "Stone, relax. That's what I wanted to talk to you about. Port Authority just found a bomb on the N Train. It was in a paper bag, with a note saying it was courtesy of the Casanova Carver. It didn't go off but it had two hours left on the timer. The trains are being shut down until the cops can search all the trains and tunnels. Just came in on the wire about forty five minutes ago, while you were out."

At this point, several things went through Stone's mind. The first was that Hardwood was living up to his report. The second was that he never intended the bomb to go off; he just wanted to generate a scare so that people would be glued to the news when he said he had a letter about it all. The third was that, without a doubt, he was going to let one detonate soon enough.

And the fourth was: winterfresh.

More specifically, misdirection.

With the cops running around the subway tunnels, Hardwood could be elsewhere doing God knew what. And if he was planning on blowing something up, it wasn't going to be the subway. It was going to be something else, something big and devastating.

Looking back at Garcia, Stone just sort of shot him a blank look, said, "Don't know anything about it. Don't know about any of this, in fact. I haven't heard from The Chef in days, as you know."

"Well, we haven't gotten a letter, if that's what you mean. Doesn't mean you don't have one somewhere and haven't shown it to me yet."

"But I haven't." Then to Mason, "Are we running with this?"

She nodded. "Sure thing, hon. Cheese sent a reporter out to get footage and feedback. It's leading off the nightly segment and we're doing cut-ins at eight o'clock. That's what I wanted to talk to y'all about. This is going to get real big real fast, and we need an edge."

"You still didn't answer about getting protection," Garcia said.

"No. I'm fine."

"Well, we're getting it for your wife. And we'll have officers staked out around her place. If you want to see her give me a call and I'll tell the boys you're coming."

"Why, am I a suspect?"

"That's a harsh word. But we have to take it seriously that you might have told this guy to pay a visit to your wife. So we're just being cautious."

He turned to Mason, his eyes wide. "They think I'm a suspect!"

"Relax, sug. If you are, that'll get us another twenty points at least."

"I know, but it still isn't funny! I didn't try to kill my wife! Twenty points? You really think it'll get us twenty?"

Garcia took out a small notebook, flipped it open and said, "Because the bomb falls under the guise of terrorism, the Feds are handling it. We're assisting, but they have the lead. I'm sure you know they're already in town, driving me nuts, but if you find anything out or have anything you want to tell us, Special Agent Mark Tucker can be reached at this number." He tore the page out of the notebook and handed it to Stone. "Or you can call me, which is what I'd prefer. I'll be in touch, okay? In the meantime, maybe stay at a friend's place or something."

He turned to leave, then stopped himself and came back. "Oh yeah, that earring we found…Remember that?"

"The one my dog shit out?"

"That's the one. I went back to your neighbor's apartment the other day because she was supposed to dig up a receipt for me to prove it was hers. She doesn't have one that matches, but she swears she bought it at Macy's. I got so busy it slipped my mind. My wife says I've got early Alzheimer's, but if you heard the crap she goes on about you'd block it all out too. Anyway, your neighbor, she's nutty as a loon so who knows if she keeps track of her expenses or not. She never found a match for the one I showed her. But it still matches the one from the cabbie. Remember him? Seems so long ago now."

"Yeah yeah yeah, I remember. What's your point?"

"Just that it's a match."

"So? Two people can't have the same pair?"

"Of course. Kind of leads us to a dead end, but we'll keep it just in case. Anyway, your neighbor—I'd stay away from her. She's got it out for you, and her memory is gone. For real gone. She swore she saw you leaving your apartment a couple times at three in the morning around the time of some of these murders. She stays up late to watch TV, says she likes infomercials, which proves she's nuts because who likes infomercials?"

Duncan poked his head in, told Mason Cheese wanted to see her, then added, "I like the one with the super disco hits of the 70s," and left.

Garcia popped another Tic-Tac in his mouth, shook his head. "My wife likes that one too. She's got this thing for Sly and the Family Stone. Me, I like Tito Puente. But back to my point. Mrs. Davis snoops around the halls and listens through people's doors when she doesn't feel like watching the infomercials. Said she saw you plain as day take a late night stroll with your gym bag the night the cabbie died."

Heartbeat commencing death roll. "Like you said," Stone replied, "she has it out for me. Not that it would be so strange, what with the hours I keep. I don't get to bed sometimes until four or five in the morning. Lots of places open all night around my apartment."

"I know. That's what I told her. Anyway, thought that if you knew she was watching, others could be too, and you'd take my plea for protection a little more serious. See you later."

After Garcia strolled out of the office, Stone ran to the desk and pulled out his flask. Normally he wouldn't let anyone see him take a pull off it—tabloids have men hiding in the walls just biding time until something like this occurs—but Mason and *The Post* seeing where he kept his booze was the least of his worries. Don't get things wrong, he still wanted to lick her body like a giant Pudding Pop, but the drink was such a requisite right then it was worth the risk. He slammed the flask down, breathed out a wall of alcohol, and then put it back in the desk drawer.

"Relax, sugar, you'll knock yourself out before we can go on air. We need to get writing about this bomb."

"Okay. Okay. But give me five minutes first. I'll be right out."

As soon as she pulled the door closed he dialed Hardwood. There was no answer.

Where the hell was the guy? Was Hardwood avoiding him or was he truly out somewhere? The Feds had to be keeping tabs on him. In fact, Stone was pretty sure they were keeping tabs on him now.

He had to talk to him, and the sooner the better for everyone involved. Especially Carlie, who, despite his constant yearning for her gruesome death, was worth more to him alive than dead, at least in terms of providing hours of angst-ridden entertainment. Hell, who was he kidding, Carlie still had some damn death grip on his insides. It wasn't that he didn't want to split her head open and swim in her brains, but a larger part just wanted back everything he'd lost.

But that was another train of thought. Right now, he needed to find out where Hardwood was.

Come midnight, he had a hunch.

CHAPTER 41

The pub was noisy, full of people in scarves and heavy jackets, people who lived in the neighborhood and people who were curious about where Roland Stone and Doug Hardwood were known to grab a drink.

Everyone was chattering about the bomb scare, and when they saw Stone enter they went nuts asking questions. He waved them all off and told them he had nothing new to report. He couldn't believe people were even out, but then New York City wasn't the type of town to take such threats lying down.

Pat hollered a hearty hello at him, and made sure everybody knew who he was just in case they missed him. "Roland Stone, everybody! The king o' the quaff, his majesty o' the media, and a right fine lad if I do say so myself. Aye, what'll it be, me boy? Bushmills on the rocks?"

All eyes in the crowd were on Stone as he took a seat at the bar. The compliments from the surrounding patrons made it hard to think or order; he spent more time thanking people than doing anything else.

"Fucking-A, Pat, the crowd's alive tonight. Didn't they hear about the bomb?"

"Aye, I saw you on the news, sitting right next to that fine piece of ass, talking about no imminent threat. Knew you'd be in tonight, like you always are after a major report. I told everyone you'd be here too, and look, you're here."

"You tell people I'm coming in?"

"Come now, you're not upset are you? It's business is all, you know that."

"I'm not mad, in fact I find it flattering. Kind of an ego boost."

"Aye, you're Roland Stone now, whether you like it or not."

Stone was considering this when the din of excited voices suddenly died out, and he saw Pat's eye begin to trace the trajectory of someone walking to the bar. If Stone were in Vegas, he'd bet the bank on who was about to sit next to him. As it was, he smelled the lingering odor of Nat Sherman cigarettes before Hardwood pulled out the barstool.

"Stone."

"Hardwood, what the hell were you doing at my wife's?"

"Perplexing inquiry. I have no idea what you're referring to."

"Bullshit!"

"Now boys," said Pat, "don't tell me you're still at each other's throats?"

"Not at all. In fact, I need to speak to you, Stone." Hardwood glared at Pat, who was leaning over the bar watching intently. "Alone, please."

"Yeah, good, I need to speak to you, too," Stone replied.

Pat took the hint and drifted over to the television, changed the channel to the *Tonight Show*. Leno was doing headlines, but when the show cut to the band, Branford was nowhere in sight.

"Not here," replied Hardwood. "Somewhere private, somewhere there are no stray ears. Care to go for a walk?"

"Yeah. Kind of. It's cold out and I didn't bring my heavy coat."

"It'll be short. I'll buy you a drink when we get back."

The last thing Stone wanted to do was go for a walk, but then he definitely wanted answers and Hardwood sure wasn't going to provide them in here. "Fine, but let's make it quick."

Outside, breath plumed in front of them as they walked toward the West Side Highway, Hardwood once again smoking his customary Nat Sherman cigarettes. Ten minutes and several avenues passed, which was far longer and farther than Stone was comfortable with. He didn't even realize they were at Tenth Ave until he saw the sign above him.

"Are we on a field trip or something?" he asked. "What'd you have to talk about? I'm fucking freezing and you'd better have a goddamn good answer for both that bomb and being at Carlie's."

"Okay, I was there. I admit. But trust me, I had no intention of hurting her. This detective Garcia has been asking questions about my son and I needed to divert his attention."

"To me?"

"Remember Gertrude's? You said you'd owe me one."

"But not that! What did happen to your son, anyway? Was it really you? That's pretty fucking sick."

"I did him a favor. He hated me, so I broke off our relationship."

"You know what, forget it. The less I know the better. But don't touch Carlie. I swear—"

Hardwood put his hand up, palm out, stopped just short of saying whoa horsey. "She's in no harm. On my word."

"And Mason?"

Hardwood chose to remain silent.

"I saw the way you looked at her at the awards."

"I admit I was frustrated. But my plans have changed. I have no intention of harming your friends."

"Well, that makes me feel a hell of a lot better. You're clearly a beacon of benevolence in what some consider a sordid and dangerous town."

They kept walking.

"Sarcasm noted, but I wanted to talk about you, not your ex-wife or Mason."

"What about me?"

For a moment Hardwood sighed, as if collecting his thoughts, then looked at Stone with the eyes of a doctor about to reveal news of a terminal illness to a patient. "The people you killed…do you regret it?"

"Regret it? What? This is what you want to talk about?"

"Yes."

"This is a dog eat dog town, Hardwood. What's to regret? I have fame, fortune, even a modicum of pride. So I sold my soul to eternal damnation. Who cares? Souls are overrated. No, I don't regret it. What's this got to do with—"

"Neither do I."

"Why are we talking about this? It isn't wise—"

The bay swam into view at the end of the street, the pallid mist above the water floating like a solid concrete wall. It was at this Hardwood pointed. "See that?"

"I see the cold. That's it. When are we going to talk about this bomb?"

"In a minute. Do you know how many bodies disappear into that murky water on a yearly basis?"

"I'm no good at math."

"Untold hundreds is my guess. I really don't know. It's been a favorite dumping ground of murderers for a long time."

"Great, thanks for the history lesson. What are you doing with bombs? What if I'm on the next train you pick? What if Carlie or Mason is? You're out of control."

Hardwood said nothing, motioned them toward the water. "Just a bit further."

"Toward the water? Fuck that, here's good. Go on, speak."

"Very well." The aging newscaster's weakness against the cold was beginning to show itself. His teeth began to chatter lightly, his eyes grew heavy, and his body shook with chills. Even with his leather gloves on, he was having trouble holding the cigarette still as he took a drag on it.

"My quandary is thus, Stone. The network called me, they want me to join them."

"You're shitting me. That's a problem?"

"Hear me out. I'll be here in New York, thank God. I start after the New Year."

"Can't say I'm not jealous, but I'm sure you knew I would be."

"Of course. That's half the fun of telling you."

"Yet you walked me to the damn river first."

"I'm changing the game. I'm giving you a free get-out-of-jail card. Different networks, different time slots, there's no need for us to compete anymore. You've earned your crown at the local level, take it and be happy with it. Leave me to run my new operations without worry that you'll try to outdo me."

"Leave you to blow up the city? Are you insane? I can't let you go around doing this. It's...it's...I have friends and family here!"

"I figured you'd say as much."

"Why not just stop? Do you feel how much heat is on us right now? They must know. They're just waiting for us to slip up. You got the network job, just end it. Don't go all bat shit."

"Can't. I have to think bigger this time. My competition is strong. Stone Philips alone—"

"Yeah, they're real journalists. They worked for it. They didn't ass rape a busdriver with a severed head for it."

"Which is why I need a new MO."

Stone caught on, preempted Hardwood's next words. "What, terrorism?"

"Terrorism is the new cosmic fear, Stone. Terrorism is what's selling the news now. Make the public feel unsafe in America's cities, and the news writes itself. People panic when they see a stray package, they tense up on airplanes, turn xenophobic and attack first. Terrorism is a hot commodity on the networks."

"You're nuts, I mean really nuts. I'm not going to let you kill people I care about. That was never the deal."

Hardwood chuckled, took a final drag on his cigarette and stamped it out under his foot in the snow. "How droll, a serial killer with morals."

"At least I'm not crazy."

"I think, my friend, we are both...what's the word...absolutely batshit."

"Okay. Maybe."

Hardwood reached into his pocket, started looking for his cigarette case, or so Stone was thinking. "You really don't regret killing all those people?"

"No," Stone replied, the hairs on the back of his neck starting to prickle. Something didn't feel right here. "I already said no."

"Then you'll understand this."

Hardwood withdrew a syringe from under his coat and rammed it into Stone's chest. Stone tried to push back, but it was too late: white hot pain lashed through his entire being. Grappling, they fell to the ground, Stone screaming and lunging at his nemesis's eyes, feeling his breath grow shorter. He tried to get an arm around Hardwood's head, but the old man was quick, and it turned out his shivers had been a ploy to dupe Stone. Hardwood landed a punch square to Stone's mouth and stopped the confrontation.

Stone went still, his body going completely numb, his muscles unresponsive to his commands. Literally.

"What the fuck," said Stone, feeling as if someone had poured quick drying cement on him. "You sonofabitch. What did you do?"

Hardwood held up the empty syringe. "Pavulon and Anectine. Don't worry, it doesn't hurt, but I can't rightly use my old methods. With this, they'll figure you were drunk, fell in, drowned."

"We...had a deal." Stone's voice was already faltering.

"I gave you a chance to get out. You turned it down. I can't have you out here knowing what's going on."

"Then why...tell...me?"

"Because I figured you deserved to know. You've been a worthy adversary. An angry one, but worthy."

"My...God, you're...truly...insane."

"No no. Just determined."

"My lawyer..."

"Is dead. I took care of that a while ago. The tapes are burnt as well. Yes, I took care of all of it. Everyone thinks he's on vacation in Thailand. Beautiful country, very few computers or cell phone towers out in the jungles. Now hang on, we need to move."

His lawyer was dead? That explained why Stone had never received a return call.

Hardwood bent down and got his arms under Stone's armpits and lifted him into a sitting position. Fixing his grip for a better hold, he began dragging Stone toward the river. When he reached the walkway that overlooked the black water, he perched Stone precariously on the waist-high cement wall that ran along the water's edge. The gray fog engulfed them, obscuring them and giving Hardwood a cloak to operate under.

"Another reason I admit: you'd probably make network anchor someday and then we'd have another war. Frankly, I'm not up for it. This time, it's just me. I know it's not how you planned it to end, but trust me, it's for the better. Your soul will get what's coming to it. It's only fair."

"But...but..."

"But nothing, Stone. But nothing. It's just business. You understand."

With a fatherly caress, he smoothed Stone's hair and gave him a pat on the head. "I really admired you, Stone. You had a good fight inside of you."

"They'll find...me," Stone said.

"Maybe. But here's the scenario they'll come to accept as true: the last time I saw you, we went for a walk, I told you'd I'd made anchor, and you stormed off. You were quite drunk. People saw you drinking in the bar. People will see me in a few minutes somewhere else, having another drink, and they'll mess up the time because that's what people do. They love me, Stone, they won't even contemplate I might have had something to do with it. That's the way it works, you know it and I know it."

"Please..."

"Now if you'll excuse me, I have a report to prepare for. It seems terrorists have blown the Brooklyn Bridge into the Hudson River."

Stone's eyes showed absolute fear. "Wha...wha...when did...that happen?"

Hardwood pushed Stone into the water. "In about an hour."

CHAPTER 42

For the hundredth time this night, Garcia read over the letters from both killers, looking yet again for some clue that might unveil the identity of the authors. The only thing he could discern was that the killers were both good spellers. Not one typo on any of the notes. Of course, they were both typed, and in this age of computers, it was conceivable that one of the many word processing programs people used had corrected any mistakes. Still, it was odd that even the grammar was impeccable. No silly mistakes like their and there. Just flawless English. Almost as if the killers had taken college level writing classes.

"George, you see these letters?"

George, who was on his way to get a Coke from the machine down the hall, reluctantly spun on his heels and made his way to Garcia's desk. "What's up?"

"You read them?"

George nodded. "Yes, four hundred times."

"There's no mistakes. That strike you as odd?"

"Computers, man. They catch the mistakes now."

"Yeah…yeah. I guess."

With that, George turned and made his way back toward the soda machine, only to stop at Garcia's voice yet again. "You know Hal never pinpointed where the Casanova Carver's emails came from."

"Yeah, so he said. Something about a bouncing IP. Hacker kind of stuff."

"You know Hardwood did some reports on hackers a few years ago? Untraceable black market goods."

"I heard that."

"Did you know Stone once did a report on dog fighting rings?"

George sighed, came back and sat in the chair in front of Garcia's desk. "And they were both at the press club awards. I know. But if you're saying these guys are doing it themselves, which, I admit, is a possibility, then we need the proof. So far everything we have only proves they're newscasters. My opinion: newscasters don't seem smart enough to pull this crap off. Not only that, but it'd ruin them if they were caught. Are they smart enough and willing to risk it? I dunno. Why don't we just shadow them?"

"We did tail them, for about a month. Nothing happened so the chief stopped it."

"You pissed?"

"Nah. I'm just tired. Just tired."

They sat in silence until George finally got up and got himself that Coke he'd been after. For the next hour, Garcia read and reread the letters. It all made sense on paper: the notes, the connections, the deaths. It had to be them. Had to be. But why?

*

Hardwood wasn't acrophobic, but standing on the wooden-planked promenade that ran above the tarmac of the Brooklyn Bridge was something he never thought he'd be doing, especially at night, especially while wearing black trousers, a black sweater, and a long black trench coat with a backpack tucked underneath. Around him, the millions of lights from the city's buildings stood in stark contrast to the onyx sky like LED buttons on a spaceship control array. If he touched the right one, would smoke and fire cough from its base and take off into the heavens like a rocket ship?

The sight began to make him dizzy, and so he gripped the handrail to steady himself and happened to look down at the driving lanes below. The humming of car engines cut loud for a moment as two semis passed underneath, then waned back into a steady drone. The sight of his dark, leather gloves caught his eye, registered as a double-edged sword in his mind: if he were to fall into the rush of cars below, who would see him? At the rate the cars were speeding along they wouldn't have time to skid away from a giant light bulb let alone a dark shadow. And, if by the grace of God the cars did miss him, would the fall onto the concrete, roughly one story down, kill him anyway? Pushing the thought aside, he made his way out toward where the massive steel cables began their arc up toward the mason towers. The Iranian demolitions expert he'd visited two nights ago on a barge out in Jersey had been very specific about finding points of stress in a target.

When he walked, the thick wooden planks beneath his feet echoed his intentions down either side of the promenade. Since arriving ten minutes ago, only two couples had walked by him, arm in arm on their way home from an evening of enchanted romance—soon to be an evening of enchanted sweat and bodily fluids if New York City paradigms had anything to say about it. It was the usual primal instinct of the city, to move brusquely through the nights with engorged genitalia, constantly seeking three minutes of satisfaction, and it was, as far as he was concerned, the foremost reason New Yorkers were falling behind the rest of the world in productive output; he'd have to do something about it soon.

Neither couple had stared at him at length, thankfully, and if they did recognize him they kept it to themselves. Still, he'd have to work fast once the best opportunity presented itself.

This is the spot, he thought, seeing that the cables were just within reach.

What he needed now was a window of alone time: no cars, and definitely no pedestrians. The first was going to be nearly impossible; the traffic in New York City only let up in the heart of winter, and even then hardly at all. Once he started to climb out on to the cross beams to place the charges, he'd have to move fast and just hope that none of the drivers looked up.

The second necessity—no pedestrians—fell under the category of unpredictable. In any other city he'd wait until early morning, maybe three or four AM, before beginning his climb, but New York City was a perpetual motion machine. More couples would be along any time now, and they more than likely would give him a quick once over.

From his pocket he pulled out a brown paper bag, sculpted it around the wine cooler that was inside. Imitating a bum seemed like the easiest way to get people to leave him alone, considering that most people here were apt to avoid making eye contact with such dregs in fear of being hounded for spare change.

Now, he spied a group of people coming his way from the Manhattan side of the bridge. Silently he cursed, but decided to use his time to figure out how best to crawl out toward the outer cables.

Four cables total held up the suspension bridge, each some five thousand feet long and fifteen inches thick. There'd been enough fluff stories about this bridge to last him a lifetime. Of all facets of this plan, the only thing that really bothered him was that he'd be destroying a work of art. Fourteen years in the making, and some 30 deaths at the result of caisson sickness, and if everything went right, he'd undo it in as much time as it takes a dog to leave a shit on the sidewalk.

The walkers were drawing closer, swaying and waving their arms, jovially shoving one another about. Two of them appeared to be having a war with gravity, as if they were seriously considering just taking a nap on the bridge. Drunk, thought Hardwood, which meant he'd have to adjust their average walking time from one mile per hour to one mile per puking session, which could take a while.

"The blood of the city is but a clot," he whispered into the paper bag, grimacing at the stench of the cheap alcohol. "Dear God, who drinks this stuff?"

While he waited for the drunkards to amble their way closer, looking up every few seconds to gauge their distance, he took his backpack off, opened it and examined the contents. Five C-4 charges, each about the size of a softball, slept soundly in the vinyl lining. Beneath them, their plastic yellow casings sticking out like children's toys, rested the blasting caps required to detonate the explosives.

He'd bought the explosive from the Iranian arms dealer he'd interviewed years ago. Told the guy he needed to blow up some trucks for a news report on faulty gas tanks. The Iranian had called him crazy, laughed at his plan, but for the price, gave him the plastic explosives without a second thought. No wonder these guys got nabbed by the FBI all the time, thought Hardwood. They were money hungry no matter how much they hated Americans for their capitalistic ideals.

"When you blow the trucks up," the Iranian had told him, "make sure you are at least five hundred yards away behind some kind of shield. The shrapnel will shoot out like bullets, and you will not have time to duck. Is pretty safe if you take precaution. Now…the fee for my silence."

That had caught Hardwood off guard; he'd assumed the price of the explosives ensured silence, but no. What was the old saying? Dance with the Devil and you're bound to get scorched. So he'd paid the man to be quiet about the report he was filming on faulty gas tanks in Chevy trucks.

Hardwood wondered what the man would think and do once the FBI released information on the type of C-4 that toppled the bridge. Chances were he'd find another place to call home, start selling his wares again from another barge in another town.

"About time," he said as the group of drunk men drew up next to him. They were walking with their arms over each other's shoulders, mimicking the opening sequence in that old *Monkees* television show. "Here we come, fucking lots of girls, we get the funniest looks from, the youngest one in curls…"

Sounds like they've got their Nick At Nite scrambled, Hardwood thought as he turned his back to them, held the backpack against his chest the way a frightened homeless man might.

"Hey, pops," one of them yelled. "We need a fourth. Jump in line!"

Just walk by, Hardwood thought, acutely aware that he had no worthy weapons on him.

"I think I'm gonna hurl," another one yelled.

"No way, dude. First one to spew buys White Castle for the rest."

There was a sickening sound of gagging followed by an accentuated gulp, then the disgusted groans of men who'd just witnessed something particularly gross.

"Oh, man, that was sick. Now I'm gonna hurl."

Hardwood continued to watch the skyline across the water, hearing the men move on past him with the indifference of the well-to-do toward the lower class. He gave it a few seconds until they were well out of earshot, then looked over his shoulder in both directions, making sure all was clear.

With a great inhalation, he slung the bag over his shoulders, threw one leg over the guardrail, then the other, and began to balance himself out onto the crossbeams toward the outermost suspension cable.

CHAPTER 43

Stone opened his eyes, saw the face of an old Chinese man hovering above him, swimming in and out of focus inside a shroud of black. Was he dead? Was this the face of the devil? "So hell is Asian," he whispered to himself.

"Tell me about it," the face answered. "You ever been to Hong Kong? Twenty million people riding around on bikes ringing little bells, and twenty million more thinking it's their cell phones ringing. Here, drink this coffee." The man thrust a tall Thermos into Stone's hands, hauled him off his back into a sitting position, unscrewed the top and tenderly helped lift it to his mouth.

The rich aromas of New York City java floated over the edge and darted up his nostrils, instantly relaxing him. There was another smell intermixed with it as well, something oaky, but he couldn't quite place it. But he was in no condition to be picky, so he drank heartily, wincing as the hot liquid ignited a fire in his belly. On the scale of good pains, this one was up there near ten.

When he was full, he tried to stand up, but discovered his lower half liked being where it was. His neck, torso, head, and shoulders were likewise staging a coup against his brain. "I can't move," he told the face, which was slowly coming into full focus and holding its pattern. A small man, maybe in his late thirties, thin goatee, silver earring, wool cap. Chinese, yes, but not fresh-off-the-boat Chinese; judging by his accent, he'd been in America a long time, maybe even born here. Behind him, a group of men stood and watched, their ethnicities varying from white to African American to Middle Eastern. All of them wore heavy flannel shirts under thick waterproof jackets. On their hands they wore work gloves; the grease and dirt on their faces spoke of hours of manual labor with heavy equipment.

A glance at his surroundings told Stone he was on a small boat, some kind of short haul vessel, probably ran things between Jersey and New York. As if he'd found some kind of visual and physical link, the floor suddenly started undulating in time with the water, a not so agreeable feeling in his current disoriented state.

"We found you floating in there," the Chinese man said, "starting to sink like a rock."

Yes, the water, he thought. It was all coming back to him now. Hardwood jabbing him with the needle, his fall off the pier, the frigid taste of briny death filling his lungs, panic and fear clouding his thoughts, and then the sweet sensation of sleep. "I was drowning."

"Drowning? Shit, I think you were dead, my man. Rocco here used to be a lifeguard. He jumped in after you, hauled you up, made out with you for a bit until your eyes popped open and you spit water all over yourself. It was a movie moment, man."

Dripping wet, Rocco held up a hand and waved. The African American man was large, pro-wrestler large, and judging by the man's wide grin, Stone wondered if he'd have to buy him dinner now. "You...you saved me?"

The Chinese man nodded. "Damn right. Rocco leapt off the bow like a cliff diver. That motherfucker swims like a shark, fast as all hell. Say, you're that news guy, right? Roland Stone. You think we'll get a medal or something?"

"Yeah, I'll call the mayor."

"You can do that?"

"I can do anything I want, I'm a news anchor."

"Damn straight you are. So did The Casanova Carver do this to you?"

"I deal with The Chef."

"Oh yeah, him too. He do it?"

"No, I, uh…" What was he supposed to tell them? They'd hit it right on the nose, it was the Casanova Carver, but he needed time to figure out what the situation was. "I slipped. No psychopaths, sorry."

"I hope they catch him soon. Cops are double-timing their patrols out here, making it a little harder to sneak a drink on the sly, you know. We got to mask it with coffee."

"I thought it tasted funny."

"A little whiskey to keep the blood flowing."

"Speaking of flowing blood, I'm freezing."

The Chinese man looked back at Rocco, said, "Yo, Rocco, go inside the wheelhouse and get my bag."

"Where are we?" Stone asked, his body overcome with shivers.

"We're near the West Side Highway. Midtown. Heading for the nearest dock. I already radioed for an ambulance for you."

Ambulance? Sure, that sounded good. Maybe they could get his body working right again, get his legs to obey him. What had Hardwood given him? He forgot the names of the drugs; the last thing he remembered Hardwood saying was something about a bridge—Oh shit.

And it came back to him just like that. Hardwood was going to blow up the Brooklyn Bridge.

"No! No ambulance!"

"Hey, chill, Mr. Stone—"

"No ambulance. Just help me up. Hurry hurry."

The Chinese man motioned for two of the other men to help, and together they lifted him to his feet. Dizziness washed over him, dots popping before his eyes, his legs still dangling like lead pipes. It wasn't like they were asleep, there were no pins and needles, just a heavy, dead weight. Willing them to move was doing little, though he could feel his toes wiggling, so that was a good sign. His arms were coming back to full use now too, and he could move his head. As they brought him into the wheelhouse, his body movements seemed to be coming faster and faster.

After slumping him in the nearest chair, the Chinese man took a small duffel bag from Rocco, opened it and took out a pair of baggy jeans and a hooded sweatshirt. "Just make sure you sign these when you give 'em back, okay? I can sell 'em on ebay."

Stone took the sweatshirt, held it up to his chest, read the front. "If this boat's a'rocking, don't come a'knocking."

"It's all I got. I hope you're a medium."

"It's fine." Stone pulled his cell phone out from his back pocket, flipped it open and cursed when he saw the black screen. He hit the power button, which seemed to be working fine if the phone's intent was to spit water everywhere. "Don't suppose you have a phone in that bag."

"Here," said Rocco, smiling like a man in love as he handed over his phone, "use mine."

CHAPTER 44

Mason picked the notebook paper up off her desk, crumpled it up, and tossed it in the wastebasket. Another failed story idea; it had seemed good at first—a list of celebrities the Casanova Carver and Chef were going to attack next—but a quick scan of *The Post's* website showed they'd beaten her to the punch.

"Assholes. Just because Andy Dick is scared doesn't make it a credible story. Shit!"

Perhaps it was time to call it a night. It was almost three AM and the rest of the late night shift had gone home already; she could take up new leads in the morning with Stone.

Speaking of Stone, she was starting to worry about him. His refusal for police protection called into question just what his current state of mind was. She'd seen enough Hollywood thrillers to know that it was possible he was being coerced into doing something against his will. As it was, the police had offered her protection as well, and she'd told them yes. Only problem was they put some cops in the building, but none around her home.

Grabbing her purse from the floor near her chair, she turned off her computer and locked her office. She spotted Duncan down the hall near the elevators and decided to wait a minute until he got in. No use getting trapped in a metal box with a weirdo like him. He'd been trying harder to get her attention. This, of course, made him the most annoying person on her personal planet, and it was better these days to just avoid him.

It was sweet on one level, the way he doted on her, got her coffee, brought her the mail, but more so it was just pathetic. She didn't want a flimsy man like Duncan, she wanted someone stronger, someone who could not only take her to new career heights, but just plain take her.

Initially, sleeping with Cheese had seemed a wise move, but Cheese had issues she could only guess at, especially a penchant for sexual deviation that went beyond anything German dominatrix professionals considered strange.

Which left Stone.

He might work if things settled down. In fact, it would be smart as hell to jump in bed with him, make it public, become some sort of WWTF sweethearts on air. At least for a while it might pull in a younger female demographic.

If only Stone would get his head straight and stop fucking around with this Chef stuff. He needed protection and he needed to get them an exclusive interview.

He was doing neither.

She made her way to the elevator as she pondered this, hit the silver dollar button and called it up from the ground floor. She shrieked as the doors opened and Duncan Willis waved back at her. "Sorry. Didn't mean to scare you."

"It's okay, sug. It's just, I thought I saw you go down already."

"I did. I forgot some stuff on my desk."

"Oh. Didn't think you worked this late?"

"Cheese has me looking at branding companies, wants to redo the logo. WYNN just redid theirs, have you seen it?"

She shook her head, stepped by him into the elevator. "Not yet. Is it good?"

"Good? It gives Cheese a hard on. Well, not that I know personally, of course. I mean, that's what Cheese said. I'm not like that. And if Stone told you different he's lying."

"Relax, hon, no use getting worked up at this hour." She watched as Duncan's eyes dropped to her chest for a second, then back up to her face.

"Can I walk you home?"

Great. This was not what she needed right now; it was late, she was tired, and a conversation with Duncan would turn off any bit of libido she had in reserve when she did slide into bed. "It's okay, I'll be fine. Really."

Looking at her chest again, Duncan said okay and started to step out into the hallway. As he did, Mason's phone rang. Duncan' hands darted back into the door, holding it open. He stuck his head in and whispered something about telling Cheese he'd left for the night.

But when she answered it, she didn't hear Cheese, she heard the frantic shouts of Stone.

"Slow down, sug," she said, pulling the phone away from her ear. "What are you saying? What about the Brooklyn Bridge?"

CHAPTER 45

The wind cut sharply into Stone's wet face as he tore out of the cab and pushed his way through the collection of people walking along the road. A car horn blared but he paid it no mind, not noticing that the car was actually skidding to a halt to avoid running him over. The Chinese man's loose clothes hung from him, making him look like a boy wearing his father's clothes, tripping him up as he made his way down the wooden planks of the bridge's promenade.

There was no sign of Hardwood up ahead, nor could he see any signs that the bridge had been tampered with. Over the side of the guardrail, more cars made the trek across the water, unaware that they might be just minutes away from becoming poorly constructed boats. There was no telling how long before Hardwood carried out this new plan, no ticking clock on the side of a bundle of dynamite with LED numbers counting down to detonation like in so many cartoons of his youth. If Hardwood was hell-bent on using terrorism to get his next big story, then he'd have studied a terrorist's methods, which meant subterfuge.

He pumped his legs, sucking in cold breath, pulling up the flapping pant legs with his hands as he ran. This made it awkward to move, but better he run funny than sprain an ankle before he could talk to Hardwood. A quarter of the way across now, and still no sign of anything out of the ordinary. Save for the fact the bridge was void of people, which was sort of a rarity for New York City, everything felt as it should. Everything was typical. A normal night.

Just like every other terrorist attack the nation had ever experienced.

September 11th had brought on a sudden sense of helplessness unrivaled in history, had led to weeks of carbon-copied news footage and ratings unlike anything the networks had ever experienced. This would be no different.

Damn, it was a genius plan when you thought of it like that. But a stupid one, ultimately, when you considered the unpredictability of it all. Who could be on this bridge right now? Mason? Carlie? Chauncey? Duncan?

Eh, screw Duncan, the prick.

The first tower drew close, began to move over him like the gateway to some Arthurian castle. He stopped in its shadow and bent forward, sucked in labored breath and realized just how out of shape he was. It was a wonder he'd been able to kill anyone with his body in this shape. "C'mon, fatso, keep moving," he told himself, hoping the pep talk would spur him on.

What really spurred him on was the thought that if he didn't move he might end up in the water, tangled up in thousands of pounds of twisted steel. Running again, the wind chiseling through the somewhat moist, baggy clothes, he scanned the distance, looking for movement of any kind. The center of the bridge was drawing closer. With the wind blowing this high up, and his body still mostly wet under the loose clothes, cold had a whole new meaning. His bones felt as cold as Carlie's heart must be.

The second tower drew close now, and he took another moment to catch his breath, all the while looking for Hardwood. Maybe he had to think like a deranged newscaster/terrorist. If he were going to blow up a bridge, where would he be?

Paris, sipping wine and letting some black ops guys do the job for him.

Keep moving, he thought, and started up once again, passing under the second tower, looking up in case Hardwood had was playing Spider-man. The site of the mason façade reaching up toward the stars gave him vertigo, so he grabbed the guardrail and slowed up for a bit.

And there, across the chasm of cross beams and speeding cars, was Hardwood, adhering something gray and pliable to the outermost support cable of the bridge.

"Hardwood!"

The old man turned, saw him, tried to figure out who he was. The clothes, and the fact he was supposed to be dead, had caught Hardwood off guard.

Stone cupped his hands and yelled, "You sonofabitch! You fucked up! I'm alive, and I'm stopping you from doing this, you crazy fuck!"

At this, Hardwood nodded, now able to place the voice with the man in strange, baggy clothes. He took his hands away from the clay on the cable—which was now stuck fast—cupped them around his mouth, and yelled back: "Stone, you look…ridiculous!"

*

Talk about a turn of events, Hardwood thought, facing away from Stone again and meticulously connecting the blasting cap to the C-4. The last person he'd expected to encounter way up here was Stone. The drug should have been strong enough to knock the idiot out for at least twenty minutes, more than enough time to drown. That's what he got for working with black market hooligans.

The fact that Stone looked like a man who'd raided an overweight teenage boy's wardrobe was disturbing enough, but what really concerned him was whether or not the twerp planned on coming after him out here on the edge of the bridge, so high above the black, beckoning maw of the river.

A quick look back showed that, yes, Stone was making his way out over the crossbeams.

"Foolish," Hardwood whispered, connecting the last of the wires to the cap. Satisfied with his work, he flipped the remote switch to the on position, slung the backpack over his shoulder once again and turned to await Stone's arrival. The man was belly crawling across the support beams like a marine in training, doing his best not to look at the speeding traffic below him, much like Hardwood had done himself. "I'm just going to kick you off when you get close enough," he said matter-of-factly. "You may as well just go back the way you came."

"Fuck you, Hardwood. This is...enough...of your...crazy ideas."

"Breathe slower, or you'll be winded when you get here and lose any youthful advantage you have over me."

"Very...thoughtful of...you." Stone pulled himself forward over the rivet-studded beam in front of him, now halfway across the gap. His loose clothing whipped about like a circus tent in a tornado.

"How'd you survive, if you don't mind my asking?"

"Rocco."

"What's a Rocco?"

"A new friend."

Hardwood nodded, checked his watch and noted the time, wondered how much longer this was going to take. "I see. So you were rescued. And here I thought New Yorkers were too smart to be out in the murky, foggy water at night. Talk about good luck, yes? I suppose you told them about my plan here. Should I be expecting the police? Because if so, might I remind you of our agreement. You will go down with me."

"Just me. No one knows. How the hell did you get across this? Jesus, it's windy up here."

"An old man's resolve can go a long way when need be. Speaking of which, are you going to be much longer? I've got more charges to place."

"Hang on, you bastard. I'll be there in a second."

"I could go place this next charge and come back—"

"I said I'll be there in a second!"

"No need to get snippy."

As he watched Stone make his way closer, Hardwood wished he had brought his gun. There was no need to leave it behind really, other than he'd planned on tossing the backpack into the water if someone started asking too many questions. The gun he'd kept at home because a) despite their benefit, he really didn't like guns, and b) he didn't trust it in a bag of C-4, and would have had to hide it on his person, which could lead to all sorts of problems if someone spotted it.

No matter, a few more feet and Stone would be close enough to kick in the head, and barring any unforeseen men named Rocco sailing by, would fall to the roadway below.

They'd be scraping him off the tarmac for weeks. No signs of struggle, no fingerprints to tie him to the crime. Just another New York City newscaster doing away with the pressures of celebrity and the malicious adoration of serial killers. At least that's how he'd report it.

Hardwood gauged the distance between them now, decided Stone was close enough. Holding onto the nearest cross cable, he place one foot out on the beam, drew his other one back and said, "Do stay dead this time, I have a lot of work to do."

And kicked.

*

Stone wasn't stupid; he knew Hardwood would have shot him on site if he had a gun, so more than likely the plan was to kick him off when he got close enough. Crossing the beams so high up in the cold wind was taking all his concentration, especially whenever he thought about the cars speeding by below, but the way he jittered and lost his grip here and there was just a ruse.

So when Hardwood kicked, Stone was ready, having positioned his legs against the beam to support all the weight of his upper body.

He caught the kick, yanked Hardwood out toward him. The old man yelped and fell on top of him, scrabbling like a cat about to fall off a window ledge. "Stone!"

Stone felt the old man's hands dig into the mushy folds of the oversized sweatshirt, grip in for dear life. Before he realized what was happening, Stone was falling sideways as well, scrabbling for the cross-beam himself, getting his arms around it at the last second.

No longer just a proverbial monkey on his back, Hardwood fought his way up Stone's torso and grabbed the beam. Together, they hung half on and half off the beam, their legs dangling above the roofs of passing vehicles.

This was not exactly how he'd envisioned the fight going. In his mind, he'd seen Hardwood bouncing off the hood of the next small car to zip along, his insides exploding into the night air like wet confetti.

"You idiot!" Hardwood yelled, doing his best to haul himself up onto the beam. The old man's wispy gray hair rose into the sky like tiny ghosts trying to flee his head. "Now look at us."

With as much upper body strength as he could muster, Stone tried to haul himself up, but was not having a very good go at it. "Me?" he huffed. "You tried to kill me, you wrinkled old asshole."

"I gave you an out, you didn't want it. What do you care if I do this? I need the stories now!"

"Not this way. If you do this one it only gets worse."

"Oh, don't act like you care, you psychopath. What, are you jealous you didn't think of it first?"

Pretty much, thought Stone. He had to admit it would be the biggest story of the year, and if Hardwood had "inside" knowledge of who'd done it, and helped catch them, he'd be eating with the president every night, using Tom Brokaw as a footstool. But then, he didn't feel like getting blown up the next time he took a cab, or rode the subway, or went to dine in a café so he was also serious about stopping it. "No," he lied, right before Hardwood gained the upper ground, sat on the beam, and threw an old man's punch at him.

It connected with the top of Stone's head and rattled his teeth. For an old coot, Hardwood knew how to hit. Another punch connected with Stone's ear and screamed down his sinuses into his chest.

"Liar," Hardwood yelled. "You want this story. But it's mine. It's all mine!"

Enough of this, Stone thought, mustering every last ounce of strength he had, hauling himself up into a sitting position on the beam. He shook his head to clear out the reverberating gong. "Report this, dickhead."

His punch caught Hardwood square in the jaw, sent him backwards into the exterior support cable.

CHAPTER 46

The cab pulled to a stop at the entrance to the bridge. "Let us out here," Mason yelled, thrusting folded up bills through the bulletproof partition's money slot. The cab driver pulled over and stopped the car, took the cash. Mason jumped out with Duncan in tow, ordered him to get his ass in gear and didn't even bother with her change.

She'd run a good twenty feet when she realized she was alone, that Duncan was still back at the cab fumbling with a small black camera bag.

It was bad enough he'd followed her against her wishes, but even worse when he'd grabbed one of the digital video cameras from the equipment room and demanded to be part of the story. With little time to spare she'd relented, because the other cameramen were either sleeping, on planes to other cities, or out on assignment somewhere, and if she was going to extemporize she needed someone, anyone, to record it. She'd phoned Cheese in the cab, just to be safe, and left him a message about Stone's cryptic call, told him something was going on at the Brooklyn Bridge and maybe the Chef had finally agreed to a meeting and could he find a suitable crew.

There'd been no answer from him yet.

"Sorry," Duncan said, now coming up beside her. "Don't want to drop the battery."

"Hurry up, this is the news, it's first come first serve."

As she raced down the promenade, she removed a compact mirror from her purse and checked her hair.

"You look beautiful," Duncan said, the camera strapped to his hand.

"Not now, Duncan. Look around and help me find Stone."

"I don't see anyone. Where did he say he'd be?"

"He didn't, he just said 'Brooklyn Bridge. Explosive.'"

"What's that mean?"

Mason paused, still fixing her hair in the mirror. She took a tube of lipstick from her purse and applied it quickly and flawlessly. After a wet, puckering air kiss to make sure it was perfect, she returned it to her purse, along with the mirror. "Don't you see. He's saying there's an explosive story on the bridge. We need something captivating, hon, something none of the other stations have. My guess is he tracked down The Chef and got us an interview."

"Seriously?"

"Seriously. So keep an eye out. He's here somewhere." She walked forward, using her hand to hold her hair down in the wind. Her jacket was long and insulating, but she'd probably have to take it off to do the report. Underneath she wore a red business suit with white trim. It was low cut and tailored to her curves, showing as much cleavage as she dared without being obscene. The middle of the bridge drew close, the Manhattan skyline glorious around them. "I don't see anything, do you?"

Duncan was silent.

She glanced back, saw him put the camera to his eye and point it up at one of the support cables. "Duncan?"

Duncan held the shot, said, "You're not gonna believe this, but I found the asshole."

*

Detective Garcia double parked near the start of the bridge, took the cup of cold coffee from the cup holder and swallowed a gulp.

"Stone and Hardwood," he said. There was no astonishment in his voice, just subtle confirmation that his gut was working as well as a cop's should.

He hadn't found enough evidence to shed light on exactly what was going on, but he'd found enough to bring them in for questioning. All he had to do was figure out how to tie it to them. In the eyes of the law, they were still just two hardworking, spotlight-hounding, newscasters, but he was sure he could open them up after an hour or two in the VIP room—as the interrogation room was known. Problem was he had to find them first; neither was home, and it was late. Maybe not late for their schedules, and New York City, but it felt queer they should both be out right now not answering their cell phones (Stone's wasn't even ringing). His cop instincts smelled something rotten in The Big Apple.

Story at eleven.

And now the strange report from a group of near-drunken river workers who claimed they'd pulled Stone out of the water before watching him run away to the Brooklyn Bridge. If the report was to be believed, Stone had possibly met his biggest fan, The Chef. Then again, considering the evidence, it was possible he'd met another type of fan, a competitor in the business. Either way, something was up on the bridge and Stone was involved.

For the first time in a while, he took out his cell phone and woke up his wife.

"Hola, mi amor," he said.

Her voice was groggy. "Boy, you haven't called me that in years. Do you have a gun to your head? How much do I get again if you get shot?"

"You get nothing. My mistress gets it all."

"Oh, really. Twenty years of cleaning your chonies and that's the thanks I get."

"Nah, she cleans 'em too, but she does it in the nude and sings Julio Iglesias."

"Must give her the clean pairs 'cause if I breathe around the ones you give me I pass out."

"It's the Chinese food I have for lunch."

Her tone shifted, became hesitant and soft. "Seriously, Ramon, are you okay? It's three in the morning. Something wrong?"

"No, no. Just going…going to get some coffee. Figured I'd kill time and…uh…ask you to tape that show for me. You know the one—"

"You already set the TiVo before you left. You getting senile already?"

"Maybe. Yeah, a little. Just…um…Okay, I gotta run. Love you."

"Ramon, don't lie to me."

"I'm not. Everything's fine. Just bored. I love you."

"Love you, too. No Chinese food."

Garcia hung up and called for back up, looking toward the spanning bridge. Stone was down there, either in trouble or causing it. Somehow he knew this night was going to end with bloodshed. He'd give it a minute and go down there himself. Maybe two minutes.

*

A good half a minute dripped by as Mason and Duncan stared across the cross beams in disbelief. Precariously perched above the speeding traffic, Stone was busy fighting with another man.

"Is that Doug Hardwood?" Duncan asked.

"I think so."

"Should we call the police?"

Without hesitating, Mason stepped in front of the camera and positioned herself for the taping. "Not until I get the story."

"But they look like they're in trouble. Not that I give a shit really, but still…"

"Duncan, help me get this report and I'll let you buy me a drink."

That was good enough for Duncan, who immediately started up the camera. He focused it and found Mason in the lens. Just as he was about to push the record button, a shadow blocked his view. He heard Mason say, "Where'd you come from?"

Duncan lowered the camera, saw that cop who'd interrogated him a while ago standing in his line of sight.

"Hi," said Garcia, "congratulations on your award, Miss Mason. I'm a big fan. Can you move? I need to talk to Mr. Stone."

*

"Everybody freeze!"

Stone had Hardwood in a headlock when he heard the command

from across the gap. He saw Detective Garcia standing there with his gun pointed at him. Next to the detective, bathed in the small key light from a digital video camera, Mason stared at him with a look of utter confusion.

"Yay," Stone said, "the police."

"I'll thank you to let go of my head," Hardwood said, his words muffled against Stone's chest.

"Yeah, in a minute." Then to Detective Garcia, Stone raised his free hand and waved. "Hi, detective, can we help you?"

"You can come back over here and let me take you to the station. I want to talk to you about some things."

"Ask him 'what things?'" Hardwood said, his face still buried in the oversized sweatshirt.

"Shut up. I'm talking to him." Then, to Garcia: "What things?"

"Oh, this and that. Mostly questions about the serial killers I've been after for so long. You know, the ones you guys have been in touch with so much. Seems every time we get a lead, it turns out bunk. But I talked to some people and I did some reading, and well, I got this little nagging voice in my head that for once isn't my wife. I don't need to tell you these killers of ours like the attention they get from you guys in the media. I'm just curious how close they actually like to get to the story."

"Writing some letters is about as close as I've seen."

"Maybe, but you need to look at some other things. Like where you got those clothes and what that funny bit of clay is on the cable there, and what's in that backpack. I'm thinking, maybe, call it a hunch, it's you two. Is Mr. Hardwood okay there? He looks to be in a rough spot."

"Yeah, he's fine. We're just talking. What do you mean, 'us'? You don't think—"

The buddabuddabudda of a helicopter's whirring rotors grew out of the silence, heading their way from the Manhattan side of the bridge. Stone saw it as a tiny dot of black against the blacker sky. It grew larger and a column of white light stabbed down from its underbelly, lit up the river like it was made of green milk.

"Shit," said Stone, finally letting go of Hardwood. "Looks like you've been made, dickhead. Cops are on their way."

With a casual shake of his head, Hardwood regained his composure, fixed his shirt, smoothed back his hair. "You forget, friend, if I'm discovered, so are you. Contrary to our current state of affairs, we are in this together whether you like it or not now. Time to ask yourself, are you a newsman, or just a civilian?"

"They're gonna have to pad the walls extra thick for you, you know."

"Can you tell me what's in the bag, Mr. Hardwood?" Garcia asked, stealing a quick look at the helicopter as well. "Is it more of that clay? Because if it's what I think it is—"

Hardwood shook his head, then thought better of clamming up and said, "Whatever this thing is on the bridge, I suspect it's just the result of some teenagers' tomfoolery. Such antics the young pull."

Garcia nodded. "Noted. But seriously, can you put the bag down and come back here. I really don't want to have to come out there. I'm no good with heights."

Raising his voice over the drumming of the helicopter, Hardwood waved him off. "No need, there's nothing much over here. I'm just investigating. I got a request to meet The Casanova Carver on the bridge and—"

"Of course. And then Stone got a message that The Chef was up here, and you two were fighting over who was getting the footage. Is that it?"

"Your deductive skills astound."

"Yeah. You should see my bullshit meter. It wins awards. So I'm asking you one last time: please come back over here and take a ride with me downtown."

"Are we under arrest?"

The helicopter was low enough now that everyone's hair began to dance wildly. "Pretty much."

Stone couldn't hear her, but Mason said something to Duncan and he raised the camera and started filming them. "Hey, prick, put that camera down," he yelled. "I'm not ready to report yet."

"But I am, Stone," Mason replied. She looked apologetic, like she didn't want to take Garcia's side in all of this, but he knew she was going to do the story anyway. It was what a good reporter did. "I know you understand, hon."

As much as he wanted to yell out that Hardwood was the Casanova Carver, he knew that the old man would do as he was threatening, and they'd both end up in an electric chair. There were no other easy outs here. No matter what story they concocted, Garcia would find the holes in it, and besides, it was pretty clear the cop had put enough puzzle pieces together to arrest them on suspicion alone. Where was he supposed to go even if he did get off the bridge and away from Garcia? He'd be a wanted man, a hunted man, and the press—as he well knew—would convict him before any real jury ever could.

Acceptance began to settle in. He felt it growing in his belly, overriding his innate need to escape. There was no way out here, none that he could think of and still be a free man.

Which left him...where? Hundreds of feet above the water, standing next to a terrorist who knew his darkest secrets. As soon as he realized it, his metaphorical fortress cracked, the stones sliding out of their holdings, the parapets crumbling, taking the stanchions with them.

"Do me a favor," he shouted to Mason.

"What?"

Taking his keys out of his pocket, he threw them to her. They plunked down on the boards besides her, and she bent down and picked them up.

"Chauncey needs a good home."

"I don't have the time."

"I thought you might say that. Detective Garcia?"

The cop had his gun trained on them both, but dipped it just a bit, the gears behind his eyes working hard, perhaps thinking there was actually going to be an easy way out of this. "I don't know what you're thinking, but I just want to talk. No need to worry about your dog."

"Will you just tell me you'll take him? He's got a good nose, he could probably be of some help."

A moment of silence passed. Garcia stuck is hand out and Mason placed the keys in them. "My wife likes dogs."

"She sounds pretty nice, your wife that is."

"She is. Now, just, you know, come on over here and we'll talk about things."

The spotlight of the helicopter fell on Stone and Hardwood, hovered still, bathing them in some form of ethereal radiance. Duncan was recording it all, and Mason finally put the microphone to her lips and started reporting, though he couldn't hear her words. The way she stood tall and proper, the way her head dipped to emphasize certain lines...she was a true professional. She'd be the only one in the city with this footage, and it would make her career. Maybe that wasn't so bad. Maybe his desire for fame and fortune really had come at the cost of something more dear.

Then again, who said he had to lose all he'd worked for just because he was exposed. There was a certain immortality in what he'd done. He might not go down in history as the most trusted name in news, but he'd go down as one of the most famous. Hell, who remembered which police officers caught Dahmer and Gacy and Manson? Nobody. But people remembered the killers. They were names that lived on forever.

Was that so bad?

Instead of securing ratings for the news, he'd be the ratings' catalyst.

"Why did you do that?" Hardwood asked, his black jacket rippling and snapping in the gusts from the helicopter. "They know nothing."

"They know everything, you moron. We got too brave, we let pride ruin us."

Something in Hardwood's eyes told Stone the man did not agree. "We can take them all," he said. "We can go across and I'll get the cop and you kill that bitch and her twerp sidekick."

"The sidekick I'd like to take out, but no, I'm not doing that."

"You can have sex with other girls, Stone. A soon as her tape gets back to the station we're goners. Let's just rush them. I'll blow the bridge, and hope it takes out the helicopter. They haven't seen our faces up there yet. They won't know it's us." Unslinging the backpack, Hardwood reached inside and brought out a small, black device with switches on it.

Across the gap, Garcia's gun came back up again, and his eyes went wide. "Drop it, Hardwood! I mean it."

Stone saw Mason reporting to the camera, unaware of what Hardwood was holding. After all this time, he still hadn't been with her, hadn't kissed her or held her or made love to her or anything. She'd been too busy with Cheese, because Cheese could get her places he couldn't, and while he resented it, he knew it was just business. Couldn't fault her for that. But it didn't mean he wanted her to meet her end engulfed in an explosion. More specifically, he didn't want her tape to meet its end. The tape needed to survive.

With a lunge, he threw himself on Hardwood, landed a punch on the man's nose. Blood arced out through the white light of the helicopter's spotlight, landed pink and soupy on the support cable.

From somewhere nearby, he heard Garcia tell Mason and Duncan to take off, heard the copter descend a little lower. Hardwood fought back, kicking him in the stomach, sending him over the edge of the cross beam. He managed to get a hand out just in time and stop his fall.

"Hang on!" Garcia yelled.

Above him, standing triumphantly, Hardwood held the remote detonator out in front of him. "I've got a story to report, detective, so I'll have to meet you later for that talk."

Garcia was a few steps out on the cross beams of the gap now, the cars below him still blissfully ignorant of how bad the situation was. With his gun still aimed in front of him, he slid his feet across the beams, tried to balance like a man on a surfboard. "Put it down, Hardwood. This story is over. The evidence is against you and you're just making it worse. Put that contraption down and back away. We'll go and have a coffee and chat and see if we can't get you some help."

A rope ladder fell out of the helicopter; a man in black fatigues started climbing down it, his eyes on Stone. How nice. They were coming to rescue him before they locked him away for life.

"Wrong, detective," Hardwood said, "this story is not over. A good reporter finds an angle when he needs to. And I'm the best newsman in this whole city. Dare I say in the whole world. Don't you remember the Winslow case?"

"Yeah, I'm wondering about that one."

"Do you know how loved I am? Do you?"

From out of nowhere, men wearing black suits and wireless ear radios were running up toward Garcia from the promenade. He turned and waved them away, as if to say he had everything under control. They had to be FBI, thought Stone, because they couldn't care less about Garcia's request. Obviously, the crew in the helicopter had called in for some serious backup. As Stone looked down between his dangling feet, he noticed the cars had stopped driving across the bridge. Sealing off the area, he thought, don't want the public to see who shoots first. Looking out toward the skyline, he saw flashing police lights running hot at the bridge entrances.

Hanging from the beams like this was beginning to tire him out. His hands were raw and chaffing, and his shoulders blazed with his weight. Chances were he could land on the ground below and suffer only a broken bone or two, but he planned on avoiding that if he could.

The man on the ladder was almost down to him, but had stopped in fear that Hardwood interpret any further movements as some kind of threat and do something stupid.

"You've got lots of fans," Garcia replied. "I'll give you that. Maybe if you put that down you can still talk to them."

"But don't you see, detective, this will be the biggest story of all time, and I have to be the one to report it. I'm part of the network now. If I don't, then that bitch there will, or some other station, and then I'm no longer useful. I have to get the ratings. Ratings equals advertising equals my goddamned life. It's all money in the end, don't you see."

"Don't you mean the Casanova Carver will report it?"

"Huh. A buffoon, that one. Useless to me now, yesterday's headlines. No, there is an even deadlier faction loose in the city, threatening the lives of every man, woman, and child who dare walk the streets. Men who use fear and terror to intimidate, who will have us locked inside our homes, glued to the TVs. Only I know when and where they will strike. Only I can warn the people. Which makes me the only name they'll trust to survive. So you can't expect me to lie down, considering how essential I am."

The men in black were shouting orders to Mason, who in turn was arguing back. Good girl, Stone thought, don't let them push you around. After all, you're the press. Get the story.

"Let it go, Hardwood," Garcia replied. "We know about your son, we know about all of it."

"I doubt you know anything, detective. You only know what I tell you every night at eleven o'clock. You know what I want you to know."

"Yes, but I have means of information too. After all, safe neighborhoods equals votes equals money for the force. It's all money in the end, like you said." Garcia flashed his eyes up to the helicopter's open door, mouthed the word NO.

Leaning out of it, Stone saw, was a man holding a long rifle. It was aimed at the back of Hardwood's head. A hand rose to the earpiece tucked under his black cap, and the man nodded. Was he going to shoot, Stone wondered. Was it loaded with real bullets or rubber ones or what? And what would happen if it hit the C-4?

Hardwood caught on, turned and saw the barrel of the rifle trained on him.

"Don't do it!" Garcia yelled, but Stone wasn't sure if he was yelling at the man in the helicopter or at Hardwood.

It didn't really matter, all things considered, because everything went to shit before either had a chance to answer. The man in the helicopter pulled the trigger, and Hardwood flipped the switch on the detonator

Stone suddenly felt intense heat engulf him, the rush of air blowing at him sideways, and finally, the smack of icy water on his face.

And he thought: not again.

CHAPTER 47

Mason straightened the notes in front of her as the station director counted down from five using only his fingers. On the monitors, the WWTF intro ended—"WWTF channel 8 news, with lead anchor Tricia Mason. Sports by Bill Greely. And weather with Claymore Swift."— and the red light came on over Camera One.

"Good evening. Tonight's top story, Terror on the Brooklyn Bridge. Here at WWTF we have exclusive footage of the deadly police encounter that has led to the disappearances of our own Roland Stone, and local news anchor Doug Hardwood. We warn you that what you are about to see is graphic."

They cut to the tape showing the small explosion and the panicked scurrying of police and FBI agents. Duncan's audible screech had been edited out.

Cheese stood off to the side of Camera One, smiling as wide as he could manage. As it stood, they were the only station to own footage of the blast, and tonight they would make ratings history.

Thanks, Stone, she thought, you did good, even if you were a psychopath.

She felt bad, sure, but only as bad as she could feel for a man who had killed like he had. And maybe she felt some fear at the notion she'd spent so much time with him, but she was fairly confident she had nothing to worry about. If he was still alive, he sure as hell wasn't in New York. What she really felt was…high. Stone's nebulous admission of guilt provided enough fuel for this station to keep going for months. It opened up ideas and rekindled the flame that had been The Chef.

When the tape ended, she faced Camera Three, spoke solemnly. "No bodies have been found yet, though police say they will continue to search day and night until they are discovered." Turning to the Camera One, she began anew: "Just how safe are our bridges? We spoke to chemical engineering expert, Dr. Naff of Columbia University, who told us that a simple bottle of rubbing alcohol mixed with the right chemicals could have us all taking the ferry before we know it."

They cut to a fat man in a white shirt demonstrating the basics of building a bomb that could be made from household cleaners. The man suggested that New York was, indeed, destined for another attack like 9/11. It was just a matter of when and where it would happen, and how they'd pull it off.

Mason thought about the real odds of it happening now that security was through the roof. They were slim to none, but it didn't matter. It made for good TV. And good TV made her who she was. Good TV was going to take her higher than she'd ever dreamed possible.
Blue bikini be damned.

*

"You're gonna be late," George Thompson said, poking his head into Garcia's office. "The cameras are all set up."

Garcia popped a Tic-Tac in his mouth and let it rattle against his teeth. "Tell them to put the juggler on instead, my assistant took off with my magic hat. It'll kill my career, and I'm so close to sawing my pension in half."

"Quit joking, you gotta get out there."

"Don't want to."

"Why not? You're a hero."

"I'm not a hero, George, I'm not much of anything. They got away in case you're forgetting."

George entered and closed the door behind him, sat down in the plastic chair under the bulletin board. "My honest opinion?"

"I don't see anyone else here."

"They drowned."

"Bullshit. You know it's bullshit. Drummed up to quell fear."

"I know the bodies are still missing, but I've seen the photos of the damage, seen the reports about the blast radius, I watched that footage on channel 8 last night, and—"

"They could have survived. It wasn't that big. I was twenty feet away and I'm still in one piece. Only a handful of burns."

"Thank God. Hardwood didn't know what he was doing or who he was buying from. The powder inside was never spread properly and he screwed up the blasting caps. Still, it was enough to blow a big ass hole in the support beams, and enough to concuss him and Stone. Think about it. With the wind knocked out of them, they'd have been sucking in water when they hit the river. No way they survived. Don't forget we haven't found that Marlin guy either."

Harold Marlin had been the SWAT team member on the rope ladder, reaching down to grab Stone before he fell to the road. When the C-4 had exploded, he'd been tossed into the water as well, the helicopter hurriedly banking away to avoid the fireball. None of the bodies had shown up yet, despite the dredging that had been going on for days.

"So unless you think one of our guys was in on it," George continued, "I'd start accepting the fact they're most likely dead."

"Some cables fell in too. They found the cables."

"Doesn't mean anything. Do you know how much shit is buried in the river? They could be anywhere."

"I'll believe it when I see it."

"Yeah, well, the cameras are ready anyway, and I passed the mayor in the hall on his way there, so my guess is you're on in a couple seconds. Fix your hair, you've got a cowlick sticking up."

"I'm serious. I don't want to go."

"You have to, Garcia. You're the hero. Now get going. You're the face everyone has to see on the news."

Reluctantly, Garcia stood up and adjusted his sport jacket, opened the office door and made his way toward the in-house briefing room where several news crews were busy checking their equipment. A blitzkrieg of flashbulbs assaulted him as he entered. At the podium, he popped a Tic-Tac in his mouth, but it didn't taste right, so he spit it into the small trashcan near his feet. He looked at the eager faces of the journalists and sighed. "I hate the news."

About the author

Ryan C. Thomas is an editor and award-winning journalist who works and lives in San Diego, California. You can usually find him in the bars on the weekends playing with his band, The Buzzbombs. When he is not writing or rocking out, he is at home watching really bad B-movies. Visit him online at www.ryancthomas.com